Praise for *Blue Diablo*

"Ann Aguirre proves herself yet again in this gritty, steamy, and altogether wonderful urban fantasy. Outstanding and delicious. I can't wait to see what she comes up with next."
— #1 *New York Times* bestselling author Patricia Briggs

"An authentic Southwestern-flavored feast, filled with magic, revenge, and romance, spiced with memorable characters and page-turning action. *¡Muy caliente!*"
— *New York Times* bestselling author Rachel Caine

"Corine has a great narrative voice—snappy and full of interesting observations on everything around her. . . . [*Blue Diablo* is] fast-paced and entertaining."
— Charles de Lint, *Fantasy and Science Fiction*

"The fast and furious pace combined with interesting characters, powerful antagonists, and the promise of romance make for a strong first entry in the series."
— Monsters and Critics

"Ms. Aguirre plunges readers into a fast-paced tale where her human characters are enhanced by their extraordinary gifts. *Blue Diablo* delivers a strong start to the series with a well-defined heroine, intriguing paranormal elements, and an emotion-filled romance."
— Darque Reviews

"Rising star Aguirre moves from outer space to the Southwest in this new first-person series. With murder, magic, and romance, this is an enticingly dangerous journey. Don't miss out!"
— *Romantic Times*

"The first Corine Solomon urban detective fantasy is a great tale filled with magic, paranormal powers, demons, and spirits bound to the necro. The heat between the lead couple is palpable. . . . This is an enthralling romantic urban fantasy."
— *Midwest Book Review*

Also by Ann Aguirre

ANN AGUIRRE

HELL
FIRE

A CORINE SOLOMON NOVEL

A ROC BOOK

ROC

Published by New American Library, a division of
Penguin Group (USA) Inc., 375 Hudson Street,
New York, New York 10014, USA
Penguin Group (Canada), 90 Eglinton Avenue East, Suite 700, Toronto,
Ontario M4P 2Y3, Canada (a division of Pearson Penguin Canada Inc.)
Penguin Books Ltd., 80 Strand, London WC2R 0RL, England
Penguin Ireland, 25 St. Stephen's Green, Dublin 2,
Ireland (a division of Penguin Books Ltd.)
Penguin Group (Australia), 250 Camberwell Road, Camberwell, Victoria 3124,
Australia (a division of Pearson Australia Group Pty. Ltd.)
Penguin Books India Pvt. Ltd., 11 Community Centre, Panchsheel Park,
New Delh - 110 017, India
Penguin Group (NZ), 67 Apollo Drive, Rosedale, North Shore 0632,
New Zealand (a division of Pearson New Zealand Ltd.)
Penguin Books (South Africa) (Pty.) Ltd., 24 Sturdee Avenue,
Rosebank, Johannesburg 2196, South Africa

Penguin Books Ltd., Registered Offices:
80 Strand, London WC2R 0RL, England

First published by Roc, an imprint of New American Library,
a division of Penguin Group (USA) Inc.

First printing, April 2010
10 9 8 7 6 5 4 3 2 1

For my children.
If I've done anything worthwhile in my life, it's you.
Each day, you make me so, so proud.
Love you guys.

ACKNOWLEDGMENTS

Laura Bradford is the best of all possible agents. What other agent would clear her schedule when I take the bus in from Tijuana and spend the day chauffeuring me around to sign stock? That was one of the best days I can remember because she is not only my agent, but also wonderful company. She boosts me when I need it, and she always has a master plan.

I also need to cheer for Mysterious Galaxy in San Diego because they make me feel like a hometown author and show such support for my books. Big thanks to Patrick at MG for telling everybody I'm destined to be a star and that he expects to see my work in hardcover one day. Words like that from a bookseller put a writer on cloud nine!

In fact, I celebrate all booksellers who recommend my work—and here's a shout to Sara of Fresh Fiction, who made my visit to Texas so memorable. I also owe her a margarita for telling readers that if they like Patricia Briggs, they'll enjoy my books.

I've mentioned Ivette before, and I don't know what I'd do without her. She makes my life easier in countless ways, freeing me up to write, which is what I love.

Others offer motivation and support when I need it. So thanks to Lauren Dane, Jeri Smith-Ready, Larissa Ione, Victoria Dahl, Carrie Lofty, and Lorelie Brown. It all helps. You're there when I need you, and I'm lucky to have such an amazing group of smart, funny, talented friends.

And hats off to Carolyn Jewel and Meredith Duran for writing books that inspire me and make me say, "Now, that's how it's done."

Thanks to Andres, who understands me after all these years, and to my kids, who are very good about letting me work.

Though Kilmer is set in Georgia, it's a fictional town, so obviously you won't find it if you drive south. I hope it feels real to you; as always, I grounded my what-if fantasy in our world, using Darien and Savannah to flavor my creation. Thanks to everyone who answered my questions about living in the South. You made it possible to enrich this book beyond what I could have managed on my own.

Finally, I must thank my readers, who are the cleverest, warmest, wittiest, and best-looking people ever to buy books. Please keep those e-mails coming; they never fail to make me smile. You can get in touch with me at ann.aguirre@gmail.com.

Home Again

I'm still a redhead.

Before we left Texas, I touched up the roots, and then I had some tawny apricot highlights put in. I guess that meant I intended to keep this color for a while. Symbolic—I'd made a commitment, at least to my hair.

Too bad I couldn't do the same with Chance. I didn't trust him entirely, and what was more, he didn't trust me, either. He secretly thought I'd leave, which I had done; die, which I'd *nearly* done; or break his heart. I just hoped I wouldn't combine the three.

Until we resolved the conflict between us—such as his luck, which might kill me, and the former lover he wouldn't talk about—I couldn't be more than a friend to him. He knew it too. I think he'd known as much even when he pressed the point back in Laredo.

The Mustang purred along, emphasizing Chance's silence. He wasn't happy about this trip to Kilmer, Georgia, but he'd promised, and I wanted answers. He owed me.

When he'd shown up at my pawnshop in Mexico City, asking for my help after our breakup eighteen months before, I agreed because he swore to turn his luck toward helping me find out what happened the night my mother died. This point was nonnegotiable. I needed to understand why it happened, and who was responsible. I wanted justice for her death. Now that I'd fulfilled my end of the bargain in Laredo, he was keeping his promise.

We passed the woods that encircled the town. Sometimes, when I was a kid, it had seemed to me that someone simply burnt a patch out of the forbidding forest, and there, Kilmer had been built. Over long years, the trees grew back in around it, overhanging the rutted road.

With the windows open, I smelled dank vegetation heavy in the air, and pallid sunlight filtering through the canopy overhead threw a sickly green glow over the car as Chance drove. McIntosh County didn't get snow or earthquakes, and the median temperature was sixty-six degrees. It was also deeply historical, containing forty-two markers. I knew all about local history: how old Fort King George was built nearby in 1721; how the Highlanders voted against slavery in 1739, not that it did them any good in the long run; and how the War of Jenkins' Ear motivated early settlers to attack Spanish forts. There were still ruins on Sapelo Island.

Just a piece up the road, there lived the only known band of Shouters, a Gullah music group. I'd seen them perform the ring shout once at Mount Calvary Baptist Church. I couldn't remember which foster parent had taken me; there had been so many, and most of them had thought I could benefit from religion in some form or another. On paper, this seemed the perfect place to live, steeped in cultural heritage and tradition.

On paper.

In Kilmer, the rules of the Deep South lasted long after laws and social expectations changed in the wider world. White men did as they pleased, and everyone else kept their mouths shut. I couldn't rightly say I'd missed it.

"This place has a weird feel," Chance said, breaking the silence at last.

"You're getting it too?" I'd always thought it was the trees, but we'd passed beyond them. Now only scrubby grass lay between us and the weathered buildings of town. Overhead, the sky glowed blue and white; it was a pretty, partly sunny day that should've warmed me a lot more than it did.

"Yeah." Before he could say more, a dark shape darted in front of the cherry red Mustang. Chance slammed on the brakes, and only the seat belt kept my head from kissing the dash. The car fishtailed to a stop.

Butch whined and popped his head out of my handbag. He was a blond Chihuahua we'd picked up along the way; I'd resigned myself to keeping him, but I hoped we hadn't scared the shit out of him. I had important stuff in my purse. I soothed him with an absent touch on his head, my heart still going like a jackhammer.

"What the—"

Chance motioned me to silence as he got out of the car. Hands shaking, I needed two tries to do the same. I checked the back, staring into the dead air beneath the tunnel of trees. Black skid marks smeared the pavement behind us.

He knelt and peered under the Mustang. Despite my better judgment, I joined him. Butch hopped down and backed up three steps, yapping ferociously. A low animal growl answered him.

Near the tires, a big black dog lay dying—a Doberman. We hadn't hit him, but all the blood oozing out of his ragged wounds told me he wasn't long for this world. He'd come from the tall grass that lined the road, or maybe from the trees beyond the field. A hard shudder rocked through me, and the air turned as cold as a northern winter night.

"Something got at him," Chance said finally. "Are there bears here? Wolves?"

I had no idea. I wasn't a wildlife expert in any location, and I hadn't been back to Kilmer in nine years. Things changed; habitats evolved. But times must be tough if wild animals had been forced to resort to hunting dogs.

I couldn't seem to look away from the shadow-dark flesh. The animal gave one final whine, as if he understood we couldn't help, and then he died. I saw the moment his eyes went liquid still, living tissue reverting to dead meat. There was a blood trail we could follow, but I didn't think that was a good idea. *Sizable claws created those wounds; nothing we need to mess with just before nightfall.*

I glanced down at the Chihuahua as he sniffed around next to my feet. "What do you think? Do you smell anything you recognize?"

He yapped twice. *Hm, so it probably wasn't a regular wild animal.* I shivered, wanting nothing more than to get off this road.

We'd acquired Butch after his prior owner was killed, and we were astonished to learn he could communicate on a basic level. There was something special about him for sure, but I had lacked the opportunity to investigate what his other talents might be. This certainly wasn't the time.

Never one to miss an opportunity, Butch scampered into the weeds and did his business. I exhaled a long, unsteady breath, and then pulled myself to my feet using the Mustang's hood. If I believed in omens, we were off to a hell of a start.

Chance went to the trunk and wrapped his hands in rags used to wipe off the oil dipstick. Before we left Laredo, Chuch—our mechanic friend—had taught him how and threatened to beat him if he didn't look after this car properly. So far Chance was doing fine.

Wordlessly, he reached under the chassis and towed the carcass to the side of the road. Without a shovel, that was really all we could do, but I appreciated the kindness. Otherwise, that poor dog would be splattered all over the road when the next car came, and he had suffered enough.

Even if we did have digging tools in the car for some unlikely reason, I wouldn't have been interested in hanging around. My intestines coiled into knots over the idea of losing the light out there, within a stone's throw of those dark trees. The whorls on the bark resembled demonic sigils in the wicked half-light, and the long, skeletal limbs stirred in the breeze in a way I simply couldn't like.

There was a reason I hated these trees. I'd hid among them while my mother died.

While Chance took care of the dead dog, I gave Butch a drink and tried to reassure him that he wasn't doomed to suffer the same fate. His bulging brown eyes glistened with what I'd call a skeptical light as I hopped back in the Mustang. Chance joined us shortly, working the manual transmission with a dexterity I couldn't help but admire.

"What a welcome." He shook his head.

"Tell me about it." As I said that, we passed a faded white sign that I knew read WELCOME TO KILMER, HOME OF THE RED DEVILS AND THE WORLD'S BEST PEACH PIE.

"Think anyone will recognize you?"

I shook my head absently, taking in the familiar sights. It was bizarre. The road into town hadn't changed at all. Ma's Kitchen, an old white clapboard restaurant, still sat just outside the city limits. The shopping plaza on the left had been given a face-lift—fresh paint and new lines in the tiny parking lot—but the general store, the dry cleaner's, the Kilmer bank, and a coffee shop still occupied it. The names on the dry cleaner's and coffee shop had changed, but otherwise, the town seemed just as I'd left it.

If we stayed on this street, we'd wind up in the town square, where the old courthouse reigned like an aging duchess who refused to admit her day had passed. The clock on the tower hadn't worked since before I moved away, and I couldn't imagine, given the faded air, that they'd come into the money to fix it since. The "historical" district simply contained the oldest houses; most hadn't been restored.

But Kilmer retained a certain turn-of-the-century charm, if you didn't know what lurked beneath its exterior. I recognized Federal-inspired houses with their rectangular structure and slim, delicate iron railings; those stately old dames mingled freely with Georgian homes with hipped roofs and quoins.

Most of those neighborhoods exuded a genteel aura of

decay. The streets hadn't been paved in a long time; they were faded to the pale gray of rotting teeth from years of neglect, and Chance had to turn smartly to avoid the deep potholes.

"It seems sadder," I said at last. "Smaller."

"Well, you're older now." To his credit, he didn't say I was bigger. That would've earned him a slap upside the head.

Anyway, I *wasn't* bigger. I still needed to lose a few pounds, but I'd been pretty chunky at eighteen when I climbed on that Greyhound bus. At the gas station–cum–video store, I'd begged a lift from a farmer headed into Brunswick. I'd known buses ran from there, so I'd used my school ID to get a discount ticket and I rode all night. The next morning, I got off in Atlanta with just a backpack and a few dollars in my pocket.

My chest felt tight, remembering. I'd gotten work at a used bookstore the following day. The owner had felt sorry for me, I think, but I loved that job. I rented a room in a boardinghouse, and I was happier than I'd ever been in Kilmer. I had been sadder than Roy to see the bookstore go under. With no friends and little money in the bank, my life took a turn for the worse. I'd left Atlanta with only enough money for a bus ticket, and things went south from there.

But I didn't want to think about that.

By the time Chance met me, I'd put myself back together somewhat. But I'd held eight different jobs in half as many years, and I seldom stayed in one place for long. There was nothing like running from your memories while trying to fit in, though I never made it. People always seemed to suss out that I wasn't quite like them.

It was more than the scars on my palms that came from a gift I didn't want. My mother's death stayed with me in the form of the pain that subsumed me each time I read a charged object. There was a name for what I did. Most people called it psychometry; *I* called it a curse.

For years, I tried to forget.

When Chance came into my life, he changed everything.

But I wouldn't think about that, either. Sometimes the past needed to stay buried; it was the only way you could move on. And sometimes you had to dig it up, because that too was the only way.

For my mother's sake, I had to deal with what'd happened in Kilmer. I'd find answers about the men who came by night to our house and burnt the place with her trapped inside. I'd discover why. Maybe then the dreams would stop. Maybe then she could rest. In the twilight, the town looked so quiet, almost peaceful, but to me, it hid a fetid air. Corruption fed in the stillness, like a pretty corpse that, when split open, spilled out a host of maggots.

I'd be the knife that cut this place wide and the fire that burnt it clean.

The Kilmer Inn

Chance parked the car because we were just driving aimlessly. He turned to me and rested his elbow on the back of the seat. "You all right?"

Well, no, I wasn't. The bruises hadn't completely healed from our last outing, and I had a fresh scar on my shoulder that'd come from a dead woman's teeth. In addition, there was a secret society of Gifted individuals that I'd only just learned about, and the mentor who was supposed to teach me how to go on probably never wanted to see or hear from me again. That bothered me on a personal level as well, as I'd shared one smoking hot kiss with Jesse Saldana the night before everything went wrong.

This wasn't the time to complain, and Chance certainly wouldn't be interested in my emotional conflict regarding another man. In fact, bringing it up would just provoke him, considering he hoped we would be reconciled before this trip ended.

So I merely nodded. "We should find a place to stay. An old woman on Second Avenue used to rent out rooms. . . . I don't know if she's still alive, or if the boardinghouse is still open, but it's a place to start."

He checked the nearest cross street. "This is Tenth and Main. Which way?"

I thought for a moment. "North, about eight blocks—I think. It's been a long time."

Kilmer was laid out in a way that made sense, so we found the house, an old gingerbread Victorian, without too much trouble. Sometime since I'd left, it had been painted a pretty periwinkle and the trim done up in fresh white. The shutters gave the windows an open, welcoming look, and the garden would've been lovely at any other time of the year.

Salt weighted the air. We weren't too far from the ocean, and maybe that had something to do with it, sandwiched in a desolate stretch of land between the coast and the Boggy Cypress Swamp. Rivers and tributaries tunneled all through this area, wandering inland from the ocean. I'd once loved going down to swim with my mama.

God, being here was harder than I'd expected. It made me miss her more. As I stood staring up at that fairy-tale Victorian house with all its fancy white flourishes along the roof, I wondered if I had the steel to see this through. I squared my shoulders. Of course I did. Otherwise I'd never know the truth, and I would've wasted Chance's time.

Time to do this.

I didn't see any sign from the yard to indicate whether this was a business or a private residence, but when we got out of the car and went toward the long wraparound porch, I saw a gleaming brass plaque that proclaimed KILMER INN. Well, that was new.

Old Mrs. Jensen hadn't bothered with any such niceties; just a pasteboard and wood stake in the yard that said ROOMS TO RENT. The place must be under new management. Just as well—Mrs. Jensen might have known me; she was a sharp old bird.

The current owners had a nice little patio set up with hand-carved rocking chairs and pretty little wrought-iron side tables. In season, the hanging baskets would probably be in bloom. I imagined sitting there beneath the black velvet of a sultry summer night, sipping a dewy glass of lemonade and watching the world go by.

Too bad it wasn't the idyllic town promised by such trappings, and we'd missed the warm summer nights, missed the sun of Indian summer; Kilmer was unrelentingly gray now and heavy with threatening rain. The clouds didn't look altogether natural to me; they were so dark, I sometimes thought I saw monstrous faces charged with lightning inside.

Kilmer was nothing like my home in Mexico. Instead of bright walls of stucco and adobe painted in vibrant shades, this town offered warped wood and peeling paint. None of the houses had aluminum siding, which seemed strange. A few were built from stone or brick, but most of them didn't look well kept. This was a town on the dirty side of decline. In fact, this home was the only one on this street that looked to be in good repair.

After a few seconds of silent debate, capped by mutual shrugs, we decided not to knock. A bell tinkled, signaling our entry into a charming foyer populated with warm mahogany and real antiques, which I priced in a single glance. Two striped damask chairs sat at studied angles from a cherry table, and the rug beneath our feet would sell for a pretty penny. I hoped Butch wouldn't pop up; I had a feeling this place wasn't pet friendly.

Before long, a platinum blond woman came hurrying down the corridor. "Good afternoon," she said without a touch of a drawl. "Did you have a reservation?"

"No, ma'am," Chance said. "But we *were* hoping to rent a room."

Her sapphire blue gaze went to my left hand. "Just one?"

Blame it on my mean streak.

I answered, "Yes, please."

Chance seemed surprised, as well he might, but he just nodded. "Do you have anything for us? We'd like a weekly rate; you have such a sweet little town here."

That seemed like laying it on pretty thick, but by the way the woman lit up, you'd have thought she'd founded the place. Since I couldn't hear any activity, I couldn't imagine she was full. I didn't know what would've brought an obviously city-bred woman to Kilmer, looking to open a bed-and-breakfast. Maybe a bad marriage or a broken relationship. Despite her well-kept skin and figure, I guessed she was past forty, so it could have been a number of things.

Truthfully, it wasn't just a desire to torment Chance with what he couldn't have that led me to ask for a single room. I also couldn't face the idea of sleeping here alone—not in this town. Wholly illogical fear clutched me tight, but then . . . fear was *usually* irrational. Most people weren't aware enough to fear the things that could *really* hurt them.

The proprietor made a show of checking her appointment book. "Oh, I think I can accommodate you. I can give you the Magnolia room for three hundred a week. You'll share a bath with the Plumeria, but that's currently unoccupied. Meals are served promptly in the dining room at nine, one, and six. If you'd like to use the kitchen to fix yourselves snacks and such, I can let you have access for another forty dollars a week."

"That sounds perfect," Chance told her, producing three hundreds and two twenties.

That changed the woman's demeanor measurably. "It's a pleasure to have you stay with us. I'm Sandra Cheney. My husband, Jim, handles the repairs and restoration around the place, so you won't see him much. Our daughter, Shannon, cleans the rooms. I do the cooking and ensure guest satisfaction." By her expression, she'd do a *lot* to please a man who looked like Chance and carried hundreds in his wallet. I wondered what Jim would say about her dedication to customer service.

Well, I was used to that. After all, Chance was worth a second look: long and lean with vaguely Asian features, smooth brown skin, and a pair of tiger's eyes that could melt your knees at thirty paces. When you dated a guy who looked like Chance, you got accustomed to women checking him out, but that wasn't my problem anymore.

"Thanks," he murmured, noncommittal. He'd gotten good at pretending not to register all the double entendres that came his way.

Sandra didn't seem to mind, as long as he had money. "If you'll fill out this card, I'll get the key to the Magnolia room."

I watched him, chuckling softly when I saw him write the name *Chance Boudreaux*. He looked about as Cajun as I did Navajo. He flicked a smile in my direction as he saw me reading over his shoulder. The man made a game out of leaving different names anywhere we stayed. People who knew him understood they'd never get more out of him regarding his true name than "Chance."

I never had, either. I didn't want to mind, but deep down, I did. It had taken this long for me to admit it, but I'd had enough of Chance's secrets. Even meeting his mother, Min, hadn't done anything to dispel the shadows around him. In fact, she encouraged the obfuscation, saying it would be dangerous for anyone to find out the truth.

But *I'd* never hurt him, at least not with a spell tied to his true name. The hurt I inflicted on him went deeper, I supposed, more than skin-deep. He still wore scars on his back, gained saving my life a few weeks earlier. Chance had sheltered me with his own body as the glass flew all around us, the result of a sending that caught us flat-footed in a warehouse, where we'd been looking for his mother.

I sighed as he signed the guest registry with a flourish. It just didn't pay to think about such things. *Better to stay in the here and now*. I hated torturing myself with might-have-beens. While he wrapped up with Sandra, I went to the Mustang to fetch our stuff.

The night offered complete calm, not even a whisper of a breeze. Dead man's hands ran down my spine as I studied the dark windows all around us. There should have been people running errands, going about their daily routines, right? I tried to talk myself out of misgivings that were probably imaginary. Most likely, people just hadn't returned from work.

Even knowing that, I couldn't shake the feeling something was wrong—bad wrong.

As I returned, she was saying, "All set. Let's go on up. You're on the second floor. You intend to check out the historical sites, am I right? You simply can't leave without visiting Sapelo Island."

We let her chatter as she led the way up the polished stairs in her twill slacks and cashmere twin set. She lacked only a set of pearls to qualify as a perfect Southern hostess. When she realized I just had a backpack, and Chance, a duffel, she looked a little put out. I guess with a money roll like his, we ought to have been traveling with designer luggage.

Still, her smile dimmed only slightly. She rattled off the amenities and then told Chance he could follow the gravel trail to park the Mustang around back. I glazed over well before she left.

The click of the door jostled me out of the innkeeper-induced coma, and I took stock. She hadn't lied; it was a nice room, done in pastels—lots of pretty pictures of magnolias and lots of Victorian lace. I liked the wallpaper with its fat candy-pink and white stripes. Sandra had done a nice job of blending colors and patterns into a sweet whole.

"I'm losing man points just by standing here." Beside the antique brass bed, Chance looked even more masculine by contrast.

It wasn't nearly big enough. We'd be all over each other in the night, but I still couldn't face the idea of closing my eyes here with a wall between us. I had to own it; being here terrified me. I'd run from Kilmer as soon as I could, and I had to be out of my mind for coming back. But at least I wasn't alone this time.

The dead dog seemed symbolic in more ways than one. If I'd had any sense, we would've called this thing a loss and just moved on. But I couldn't. Running would mean I was letting them win. I deserved answers—and closure. Once I put this behind me, I hoped the dreams would stop. I'd go back to the pawnshop; go back to enjoying my quiet life.

Butch stuck his head out of my bag and whined as if in sympathy. I forced a smile and petted him in reflex. "I'm fine; don't worry."

Chance quirked a brow. "Saying it repeatedly doesn't make it true, Corine."

Because I felt hunted, fragile, I bit back. "Fine, but my mother *died* here. How would you feel about Mexico, Chance? If that mountain had been Min's grave."

He didn't move; didn't flinch. Dammit, I'd never known when I wounded him, and I still didn't. I hated that he could read me like a book, whereas he was microfiche to me, and I didn't know how to work the machine.

"Like you do now. And I wouldn't stop until I had the people responsible for it. I *do* understand your reasons; I just want to make sure you can bear up. It isn't likely to get easier, if just being here unsettles you."

He had a point.

I exhaled. "I'm sorry. That was uncalled for. Yeah . . . I'll hold. Don't even worry about me."

His smile came sad and sweet, like the dying notes of a blues sax at closing time. "I can't help that."

Well, I knew. I'd always think about him too. Some things just never stopped being true. My heart ached at his expression, quietly resigned but hungry for what I couldn't give. Not when he couldn't offer what I needed back.

More as a distraction, I set Butch down and let him run around, sniffing. He pronounced the room clean with a little yap and jumped into the armchair by the window. The little dog circled three times and then lay down on the pale yellow cushion. He'd eaten and had a drink at the last place we stopped for gas, and done his business outside town, so I expected him to be good for a while.

With the last light gone, the sky looked like a bruise over the treetops in the backyard. I gazed outward, wondering what they were doing—the men who'd murdered my mother. Were they eating their dinners and then settling in with their TVs? What the hell *happened* all those years ago?

Chance came up behind me, but he didn't touch. I could feel his warmth just beyond my personal space, and I wanted to turn into his arms; let him hold me and kiss my throat until the hurt receded into heat.

I didn't.

When I finally spun round, I managed to move back in the motion. "We'll get started in the morning." I made my tone businesslike as I checked the time on a reproduction vintage clock. "You feel like rummaging in the kitchen for us? Looks like we missed dinner."

"Anything special you want?" Why, oh why did he have to put it that way?

"Fruit and cheese." I hesitated. "Thanks, Chance."

Not just for getting dinner—for everything. Without him, I had no hope of getting at the truth. We'd always possessed a symbiotic relationship, where our gifts were concerned. It was all the emotional stuff that tripped us up.

He went out the door smiling, as if he knew I'd meant more than I said and felt more for him than I wanted to admit, even now.

But then, I always had.

Out of Luck

I'd like to say things looked better in the morning, but since it was pouring rain, that would be a lie. I smuggled Butch out in my bag first thing, and we both wound up drenched. After wrapping him in a towel, I took a quick shower, which made me feel marginally better.

I gave Butch his breakfast while wondering where Chance had gone. Since he hadn't left a note or taken the Mustang, I could only assume he'd return soon. By the time I finished braiding my long hair, he showed up with coffee. That was when I figured out he must've vacated the room to give me some privacy.

"Thanks." I took the steaming mug and noted he'd doctored it with cream and sugar, just as I liked.

He was trying so hard, and sometimes I felt tempted to give in, but we hadn't *resolved* anything. The reasons I had for leaving in the first place still resounded with truth. His luck might very well be the death of me.

Chance's talent was also unique, which was why I'd blackmailed him into coming to Kilmer with me, after I helped him find his missing mother. He had what I called uncanny luck; with a little focus, he could shake loose whatever he needed from the cosmos. Sadly, that ability came at a terrible price. Because he got all the lucky breaks, the world balanced itself out on the person closest to him, which meant all the bad karma stuck to me when we were together.

His lover *before* me died. He'd never mentioned that . . . until a few weeks ago in Laredo. And that just underscored my wariness about him. How could we have spent years together—years!—and he'd never seen fit to tell me?

When I remembered all of that, it became easier not to succumb to temptation. The problem was, I couldn't cut him out of my heart entirely. A certain heated look from him still had the power to turn me into hot butter.

I grabbed Butch and slid him into my bag. "Be good. Don't make any noise."

In answer, the dog snuggled down on top of my wallet and made himself at home. Downstairs, we ate a good break-fast of fried eggs, bacon, and biscuits; I slipped tidbits to Butch whenever the coast was clear. And on the way out, it occurred to me that Chance and I needed only another cou-ple to qualify as a Scooby-Doo unit. I was grinning as I got into the Mustang.

"What's so funny?" A smile started in Chance's eyes, as if he wanted to share the joke but feared it might be at his expense.

That stung a little. I'd *never* hurt him on purpose. "We should call Chuch and Eva to join us." I explained my ra-tionale, and then he laughed too.

"We'd need a painted van, and Chuch would kill me if we traded the Mustang. He still loves this car, even if his name isn't on the deed anymore."

Subtle, Chance. Very subtle.

Not being an idiot, I didn't touch that line. "So, where do we start?"

Chance closed his eyes for a moment, and the car livened with the thrum of a charged wire. Use of his gift never failed to prickle the hair on my forearms, rousing a little chill that hinted at arcane energy in play. Rain tapped away at the Mustang and cloaked us from the wider world. I felt I could sit all day and gaze at the purity of his profile.

When his long lashes unfurled, I caught my breath a little. His striated gaze, amber, topaz, and sherry brown, just never lost its magic. I forced myself to sound brisk, no matter what my pulse was doing. "Got something?"

"I have no idea," he said finally. "It's faint, really faint. But *if* I do, it's west."

Well, that was odd. Generally, his ability worked like dowsing, and the pull got stronger the closer we came. I'd only seen him blocked one other time, which didn't bode well. To date, only demon magick had proved stronger than what Chance could do. He put the car in gear, looking uneasy.

"So I was right. There *is* something wrong here."

Chance nodded. "Wrong and *old*. Whatever's happening in Kilmer, it isn't recent."

By my reckoning, it was at least fifteen years old, and might hark back farther still. Tragedy had a way of running under your radar if you weren't personally affected by it. Maybe other families had been torn apart as mine had; I just hadn't noticed.

"Well, don't just sit there. 'Go west, young man.'" I forced a smile.

He didn't offer one in return, just started the car and waited long enough for the windows to defog before he circled around the inn. This late in the morning, there were no cars to challenge us when we pulled into the street. Driving west offered no answers, though, just took us to the road that led out of town.

Chance frowned at the wet pavement as he pulled into the parking lot of what had been a used-car dealership. Now it was just a sea of broken cement with a small vacant building at the far end. The chains had long since rusted away.

"I hate to say it, Corine, but I don't think I can be your Magic 8-Ball. I think we're going to need old-fashioned legwork."

I should've known it wouldn't be as easy as I wanted,

but some part of me wasn't even surprised to find my suspicions confirmed about Kilmer's rotten core. My flesh had been crawling ever since we drove through the tunnel of trees leading to town. It didn't look like things would improve any time soon.

"There are two obvious places to start. I can make a list of all my old foster parents and we can drop by to see how they're doing . . . and pick their brains." My tone expressed how much that notion pleased me. "Or we can do a little research at the library. We may end up doing both, anyway, but I know where I'd prefer to start."

"The library it is. Which way?"

"It used to be downtown, near the courthouse."

It still was, a pale stone building set along the square. For the first time, I noticed it possessed a Gothic air, ornate stonework and bizarre symbols etched into the rock. Most people would call this Gothic Revival style, as it even had gargoyles on the roof. If I watched them too long, they might even have moved, and I didn't want to see that. Chance parked, and I climbed out of the car.

The rest of the square was less dilapidated. Outlying regions had gone positively seedy, but here, the rectangular brick buildings were in pretty good shape. Too many of them sat empty, though, the small, striped awnings blowing over businesses that had closed or moved out of town. Faint gilt lettering had been half scraped away on some of the windows, so they said things such as AILOR and OOKSHOP. The death of a bookstore always made me sad.

In front of the courthouse, there was a Grecian-inspired lady carved out of marble; the folds of her robe were filthy now, stained with a combination of dirt and dead leaves. I knew she was supposed to be Themis, the goddess of justice. Many towns had a similar statue near the courthouse, but she was usually depicted with a sword in one hand and scales in the other. Maybe the sculptor knew something about Kilmer, because he'd depicted her sitting on a rock, sword slack, and the scales beside her. Maybe it was just my imagination, but she looked sad, frozen in that pose.

Everything smelled wet, and the air was heavy in my lungs. Water pooled on the small brown lawn out front, so we picked our way carefully up the path. Three steps led up to a glass door. A posted sign read OPEN, but I could only see our misty reflections; no lights within.

"Stay down," I instructed Butch, who complied with a little huff.

It was weird and eerie, how little this place had changed. In some ways, Kilmer struck me as the town time forgot. There were no restaurant chains, no big stores, not even a single Micky D's. Common sense offered "no money to be made" as the reason, but I wondered if there was more to it. The lack of modern touches seemed unnatural, creepy, rather than comforting. *This* small town offered the feeling of "I know where you live" instead of the security of recognizing all your neighbors.

A grungy gray runner waited for us just inside, so we wiped our feet and let our eyes adjust to the dim interior. Immediately to the left sat the checkout desk, where a gimlet-eyed librarian studied us with disapproval. I guessed she thought we should be at work.

Well, we were.

"Where's the microfiche?" I asked.

The old woman's mouth pursed as if I'd given her a persimmon to suck. Then I realized I'd done something worse—I hadn't greeted her or rambled about the weather for ten minutes. "In the back. Are y'all wanting to look at something special?"

I could've made up some story about writing an article, but that would have made the rounds faster than some random woman poking around the periodicals. Sooner or later, people would start asking who I was and why we were here. I just wanted to put it off as long as possible.

"Just the daily paper to start, the back issues. Are those still in a file cabinet by the machine?"

Her eyes narrowed behind granny-framed glasses. "Have you been in before? Do I know you?"

Beckoning to Chance, I chose not to answer and wove my way through the stacks. I'd once spent a lot of time in here, reading old mysteries. She called after me. "Copies are ten cents and I don't make change!"

"Nice," Chance whispered. "I'm glad I let you do the talking. I'm sure *I* couldn't have done any better."

I waved a hand at him. "She's too old for you to seduce with a few charming words and a killer smile. It wouldn't have been worth the time."

His smile widened into a cocky grin. "You might be surprised."

"Aw, come on. Did you have to put *that* image in my head?"

"No. It was just fun. So what're we looking for exactly?"

As I fired up the machine, I thought about that. "We need dates before we'll get anything out of the local paper. So let's start with the day my mom died."

The winter solstice, December 21. Men had come in the night, bearing flaming brands. She'd shooed me out the back door and then gone to face them in her white nightgown, her hair streaming loose. All night long, while I crouched in the woods, I could smell the flames, curling up into the ink-dark sky.

And ever after, I'd smelled smoke in times of trouble.

"Good idea. We might turn up a pattern." Chance sat down beside me while I pulled Butch out of my bag and set him on the floor.

"Not a peep," I told the dog. "I know this sucks, but if we get kicked out because of you, before we find out anything, I'm totally tossing your bacon snacks."

I thought he believed me, because he didn't even yap in protest. Instead, he curled up and went to sleep. I guessed he wasn't heavily invested in our research.

"Don't most libraries have free public Internet?" Chance asked.

Following his gaze, I peered around the reference section. Yeah, they usually did. But this place looked like it had last been updated in 1967, and there was no PC terminal anywhere to be found. We'd done so much investigating on the Net over the years, I wasn't sure how we'd function.

And then it hit me.

"Let's call Booke. He can research the date and see if there's anything unusual." I had my doubts events in Kilmer would've made the bigger papers, but you never knew.

We'd met Booke through Chuch, although not in the strictest sense. I only knew him from online chats and telephone calls, but he'd proved invaluable in research matters before. I had his number programmed in because, as he lived in the UK, there were a lot of digits—too many for me to remember. After I hit the button on my cell, I waited for it to dial. It should have been early afternoon there. The phone rang four times before he picked up.

"Booke?"

"Corine! How fantastic to hear from you." He had a great voice, deep and plummy. "How are you? Did you make it to Georgia?"

I felt a little sheepish because I hadn't called just to see how he was doing. Then again, he probably knew that. Still, I figured I'd respect the niceties. "I'm fine, and yes, we're in Kilmer now. Long drive. How are you?"

He made a noncommittal noise, as if he'd rather not lie to me, but he didn't want to burden me with his problems, either. "Glad to hear you're safe. Can I help with something?"

Busted.

"Possibly," I said. "Would you mind doing a little research on Kilmer, Georgia? Let me know if you find anything interesting. I'll call you back tomorrow to check in."

Before he answered, I heard keys clicking. I guessed he must be wearing a headset or an earpiece. "Huh." He sounded puzzled. "How do you spell the name of the town?"

I enunciated each letter, and then more keys clacked on

his end. His keyboarding sounded very impressive. And how much of a dork was *I* for noticing?

"What's the problem?" I asked when the silence became extended.

"Well . . . there's *nothing* about Kilmer, Georgia," he told me at last. "Nothing. I've checked six different search engines to be sure. They offer me Kilmer as a last name . . . and ask if I mean Kildare, and finally suggest a swine farm in Monticello, Indiana. According to the Internet, Kilmer doesn't exist."

"But I'm standing here in the public library," I protested. "I grew up here."

How was that even *possible* in this day and age?

"I can't address that. If you can give me latitude and longitude, I can try to scout the place. I'll proceed as if it's dangerous and get back to you."

"Jesus," I said, shaken. "We've got our work cut out for us."

Booke sounded worried. "Be careful, Corine. I don't like the feel of this."

"You and me both."

Once I promised to call him in the morning, I rang off. He said he'd contact us if he learned anything we needed to know before then. I stared at the microfiche machine with equal blankness until Chance brought me out of it with a tap on the shoulder. I had to fight the urge to lean into his arms. I knew he wanted me to. Instead, I filled him in.

"Weirder and weirder." Chance touched my cheek lightly, drawing my face up. "I suspect we've got a hell of a mess here."

"No kidding." I couldn't imagine the scope of whatever had scrubbed all traces of Kilmer from the outside world. Maybe we should talk to Sandra Cheney and find out how she'd ended up here. She might be the last new blood the town had seen.

His fingers trailed down my jaw and curled around the

nape of my neck, as if he meant to lean down and kiss me. Instead, his gaze fixed on mine, steady and reassuring. "I just want you to know I'm in, just like you were in Laredo, no matter how bad this gets."

I smelled something burning.

Familiar Strangers

The light had shorted out in the microfiche machine, as if somebody didn't want us reading the article written about my mother's death. As discouragement went, the dead dog offered more punch. But I was probably reading more into a minor mechanical failure than it warranted. After all, it had probably been years since anyone had used this station at all.

So I wrote it off as an odd coincidence, though the librarian made such a big fuss about calling the maintenance man, you'd have thought he was flying in from New York instead of coming up the basement stairs. When Mr. McGee finally presented himself, I understood her concern a little better. With his long white handlebar mustache and unruly head of hair, he looked like a Civil War relic himself.

This repair could take a while. The librarian frowned at us and returned to her post at the front desk. Thank God she hadn't noticed Butch napping in the chair beside me; that would have gotten us tossed out on our collective ears. I tried to block him with my body, but Mr. McGee said, without glancing up from his work, "I don't care a bit about that little dog. He ain't harmed nothin'."

So he wasn't quite as blind as he seemed. "Are there archives downstairs?"

"If you wanna call it that. We got some boxes of junk

that don't go nowhere else. Don't let Edna see if you're fixing to sneak down there. You'll get her blood pressure up."

I took that as tacit permission, and tucked Butch beneath my arm. He whined a little but had the sense not to make a big fuss. Chance followed me as we wove through the shelves, angling toward the door Mr. McGee had emerged from. In a small town like this, it wasn't locked, so we headed downstairs unnoticed.

The basement smelled of dust and mildew. I wrinkled my nose; Butch sneezed. Old brown boxes sat piled on green industrial shelving. Numerical codes had been scribbled on the front, but I had no idea what they meant. I felt sure Dewey wouldn't approve.

We each opened a box at random and prowled through the contents. It was worse than it appeared. Old deeds, marriage licenses, letters and diaries had all been tossed together without rhyme or reason. As far as I could tell, the numbers on the outside of the boxes seemed to indicate a range of years for the junk contained therein. If I cared about quantities of cotton ordered by the general store in 1887, I'd be in heaven.

The air felt heavy and still, not even a hint of ventilation. Noticing that made me pause and look at the walls. "Chance, how many feet of rock would you say lie between us and the street?"

He shrugged. "A lot. Why?"

"Seems to me it would take an awful lot of power to block you in here. Why don't you try your luck again and see if there's anything we can use?"

"Worth a shot."

Chance focused. The room came alive with that raw static feel, as if we were mere moments away from a thunderstorm bursting to life around us. When his eyes opened, I saw tiny sparks of lightning. There was something deliciously elemental about him when he used his talent. I shivered a little, following him over to a metal filing cabinet shoved up against a wall.

He pulled out a manila folder with the initials *J.M.* scrawled on the front in red ink. "This is it."

"Whatever *it* is," I muttered.

Chance flipped it open, looking dubious. *Score.* He'd found a bunch of random newspaper clippings. Most of the articles had yellowed with age, and they didn't relate to any one subject, either.

I plucked out the top one and read aloud. "'Highway Built Ten Miles West of Proposed Route; Town Council Irate.'" The next one was even less interesting: "'No Cable for Kilmer.'" If we'd found someone's secret research, I had no idea what they were doing, except maybe documenting how sad and boring this town was.

Huh. Maybe Chance's gift just wasn't working right.

He closed the folder with a snap. "We should just take the lot and read them later. We don't want Edna to catch us down here."

That seemed like a good idea, so I slipped the file into my bag. Butch went in on top of it, and then we headed back up the narrow, spiderweb-clogged stairs. My heart almost stopped when I ran into Mr. McGee. He steadied me with strong, gnarled hands, but his eyes looked weird and filmy in the half-light.

"She's gone to the lavatory, young 'uns. Thinks y'all already left." He sounded oddly urgent. "Don't let her catch you messin' around down here."

His fervor took root in the form of dread. I had no idea what a withered old librarian could do to us, but if I'd learned anything over the years, appearances could be deceiving. We quick-stepped to the front door and out into a dismal, drizzling rain.

To my consternation, a woman I recognized met us on the way out. Miss Minnie had offered me a home after my mother died. I'd been happy there for a time. She respected my need to grieve, but she drew me back into daily life with irresistible requests for me to do this or that because she wasn't as spry as she used to be.

Together, we baked pies and cookies, cleaned out her attic, and refinished an old wooden dresser—pretty much anything she could think of to keep my mind off my loss. And I got better in her company, crying less in the night and talking more during the day.

But the respite didn't last long—just a few months. In the evenings, Miss Minnie would let me look through her jewelry box and tell me stories about the people they used to belong to—and I liked that. It made me feel rooted, part of something for the first time since my mama died.

And it was good until my gift sparked to life. I was handling a jeweled hair clip, a pretty piece that I'd long admired. That time, it singed my fingers, and I said without thinking, "This belonged to your great-aunt Cecilia. She was wearing it when she died."

Miss Minnie had gazed at me, her face pinched and gray, before snatching the clip away and fussing over burns she couldn't figure out how I'd gotten. That night, she called the social workers and said she wasn't equipped to deal with "a child like me." By the time I left Kilmer, she was the only one who was still halfway nice to me. Though she hadn't wanted me living in her home after that, she never stopped trying to get me to attend the Methodist church with her, as if religion could fix what ailed me.

At our near collision, her head came up. I smiled to see her white hair wrapped up in a cheerful rain bonnet. I remembered her saying bright colors made us miss the sun a little less. She returned my smile on automatic and started to brush by me with a quiet apology for her woolgathering.

I wasn't surprised. I'd been dishwater blond when I lived here, a mousy shade that made me fade into the woodwork. Back then, I'd wanted exactly that. I didn't want to be noticed or discussed. I only wanted to get away.

Then she hesitated, her hand on the door. "Do I know

you?" Miss Minnie squinted. "Yes, I'm sure I do. Why, Corine Solomon, as I live and breathe! I'd never forget those pretty blue eyes. It's so good to see you."

Reflexively, I curled my fingers into my palms and tucked them into my jacket pockets. "You're looking well, ma'am."

"Well, it's a rotten day to catch up, but I'd be obliged if you came for dinner before you leave." Her smile seemed warm and genuine. "Your young man's welcome too, of course."

From the confines of my bag, Butch whined. I heard the papers we'd stolen crunch as he tried to get comfortable. That gave me the excuse I needed.

"Yes, ma'am. Your number's still in the book?"

"Same as it ever was," she agreed.

With a wave, she passed by into the library.

The Mustang looked brighter and shinier than anything else on the street. Perhaps it was the damp or the wan winter light, but Kilmer looked as if the life had been leached out of it long ago, leaving a pale facsimile as its anchor in the real world. That thought weighed on me as I climbed into the car. Something about it resonated, but I couldn't connect it to anything else; it was more of a feeling than a certainty.

"I can't picture you here," Chance said, starting the car.

"Me either." It seemed a lifetime ago. In some ways, it was *more* than a lifetime. "But this is where it all began."

He paused long enough to maneuver onto the road, though I didn't know where we were going. "You never talk much about your dad."

For me that word conjured up images of a man who wore a panama fedora and a two-tone shirt. He always smelled of pipe tobacco and Old Spice, and he used to sing in the shower, silly songs he made up as he went along. More than that, I couldn't remember, any more than I could recall why he'd left. My mother never talked about it, and I figured she had her reasons.

"Neither do you," I said pointedly.

I suspected Chance knew more than he'd revealed. More truth he hadn't entrusted to me. I wasn't sure where the line should be drawn, or whether I wanted his deep, dark secrets at this late date.

"Does that bother you?" He drove as he did everything else, expertly and with complete control.

It had, once. Chance was like an iceberg, only its tip showing above the water; sure, it was beautiful and bright, but you never knew what lurked beneath the surface. He'd never made any attempt to share that with me, even though he wanted me laid open for him like a watermelon at a Fourth of July picnic.

The double standard had gotten old a long time ago, and I didn't have any interest in changing him. Maybe we'd both be better off if we just forgot about each other. Only I couldn't do that, damn him.

"It doesn't matter now."

"I *hate* when you do that." Though his tone was gentle, the words were not. "You expect me to know everything without your ever saying a word. You always did. You expect me to have some magical way of divining what you need from me, and that's just not fair. How can I offer it when I don't even know what it is half the time?"

The wipers scraped on the windshield, underscoring his muted frustration. I'd like to say I disagreed with him, but he had a point. I *did* have trouble articulating my needs, because the minute you told a person what you wanted, you made yourself vulnerable. They had the power, not you. If you never asked, you could pretend you were never disappointed.

But that only works if you're happy living a lie.

I exhaled unsteadily and reached for Butch, who nuzzled my hand. I could've said nothing, but that was the same as an admission. I decided I might as well go all the way.

"Point to you. But I never said I'm easy to be with, Chance." I tried to keep my voice even. "I told you before . . . I don't blame you for anything."

I didn't want this to turn into an argument, as we'd never been any good at those. I got shrill and defensive; he went icy and remote. Then we made up in bed before we agreed on anything. As fruitless cycles went, it had its perks.

"That's not entirely true."

I fell silent, refusing to discuss it further. But he was right again, dammit. I *did* blame him for not explaining the risks of being with him. Maybe it wasn't fair; I mean, how could he date someone while simultaneously telling them it wasn't safe? I could see his point of view—what was the point in having that conversation until he was sure the relationship was going somewhere? But once he knew . . . I should've been clued in and given the option to choose.

That summed up my key complaint about Chance. He always seemed to think he knew what was best for me and never bothered to confirm it. Well, after I fell through the floor of a burning building, I'd put the pieces together myself.

And then I walked away, as soon as I was able.

It wasn't just the danger of bodily harm that had driven me off. I felt as if I had to leave a relationship where I wasn't a full partner. I didn't want him to be my guardian; just my lover. I remained unconvinced he knew how to separate the two impulses.

We passed few cars. It was around lunchtime; there should have been people on the road heading home for a bite or looking for a likely dining spot. So far as I could tell, there was Ma's Kitchen, the coffee shop, and the Kilmer Inn. I hadn't seen a single restaurant otherwise—more hallmarks of a dying town.

The silence between us stretched taut, emblazoned with the inability to connect that had destroyed our relationship. He couldn't let me in all the way—and I was afraid of giving more than I got. My heart hurt with the futility of it.

When we pulled up to the periwinkle Victorian house, I realized we'd come straight back to the bed-and-breakfast. Chance circled around back and put the car in park. Before

I could move, he came around the front of the car and yanked my door open. With a start, I saw he'd gotten his expensive leather shoes muddy.

Rain trickled down his brown face, but he paid it no mind. I slid out of the car, suddenly uneasy with the intensity I'd evoked, but instead of telling me what was on his mind, he only muttered, "Let's get inside before you catch your death."

Disarmed Conflict

We ran through the rain toward the porch and tried to stamp off some of the wet before going inside. Sandra came down the hall to meet us. She tried to look welcoming, but instead her expression looked brittle. "You two got caught out in it, did you? Well, you should have time to freshen up before lunch."

Translation: *You're dripping on my rug, so get your asses upstairs.*

I didn't know whether we rubbed her the wrong way or whether she just wasn't cut out for customer service. The diamond-sharp edge to her manner made me uneasy. What would she do if she found out about Butch?

Maybe the stress of being back in Kilmer had gotten to me. Surely I didn't suspect a middle-aged innkeeper would murder my dog. Still, I made sure he was out of sight as I hurried toward the stairs.

Chance came hard on my heels. "There's something off about her."

I didn't feel safe to answer until we'd locked the door behind us. "You think?"

We still hadn't met her husband or her daughter. The inn seemed eerily quiet, no sounds within to indicate a meal being served; just the rain drumming on the roof and our breathing. I would have liked to blame my wet clothes, but my skin just crawled.

And the idea of getting naked and stepping into that old-fashioned tub, then drawing the curtain so I could take a hot shower? My teeth chattered.

"You're freezing," he said. "You take the bathroom first."

"Come in with me." The words shot out before I could stop them.

He froze. "You want me in the tub with you? Naked bodies, hot water, steam . . ." Chance's look turned dreamy for a moment; then he seemed to gauge my expression. "Jesus, you're scared to death. What's wrong?"

I could only shake my head. "I don't . . . I don't know. Please, will you sit in there with me? Keep me company?"

Score points for Chance—because he didn't question my unusual, neurotic behavior. It felt . . . good. I said, *Thank you*, with my eyes. And he smiled. God, he was so beautiful. Men had no right to look like he did, especially dripping wet.

Shivering all the while, I gathered up my toiletries and made my way to the bathroom. The hinges creaked as I pulled the slatted door wide. A door on the other side adjoined the Plumeria room. However crazy it sounded, I wanted Chance parked in between, watching my back.

My breathing slowly settled. He wouldn't let anything happen to me. I undressed in the tub behind the shower curtain, knowing he could see the sexy shadow play of my movements. His muffled moan verified that notion.

"Cruel and unusual," he muttered.

"You always did say I have a mean streak." I sounded almost normal, thank God.

"Do you ever."

The pipes groaned, and then the hot water gushed out, no warm-up period . . . unusual for a place this old. I derived a certain amount of satisfaction from washing myself with him only a few short feet away. I imagined him watching my hands with rapt attention, and my pulse spiked. Okay, I didn't want to tease *myself*, so I finished up quickly.

But when I stepped onto the bath mat, safely wrapped in a towel, I didn't receive the sizzling welcome I anticipated. I started to make a joke about finding him frozen in the middle of the room, but Chance motioned me to silence. At first I didn't know what I was listening for. Then it registered.

Creak. It came from the floorboards in the Plumeria room. For reasons I couldn't articulate, the sound chilled my blood. I stilled too, listening to light, furtive steps coming closer and closer. Steam twirled in the air between us like a fiendish fog.

I held my breath, every muscle coiled. And then . . . the decorative brass doorknob turned ever so slowly, side to side. Nobody knocked. The door didn't rattle. I heard no steps going away, but they might have been drowned by my thundering heart. After what seemed like an eternity, I had to inhale. Stars sparked in my field of vision, and the terror I hadn't been able to explain before returned twofold.

Would they come into our room? Would they try the door from the other side? There might be a perfectly reasonable explanation, but my twitchy nerves screamed no.

"Whew. Either we're both crazy, or . . ." Chance wrapped his arms around me, rubbing my back through the damp terry cloth of my towel. "We should find somewhere else to stay."

While Chance stood guard, I scrambled into clean clothes. Butch trotted into the bathroom and whined. I tried to shush him, but he ignored me, scratching at the bottom of the door that led into the Plumeria room. Against my better judgment, I hunkered down on all fours and peered to see what had the dog so riled up. I spied something through the little crack beneath the door, and a foul smell told me the powdery residue wasn't dust.

"Chance, come take a look at this."

He crouched down. "Smells rotten."

"We've either been visited by something nasty or this is a spell component." Dammit, I wished I had my mother's books. "Let's get out of here."

"First . . ." He got a zip bag out of his duffel and used a comb, wrapped in toilet paper, to scoop up a little of the powder. I didn't know what he planned on doing with it, but it didn't seem like the time to question him.

We snatched our belongings, and I opened the door into the hall. Another line of evil-smelling powder ran across our threshold. I remembered the way Chuch and Eva had warded their house with sea salt and wormwood and I hesitated, wondering if we'd been hexed or blessed.

"Could this be for our protection?" I wondered aloud. "A country tradition?"

"Either way, step over it. Don't get it on your shoe."

That sounded like a wise idea, if only to avoid the smell, so I did just that. Chance followed me, closing the door behind him. I stifled a little scream when Sandra Cheney came around the corner.

"Lunch is ready," she said. "I wanted to make sure you didn't miss it. I made a lovely pot roast with potatoes and carrots. Peach pie for dessert."

Somewhere in the distance, thunder rumbled, but no lightning flashed afterward. To me it sounded like a portent of things to come.

"Thank you, but we have an engagement," I returned as politely as I could manage.

Something flickered behind her pale blue eyes. "An engagement? I didn't realize you knew anyone in Kilmer. I took you for tourists, not that we get many these days."

I dodged her question. "Why is that?"

She made a vague gesture. "Oh, you know. People just bypass the town, since the highway doesn't run by here."

"What made you open a bed-and-breakfast?" Offense seemed like the best defense. If I questioned her all the way to the foyer, she wouldn't be able to do the same. Chance walked ahead, apparently trusting me to deal with the situation. I had to admit; I liked the sensation.

"It was always here," Sandra said. "My husband's maternal grandmother used to run the place. Jensen's Boardinghouse, she called it. We just updated the look and changed things a little when we took over."

We reached the stairs and I let her pass. I didn't want her thinking too hard about why I had both my backpack and my purse; nor did I want her getting a glimpse of Butch.

"How did you wind up in Kilmer?"

Sandra cut me a surprised look. "Why, I've always lived here. Before I married Jim, I was Sandy Prentice."

Said as if the name means something to me. I tried to appear suitably impressed.

"Nice."

Her expression morphed into a tight-lipped courtesy that said *I just knew you weren't from around here.* Good for me.

"Reverend Prentice is my father," she went on, "and the minister at the Methodist church."

The same one Miss Minnie always tried to drag me to? No wonder I didn't recognize Sandra. I never went inside churches if I could help it. The whole witch's daughter thing made me uncomfortable.

As I cast about for something to say, Chance put in, "Well, no wonder you have such a knack for setting people at home. As a preacher's daughter, you must've helped host a lot of get-togethers."

Sandra flushed, obviously delighted. I struggled not to snort.

"Yes, I *did* help my father when he'd have the deacons over to Saturday breakfast. And aren't you a sweet thing to notice?" Her newscaster accent finally stressed and broke, giving way to a drawl as she flirted.

"I could hardly help it."

"I hope you'll stop by the dining room and meet Jim and Shannon before you leave. That way you won't be disturbed if you run across them at odd hours."

Now why would she put it like that?

"We'd love to," Chance told Sandra.

His palm settled into the small of my back, nudging me

toward the dining room. I could only assume he wanted to get a look at her family. I didn't remember Jim Cheney, but if he was Sandra's age, they would've been well out of school before I got there.

To my surprise, the dining room table was set for a meal, laid with fine china and good crystal. The food had obviously been prepared with painstaking care, but there wasn't a chance in hell we'd eat it. In fact, I wished we hadn't eaten breakfast.

A man with dark hair and silver at his temples sat in a wine velvet wingback chair, staring at his hands. His worn chambray shirt and slightly stained jeans clashed with the pristine, if slightly fussy, décor. He seemed miles away, or maybe he just wanted to be.

"You must be Jim," I said, forcing a smile. "You have a lovely place here."

His head came up, revealing haunted, gunmetal gray eyes. "That's all Sandra's doing," he answered. "I just keep things from falling apart. But thank you."

Maybe I was just overly attuned to nuances and searching for weirdness, but this family offered it in spades. Oddly, the daughter provided a much-needed link to normalcy.

Shannon wore her hair dyed black, tipped in electric blue. She was skinny, swathed in black clothing, and she had a ring in her nose. When her mom made the introduction, she scowled at us. I'd never been so happy to see a punk-Goth kid with a bad attitude. Based on what we'd glimpsed thus far, I'd feared Kilmer was permanently stuck in 1962.

"Mind your manners," Sandra snapped. "And be polite to our guests or I'll take away that iPod your uncle Kenneth sent you."

The kid mumbled something, and then said grudgingly, "I'm pleased to meet you."

She offered her hand, and when I shook it, we threw a tiny blue spark. Shannon frowned as she drew back, rubbing her fingers as if she suspected me of shocking her on purpose. *Interesting. Very, very interesting.* I didn't know yet what

I intended to do with the information, but Shannon was Gifted.

"That's better," Sandra said with an approving smile. Something about her put me in mind of *The Stepford Wives*.

Jim said nothing at all. He'd returned to staring, although now he gave the impression of gazing out into the rain and wishing himself a thousand miles away. His misery felt tangible as an extra presence.

Well, I'd had enough. "Enjoy your lunch. It looks delicious."

"I'm a vegetarian," Shannon snapped.

Of course she was—probably Wiccan too, and possibly a lesbian as well; anything she figured would get her mom good and riled. She might have been the one sneaking around, practicing faux spells as part of her teenage rebellion. Maybe she thought if she ran off all the guests, she wouldn't have to clean the rooms. Maybe that incident in the bathroom was nothing to worry about at all.

And maybe I was Miss Universe.

Between the daughter's rebellious scowl and the husband's quiet despair, I felt sure there was something wrong in this house. Whether it had anything to do with my mother's death remained to be seen.

Shannon watched us go. Chance waved as he went, and I followed him out. I didn't say I'd see them later because I knew that, unless something went heinously wrong, we wouldn't be back.

The way our luck had been running, I figured we'd probably return before dinnertime.

Gone Fishing

Butch was none too pleased at going back out into the rain.

I couldn't say the notion pleased me mightily, either, but something was wrong at the Kilmer Inn. I didn't know where we'd get lunch or where we'd stay, but it seemed like it was time to start knocking on doors. Much as I loathed the idea of seeing all my foster parents again, I couldn't think of anywhere else to start.

"Head for that filling station," I said, pointing at a rundown building on the right.

It wasn't a chain, either. A faded sign read CHUCK'S GAS-N-GO. Near as I could tell, there were no chains at all in Kilmer. I couldn't remember if there ever had been, come to think of it. My memories of the place, apart from ones about my mama, seemed odd and fuzzy.

While Chance topped off the tank, I lowered my head and dashed for the dirty white building. Rain pelted me, trickling down my neck to the small of my back. I went up a cement step into the office. To the right stood an attached garage with two repair bays. A guy in a filthy coverall came through the connecting door, wiping his hands on a rag.

"Something I can do for you?" He touched the brim of his yellow cap, but I wasn't sure whether he meant it as a courtesy or if he was just wiping his fingers some more.

My gaze went to the soft drink cooler on the left. "Just need a couple of these." I snagged two cans at random. "And to pay for gas, whenever he gets done."

The guy nodded, folding his arms across a spindly chest. He sported a fierce red hickey on his neck. He preened a little when my gaze lingered on it. *Yeah, buddy, you're getting some. We're all proud of you.* I then noticed that the station lacked a console to tell him how much gas was being pumped, and the cash register didn't have a place to scan a credit card, either. Behind the register, I spied an old sliding imprinter. Holy crap, they still used paper and carbons here.

"Looks like he's set," the guy said. "I'll just check how much."

The attendant stepped out into the weather like it didn't bother him, though maybe he reckoned a drenching as good as a shower. It sure couldn't do his coverall any harm. I stared out over the cracked cement into the storm; rain fell in sheets spattering in rhythmic bursts driven by the wind. Beyond the gas station, no cars passed at all, the road an empty gray ribbon that threaded through town.

I reached across the counter and snagged the directory sitting next to the phone, and then I rummaged through my bag, looking for a pad and paper. If nothing else, I remembered their names. There had been ten of them. I never stayed in one home more than a year after my mother died, and the quality of my foster parents had declined as the social worker lost patience. As I recalled, she was less interested in the quality of my placement than checking me off a to-do list. Unlike most small towns, Kilmer had its own branch of social services, independent from the county. That had never struck me as odd before now.

The cashier came back in while I was writing and named a sum for the sodas and gas. Absently, I paid the amount, still flipping through the phone book. It took me another five minutes to finish the job. As I closed the cover, I noticed it was printed locally by the same company that owned the newspaper. I tapped the front thoughtfully.

"Who's in charge of Paragon Publishing?" I asked, not expecting him to answer.

"Well, I reckon that'd be Augustus England. Did you want to put an ad in the paper? You don't need to talk to him, if you do. He's got an office assistant."

I tried to imagine a publishing empire being run by one guy and an office assistant. Clearly that would only work in Kilmer. On impulse, I checked for a personal address for Mr. England and found him unlisted. *Well, of course.* I probably wouldn't find a single town councilman in the book.

I did scrawl the address of the business offices for Paragon Publishing, however. The town reporters might know something about the weird stuff going on. At least, they always seemed to in movies . . . right before they died horribly as a result of their meddling ways. With a smile, I slid the directory back over the counter and stepped out into the rain.

I dashed for the Mustang, where Chance sat waiting in the driver's seat. His smile twanged my heartstrings as I hopped in. "Get the addresses?"

"Yep. This would be easier if we could map them online," I said. "Some of these are out in the country, so I suspect this is going to be a long day."

He sighed. "Then let's start with the ones here in town. Maybe the rain will let up."

I surveyed the list.

The third address on the list belonged to Glen and Ruth Farley. I'd stayed on their farm for about nine months. They worked me hard over the summer, but I had no complaints. They'd let me be, otherwise, which was more than could be said for some. It looked liked they'd sold off their acreage, though, and moved into town. I tapped the paper.

"This one isn't too far. They're over on Twelfth Street now."

Chance acknowledged that with a nod and made a left. He'd already learned the layout, and within five minutes, we pulled up outside a small brick house. A black wrought-iron fence separated the yard from the sidewalk. It was identical to its neighbors in every respect, except for the statues on the front lawn. I thought it odd to see a full Nativity scene out already, before Thanksgiving. Lights twined around the rustic wooden frame, twinkling in a weirdly festive cascade of white, gold, red, and green. They cast fey shadows over the wet brown blades of grass.

"Shall we?" He arched a brow at me, lips quirking into a wry half smile.

I had no idea what I was going to say when we got to the front door. Butch gave a little woof of disapproval at being dragged out again. If we had a safe place to leave him, I would have, but since *we* were the reason he'd been orphaned, I didn't want anything to happen to him.

Chance didn't wait for me to muster my nerve. He opened the screen, and then rapped on the door, as if he had everything figured out. I guessed our tack depended on whether they recognized me. With the red hair, I didn't know whether they would, although Miss Minnie had said she knew me by my eyes.

After a minute, something rattled and the door swung open slowly, like monsters might lurk on our side. A small woman with faded gray and brown hair peered at me around the crack between the door and chain. Her gaze flicked nervously to Chance. "I'm not interested," she said, "whatever you're selling."

She started to slam the door, but I caught it with my palm. It would have to be the truth, or some close facsimile thereof. "Miz Ruth, it's Corine. Solomon? May we come in for a minute?"

"I declare," she exclaimed. "I haven't seen you in a coon's age, girl. Look at you with that wicked red hair. Come in, do come on in, and get out of the wet." With that, she unhooked the chain, but I noticed she gave the empty street a long, hard look before stepping back to let us in.

I murmured something noncommittal. Chance gave me a look as we followed her into the parlor, furnished in country blue with lots of homemade throw pillows. Her furniture had big fat cabbage roses, and the arms were threadbare. She'd tried to cover that with lace doilies, but as I sat down, I saw the loose threads through the holes in the lace.

The carpet was worn and yellow; I could see the paths where she had walked in the years they'd been living there. Most people would lay down runners to prevent that, but I found it comforting to see evidence of passage. Someone, probably Miz Ruth, had hung cross-stitch on the wall. I read the messages with disquiet: BLESS THIS HOUSE and SAVE US FROM THE TIME OF TRIAL and DELIVER US FROM EVIL. I recognized the latter from the Lord's Prayer, but I found it ominous she would have excerpted those lines and nothing more.

Chance sat beside me on the love seat while she perched opposite us in what was probably her husband's recliner. It was plain blue velour or velveteen, whatever they called that fabric, and it had scuff marks on the bottom. She didn't pop the footrest up, though she did look tired—or maybe worn would be the better word. Miz Ruth couldn't be more than fifty-five, but she looked ten years older. Purple bruises cradled her eyes, the kind that only came from many, many sleepless nights.

Miz Ruth folded her hands in her lap, as if stilling her nerves with conscious effort. "So what brings you back? It's been ages now, hasn't it?"

"Yes, ma'am," I acknowledged with a nod. "Nine years, to be exact." I didn't know what I was going to say until it came out in a rush. "Well, I reckon I wanted to show Chance where I grew up. Introduce him to the people who raised me."

That was inspired. They'd had years to forget how much I freaked them out.

Her expression softened. "Well, if that isn't the sweetest thing." Miz Ruth turned to him with a smile. "You must be Corine's young man. It's a pleasure to meet you . . . Chance, is it?"

"Yes, ma'am." He stood up to shake her hand, earning an approving nod.

"Well, I'm Miz Ruth. We had Corine, when she was, oh, fourteen or so, I guess. She was a great help around the farm, particularly with the animals."

I correctly interpreted his look. *Yes, I* do *know how to milk a cow. No, I won't be doing it again any time soon.*

The older woman probably didn't even remember why they'd called the social worker and had me reassigned. But I did. I'd touched a gun and experienced a hunting accident that scared the bejesus out of both me *and* them. My inexplicable burns frightened them the most, making them think, as most decent, God-fearing folk did, that my powers must be infernal in origin. I curled my hands in my lap, not wanting to remind her.

"I bet she was," Chance said with an especially winning smile. "I don't suppose you remember any stories to embarrass her with. She's met *my* mother more than once, but—"

"Oh, I'm sure I can come up with something." Miz Ruth blushed girlishly. She probably thought I'd told him she had been like a mama to me. If she felt flattered by the notion, well, that was all right; better if we softened her up so she wanted to talk.

And *Lord*, could she talk. She told a good ten stories about me, half of which I was pretty sure weren't true. She just didn't want to disappoint Chance, I suspect. He listened with every appearance of fascination, leaning forward so he didn't miss a word. Miz Ruth probably hadn't held a handsome man's attention this long in years. I sat quiet, understanding he was gaining her confidence, so I could work around to my questions. Those would be hard and horrible, and they'd go better if they felt like normal curiosity over the course of a friendly visit instead of the inquisition I wanted to invoke.

She broke off at last to say, "Whew, I'm parched. Have y'all eaten? I have chicken and dumplin's left from last night. I could heat some up in a jiff."

As if summoned, Butch poked his head out of the top of

my bag. He yapped, letting us know he could eat. I hoped Miz Ruth wasn't allergic or afraid of Chihuahuas.

"Sorry," I started to say.

"What a darling animal!" She came over to pet him on the head.

Butch consented to her attentions with great dignity. Then he leaped down from my purse and trotted around, sniffing here and there. "Don't worry," I told her. "He's house-trained. He just wants to explore a little."

"That's just fine. He might even smell the cat," Miz Ruth said. "He's been gone a year, but . . ." She shrugged.

"I'm sorry to hear that. What happened to him?" I wondered if pets had been disappearing. After all, that Doberman on the road into town had to belong to someone.

"You know, I have no idea." She spoke over her shoulder, and we followed her into the kitchen, done in faded yellow and white gingham. "One morning, he just didn't come home. I'd let him out of a night, and usually he'd show up like clockwork at six a.m., crying for his breakfast."

I grinned. "Isn't that just like a man?"

She laughed softly as she got out a pan. "Oh, I'm sure your Chance has good reason to stay in, so they're not all like that."

"Thank you." He favored her with another warm smile, and I swore she almost melted into syrup on the floor.

Butch trotted in and curled up at my feet; his calmness actually reassured me. He had a solid track record for sensing danger, knowing when to panic, and when to take a nap. Miz Ruth hummed as she whipped up the noon meal, chatting about this and that. She seemed to have taken heart from our presence, which made me wonder what was wrong, and where her husband was.

We sat at the kitchen table, a genuine antique I valued at nearly a thousand dollars. You didn't see woodwork much like this anymore. She didn't even have a tablecloth on it— just woven placemats. The pawnshop owner in me wanted to make her a lowball offer. I stroked my fingertips across the burnished wood and let the images come.

If I didn't block them, every item I touched would singe my skin and whisper to me about what had happened to it. This time, I was curious enough to risk the gentle burn, but I saw only a pale collage of meals, first with Ruth and Glen, and then Ruth, all by herself. Then I glimpsed a woman in Phoenix who wanted a table like this more than anything, and she'd pay a ridiculous price for it too. When the images flickered out, I was grateful they hadn't delivered a scene of heel-banging sex. It would be hard to sit and eat chicken and dumplings after that, but I'd manage. Of all my foster mothers, Miz Ruth had been the best cook.

Since I didn't want to upset her before she fed us, I sat quietly, letting Chance charm her. The warm and homey aroma wafted from her cook pot, better than a big country hug. I could use a little comfort; that was for sure.

After lunch, it might get ugly.

Catch of the Day

I thoroughly enjoyed the chicken and dumplings. Southern women knew how to cook them from scratch, and I hadn't eaten any this good in years. Miz Ruth was kind enough to offer a little plate to Butch, who looked properly appreciative. He gave her the *happy* bark and wagged his tail as he dug in.

We declined the offer of leftover brown Betty but accepted some fresh coffee. She made it fancy for us with ground chicory and cinnamon, and it made me homesick for a place that had burnt to the ground years ago. I remembered sitting with my mama on the front porch, that wondrous smell wafting up from her cup. We'd watch the sunrise together over the trees, sharing the colors slipping from pearly to passionate to happy-summer blue. Birdsong, trilling wrens and finches, filled the air at the birth of the new day. We didn't need to talk; we had the call of the meadowlark and mockingbird to keep us company.

At full light, my mama would head to the kitchen and start breakfast. Afterward, we would prowl the woods or work in the garden. Sometimes we'd take her battered old Duster to town to do a little shopping, but mostly we kept to ourselves. We always had a parade of visitors: hurly-burly men, peddlers, Gypsies, witches, and one man who told me he was a king in hiding. I always thought he was funning me, but now I had to wonder.

While I was woolgathering, Miz Ruth had laid out a plate of cookies. She seemed inclined to linger. She nibbled at a sugar cookie with the air of someone who was indulging a habit more than a desire; in the South, dinner wasn't over until people had coffee and a taste of something sweet.

And maybe she didn't have anything better to do today. I wished we could afford to sit and be social, but we had nine more houses to hit. I started looking for a segue.

It came in the form of her husband, Glen. She had danced around the subject of his absence, casting looks back to the easy chair that still bore an imprint of his behind. At first I thought he must be running errands, but when she said, "It hasn't been easy with him gone," I knew he wasn't coming back.

"What happened?" I asked gently.

"Don't know," she answered with an unhappy shrug. "He went hunting, maybe two weeks back, and just never came home."

Like the cat. Thankfully, I had the sense not to say it out loud.

"Did you file a missing persons report?" Chance asked.

Like that would do any good in this town, but Miz Ruth nodded. "The sheriff sent a deputy around when I called in. He wrote it all down in his notebook and said they'd have someone troll the woods, but nobody ever found anything." Her tone said she was none too sure a search had ever been conducted.

The way I'd felt driving through the woods, I couldn't imagine anybody being eager to go out and prowl around in them, so I figured she was right.

"I'm sorry to hear that," I said sincerely. "You must miss him."

She smiled, a touch of sadness in her eyes. "I do. But you know all about losing somebody, don't you? And you just a child at the time."

Perfect. I couldn't have asked for a better opening, but I had to be careful or she might get suspicious. "What do you remember about that, Miz Ruth? Nobody told me much. Like you said, I was a kid, and people don't tend to explain things to children."

"Such a shame." She shook her head. "There was a terrible fire," she added for Chance's benefit. "Your mama, God rest her soul, fell asleep with a lit cigarette. That's what I heard, anyway."

A lit torch, more like. I set my jaw. Nobody knew I'd *seen* the men in our front yard, or I'd probably be dead too. When they realized I'd survived, I told them I sneaked out hours before to meet a boy in the woods behind the house. Even then, I had a strong sense of self-preservation, and I never felt safe in Kilmer after my mama died.

"My mother didn't smoke," I said with deliberate bite, knowing I shouldn't contradict whatever story had been given out. "Never did. She was a vegetarian too."

Worry stirred in Miz Ruth's tired eyes. "I hope you don't mean to go poking around, Corine. Stirring old ashes doesn't do nothin' but throw sparks, and it just might get the wrong people riled up." It sounded more like a warning than a threat. I wondered if she'd bring up my mother's home business selling potions and charms, but she just shook her head and sighed.

"Would you care to tell me who those folks are?"

"I've wasted enough time jawing," she muttered. "I have to get to the washing up, and then there's more housework. I hope you don't mind seeing yourselves out."

I had no choice but to scoop Butch off the floor and acquiesce with a nod. She knew something she wasn't telling; I'd stake my life on it. And she was frightened, as well she might be. Her hands shook as she carried our coffee mugs to the sink, porcelain chattering in her grasp like gag teeth.

"I'm sorry for bothering you, ma'am."

I think she knew then that everything before had been a pretext. She turned with a sharp look. "No, you're not. You'll poke around until—well." Her shoulders slumped. "Maybe I'd do the same thing in your place, if I were younger and had somebody to help." She glanced at Chance. "Please be careful, Corine. This town isn't like you remember."

Her words chilled me. Given my history, I didn't recall Kilmer as the pinnacle of warmth and security. When we stepped out onto the porch, I saw the rain had abated some. Now it was no more than a miserable drizzle, misting my hair. I glanced over at Chance, who looked pensive.

"What do you think?" I asked.

He fell into step beside me as we descended the porch steps. At hitting the sidewalk my heels skidded on some wet leaves, and Chance steadied me, but he didn't take the opportunity to sweep me against him. I appreciated his restraint; he wouldn't pressure me about the relationship thing, which meant he'd learned something about me. Which made me want to throw myself into his arms—and by his maddening smile, he knew it too.

"Honestly?"

I nodded.

"It sounds like there's a monster loose. Missing people and pets? That mauled dog? The whole town stinks of dark magick."

"A monster," I repeated. "Like something out of *Creature Feature*? That's an awful lot of ground to cover."

"Don't be a smart-ass. As a hypothesis, it doesn't make a lot of sense, but we've never come across anything quite like this place before, have we?"

"I meant the woods, you know, ground to cover? If there's a monster in Kilmer, where else would it be?"

Chance slid me a look that said he wasn't convinced.

Butch whined. "All right, already, I'm getting in the car."

"My other guess would be a black coven," Chance said after we'd slammed both doors. The rain pattered on the Mustang, lending credence to the impression we were safe from the world within its metal frame. I locked my door nonetheless.

A black coven. That made more sense and might even offer a clue as to why they'd gone after my mother. The answer might be as simple as opposing hermetic traditions. That gave me no comfort, mind you, but at least it was comprehensible, when otherwise I'd only been dealing with intuition and ominous foreboding.

It didn't help us put the pieces together, however.

Only legwork could do that.

By the time the dismal gray sky filled with the diffuse, muted rays that signaled sunset, we'd visited four houses. At the first two, nobody answered, and at the second two, they pretended not to recognize me (or *really* didn't) and wouldn't let us in. They had *all* been afraid. That offered a clue we would be fools to ignore.

Unfortunately, we had no place to stay for the night, unless we returned to the bed-and-breakfast, where somebody might try to kill us. That possibility wasn't new, but usually I had some idea why. I suspected Sandra, if for no reason other than because she made my flesh crawl. Somebody in that house was making Jim miserable, and I didn't think it was Shannon.

"If we're going to be here a while—"

"Then we need a base of operations," I finished.

The streets were eerily quiet. I didn't even bother to look as I crossed toward the Mustang. Only Chance's choked cry gave me any warning of the car bearing down on me. He dove for me, shoving me out of the way, and we rolled across slick, leafy pavement to collide with the Mustang's solid tires. I could feel a huge, throbbing bruise on my shoulder where I'd hit, and there would probably be other marks as well.

It would've been considerably worse if the car had hit me.

Chance shoved me half under the Mustang, as if to protect me, and then bounded to his feet. From my vantage point on the ground, I saw him drop into a fighting stance, probably in case the car stopped and the driver tried to finish what he'd started. Instead, the vehicle fishtailed around the corner, squealing as he—or she—peeled out away from us.

I checked on Butch, who whimpered up at me. Overall, he seemed less frightened than me. The stupid dog probably trusted me to take care of him.

Chance helped me to my feet with gentle hands. I found myself shaking at the unexpectedness of it. No dark magick, no chill in the air—a pretty mundane murder attempt, when you came right down to it—and there was nothing to ward off, and nothing I could do to protect myself except pay better attention.

"It was an Olds Cutlass," he said grimly. "Dark blue. Mud all over the plates. Are you all right?"

"Yeah," I managed to say. "Thanks. I guess word's gotten around, and somebody isn't happy."

"Understatement." As if he couldn't help it, he wound his arms around me and rested his chin on my hair. His heat seared me through our damp clothes, the lines of his body strong, beautiful, and heart-wrenchingly familiar. "I don't think my luck had anything to do with this, though." He sounded hesitant, as if I might blame him for the latest close call. "It feels like it's hardly working at all here."

I thought about that and agreed. "Don't worry, Chance. This one's on me. If I hadn't come back, the driver of that car wouldn't have targeted me. Since I'm back here asking awkward questions after all these years, it means I know something about the night my mama died—and *they* have something to lose."

"So do I," he muttered, running a thumb down my cheek. "I guess it's pointless to ask you to take the warning and go?"

I answered that with a look. He sighed, let go of me, and opened my car door. As I got into the Mustang, I swept the street with a final glance and noticed twitching curtains on five different houses. They'd seen the near hit-and-run, but nobody came out to see if I was all right. People either hated me a lot more than I'd remembered or they didn't want to risk being on the streets after dark.

I didn't think I'd made that many enemies as a kid.

Chance checked his watch as he put the car in gear. "So . . . we've had our daily dose of adrenaline. It's not quite five yet, despite the weather. Let's see if we can find a real estate agent on the square somewhere."

I couldn't remember seeing anything of the sort, but we drove downtown, keeping an eye peeled for anything remotely helpful. Most of the stores were closed already, or had never opened for the day. At ten minutes to the hour, I spotted a small white sign that read REGIS PROPERTY MANAGEMENT.

"That looks promising."

As Chance parked in a metered spot, I glanced down. Yuck. We'd be hard-pressed to convince the real estate agent we weren't vagrants, given my current state. While I tried to brush the worst of the dirty leaves off, he came around to open my door. Despite my determination to sort my feelings without letting him influence me, my heart gave a happy little jolt. He *knew* I was a sucker for such courtly, old-school gestures.

Butch pawed at me from inside the bag. I knew what that meant, so I set him down near the drain beside the curb. He did his business, and then we went on into the office. No bell jingled to sound our entry, but a middle-aged woman sat at a pasteboard desk, writing a memo by hand. There was an old typewriter on the table on the wall to her left. Dreary landscape photos lined the walls, and brochures about property taxes lay scattered on the table.

All told, it was a typical front office . . . if you'd flashed back to 1963. The woman looked mildly annoyed to see us, as it was nearly closing time. She reminded me of a cow, although not in a bad way; she was just placid and well fed. A fake walnut plate in front of her appointment calendar read AGNES PETTIGREW.

"Did you have an appointment to see a house?" she decided to ask when it became clear we weren't going away.

Chance shook his head. "We were hoping to talk to Mr. Regis about a rental. Are there any apartments or houses to let in town?"

She bestirred herself for him. All women did. "Let me check the books."

"We have two properties that might qualify," she told us after a moment. "And a couple of owners might be amenable to a long-term rent-to-buy program. They're very motivated sellers."

"Are they?" I asked, exchanging a look with Chance.

Desperate to get out of town, you might say.

Agnes took that as a polite rhetorical question. "But you'll need to make an appointment. Mr. Regis can't—"

"What can't I do?" A booming voice came from the back room.

The door burst open, rebounding against the opposite wall, and the doorway filled with the largest man I'd ever seen in real life.

Destiny for Sale or Rent

Agnes stammered. I didn't blame her. I wouldn't have wanted to be caught trying to organize this man's life for him, even if I did know best. But she didn't look frightened; instead her gaze gobbled him up. As she stared up at him, her mouth went soft and she propped her chin in her hand.

Curious, I brushed her jacket with my fingertips. I didn't expect much of a burn; there shouldn't be any trauma associated with this object. The pain was slight, and the coat showed me that they usually walked out together. He made sure she got to her car safely each night, and he sometimes stood by the driver's side, chatting to her, after he shut her door. *Wonder if he knows how much that means.* I could see her face tilted up toward him, reflected back in the rearview mirror, and these moments meant everything to her.

"You don't have time to talk to these folks tonight, Phillip," Miss Pettigrew said then. "They should schedule a proper appointment."

And you won't miss your nightly date.

The real estate agent dismissed her concerns with a wave of one meaty paw. "Go home, Agnes. I can talk to these folks without you hovering, so don't worry. You won't miss *Wheel of Fortune*. Lock up on your way out and flip the sign to 'Closed.' I can surely handle this myself."

Her lips drooped as she gathered up her purse, but she didn't waste any time in getting herself out the front door. She probably wanted to make it home before dark. I offered a pleasant wave, and she frowned before turning to hurry down the walk, head down in anticipation of a coming storm.

"Thanks for your help," I said with a polite smile. He was the first normal person we'd met in Kilmer. He didn't seem nervous or frightened—just eager to sell us something, which fit the real estate agent profile to a T. His face was broad as an iron skillet, pink skinned, and smooth. His eyes shone like blue stones, but with considerably more warmth.

"Not at all. I'm Phil Regis." He shook my hand with a grasp that ground my knuckles a bit, and then he ran a hand through his salt-and-pepper hair, sheepish, as if he constantly forgot his own strength.

Mr. Regis stepped back and waved us into his office, a good-sized space with a big cherry desk littered with pens and paperwork. The pictures in here were prettier than the ones in the waiting area, good watercolors that might be worth something. I'd need to look at the signatures before I could say for sure. Chance and I settled into padded vinyl chairs on the other side of the desk.

"Now then," Regis said, "I heard something about y'all needing a rental. Are you newlyweds? Because I could probably get you a mortgage cheaper than you'd expect. It's a buyer's market, you know." He gave a deep laugh that swelled his chest like a bellows.

Chance shook his head, though I don't know whether he was disagreeing with the buyer's market, the mortgage, or our being newlyweds. "We're just vacationing in the area. I'd like to let for a month while we're exploring all the historic sites nearby."

"Huh," said Regis. It was a thoughtful sound, not a doubtful one. "We don't have much to rent, but I do manage a couple properties that might fit the bill."

"The receptionist mentioned as much," I said. "Can we take a look?"

"Sure, sure." He stood, crossing past us into the waiting area. We heard him rummaging through Agnes's desk; then he returned shortly with a black three-ring binder lofted in triumph. "She tries to hide it from me. Fool woman thinks I'll put the pages out of order or something." Regis shook his head, but I noted underlying fondness in his tone.

"She did seem protective," Chance observed.

"And isn't that a hoot?" Regis laughed. "She seems to think the world will come to an end if someone sees me without an appointment. It's beneath my consequence, according to Agnes."

"Thanks for seeing us," I said again, hoping to nudge him back on track.

The real estate agent flipped through the binder, then tapped a white piece of paper with handwritten notes. I admired the penmanship, even upside down, and imagined Agnes deserved the credit. A picture had been stapled to the top of the listing. He spun the book so we could take a look.

"This farmhouse belonged to Mrs. Everett. She passed away, oh, a good three years ago. She had no kin, so I bought the property myself for a song. I intended to flip it—" At our blank looks, he explained, "Renovate, then sell on a markup. So far I've had no luck."

"How come?" I asked.

"Superstitious idiots. Mrs. Everett passed away there. In her sleep," the real estate agent hastened to add. "There's nothing to be afraid of, but I can't even get anybody out there to remodel the place. So other than having it dusted and aired out every few months, I haven't been able to do anything with it. So it's still mostly furnished."

I wondered if it would still be full of old-lady smell, lavender, and Vicks VapoRub. I hoped her possessions didn't clutter up the place as well. Old ladies were notorious pack rats, keeping boxes of rubbish nobody else could see a use for.

"Her personal things?"

"Gone," Regis assured me. "I'm sure it just needs a good airing. Leave a window or two open, and you'd be just fine out there. I could lease the place to y'all for a month . . . and I'd be willing to go longer if you decide you want to stay. We could work out a rent-to-buy program, if you don't have a down payment." He sounded so hopeful; I didn't have the heart to tell him there wasn't a chance in hell of that happening.

Chance studied the picture with such concentration, I took another look: white house, windows on either side of the front door, and red steps leading up to a wraparound porch. Ten thin rectangular columns supported the roof over the porch. The downward slope gave the black tile roof a tiered but pointy look, like a witch's hat.

All told, it appeared habitable enough, but I didn't like the weird triangular window I assumed led to the attic or other unused space. Why else would it have been boarded up? But maybe those were just creepy storm shutters. I read the amenities with half attention: three bedrooms, bath and a half, bi-level with storm cellar and artesian well.

"What's the other option?" Chance asked, as if he sensed my hesitance.

If Regis was disappointed we didn't leap on the house immediately, he didn't show it. Instead, he flipped through the binder some more and then turned it so we could see. "This is a bachelor apartment, above what used to be an accounting business. But he left town, and I haven't rented that space to anyone yet."

From what I'd seen of Kilmer, he wasn't likely to, either.

"Do you own that building too?"

"No, but I manage the property for August."

For a moment, I thought he meant the month, and it was November. Then it hit me. Augustus England, publishing magnate.

"He runs the newspaper and prints up the town phone

books, right?" The question spilled out before I thought better of it.

Stupid. Regis's gaze sharpened. I could tell he wanted to know why I knew that much about the town, if we were just tourists passing through. For the first time, I saw steel behind his bluff, friendly exterior. The very air in the office seemed to chill.

"We looked you up in the directory over at the filling station," Chance said easily. "Corine has a head for trivia. I'm sure she read the information page, the credits, the emergency numbers, and who knows what else while she was looking for a real estate agent."

I made my smile sheepish. "I read the copyright page in books too. I love finding out real names when authors write under a pseudonym."

I hoped I looked properly guileless. I had the feeling he wouldn't rent us anything if he knew we were here to poke around. Sure, he'd find out sooner or later. Such was the way of small towns, but once we had a contract, he couldn't boot us out.

Regis seemed to relax. "Oh, my wife's the same way. She'll read anything, even the cereal box."

Wife, huh? I wondered whether the woman knew Agnes Pettigrew would dearly love her job. Filing that away under relatively useless information, I said, "So, tell us about the apartment."

"Well, it's cozy," said Regis. "All utilities included, of course. It has one bedroom, a sitting room, full bath, and a kitchenette with two electric rings for cooking."

Real estate agent to real-world translation: Cozy equals claustrophobic.

"Could you break down the pros and cons of each?" Chance asked.

This should be funny. I didn't think salesmen ever admitted anything had cons.

"Well, the farmhouse has a lot more space, but it's outside town, less convenient, but private and nicely wooded. The bachelor apartment is small, but it's centrally located. You'd be in walking distance to a little corner store and a couple of nice shops on the square."

"What's the rent on them?" The fact that we hadn't asked before now probably told Regis we had more money than sense; a couple of yuppies fresh from the big city, curious how the other half lived.

"I can let you have the farmhouse for seven hundred dollars," Regis said, after pretending to run some numbers on an adding machine. "Since it's smaller, three hundred seventy-five for the apartment."

"Could we have a minute to discuss it?" Chance curled his hand around the nape of my neck. The gesture looked possessive, but I knew it was mostly for show.

"Of course. I'll just run down the block to get coffee. Would y'all like anything?"

We both shook our heads, bemused by this small-town mentality. We could have rifled his office looking for cash and valuables and taken off long before he returned, if we were lying about wanting to rent property in town.

"Town or country?" Chance asked after we'd confirmed Regis's departure.

I sighed. "Hell, I don't know."

"I think it'd be harder for someone to sneak up on us out at the farmhouse, and it's easier to ward a house than an apartment inside an office building."

"You don't want to stay in town," I guessed.

"I'm not crazy about shoe box flats, and I don't want people to be able to mark our movements so easily."

"The house it is," I said. "Though I'm none too excited about the prospect of a ghost and the proximity of those woods."

Chance grinned. "We're safe unless Birnam Woods marches on Dunsinane?"

"Funny," I grumbled. "The yard will be better for Butch, anyway."

By the time Regis returned, we were sitting quietly, hands

folded. The rich, slightly bitter scent of coffee wafted from his Styrofoam cup as he rounded his desk. He set it down on the edge and regarded us expectantly. "Did y'all decide?"

"The house," Chance told him. "But Corine is a little nervous about the prospect of staying where someone passed away. I'm afraid I can't offer more than five fifty. If you can't help us, I'm sure there's another little town down the road."

Even when he had plenty of money, Chance was always a businessman. I could hear him saying it now: *Never take the first offer.* Regis's face fell.

"Now, let me run the numbers again, sir. Don't be hasty."

I stifled a smile as Chance offered his impassive look. "If you think it would help."

"Six hundred," Regis finally said, sweating. "Final offer. I pay the utilities on the house, you see. The power is still on, though I had the phone cut off. And if you're out there, using up the juice, I just can't afford to—"

"That'll be fine," I cut in. I didn't want to stroke the man out.

"The cook stove is gas," he went on, "but there's a propane tank out back. You should be fine for a month. I'll need one hundred down as a damage deposit. If you want to write me a check, I won't cash it. I'll just hold it until the month's out."

Regis seemed to think, probably based on my messy, disheveled appearance, that we were strapped for cash. Well, I defied *him* to look any better after being shoved across a wet, muddy street. I set my jaw.

"Cash is fine," Chance said. He drew out his expensive leather wallet and counted seven bills. "Here's the deposit and one month's rent."

I could see Regis revising his initial impression of us, but Chance didn't have much ready cash left, between the bed-and-breakfast, and these alternate lodgings. I didn't know what we were going to do with the stinky powder we'd found there, or what had become of Booke. When I checked my cell phone, I was a little worried we hadn't heard from him yet, considering he'd intended to scout the place.

"Is there an ATM in town?" I asked.

The real estate agent looked blank for a long moment. "You mean a money machine? I don't think so. People just stop by the bank during business hours or write a check. Some folks get a check-cashing card from the supermarket, I guess, if their paychecks aren't too big."

He had to be shitting us. I felt like we'd slipped through a gap in time, or taken a wrong turn to wind up in Mayberry.

"Okay," I said, feeling dazed. "Thanks."

"We'll have to make this last," Chance murmured, tapping his wallet.

Damn, that absolutely meant grocery shopping . . . and cooking. I sighed. Kilmer didn't seem to have a limit in the ways it would torture me.

It was almost, almost enough to make me turn tail and run.

Almost.

I accepted the key while Chance signed some paperwork for Mr. Regis. He drew us a map on a yellow legal pad, giving good directions on how to reach the place. "You'll pass Ma's Kitchen on the way out of town. That's how you know you're on the right track." Then he began outlining all the twists and turns. It sounded like the house was really in the middle of nowhere, like a witch's cottage in a fairy tale. He hadn't been kidding when he said "deeply wooded and private."

"Shall we?" Chance asked.

"I guess." We thanked Mr. Regis and stepped out into a heavy, purple twilight. The horizon seemed oddly dark and devoid of color, with none of the usual fiery streaks. I shivered as I got into the Mustang. "Let's see if Ma does takeout. We'll need something to eat while we go over that file."

Butch popped his head out of my bag—I needed to reward him for sleeping through the meeting with Regis— and yapped once in agreement. He could always eat.

Alone in the Woods

There were no lights for miles. Everywhere I looked, there were only the trees and the dark. In daytime I could tell you the names of them and what medicinal plants grew in their shadows. My mother meant me to be a witch when I grew up, and she had been preparing me for it. I still had my grimoires back in Mexico, but I had no magick.

The house we'd rented sent a cold chill through me. Most likely, it was the light slanting through the trees that gave the place such a desolate, devilish look. It could also be the way the rough gravel drive snaked through the woods, rounding a corner and opening into a cleared field, like a witch's cottage from children's stories.

This house was bigger than a cottage, of course, and more run-down than it had been in the photo. The roof over the porch sagged a little, but it appeared structurally sound. I hefted my purse as I got out of the car. Call me a coward, but I immediately set Butch down and let him go sniffing around the exterior. I trusted him to find anything we should know about, like, say, a reanimated corpse crawling around the perimeter.

He trotted around the side of the house and out of sight. I clutched the paper bag full of takeout from Ma's Kitchen, waiting for the dog to reappear on the other side. When

Chance touched my shoulder, I almost threw our dinner at him.

"Whoa," he said softly. "We're okay, Corine. We can handle this. I admit, the place is a little creepy, but we've been in worse spots."

I didn't know whether he meant this house in particular or Kilmer in general, but I was worried about our stupid dog. To my vast relief, Butch came trotting around the other side with nothing to report. He climbed the stairs and sat waiting beside the front door.

Chance smiled. "Our security expert has approved the place, it seems. Let's go see what seven hundred dollars bought us."

I gave him the keys, and he led the way, carrying both his duffel and my backpack. Trailing behind, I cast a nervous glance over my shoulder as I went into the house. We stood inside a sitting room, furnished only in the most basic sense. All the pictures had been stripped from the walls, but they'd left a flowered sofa and matching settee. The place smelled musty and damp with a hint of old-lady lavender. Butch poked his head beneath a chair and sneezed.

"Is there a lamp or an overhead light anywhere?" As I said it, a dim circle of gold dispelled some of the shadows. Chance had found a side table with an old-fashioned glass lamp. It must not have been worth anything, or it would've been removed along with the paintings. A fine layer of dust covered everything, so it had been a while since anyone cleaned.

"It has a hairline crack," he told me over his shoulder.

It was scary how well he knew me.

Learning the layout didn't take long. The downstairs was arranged in a semicircle, connecting parlor to dining room to kitchen. A hallway branched from the parlor, forming the other side of the circle, leading to the bedrooms. The corridor terminated in a bathroom, and what I took to be the master "suite" had a half bath attached.

I flipped a light switch, and a dim overhead light came

on. Whoever removed Mrs. Everett's personal effects had done a haphazard job. They'd hauled off the bed frame and headboard, and left the mattress on top of the box springs on the floor, but they hadn't taken an exquisitely carved armoire, just because it had been painted a hideous green and dinged up a bit. If someone put a little effort into refinishing that piece, it would retail for nearly a thousand bucks. I resisted the temptation to find who might be willing to pay it.

Before I lay down on that bed, I had to know, though. I wiggled my fingers in preparation for contact with the mattress and relaxed my mental grasp on my gift. Heat rocketed through my palms and up into my arms, but I didn't receive the impression of death. Instead, I saw a mosaic made of many nights: just an old woman sleeping or reading, or lying awake and staring at the ceiling. Whatever became of her, Mrs. Everett didn't die in bed. Thank the gods.

I felt more like a squatter than an honest renter, but we could make do here. I checked the bathroom and found a toilet, a stained, once-white pedestal sink, and a shower stall; nothing fancy, just blue tile with a green tinge to the grout. I hoped we wouldn't be here long enough for that to bother me.

"Finishing scoping out the place?" Chance asked from behind me.

This time I didn't jump. "Yeah. It looks bearable."

"Let's eat before the food gets cold. There's no microwave." He led the way into the kitchen, Butch trotting at our heels. Apparently Chance had flipped light switches wherever he found them, as if he could banish the ocean of night that surrounded us. He caught my look and added, a touch defensive, "What? It's really dark out there."

I knew what he meant; without city lights and noise, this place freaked me out too. Add in the looming threat of the trees, and I could hardly think, but I couldn't help teasing him. "You're scared of the dark, Chance? *You?*"

"I'm not scared of anything as long as you're beside me."

Call me an idiot, but I melted a little over that. I covered by unpacking the food. I found it unspeakably sad that the old woman who'd lived and died here had probably spent her mornings sitting at a table with placemats laid for two. The kitchen was small, old-fashioned, and painted a pale, streaky yellow. The fridge looked like it had last been updated in 1945—a squat Hotpoint unit with rounded edges and a silver handle.

Before we sat down to eat, I set out Butch's portable dishes. After the dumplings earlier, he wasn't too interested in dog food, but he did take a drink, and then he came to sit on the floor by the table, telling us via big bulging eyes he thought we sucked for not giving him more people food. The waitress at Ma's had packed us two blue plate specials, which turned out to be meat loaf and green beans. Good packaging had kept it warm while we drove around country roads after dark, looking for our destination.

Chance tucked into his food, but I had a phone call to make first. To my surprise, I had twelve text messages and four voice mails, but the phone hadn't rung. I checked the settings, and it was programmed to vibrate *and* play J.Lo's "If You Had My Love." My cell hadn't made a peep all day.

I tried to dial out, but even though I had two bars, I couldn't get a call to connect. A dark, dreadful feeling crept over me, as if I were marooned on a broken log with floodwaters rising all around me. We had to find a way to contact the outside world. Jesse would go nuts if he didn't hear from me, and what about Chance's mom? Not to mention Chuch and Eva. We would *not* disappear in Kilmer, an unsolved mystery.

Taking a deep breath, I started wading through my text messages. The first one astonished me. Jesse—the man I'd left to clean up the mess in Laredo—had simply written, *You ok?* That might not have been so shocking if it hadn't also been time stamped around the moment when I'd been so terrified, standing in the bathroom at the Kilmer Inn. Things got weirder as I read the next message.

Corine, what the hell is going on? This one bore a time stamp just after Chance pushed me out of the way of a rampaging Cutlass. Even in text, Jesse's tone grew increasingly more agitated as he asked why the hell I wasn't answering. The tenth just said, *Where are you?*

I read the last text message with a growing sense of foreboding. Jesse had written in shorthand, as if he were driving, or in a hurry: *Omw. I dont hear from u in 24, I report u missin.*

He'd packed up and was coming to look for me? From that, I extrapolated he'd sensed my emotional state from hundreds of miles away. Jesus. I didn't know how he expected to find Kilmer when it wasn't on MapQuest, but I didn't imagine that setback would deter Jesse Saldana. But what would an unexpected trip mean to his suspension from the police department? Dammit, I had enough to worry about.

The last message came from Booke. A weight lifted when I realized he was all right. *I've been ringing all day; left messages. Hope you get this. The astral over Kilmer is like a wicked dark scar. I tried for hours, but I couldn't see a thing, just swirling, inky fog. Do be careful, and get in touch if you can.*

As I closed my phone, Chance called, "What are you doing in there? Eat your dinner, woman."

I smiled at his faux-peremptory tone. He was trying to keep the mood light, dispel some of the shadows, but he didn't know the worst of our problems. I decided to let him finish his food before addressing the issue, so I came back to the kitchen and sat down with the folder we'd stolen. While I ate cold meat loaf and green beans, I skimmed through the collection of yellowed articles, most of which dealt with the town losing bids for contracts, developers building elsewhere, businesses closing down, and other crappy developments.

None of it was helpful.

Before I knew what I meant to do, I slapped it from the table and lunged from my seat, stomping on the articles.

Chance cut me a worried look, but I didn't care. A storm of words rose, tangling in my throat until I couldn't tell one from another, and it became a voiceless scream. It took me a moment to recognize the pain I'd been repressing; then it drowned me in a red wave.

"This stuff is worthless! Your luck doesn't work here, because *nothing* here works the way it's supposed to. This is the ass-end of hell, a stupid Southern Bermuda Triangle!"

Chance put out a hand, as if he might try to calm me, and I took a step, wanting to fight. I wanted to hurt someone, *break* things, because here I stood, a grown woman surrounded by the woods where I'd hidden as a child, and I felt as helpless as I had then.

My mother died in this town, and I didn't know where to begin. I had no ideas, no leads; just a certainty something was wrong. We had no object for me to handle and find the answers. He backed off, looking worried.

For a good ten minutes, I ranted at Chance about broken cell phones, evil trees, murderous Cutlass Supremes, and black astral mist. I'm sure I made no sense, but he gazed at me steadily all the while. When the storm blew itself out, I crumpled amid the fallen clippings, tears burning at my eyes. I never had the luxury of crying as a kid. I'd dedicated my energy to dealing with the stress of living with strangers.

He came to me then, quietly. Maybe he didn't think he could offer any words to assuage my feelings; he would've been right. Instead, he wrapped his arms around me and drew me between his long legs, cradling me against his chest. He rocked with me, ever so slowly. Butch crawled into my lap, and I half hiccupped, half laughed.

"This place is evil," I whispered. "And I don't know what to do about it. Jesse is on the way here. I'm afraid something terrible's going to happen to him while he's looking for us, and it'll be my fault. I won't be able to stop it. I won't be able to save him." The words just kept spilling out of me.

I felt Chance tense, and I knew he had to wonder what

Jesse Saldana meant to me, but those feelings had tangled with old guilt.

"It seems worse," he said at length, "because we don't have any idea what's wrong. We have no clue what we're fighting—or whom." Despite his closeness, I heard distance in his voice. "From a psychological standpoint, the unknown threat always seems worse. Identifying patterns and putting pieces together would allow us to construct a strategy. Right now we're flying blind, and you're exhausted."

"Okay," I said, leaning my head against his shoulder. "Tomorrow we make a list of everything we noticed about the town. We ward this place, and we see about getting messages out. Booke might be able to figure something out if we tell him exactly what we've encountered."

"That's a plan," he agreed, stroking my hair. "We won't get this done in a day. I have no idea how long it'll take for us to get to the root of the problem, and . . ." He trailed off in hesitation, then continued. "I'm sorry my luck isn't more use, Corine." He sighed. "Here, it's like a magnetized compass where the needle never stops spinning."

Magnetized . . . That word hung in my thoughts but never found purchase. My mind was tired, but I couldn't imagine snuggling down and falling asleep. After a moment, I pushed away from him and climbed to my feet.

"Thanks," I murmured. "I didn't mean to—"

"It's okay." As he stood, he dismissed my uncharacteristic meltdown with a shrug.

I wanted to get away from him, so I left the kitchen, passing through the dining room and then the parlor. Wondering how the old woman had died ate at me. Did we have a resident ghost?

If Chuch had been here, he could have told me, but I had zero aptitude for such things. Like a spirit myself, I passed through silent rooms, touching this or that. Deliberately, I shut down the filter that kept everyday life from turning into a barrage of searing pain and maddening impressions. If Chance wondered what I was doing, passing in and out of the kitchen, following threads of energy stored in objects she'd used on a daily basis, he didn't ask. He sat at the table, poring over the clippings I'd spilled on the floor.

The pain was bearable. Bit by bit, I built a picture of Mrs. Everett's daily life. She did crossword puzzles in the morning while drinking her coffee, and she sat in the rocking chair in the parlor, reading the Bible in a spill of sunlight in early afternoon. Evening found her staring out at the woods, fingers pressed up against the windows. I could feel her layered beneath me as I stood in her place, gazing at those dark trees.

And then I saw her crumple beneath the picture window in the parlor. Everything went dark, and I swayed. *I'm Corine. Corine Solomon.* My heart hammered as I extricated myself from her quiet death, feeling I'd narrowly avoided a patch of quicksand. None of her experiences caused the agony I associated with violent death, so I concluded she'd died naturally, a consequence of her worn body.

"Well," I said to Butch, "at least the house seems to be phantom free."

As if in response to my words, heaviness seeped into the air. The dog pressed close to my ankles, and I felt him trembling. Ice prickled along my nerve endings. This was similar to what I'd felt in Laredo, just before the shades appeared. But we'd killed the warlock responsible. This had to be different.

Movement in my peripheral vision had me jumping at shadows. I felt a presence, something watching us. The cold intensified until I could feel my skin prickling into goose bumps. Butch whined, so I spun to face whatever had frightened him.

Carmine bled from the parlor wall, coalescing into the words WELCOME HOME.

In Dreams

For a long moment, we stood frozen, and then I bent to pick up Butch. He nestled in my arms and hid his face. The heaviness in the air grew more profound, as if there were a giant hand pressing down on the top of my head. Frost crackled on the windowpane, and when I called for Chance, my breath swirled like white fog before my face.

"Coming!"

When he stepped into the room, there was a localized boom, as if he carried enough heat in his body to offset the chill. I could swear I saw storm clouds around him for just a few seconds, as if two powerful weather fronts had collided in the front parlor. Then the weight went away, and I could move again. Without speaking, I pointed at the wall. With Chance here, my fear was subsiding.

"It's not blood," he said after a short inspection.

No real surprise there. Bleeding walls rarely spilled the liquid of life. That didn't decrease the creepiness of the timing—after I'd said the house held no ghosts, as I recalled.

"What is it, then?"

"If I had to guess? Berry juice."

"Like from the woods?" I went back to the window, staring out at the dark, and received the disconcerting impression it stared back.

What was it Nietzsche said? "If you gaze long into an abyss, the abyss will gaze back into you." And so it did. I became convinced something sat out there, judging our movements. My scalp prickled. I didn't know whether to take heart from the message or consider it a warning meant to frighten.

I refused to let it.

"Maybe," he said, still staring at the writing on the wall—literally. "You think someone lives out there? It would take a precise, sympathetic translocation spell to achieve this." He pointed at the dripping letters.

I wasn't interested in the practical aspects. If this was an intimidation tactic, it was doomed to fail. Instead of dwelling on how the unsettling effect had been achieved, I found a bucket and some rags, and started scrubbing it off the wall. That morning I'd been accosted in a bathroom and nearly run over by a car. They'd have to do better to get me riled up. The fact that I'd cried earlier probably had something to do with my steady emotional state too.

Enough was enough. We wouldn't solve anything today, and I was no longer worried about Mrs. Everett's lingering spirit, so I located some old sheets not taken in the haphazard packing and gave them a good shake. They were faded and ragged at the edges, but soft from many washings. I went into the master bedroom and tucked the flat end between the mattress and box springs.

A quick rummage through the dresser unearthed an ancient quilt in the bottom drawer. I retrieved my bag from the parlor and changed into loose shorts and a T-shirt. Once I brushed my teeth, I was set to get some sleep.

"Let Butch out before you go to bed," I called. "Night, Chance!"

I didn't know where he would crash, but I felt safer here than I had at the bed-and-breakfast, so I wouldn't ask him to bunk with me. His dangerous luck aside, he had to get better at talking about his feelings. It couldn't be all about me any more than it should've been all about him the first time. I'd driven myself half mad trying to please him, and now he was doing the exact same thing. We needed to strike a balance, somehow.

Maybe the pendulum would eventually come to rest between us. Maybe—

There was no gentle rollover from waking to sleep, no dreamy, hazy lassitude. I didn't even remember closing my eyes. Then . . . I was somewhere else.

Given the day I'd had, if I hadn't been to this room before, I might have panicked. From the mahogany shelves to the cream and ivory wingback chairs, this gentleman's library suited my impression of Ian Booke, who sat at a heavy antique desk, brow furrowed in concentration.

Our man in the UK had perfected lucid dreaming, and we'd talked this way once before. Relief washed over me when I realized he'd been trying to get in touch when I went quiet. He must have been at it for hours.

In my dreams, Booke had a shock of nut-brown hair and charcoal eyes. His face was narrow and clever rather than attractive. I didn't know anything about him in real life; nobody did.

I came toward him clad in the Wonder Woman body Booke envisioned for our dream encounters. He glanced up at my movement, his expression revealing visible relief. He left his desk and took two steps in my direction before apparently remembering we couldn't touch or I'd wake up.

"You're all right? I've left five messages now."

"Depends on what you mean by that," I said ruefully. "I'm glad to see you—er, talk. You know what I mean."

He inclined his head with a half smile and led the way over to the chairs. I sank down gratefully, unused to the height of the form I wore in the dreamworld. After taking a deep breath, I summed up everything we'd noticed about Kilmer: the unusual behavior of the citizens, a maimed dog, the lack of modern conveniences, dying business, broken cell phones, strange, stinky powder, murderous automobiles, and bleeding walls.

Damn. The recitation alone made me tired.

"So," I concluded, "the only place we've gotten the cell phone to work is the library. I have no idea why."

"I might be able to help. If you can, use your cell phone to snap some pictures, interior and exterior views, and send them to me via e-mail. Do you have a Smartphone?"

I rather doubted it; unlikely the device would be any cleverer than its owner. "Chance does, I think."

"Get those to me as soon as you can, and I'll see if I can sort why the library prevents the technological failure that plagues you elsewhere."

I smiled with genuine warmth. "Thanks. That could really help us devise some defense. I'm glad you found me like this."

"I wasn't sure I could," he admitted. "Not with the bizarre shroud encircling the coordinates you gave me. But this technique focuses on the person more than the place, so I think I could find you anywhere."

That statement carried an oddly reassuring resonance. "Can you help? Kilmer feels so cut off from the real world."

Booke frowned. "That would take some doing, serious power, there. I wonder if the dark spot in the astral has anything to do with your isolation."

I could only shrug. "That's your stomping ground, not mine. But maybe you could research what rituals might achieve that effect."

"I'll get on that as soon as we've finished here," he said with a nod. "I can't scout as I did in Laredo, so that's right out. But I can relay messages. Today"—he hesitated, ducking his head—"I just wanted to make sure you were all right."

A flicker of pleasure washed over me. "I am. Just a bit bruised. By the way, could you call Chuch and let him know we're fine? He'll pass the word to Saldana, who's riding to the rescue like a white knight."

"Must be nice," Booke muttered.

I raised a brow. "What?"

"Getting to play the hero."

"Well, he hasn't done anything yet," I said. "He might just make things worse."

But he wasn't looking for sympathy. By his expression, his agile mind had already moved on to something else. "You mentioned a strange residue."

"From the bed-and-breakfast. We figure it's a component, but we don't know what it is or whether it's used in a baneful or beneficial spell."

"I wish I had a sample. *I'd* know," he added without false modesty.

"There's no FedEx here," I grumbled, "and it would take forever in the mail, assuming they'd even send it out."

Booke sighed. "Rotten you can't just wish it here."

His casual comment gave me an idea, possibly a stupid one, but nothing ventured and whatnot. "This . . . pocket world, how real is it?"

"Real enough to communicate ideas, not facilitate touch." He shrugged.

Well, I wasn't asking so we could make out. "Can I change it?"

Booke sat forward, arms resting on his knees. He'd caught on, and his expression reflected keen fascination. "As I said last time, Corine, what you see depends upon your expectations. What *I* see is quite different. Only our thoughts intersect as an absolute. What exactly do you have in mind?"

I struggled to articulate it. "I want to bring you here, where I am. And then I want to try to make this . . . shared space . . . real enough to give you that plastic bag. We wouldn't have to touch."

"Dream translocation?" he asked, thoughtful. "I've heard of it. Legends say devoted lovers gave each other tokens over long distances . . . not that I think you and I—"

I waved away his embarrassment. "Thing is, you need to share the setting with me, so we need to build the image together, right?" He nodded. "So how do we go about that?"

Booke considered for a long moment. "I'd say describe

your current location in great detail until it becomes real to me."

What the hell? I didn't have a better idea.

I couldn't have said how long I spoke, but the room re-shaped around us as I built the house in my mind's eye as well. Eventually we had a complete replica of Mrs. Everett's farmhouse, except for the view of the woods. We sat in the parlor, and Booke gazed around with apparent absorption. He got up to explore and came back to report in a few minutes.

"This is brilliant," he exclaimed. "I can even smell the dust."

"So let's test the rest of my theory," I said. "At worst, we fail."

He shook his head. "At best, we make history."

With a nod, I stood and went to fetch Chance's back-pack, which had been near the front door the last time I saw it. I unzipped it and brought out the zipper bag. I shook it a little and the powder danced inside it.

Before handing it to Booke, I said, "I'll call you from the library tomorrow. Don't worry if you can't get a hold of me, because—"

"You're in a black hole," he finished.

"Near enough."

We fixed the combined force of our wills on the bag, mak-ing it real in a joint effort. This wasn't some mental repre-sentation of the bag; it *was* the bag. I knew every crinkle in the plastic, every ounce of its weight. When I let go, it would no longer be here, but there, across an ocean.

At last, I extended my hand toward him. He took the powder from me, but our fingers brushed in the transfer, a little flicker of warmth, and—

I woke to late-morning sun streaming onto my face. In another room, I could hear Chance ranting. A thunk told me he'd kicked something. Rare—and enjoyable—as it was for him to lose his cool, I should go see what had him so agitated. I slid off the mattress and padded down the hall into the parlor, where he was pacing.

"What's wrong?"

I thought I knew. I prayed I knew.

"The powder's gone! I'd love to know how they managed *that* trick. Well, that and the bleeding wall too. We're warding this place first thing, assuming we can even find what we need in this godforsaken backwater."

"I took it."

Chance drew up short, mouth half open. "Why? What'd you do with it?"

Pride put a huge smile on my face. "I think I gave it to Booke to study. He should be able to tell us what it's used for."

For a moment, he struggled for words, trying to articulate how crazy I sounded. He listed a few reasons why that was impossible, and I smiled. I felt like the Cheshire cat, irritatingly pleased with myself.

Eventually, I gave him the explanation I knew he wanted, but that didn't seem to make him feel any better. It took me a moment to figure out why. He'd thought he knew everything about me, and here I managed something like this. He wouldn't like feeling out of the loop; never had.

Chance studied me for a long moment. "I thought you couldn't do magick. You told me you practiced with your mother's books and never got any spells to take."

"I'm sure it was Booke's doing." If it worked; if we hadn't banished the evidence to some weird pocket dimension where demons would eat it—and hopefully suffer indigestion—and where the powder would do us no good at all. "We can call him later to confirm our success."

"I thought the cell phones weren't working." Why was he acting so suspicious? The way Chance eyed me, you'd think I made a habit of keeping secrets from him instead of the other way around.

"They worked in the library yesterday," I reminded him.

"You need to check on your mom too. So we'll stop there after we shop for the sea salt, but I don't know where we're going to find agrimony, wormwood, cedar, dill, and coriander in bulk around here."

"I'd include pine, heather, marjoram, and slippery elm, but we'll have to make do with whatever we can get."

Chance's mom had taught us about protective herbs, and living with Chuch, we'd received a refresher course in good wards. The mechanic layered them inside and out for double coverage. We'd do the same—and I wouldn't leave Butch out there until we did.

That morning, I felt energized. Though things weren't any better than the previous day, I had a handle on them. We'd go shopping for supplies, and then we'd make phone calls. Booke was on the case, and if I knew Chuch and Eva, they would want to do some legwork if they could. Jesse was on the way.

If Kilmer thought they could frighten me off, they had another think coming.

This was for my mom, Cherie Solomon.

We had not yet begun to fight. Sure, they'd crippled us by taking away the tools we generally used to solve problems, but we'd find ways around the obstacles they threw in our path. No matter how many times they knocked me onto a dirty road, I would rise. I'd ferret out their secrets and then handle the objects that would spill them.

In other words, Kilmer, game on.

Luckless Bastard

By one p.m., we had a trunkful of bulk spices. We'd driven to a neighboring town to pick up most of them. More interesting, twenty miles away, nobody seemed to have heard of Kilmer. They'd never even driven through.

We stood outside the public library while I snapped pictures of the building's exterior with Chance's phone. When I thought I'd gotten all the angles, we went inside. I studied the screen and, sure enough, as the door closed behind us, five bars lit up on the device, as opposed to the straggly one or two we got anywhere else in town.

I gave it back. "Can you take some pictures of the inside and then send the lot to Booke? Do you have his e-mail?"

"Sure," he said, and glanced around the interior as if deciding where to start.

Once he'd gone, I dug my cell out of my pocket. The librarian glared at me from the desk, so I moved away from the front door. Somewhere in the middle of History and Philosophy, I took a look. I had more messages from Jesse, but none from Booke. First thing, I called Saldana, knowing he was probably here—or nearly so—by now, depending on what time he'd left Texas. I had never been so happy to hear a call connect.

He answered on the first ring, his voice warm, worried,

and touched with a Texas drawl. "Corine, are you all right?
Where are you?"

"At the library," I told him, keeping my voice low. "It's
the only place my phone works. Things are weird. I'll tell
you more when you arrive." I wanted to say I was touched
that he'd drop everything to come looking for me, but I
couldn't find the words, so I went with a question instead.
"Where are *you*?"

A long silence followed, but background noise told me
he was driving. "I have no idea," he said at last. "I can't
find the town. GPS has never heard of it."

"Booke said there was no reference to Kilmer anywhere
online, either. If you're totally off course, I suggest finding
a library and looking for archived maps, anything before
1900. If that doesn't work, go earlier . . . until you find it.
It's here." I paused. "Even if the rest of the world seems to
have forgotten about the place. For now, though," I went on,
"look for a road sign. There should be something posted
about the next town."

"Yeah. There's one coming up—looks like Darien. I'm
five miles away."

"You're fairly close." I gave him directions to the house
from the road he was driving on. "We'll meet you there in
two hours. If you have trouble, text me. If I'm not here, I
may not be able to answer, but I can come looking for you."

"And vice versa." I heard the smile in Jesse's voice as he
rang off.

Then I called Booke. It was so weird that we couldn't
call out anywhere else. Come to think of it, I hadn't seen
pay phones anywhere in this godforsaken town.

"I have bad news, good news, and maybe more bad," he
reported.

"Bad first, then good, please."

"You sent me a mixture of burnt cat hair, ground bone
dust, powdered stinkweed, and . . . one thing I can't seem to
isolate. If it's been transmuted as a result of the spell, I may
never know what it was."

"The spell or the component?"

"Both," he said, sounding unhappy. "Right now, it could be a spell meant to cause genital warts, prevent attacks from unfriendly spirits, make you grow hair on your back and develop unpleasant body odor, or summon a demonic cat to smother—"

"And that's the bad news?" I figured he could go on like that for a while. "What's the good?"

"Well. None of those things has happened, right?"

Only Booke would ask that, though I did give my armpits a tentative sniff. "Nope."

"Then the spell might have been interrupted when you fled the bed-and-breakfast."

"Great. Finally, something swings our way."

"Or . . . ," he said, hesitant, "it might have been cast with a timer or trigger."

"So it could go off like a bomb if we put a foot wrong." I rubbed my forehead. I'd never wished harder that I had my mother's abilities instead of a relatively worthless and limited gift like the touch. "That'd be the other bad news, right?"

"Unfortunately, yes. You need someone to cleanse all your possessions, but I suspect you don't have anyone handy who could."

"Not right here, no."

I thanked him and rang off. If we were to get a witch out here, I'd need to visit Area 51—a message board that the Gifted used to communicate—and ask around. We might be able to use Chance's phone to connect to the Net and do it that way, but it would have to be before closing time. After five p.m., we were on our own.

Chance found me a few minutes later. "Anything?"

First I relayed what Booke had told me; then I borrowed his phone. It took fifteen minutes for me to log into Area 51 and post a request for someone to perform a cleansing. Maybe we'd get a nibble, maybe not. If nothing else, before we left the library, we should talk to the handyman again.

Mr. McGee might remember something from years ago, and he looked ornery enough that he wouldn't care about keeping other people's secrets.

"Quick," I said. "Downstairs. Don't let the librarian catch us."

We ran Mr. McGee to ground in the basement. It wasn't hard. He was sitting at a table, listening to an old transistor radio. To my ears, it sounded like the whispers and hisses of mechanical failure—no music or words broke the soft, sibilant hiss.

"What're you listening to, sir?" Chance spoke first, politely announcing our presence so we didn't startle him.

We came around the other side. I find it difficult to hold a conversation with someone's back. In this case, it didn't help any. Whether some trick of shadows or light, his eyes appeared blind, all darkness devoid of iris or pupil. He turned his face toward us.

The old man said in a vacant voice, "Dead people."

If he intended to frighten me, well, it worked. Icy fingers crept down my spine, and I could imagine I heard ghost whispers buried in the mechanical static—broken phrases and pleas for salvation. Now and then, I could almost make out the words. It felt as though the sound burnt itself into my brain, as if my flesh fused with the signal. Despite myself, I edged closer to Chance, who wound an arm around my shoulders.

"Can you understand them?" I asked quietly.

Mr. McGee tapped his gnarled fingertips against the table, yellowed nails sounding like chitin-shelled insects beneath a boot. "Sometimes," he said at last. "More often than not, these days. They say you can only hear them if you're near death yourself. Can *you* make out what they're saying, missy?"

The question hit me like a fist in the chest. My lips felt numb. A charged tingle shot up my spine and out the top of my head. I felt compelled to answer; the truth spilled out of me like a black ribbon, linked to the awful ink of his eyes.

"Help us." I mouthed the words, nearly soundless. "They're saying, 'Help us.'"

Chance cut me a sharp look, as if wondering whether I was playing along, humoring the old bastard. I wished to hell I was. The infernal chorus had coalesced for me; I heard a thousand souls moaning in torment, begging for deliverance.

"Ah," McGee said, nodding. "Ah. Poor pretty thing." If he hadn't been so damn terrifying, I would've dismissed him as nuts and walked away. But I couldn't seem to move. "I wondered when y'all would come back," he went on.

"You knew we'd be back?" Chance asked, lofting a brow. He didn't seem afflicted with the same raw horror that weighted my bones.

"I know everything about this town worth knowing."

"Then you know what happened at the Solomon house," I said. It wasn't a question.

He peered at me, seeming surprised for the first time. "You're *her*. The one who got away. Oh, missy, you ought not to have come back. They'll do for you this time for sure."

Excitement shivered through me. "They, who? I need names, Mr. McGee."

But he seemed lost in a fit of dementia. "They thought I didn't know. And I didn't, not for a long while, but I heard it on the radio. I know. I know—" He began to choke, a hideous red froth burbling from his tobacco-stained lips.

Chance grabbed for the old man as he fell, and I ran, screaming, for the stairs. When I got back, Chance had given up on resuscitation. I stood there, trembling, soothing Butch with a touch to his head. He scented death in the air and gave a little whimper. I knew he wanted to leave. So did I.

The basement turned into a confused nightmare of agitated questions and implications of blame. Two young men from the funeral home arrived first, followed by the sheriff, and then the doctor. As they argued, Mr. McGee lay stretched out on the basement floor, dead as a doornail. He gave off a faint odor similar to the powder we'd found lining our doorway at the bed-and-breakfast.

Chance had the guy's blood all over him. He'd done his level best to save him, but whatever got him had been inexorable.

The country doc knelt, gave a cursory look, and then pulled out a notepad. "John McGee, aged seventy-six. Apparently suffered a seizure, possibly stroke related. Time of death"— he checked his watch, an old-fashioned wind-up one—"one forty-five p.m."

I could hear the librarian trying to keep order upstairs. Chance, the sheriff, and a couple of guys from the funeral home stood watching the doctor complete his rudimentary exam. To me, it looked like he just poked McGee here and there to make sure he was deceased.

There were no body bags here. While they wrapped him in a sheet, I edged closer to the worktable. Expecting to be caught at any moment, I edged McGee's old cream and chrome radio into my bag. Butch yelped a little, which drew their attention back to me. It didn't take much to look as though I were restraining loud, noisy sobs.

The sheriff put me in mind of a basset hound. Robinson had thinning brown hair, a weathered face with generous jowls, and a sizable gut on a short, spindly-limbed frame. Our chance of getting away without trouble seemed slim.

"Let's go on up," he said. "I'm going to need to ask y'all some questions."

"Yes, sir." I made my voice meek as I preceded him up the stairs.

We sat down at a library table near the back. They hadn't yet taken us down to the courthouse, but I was pretty sure they would—in time. Chance told our story concisely, which was good, because I had a wiggly dog stashed between my knees and stolen goods hidden in my bag.

Robinson listened without comment, and then he turned

to me. He couldn't seem to grant Chance as much as a glance without going green around the gills. Admittedly, my ex did look a sight, blood-spattered as he was. "I'd like it in your words now, miss."

In the background, I heard the librarian shooing townspeople away. She'd managed to get the doors locked after the man from the funeral home took the body away. Apparently they wouldn't be calling a CSI unit to the scene. Imagine my surprise.

"We went down to visit with him." That seemed nice and innocuous. "I lived here, years ago, and I've been paying respects to folks I knew back then."

They could verify that part with Miz Ruth, at least. I hadn't known Mr. McGee from Adam, but I didn't see any point in advertising the fact. It wasn't like the maintenance man could contradict me at this point, poor old soul.

"You're from Kilmer?" The sheriff pushed up the brim of his hat, eyeing me with bloodshot eyes.

"Yes, sir." I opened my eyes wide. Older Southern men were often suckers for respectful manners. Maybe it would work here, though cops generally hated me on sight—and the antipathy was mutual. But my twin plaits and lack of makeup probably made me look younger; another good thing.

"I need your name for the record, honey."

Nothing like announcing yourself to your enemies, but I did wish it hadn't killed Mr. McGee. After this, nobody would doubt who I was or what I wanted. Chance tensed, and his hand went to my knee, squeezing, silently begging me to lie.

I knew why. This was dangerous, dangling myself as bait. To his mind, I might as well rub sirloin on my bare ass and run around in the woods yelling, *Here I am.*

"Corine Solomon," I said deliberately, watching the sheriff's face.

He wrote it down dutifully in his little notebook. "Sounds familiar."

I let that go. If he didn't know and did some digging, he'd find out soon enough. "I lived here until I was eighteen. Now I'm on vacation and catching up with folks I haven't seen in a while. It's such a pretty little town."

Robinson practically glowed. "That's surely true. You just don't find places like Kilmer anymore."

Not outside of hell, anyway. My smile didn't falter.

"I'm sorry if we broke the rules," I said quietly. "Mr. McGee had told us to come see him anytime we liked."

Also not true, but again, who would know?

"Did y'all talk about anything that might have upset him?" Robinson asked, clearly trying to be delicate.

I pretended to think about that. "No, sir. He was telling us about wanting to start a home repair business, when he started to choke. I got scared and ran for help. I think Chance tried to revive him, but he's not a doctor or anything." I sounded ridiculously guileless, but Robinson seemed to be buying it, lock, stock, and barrel.

"Well, I guess it's not so unusual for an old gent like McGee to keel over. I'm sorry you had to see it." He patted my forearm. I tried not to tense, but I was terrified he'd notice the scars on my palms and start looking closer at me in other regards.

"It was scary," was all I could think to say. To my vast relief, he took his hand away and closed his notebook.

"Here's how it's going to have to be," he told us. "The doc will check out old Mr. McGee down at the funeral home in the morning. I'm sure things happened just like you said, but just in case Doc finds evidence otherwise, I'm going to detain one of y'all overnight, just to make sure you don't run off." He offered a friendly smile, but it didn't reach his eyes when he looked at Chance. "That would surely make fools of us, if y'all got away with murder."

That was crap, but I knew Robinson didn't have to be polite or reasonable about it. Here, the law operated however he wanted it to. Hell, even in big cities, they could hold a suspect for up to twenty-four hours for "questioning." I wasn't sure about these circumstances, but personal rights seemed to be shrinking all the time. I started to object, but Chance silenced me with a gesture.

"I don't mind," he said quietly. "In the interest of full co-operation, I can take a night in custody."

As Sheriff Robinson led Chance away, I had a cold feeling in the pit of my stomach.

Divide and conquer, right? I wondered if either of us would last the night.

Lost Cause

I followed them to the courthouse, where they had a tiny jail in the basement, but it didn't do any good.

"You can pick him up in the morning," the sheriff said with a jovial smile. "Once I've heard from the doc. Don't fret, miss. We'll take good care of him."

I was *afraid* of that. I gave Chance a desperate look from across the room. He sat, quiet, on a cot. As if he felt the weight of my gaze, he glanced up from his clasped hands. "I'll be fine," he said, obviously trying to reassure me. "See you tomorrow, Corine."

I wished I could've said something that would've made a difference. If his luck worked there, then I could believe he would be fine but, like the cell phones, so far it had only functioned in the library, which was closed to us for the duration of our stay. Edna had made it clear that if we came in again, she'd call the sheriff.

Dispirited, I turned and trudged back up to the street, where the Mustang sat at a metered spot. I got in and mangled the manual transmission as I drove out of town. My speed gradually accelerated. I'd lost track of time and thought I might find Jesse waiting for me, but there was no Forester parked in front when I arrived.

Butch hopped out of my purse and did a perimeter check.

That meant peeing at various corners of the house, but he seemed calm enough when he returned. The weather was better than it had been, cool and temperate, but not rainy. I didn't know how I'd like being out here after dark, but before night fell, I had work to do. It kept me from thinking.

With a lot of heaving and huffing, I managed to get all the supplies up on the porch. I had no idea how I was going to get all the herbs mixed and then poured around the foundation of the house. Chuch used a wheelbarrow. I'd never done wards by myself before. In fact, I wasn't even sure what ratio to use. I couldn't call anyone to ask, either.

I'd never felt more alone in my life.

Trying not to think about Chance, I unloaded the staples we'd purchased: coffee, tea, sugar, instant milk, raisins, peanut butter, jelly, rice, bread, and a bag of apples. I assumed we could survive for a good long while on this kind of thing. In fact, I remembered my mother making rice pudding out of sugar, rice, raisins, and instant milk. I stashed our groceries in the cupboard, where I found unexpected bounty, a tin of unopened powdered eggs.

I topped off Butch's food and freshened up his water, then stood staring out the window above the kitchen sink for a moment. Oddly enough, I felt safer in a house where the walls bled berry juice, close to woods that used to terrify me. My dread had solidified, and what I needed to fear lay inside the town borders, not out here. These . . . were just trees, however skeletal and imposing.

I explored the house, looking for a big bin of some kind. Butch trotted along behind me, not seeming to want to let me out of his sight. I couldn't blame him. He'd whined all the way back to the house, trying to tell me we were a human short. Unfortunately, I couldn't do anything about it.

"I'll have to check the attic," I told him.

He yapped twice, disagreeing. I guess he thought we should get back in the Mustang, get Chance, and blow this creepy town. For a dog, he had good instincts.

After some searching, I found the pull cord and tugged the

stairs down in a puff of dust. I stared up into the dark, slanted maw, and then gathered my courage. I climbed slowly, hands on the upper steps, until my head and shoulders emerged into the eerie twilight created by the triangular slatted window.

My imagination too easily created a scenario where a madwoman was locked up there. I felt loath to enter, mainly because the space seemed to be unfinished, boards laid in a lattice across visible insulation. Even at the best of times, I didn't qualify as coordinated.

Still, the house wasn't going to ward itself, so I inched up the ladder and onto the first plank. It bucked under my feet, and I let out a yelp that would do the dog credit. As I windmilled my arms, I imagined myself splattered at the bottom of the ladder. That didn't help, so I skip-hopped forward three paces, and my weight distribution steadied the board.

That was key to walking around up there, sort of like being on a balance beam, except I couldn't step on the ends. As long as I kept to the middle, it seemed sturdy enough. There was a fair amount of junk up there, most of it worthless. I bypassed a chest full of old clothes and a dressmaker's dummy, shoved up against the wall.

I couldn't help my fascination with that triangular window, so I shuffled over to look at the slats nailed across it, definitely not storm shutters. But then, I'd known that, even from out front. A tiny shriek escaped me when I realized what I was seeing.

Scratch marks on the white paint, rusty streaks. Someone had clawed at these, desperate to escape. Someone had been imprisoned.

I shouldn't. It wouldn't give me any peace, yet I found myself unable to resist touching my fingers to the scars. I screamed.

Pain subsumed me, and in a fiery rush, the world melted.

She's not more than twelve or a tiny thirteen, a child, really. Her dark hair hangs lank around her sallow face, all eyes and jutting bone. She's starving, eating insects to supplement the bread and water. She knows pain, grief, and in-

*comprehension. They think she's mad. They won't listen to
what she knows is true. They say she's demon touched.*

*She scratches at these boards, day after day. One day,
she will break free. One day, she will fly. Then she turns from
the window, and—*

I lost her. I didn't know what became of her. Nothing
else I touched yielded a flicker of charge; nothing else had
absorbed enough of her energy. I felt sick, shaken. The weight
of conspiracy seemed too much for me to bear; this town
had a hundred years of them, not just what happened to my
mother. I envisioned them as blood soaked into the red Georgia dirt, bones buried beneath the stones that paved the streets.

I staggered, hardly remembering why I'd come up. At
last I spied a galvanized metal tub, probably used for laundry a hundred years ago. Butch barked somewhere in the
distance. I called, "Heads up!" before letting go. The tub
clanged when it hit the floor, but I didn't hear anything else.

The house sat weirdly still and silent, waiting, as I came
down the ladder. I felt like I was no longer alone, and yet,
conversely, Butch had stopped barking. I didn't know where
he'd gone.

Did I leave the door open?

Tub forgotten, I pressed my back to the wall and inched
my way along toward the parlor. I found nothing so convenient as a candlestick to use as a weapon. Whatever waited
for me out there, I'd have to face it bare-handed. I heard the
unmistakable sound of a gun being cocked.

Then I went boneless as a familiar voice said, "Come
out where I can see you. Slowly. I have a weapon. I will not
hesitate to use it."

"Jesse?" I breathed.

"Corine?" He stepped around the corner, and he seemed
to slump a little in relief. Nothing like fearing for someone's safety to make a man forget he was mad. After the
mess I'd left him in Laredo—a dead partner and a field full
of bodies used in necromantic magick—it was a wonder he
would come looking for me at all.

Jesse Saldana was an intriguing mix of long, tall Texan in battered boots, touched with Latin heat. He had a nice face, if scruffy and unshaven. He looked tired, as if he'd continuously run his hands through his tawny, sun-streaked hair. Ostensibly my mentor, in charge of introducing me to Gifted society, he'd hinted that he wanted to be more. Empathy was his particular gift; sometimes it was nice to have a man who knew how you felt. Right then, it was damn convenient.

I managed a smile. "The same."

"Your dog was out front in hysterics. I came in, saw your car, but couldn't find anybody. I had a feeling something was wrong, but I couldn't get a fix on what. I pounded on the door, but it was unlocked, and—"

"You got worried." Up in the attic, I hadn't heard a thing, lost in someone else's memories.

"To say the least." He came toward me then and swept me up in a big hug. A small blue spark showed when we touched, not unpleasant—just the reaction of our two gifts renewing acquaintance. I let myself lean for a moment, so glad to see him I couldn't speak. He stood back and took a look at me. "You seem to be in one piece . . . but I wonder what had that dog so worked up. Where's Chance?"

A strangled laugh that wanted to be a sob hiccupped out of me. I backtracked to where the tub lay on its side in the hall. "Put the ladder back up, help me with the wards, and I'll fill you in."

If Jesse thought my priorities strange, he didn't say so. Instead, he gave me a quick and dirty course on what herbs we should mix and how much, along with the spoken words. He explained, "This would possess more power if we were practitioners, but the herbs alone should work. You bought just about every protective plant known to man."

"That was the idea."

"A good witch can ward a house without the herbs," Jesse told me, "weaving protective energy in place like a net."

He'd know that because of Maris, an ex-lover who died because she could have identified the warlock involved in a kidnapping we'd investigated in Laredo.

We went around the house three times, intoning, "Three times around, three times about, the world within, the world without; we deny all access to any who mean us ill, whether through doorway, tiny crack, or windowsill." I made sure we wedged the ward mixture well up against the foundation, where it would theoretically bond with the stone. The last step sometimes failed in newer houses where there was often too much inorganic material.

Not content with that, I went through the interior of the house and lined the windows and doorjambs. I had mixed feelings about protecting a house where that poor girl had been locked up . . . but maybe she hadn't died there. By the time we finished evil-proofing the place, I'd filled him in on everything that had happened.

Saldana got out his cell and dialed. At first I thought he didn't believe me; then I realized he meant to test our wards. To my delight, my phone rang.

"Well, there's one problem solved," he said, ending the connection. "As for the rest, it's a hell of a mess, sugar. We should get back to town and see what we can do for Chance. We can't leave him there overnight."

Tell me something I don't know.

With Jesse, a cop from Texas, by my side, they might listen. He knew the law better than I did, and he had physical presence to back up his claims. We just needed to grab Butch and . . .

The silence troubled me. For a moment, I couldn't decide why, and then it hit me. I hadn't heard or seen the dog since Saldana arrived.

"Have you seen Butch?"

Jesse cocked his head. "He was outside, watching us work, wasn't he?"

"*Was* he?"

We scoured the yard, calling for him. I grew more fran-

tic with each passing moment. I would've given a year of
my life to see Butch come bounding out of the woods. I saw
only stillness, trees wrapped in autumn skins.

"Should we go looking for him?"

Definitely, we should. I just didn't look forward to thrash-
ing around in the woods. This felt like a trap, like we were
being herded, but I couldn't just leave him.

I sighed. "Let's make a couple peanut butter sandwiches
and then take off. Looks like we're going for a hike."

The forest stood watchful, as if it had eyes trained on us.
Trees tangled their limbs together, creating a thorny wall, ringed
in deciduous greenery. Inside, it would be cool, shadowed, dark,
with soft things squishing underfoot. I remembered well.

If I'd *ever* wanted to do anything less, I couldn't remember.

Secrets Dark and Deep

My bag felt too light on my shoulder.

I'd gotten used to Butch's slight weight on top of my stuff. He was a good dog, well trained, polite, and he listened uncommonly well. In fact, he was almost too smart.

For that reason, it made no sense for him to run off into the woods with the sky scowling thunderclouds. It looked like it might pour buckets on us any minute. That didn't stop us from setting out, calling quietly.

Skeletal trees closed in around us as we passed from the overgrown yard into the woods. A small animal like Butch wouldn't leave a trail. He could cut right through the underbrush and go any way he wanted. I'd never noticed a propensity in him for chasing squirrels, but he *was* a dog.

I felt half a step from coming unglued. *Find Butch. Get Chance.* I repeated the four words like a mantra as we passed deeper into the forest. Even in late fall, it felt dank and oppressive, as if it had been years since sunlight had last touched the ground. We had no choice but to follow the rough trail, which came to a parting of ways, east and west, at a big lightning-scarred tree. The limbs were twisted and blackened, dropping away in dead chunks of wood. Ahead, the trees formed a nearly impenetrable barrier, ancient live oaks grow-

ing in tight knots, shrouded in Spanish moss in funereal
fashion.

"Any idea which way?" Jesse asked.

I shook my head. I couldn't read the forest, a network of
living things. My gift applied only to inanimate objects. To
make matters worse, if we went deep enough, the area shifted
to swampland, and then we were talking about an enormous
ecosystem full of creatures, some of which could devour Butch
in one bite. A sick feeling coiled in the pit of my stomach.

"Can you feel him?"

Saldana gazed at me with an expression that said he
thought I'd lost my mind; then he shrugged. "I can try."

His bitter chocolate eyes went odd and distant, much as I
imagined I looked when I handled something. I tried to be
patient, but I didn't know much about his gift. Should he be
able to tune right in? Did he visualize the person (or animal)
and then try to pluck an emotional state out of the ether?

At last he came out of it, looking dazed. "Never tried
that before. I'm not eager to repeat it." Jesse rubbed his head
and pinned on a smile, but I saw it had caused him pain.

"You all right?" I reached out a hand, tentative, and he
took it, pressing my palm to his temple. That roused defi-
nite warmth. I liked his simplicity. He didn't prevaricate or
pretend not to hurt when he did. I wasn't used to things
being that uncomplicated.

In response, I shifted and cupped his head in my hands,
massaging with my thumbs and fingertips. It seemed like
the least I could do, given he'd hurt himself trying to find
my dog. Jesse leaned down into my touch, nuzzling his head
into my hands. We spent a few moments like that before he
groaned and rolled his shoulders, as if I'd given him a full
body massage.

"Better," he said, smiling. "Nothing a few Advil won't
cure."

But he didn't step back. Instead, he leaned his brow against
mine, as if I held his head in anticipation of a kiss. Awareness kindled. I remembered how sweet his mouth tasted

and how he knew exactly where to touch me. Such knowledge came from his empathy, no doubt, but that made it no less delicious.

"You came all that way," I whispered. "Are you going to get in trouble?"

He shrugged, his hands coming up to frame my waist. "Maybe, but it doesn't matter. I knew you were hurt and scared."

"And you had to come riding in like the white knight?"

"It's not about my being a hero, Corine. It's about keeping you safe."

That struck a deep chord; I'd been on my own so long. "You think you can do the job? I can be a handful."

His voice deepened, roughening with desire. If only I could be sure he wanted *me*—and not because of my feelings. "I'd like to try."

"I . . ." *This is not the time. Focus.* "Did you find him?"

Jesse stepped back, accepting the deferral. "I think . . . he's to the east. And he's excited about something; not frightened at all. I got the impression he's *waiting* for us."

Astonishment washed over me. "You're kidding."

"I could be wrong." He spread his hands. "But unless a wolf smelled us coming and is looking forward to eating us, I'm pretty sure that was Butch."

I smiled reluctantly over that. "East it is."

Our steps turned in tandem, crunching over fallen tree limbs that sounded like bones breaking underfoot. Navigating the trail took most of my attention as I tried not to get caught on stickers or slapped in the face with a wayward branch. The wan sunlight didn't penetrate in here, and I snuggled deeper into my jacket.

My tennis shoes would be worthless after this, stained green and black. I didn't even want to look at the hem of my jeans. I sensed he wanted to say something, but I didn't hurry him. I'd like to know how he'd sensed my feelings from so far away—and whether it had hurt him like scanning for Butch, but I'd let him go first.

After a few minutes of walking, he finally spoke. "What's next for you? After this?"

"Home," I said, right off.

That word conjured an immediate image of mountains, terraced houses, winding roads, and blue skies. I lived in a white adobe building that housed a pawnshop on the lower level and my bi-level flat on the upper two floors. I loved the glorious, sun-drenched warmth of Mexico City, nestled in the northern end, near Atizapan.

It had been far too long since I'd been there, and I would be lucky if the man I'd asked to run the place hadn't absconded with all my profits by now. Sadly, Senor Alvarez probably made up the most reliable aspect of my life. When I got back—if I ever did—he'd give an honest accounting of business since I left, and go on his way.

He showed a flicker of disappointment, quickly masked. "So back to Mexico?"

I raised a brow. "Yeah. Where else?"

"I thought you might consider settling in Laredo."

"Why? Because you're there?"

"Not *only* that," he muttered. "It's just not a good idea for you to stay in Mexico. You know how easily Montoya can get to you there?"

Montoya. The name chilled me. We'd made an enemy when we rescued Chance's mother from men with a score to settle. If Diego Montoya ever figured out who I was— and he would in time, as the man had limitless resources— my life wouldn't be worth as much as a fake Versace shirt in China. I knew we were running on borrowed time. That's why it was so important for me to figure out what happened here in Kilmer; I might not get another chance.

"He can get to me anywhere," I pointed out.

I tried not to think about all the reasons I had to worry. Right now, I could focus on only one problem at a time. *Find Butch. Then go get Chance.*

Saldana narrowed his eyes on me. Nice to know I could

cut through his patient persona. "Oh, right. Thanks for pointing that out, Corine. I'll just stop worrying."

I made my tone flip as I pushed through a natural archway of entwined branches. "Are we fighting already, honey? You just got here."

"You drive me out of my mind," he bit out. "I can tell you're scared to death, and here we are, marching through trees that terrify you for reasons I don't even understand, looking for a dog that—"

"What am I supposed to do, Jesse?" I stopped walking then and whirled on him. "Melt, just because you know how I feel? Is this where the little woman confides in you, making you feel strong and manly because you can shoulder her problems? Well, listen up: That approach doesn't work for me. Not on any level."

He glared at me. Between his sugar-sweet drawl, his tawny good looks, and his gentle charm, I was sure women rarely responded to him this way. But I couldn't let past precedent inhibit a really good rant; I was working up a good head of steam, and that anger was distracting me from my worry, so I encouraged it.

"I just met you. You come running because you felt something about me from *miles* away? Okay, so that was nice, but—in general, I don't *like* your knowing how I feel. I don't like anyone knowing anything about me that I didn't choose to tell them. How would you like it if *I* invaded your privacy?"

Running on automatic, I grabbed his wrist, ignoring the tiny shock, and permitted an impression from his watch. It stung—there was always pain—but the intensity depended on what memory was stored in the charge. His emotions surged into me, raw and tumultuous. I'd suspected that he felt things more intensely as a result of his gift and it charged his personal effects right off, but now I had confirmation. I was too angry to let a little pain stop me from making my point.

"How would you like it if I found out—*without* your tell-

ing me—that you think I'm cute when I'm mad and you
want to kiss me?" I'd meant this as an object lesson about
invading other people's privacy, but he didn't look discom-
fited.

Instead, he smiled. "I don't mind at all. I guess you have
something to think about while we walk, don't you? Unless
you're angling for that kiss now?"

Ten minutes ago, yeah, I'd wanted it. Now I was too
angry.

Wordless, I spun and stalked along the overgrown trail,
hoping we were, in fact, headed toward Butch and not a
hungry wolf. I found myself grinding my teeth in frustration, which was in some ways better than blind terror, but
not good at all for my dental work. I forced myself to calm
down and put one foot in front of the other. All too soon,
the outrage started draining away, and I was left with gnaw-
ing worry once more. It was impossible to stay mad at Jesse
Saldana for acting according to his nature.

We walked another fifteen minutes in silence. I noticed
belatedly we had come into a tomb, or at least, it felt that
way. The ambient forest noises had died away; no animals
skittering through the brush, chattering, or birds chirping.
Even the wind seemed loath to stir the trees.

I could smell the dankness of the swamp from here. We
were close to the border, where the ground could give way
suddenly, sucking you into hidden sinkholes. I studied my
feet as we walked, cursing Butch silently. When we found
him, he was in *so* much trouble. How did you punish a dog
for running off, anyway?

We passed another of those natural arches; this one reminded me oddly of a gazebo, as if we were entering someone's yard. I stepped into a small clearing. I saw evidence
of passage in flattened grass and churned earth; nothing so
subtle as paw prints.

Something big had traveled this way, though I didn't know
how long ago. Judging from the depressions in the dirt, it
was heavy, as the channels sank almost six inches. I didn't

want to think about what could have made them, although
to my morbid imagination, it looked like massive talons had
raked through the soil.

I so didn't need to be thinking along those lines.

Plants had been blackened all along this unholy trail,
and a low-grade stench wafted from the dead greenery. Apparently this thing killed whatever it touched, causing wilt,
wither, and rot. Where the *hell* was my dog?

Bile rose in my throat, preventing me from calling out.

As if in answer, Butch pranced around a huge split tree
that was covered in gray-green lichens. The ground around
the dead tree sank inward, as if a meteor had crashed there.
He barked as if to say, *What took you so long?*

It was nice to know the dog had so much faith in us, but
why had he brought us out here? I took a step toward him.
Then I knew.

Inside the dead tree sat a madman's jumble of lost possessions: necklace, bracelet, ivory hairbrush, a china doll with
its face half charred. Every item looked as though it had
been plucked from a conflagration. I could almost smell the
smoke.

"They're trophies," Jesse whispered.

"Yeah." Even from a distance I could tell that.

This place reeked of death, solitude, and decay. I felt
numb as I came forward. I thought I recognized one of the
items half buried toward the back, and I could no more resist kneeling than I could have stopped breathing. Jesse stopped
me from reaching out with a hand on my arm.

"You don't want to touch those, Corine." He left the subtext unspoken, but I suspected he was right. I'd never seen
so much evil heaped in one place.

"No. I'm sorry," I said. "I wasn't thinking. Will you get
it for me? Please?" I pointed to a delicate chain. If I was
right, when he pulled it free, it would have a flower pentacle on it.

As if he sensed the import, Saldana didn't argue, though
he had to be reluctant to poke through the pile. Butch actu-

ally brought him a stick, which drew a second look from both of us. Jesse leaned in and raked a few items aside, and then, after a few abortive attempts, raised the necklace into the light.

I forgot to breathe. Tears rose in my eyes, hot and searing. The last time I'd seen this, it shone silver at my mother's throat. Fire blackened now, yes, and filthy from the years it languished in this unholy place, but it was hers, undoubtedly.

"Oh God," I whispered. My lower lip trembled, and I snatched the chain before Saldana could stop me.

The world dissolved in fire.

Derelict on Memory Lane

I lost myself.

First in pain, and then darkness, and then—

My daughter would die if I failed here. I knew it. Terror lent me speed, and I hurried to the chest of drawers where I kept my spell components. One mistake would be fatal. I didn't have much time.

I cast the circle and had spoken most of the words when I sensed approaching peril. Corine was asleep upstairs; I ran to rouse her. For some reason, my frantic words made no sound, but she seemed to hear me. She argued with me.

I hugged her fiercely and then shoved her out the back door. I hoped she knew how much I loved her. I went to meet the men who wanted me dead.

My ears rang. I couldn't hear what they said. There were twelve of them, like a jury of my peers, come to judge me. I didn't need to see more than the torches. I slammed the door and locked it.

Then I ran back to the circle I'd drawn on the floor. My hands shook as I sealed myself inside it. I had one last thing to do.

Protect her, I begged. Give her the gifts she needs to sur-

vive. Let her live as my legacy to the world. I poured every-thing I was into the working.

The door flew open. A tall man stood in the doorway, and I would never forget his face. May you burn in hell for what you do this night. Turn and burn, you dark one in human skin. Licking flames threw weird shadows around the house that had been our home. Never again. Raising the athame, I gave myself over to the Lady.

And I died.

"Corine!" The voice came from a long way off, desperate, terrified. I didn't want to heed the hands pummeling me.

At least they seemed to be. No, they were pressing down, not pummeling. Someone was performing CPR. Was I dead? My flesh felt odd and heavy, almost entirely inert.

I felt a mouth over mine, then breath being forced into my lungs. I couldn't seem to open my eyes. And then I coughed. If dying hurt, living was worse. Butch nuzzled me, whimpering, but I couldn't lift a hand to reassure him.

Jesse brought me upright. His hands rubbed over my back, and when I finally managed to lift my eyes, I found him looking wretched, almost as bad as I felt. The burn on my left palm felt as though it might never heal.

"You died," he whispered, raw.

I couldn't work up any concern over that. "So did my mother. She—she killed herself. Why didn't she run? We could've both—" A sob tore free.

I didn't need an answer after all. I'd *been* Cherie Solomon for the last few minutes of her life. She hadn't run, because the men would've come looking, and she'd loved me so much I ached with it. My tears ran freely, slipping down my cheeks. I felt dire and bloodied. All these years, I'd thought she died in the fire.

But the truth was somehow worse. She'd died by her own hand, part of that final spell. I had always assumed they'd come upon her before she finished—and that was why my powers were incomplete. Based on what I'd just seen, that obviously wasn't true, so the fault must lie in me. I was a faulty vessel.

"Oh God." With gentle hands, he unfolded my fingers from around her necklace.

It fell from my grasp into his palm. Numbly I noted a new scar: The flower pentacle had been branded into my palm. The wound showed livid and purple with little white blisters around the edges. I'd never seen anything quite like it, and what seemed stranger—I had *no* other marks on my left hand anymore.

Jesse followed my gaze and registered the change as well. "What does that mean?"

"I'm not sure."

"We should get you to a hospital."

I shook my head. "That's fifty miles away. I'll be fine, but Chance won't."

Before he could argue, Butch lifted his head and growled. The heavy chill I'd noticed before the letters appeared on the wall returned. Everything stilled, even the wind. It felt like too much work even to move. Something was coming. I sensed the vibrations in the earth.

Something huge and heavy would burst into this clearing and roar over finding us toying with its trinkets. It must have an awful reason for keeping mementos of the dead and would most likely add us to its collection. I knew I should be frightened, but I felt as though my emotions had been burnt at the sockets.

Was it possible I hadn't returned all the way? Perhaps I was undead; that would be mightily inconvenient. I pinched myself, just in case. No. It stung a bit.

"Corine, we have to go now. Can you walk?"

I didn't know. When he pulled me to my feet, I discovered I could, clumsy, stumbling steps. Saldana snagged Butch, who wisely didn't protest. Before I hardly knew what had happened, he tucked me behind him and drew his weapon.

I had a feeling it wouldn't do us any good against what shared these woods with us, but men always seemed to feel better being proactive.

As we moved through the trees, trying unsuccessfully to be quiet, the distance between reality and me receded. My skin started to feel like my own again. The pain in my palm anchored me, and I tried to banish the memory of my mother's death. In a way, it was *my* death too, for that touch had killed me. Only Jesse's hands and mouth had kept me from slipping away into the dreaming dark.

He appeared to be doing his best to save a life I didn't want as much as I should right then. Reaction got the best of me. It seemed easier just to wait for the thing to find and eat us, or whatever it did to its victims.

"I'm not going to hurt you." The insanely deep voice came from everywhere and nowhere. At first, I thought I must be losing my mind. It rumbled all around me, shivering the earth as if with a happy sigh.

I stopped walking and glanced at Jesse, who looked like I felt. "Did you—"

"Hear that? Yeah."

He spun in a circle as if trying to find the microphones and bass amps. The way dark mist rolled in around us, he might want to check for a smoke machine too. I smiled slightly over that. For someone who was introducing me to Gifted society, he didn't seem to have run across as much weird stuff as I had.

I wondered if the unseen thing wanted some response. "You aren't?"

"No," it rumbled. "You are precious to me. Poor pretty thing. I wondered when you would come back."

A cold shudder rolled through me, and dead man's hands slid down my spine. I'd heard those words straight from Mr. McGee, just before he died. Beside me, Jesse froze. Clearly he'd made the connection as well from my recitation of the story.

"You know me?" I forced the words through numb lips.

"Darling child," the dark thing crooned, "I hid you. Sheltered you. You slept in my arms on blood night." For a mad moment, I thought we must be speaking to the dark spirit of the wood. My breathing grew labored, fear oozing out my pores in acrid sweat. "I kept your mother's legacy *safe* for you."

The necklace in Saldana's grasp suddenly seemed tainted. I wanted to grab it from him and throw it as far from us as my pitching arm could manage. He seemed to share the instinct, but after that first twitchy impulse, I shook my head. If there was evil in it, then it had already infected me. I gazed down at my marked palm with a dry, aching throat.

My chest felt as though I might be suffering the beginning stages of a heart attack. "Does that mean you will let us go?"

"Gladly," it rumbled. "Go from here and do not return. There are others in this place who mean you ill."

People, I guessed. But sometimes people were the worst monsters of all.

"Let's go," Jesse said beneath his breath. He started walking, fingers white-knuckled on his gun, as if to test the offer of free passage.

Butch never even twitched. I was afraid the little dog might have died of fright.

Getting away couldn't be so easy; it was never a matter of asking nicely not to be devoured. The monster must be playing with us, for I couldn't be misconstruing the air, thick with hunger and malice. It wanted us in ways I didn't understand.

I never lost the sense of it as we passed back through those arches on this profane path. If nature should be a temple, then this one was desecrated. The monster kept pace with us, an unseen presence slithering through the underbrush. I decided it could shift shapes, whatever it was. It did not have to be huge and heavy; it could be whatever it desired. That knowledge shook me in ways I didn't like to think about.

"Your friend will die in the dark," it said in parting as we came to the thinning trees that marked the end of its dominion. "Farewell to you, precious child. Farewell."

My breath whooshed out of me. *Chance.* Though I told myself I couldn't believe anything that creature told me—it was probably born of lies and darkness—I nonetheless tasted the certainty in its words. Sometimes truth tormented best of all.

As we stepped into the yard at last, I felt cold and dirty, weary beyond all belief. The fire in my left hand went beyond any hurt I'd previously suffered or imagined. Tiny lightning worms gnawed at my nerves, writhing in devilish sparks all the way up to the pain centers in my brain.

I desperately needed a good night's sleep, but there was no time. It was already late afternoon. If we delayed any longer, we would lose all hope of springing Chance before dark.

Because Jesse insisted, I washed my face and hands before we headed back into town. I also changed my clothes, not wanting to look like I had been rolling around the forest floor. We took his Forester because it was parked behind the Mustang and I didn't want anyone to recognize us.

He also demanded I eat one of the peanut butter sandwiches we'd packed for lunch. I didn't want it, but I didn't complain, munching mechanically and washing it down with tepid water. Afterward, I pulled Butch out of my bag and cradled him to my chest. As if he knew I needed comfort, he nuzzled his cold nose against my neck.

"Here's how it's going to be," Jesse told me as he parked in front of the courthouse. "I'll do the talking, and you agree with whatever I say. Got it?"

If I'd possessed the wherewithal to get Chance out earlier, I'd have done it, so I didn't mind letting Jesse call the play. I merely nodded and led the way downstairs to where they were keeping Chance. It was a makeshift jail at best, a small area barred off for town drunks. Sheriff Robinson looked slightly annoyed to see me back. His eyes narrowed

when he realized I'd brought backup and wouldn't be inclined to play ball with his "good old boys make the rules
in this here town" party line.

Chance had been sitting on the bunk, but he stood up,
looking puzzled, and a little glad, I think. Surely he hadn't
thought I meant to leave him in there all night. A little tremor
of relief ran through me. We'd gotten there in time.

Jesse planted his feet and stared down at the sheriff. A
long minute passed without anyone saying anything, and
then Robinson got heavily to his feet. "Is there something I
can do for you folks?" He tried on a smile like it might fit.

"I'm with the Laredo police department," Saldana said.
He wisely didn't mention his suspension.

The sheriff's smile lost its curl. "You're outside your jurisdiction, son."

The set of Saldana's jaw said he didn't like being called
"son" by a man he hardly knew. "I'm on vacation, but I do
know something about the law. You have the right to hold
someone for twenty-four hours in conjunction with a crime.
Has Chance been questioned, sir? What crime took place?
Has he been charged? Or do you intend to claim this incident
somehow relates to Homeland Security? As I see it, that's
your only hope of keeping him behind bars."

Robinson scowled. "I could make trespassing stick on
both of them."

"And I could call down a dozen human interest groups
on your little town." Jesse's smile showed teeth, but it wasn't
charming or pretty. "Would you like that? Reporters everywhere, poking around? Everybody has secrets, don't they,
Sheriff? Could yours stand up to close scrutiny? I can get a
film crew here from Savannah in—"

Pure dislike flashed in the sheriff's hound dog eyes, but
he offered his hands in what was meant to be a placating gesture. "There's no need for that. It's a simple misunderstanding. Since they're new in town, I thought they posed a flight
risk; that's all."

"It's called due process," Saldana bit out. "You don't get

to detain American citizens without it. Now let that man out of the cell before I get mad."

Jesus. I was impressed. No wonder he hadn't wanted me to talk.

Without a word, Robinson stomped over to the cage and unlocked the door, which swung wide on its own, making me think the floor had a slope too delicate to perceive with the naked eye.

"Get that dog out of here," the sheriff growled. "You can't go dragging animals into public places."

"You came back." Chance said it like I always left him in the lurch. And maybe he thought I did. I'd certainly left him once.

"Yeah," I answered thickly. "Brought the big guns too."

The idea that he'd needed Saldana to rescue him seemed to make him unhappy, so I hugged Chance hard. Whatever else, I didn't want to lose him for good. I did know that.

"I hate bullies," Jesse muttered as we went back up the stairs. "He loved knowing he had the power to keep you caged, Chance. Just on his say-so. God knows what would've happened after lights-out."

I shivered again and led the way out to the car. I had a feeling we wanted to be snug inside the wards before dark.

Stolen Kisses

We reached the house just before nightfall.

Chance seemed subdued. If I knew him, his mood related to Saldana coming to his rescue. That had to be a blow to his ego. There was no telling how he'd react to finding out I died in the woods; if it hadn't been for Jesse, I would have still been lying there.

After a quick perimeter check, we went inside. The place seemed secure, but I was glad we'd taken care of the wards. It occurred to me that we might want to mark the windows too. I didn't know if it would prevent glass breaking—probably not, in fact—but it might keep bad things from crawling over the sills.

I put Butch down, and he went into the kitchen to see if there was any food in his dish. Shortly thereafter, I heard crunching, so I guessed there was. No question, I should tell Chance what had happened.

Instead I mumbled, "I'm going to see if I can coax some hot water out of the shower."

"I'll check the water heater," Saldana offered. "The pilot light may have gone out."

"Thanks."

Jesse knew I didn't care about the shower. I was beyond

that. I needed comfort and privacy, but I leaned toward the latter because the former would involve choosing someone to console me, and then I would feel guilty about the guy I *didn't* turn to. And it was hard enough for me to open up in the first place.

I found a pair of worn jeans in my backpack and a clean shirt, a pink cotton gauze blouse that should've clashed with my hair, but didn't. Then I unearthed my polka-dotted cosmetic bag. I'd need soap and shampoo if I went through with the notion of cleaning myself up. Too bad I couldn't hose myself off where it counted. I could still feel the dark thing's presence, like it was peering at us from the forest.

The house is warded, I reminded myself. *Nothing can get in.*

Then I remembered the way the warlock had sent the undead thing to crawl around and around the house, breaking our wards at Chuch's place with its fetid blood. I shuddered. Surely Butch would let us know if anything like that arrived. The one good thing I could think of about being in Kilmer—we were so far off the grid, I couldn't imagine Montoya tracking us down via mundane means, and it would take him a while to hire a decent practitioner to employ any finding spells.

Thinking along those lines just gave me another set of worries. *Did we leave blood at the scene back in Laredo? Anything they could use to track us?* But the crime scene at the compound had been such a mess that it would take a CSI unit weeks to sort out the bodies. There shouldn't be any mundane clues.

When I went down the hall toward the old-fashioned bathroom, I saw Chance sitting in the parlor. He stared at his folded hands, much as he'd been doing on the cot in the makeshift jail. I knew something was bothering him, but I lacked the emotional fortitude to help him through his issues when I had so many of my own.

I stripped out of my clothes and left them piled on the bathroom floor. For long moments, I let the water run and stood staring at my left palm. The blisters around the brand looked oddly like petals adorning the flower pentacle, and the mark throbbed steadily in time with my heartbeat.

It meant something. When I'd touched my mother's necklace, it triggered a spell, but I didn't know exactly what it had done to me—or who left it for me to find. I wanted to think it must be something good, and that it came from my mother, but given the dark place where it sat waiting, I couldn't rid myself of the fear I now carried a taint.

In response to that thought, I stepped into the shower beneath tepid water, taking my soap and shampoo with me. The water felt strange and soft; it lathered too much and took at least two minutes to rinse out of my long hair. Soon the stream went from lukewarm to chilly, so I soaped up quickly and got out even faster. This wasn't the place to sit down under the hot water and fret. I'd have to do that somewhere else.

When I emerged, dripping onto the cold tile floor, I realized I didn't have a towel. In this place, we'd been lucky to find any linens at all. I didn't want to wiggle into my clean clothes all wet, and I shied from the idea of drying off on the dirty clothes I'd just removed. Dammit, I was tired of living like a squatter.

Someone rapped twice on the bathroom door. I cracked it and found Chance waiting, face averted. In his hands he held a fluffy white towel; I recognized it from the Kilmer Inn. I could feel a smile building at the corners of my mouth. As I lusted for that symbol of civilization, I pretended nonchalance.

"You stole a towel?"

"Three," he corrected with a half smile. "They owe me more than three towels too. I paid three hundred and forty bucks for one night! You want this or not?" He held it beyond my reach so I'd have to open the door to get it.

"Oh, I want it." Maybe he didn't think I'd do it, but I swung the door wide and stood there, water trickling from my hair, running in rivulets along my bare skin. I showed nothing he hadn't seen before, but I succeeded in shocking him.

Chance went still as I snagged the towel and wrapped it around myself. "You have no shame," he said huskily.

"None," I agreed with a smile that felt wicked.

I shouldn't tease him. I really, really shouldn't.

"And a mean streak wide enough to put the Mississippi to shame," he went on, still studying the curve of the white cotton covering my breasts.

I nodded. "That's true too."

Life sparked through him. I couldn't explain it, but he shook off whatever had been bothering him before. A smile shaped his sinfully lovely mouth.

"You have ten seconds to close the door, Corine."

"Or what?"

I watched his mouth move as he counted. Nerves clenched my stomach in a good way. I needed the distraction, and I'd probably like whatever he meant to threaten me with.

Nine.

I didn't shut the door.

Quick as a lightning strike, he knotted his hand in the slick rope of my hair and spun me toward him. Breath left me as he buried his face in the damp skin between my neck and shoulder. As he nuzzled, he let out a little growl that thrilled me in ways I shouldn't allow.

"You smell so good," he whispered.

I hadn't even put on the frangipani perfume he loved yet. This was just me, and somehow, his reaction stirred me all the more, making me feel like he craved the unadorned essence of me. What woman didn't want to feel she could drive a man wild with only her skin and her smile? Power thrummed through me in a heady rush.

I used to find him an immensely civilized lover. I used to fret about making myself attractive to him, making him desire me. Right then, he didn't seem remotely in control. Molten gold sparked in his tiger's eyes. Maybe I wasn't ready to commit, but I *wanted* him. I always had.

Chance backed me into the bathroom, spun me, and pressed me up against the bathroom door. I felt every inch of my nakedness in contrast to his sleekly clothed muscles. He'd grown even harder since I left.

When his mouth took mine, he didn't ask if I wanted it, or if I'd permit it. Heat sparked between us like two live wires, and I came up on my toes.

Part of me knew how easily he could finish it—rip off the towel, unfasten his pants, and do me up against the door. He kissed me, all urgency and raging need. As our lips clung, he rocked against me, letting me know how close he was to doing just that.

A kiss became ten, and then twenty. He kissed me like he had nothing better to do for the rest of his life, and I twisted against him. I didn't know if I wanted more or to get away from his wonderful, merciless mouth. He ran it down my throat to my shoulder, alternating lips and teeth, and I wanted him to do that everywhere.

I shook, but *he* trembled too.

His breath came in great, harsh gulps as he pulled me against him, tighter. My hips moved. I probably wouldn't have objected if he had raised me up and finished us. But he didn't. He continued to tantalize us both with sweet, slow movements, hip to hip.

"I want you so," he whispered. "You have the softest damn skin"—he ran his fingertips down my bare arm—"and your hair, I haven't had you with this hair. You're fire and ice, and everything about you is burning me up."

I think he wanted me to give permission to take the last step, but I couldn't. Before that happened, I needed him to tell me things it would never occur to Chance to say. He'd broken his sexual restraints, but he had emotional bonds to slip as well.

I also needed to know his gift wouldn't kill me before breakfast the next morning.

No matter how much we wanted each other—and I could no longer deny that was the case—we had issues to resolve.

I let out a shivery breath and couldn't resist taking one last bite, right behind his ear. He'd always been a sucker for that. Chance tensed, letting out a sound that half excited, half alarmed me.

He dropped his head on my shoulder and groaned. "You're not going to say yes, are you? Heartless. You're a heartless woman."

"I'm not the one who knocked on the bathroom door while you were naked. Seems like you shouldn't have put yourself in line to be tempted."

"That happens when you breathe," he muttered. But he stepped back, taking my hand instead of my whole body. Before I could warn him, he pressed a kiss to my newly branded palm.

A whimper escaped me. "That's not good for me."

"Jesus, Corine. What happened? Did you handle something? Didn't Saldana know to get you the salve?"

I barely refrained from snapping at him, *No, we came to save your ass instead.* I didn't want to tell the story naked. Some things were bad enough without being made worse by extraneous circumstance.

"I'll tell you later," I muttered.

Secrets that I shared with Jesse didn't sit well with him. Jealousy flared in his lambent gaze, quickly suppressed. "Just . . ." His hands fisted at his sides. "Don't let me catch you making out with him again, or I swear to God—"

Talk about a bucket of cold water. "So that's what this is about. Jesus, Chance."

Apparently he hadn't been overwhelmed with desire. This was vintage Chance. He wanted to mark his territory, so he put on a passionate display. And I should have known the difference. After all, he found me plenty resistible until Jesse showed up.

"That's not why I kissed you."

I flung open the bathroom door. "I need to get dressed."

I never learned. I berated myself as I rubbed the towel all over, trying to forget how easily he'd made me want him. I hated being stupid, and I never seemed to learn from my mistakes where Chance was concerned. By the time I had my clothes on, I only wanted to smack him a little bit.

I stomped out of the bathroom, hoping Jesse had told him about our encounter in the woods by now. By Chance's dead expression, he had. My ex looked cut to the core that I hadn't bothered telling him what happened. I'd *died* and hadn't seen fit to confide in him.

And it hurt him. I saw the shadow of it in his eyes. It was more than the fact that I'd shared something with Jesse—that he'd saved me. Chance felt iced out, treated as peripheral when he wanted to be center stage with me. Well, good. Let him see how it felt to be manipulated and kept in the dark.

And Jesse was a son of a bitch too. He would've sensed what was going on in the bathroom, so he'd informed his rival how he saved my life, a talent Chance seemed to lack. In fact, sometimes he actively endangered it. He'd probably also reminded Chance how he rode to my rescue, coming a thousand miles to save me.

"You're both assholes," I said aloud.

They jumped. There was oil in the next room if they wanted to play at Greco-Roman wrestling. Hell, if they enjoyed it, they could always settle down together, and leave me alone.

Before either of them could reply, three things happened at once.

Thunder boomed so loud it shook the house, but there was no resultant lightning, no onslaught of rain. The night felt deadly quiet.

A young girl's voice called out, "Is anyone there?"

And a dead man's radio began to play.

The Wrath of John

The house filled with the bizarre but crystal clear strains of "Fools Rush In," Sinatra's version, if I wasn't mistaken. It fit Kilmer's air of yesteryear perfectly.

I didn't call, "Come in" to whoever—or whatever—waited for us outside. A knock sounded at the door, and I went to investigate. The guys fell in behind me as I peered around the chain like Miz Ruth.

Shannon from the bed-and-breakfast stood on the front porch, looking nervous. She wore a black hoodie and a plaid miniskirt over black leggings. At first I wondered how she'd gotten here, and then I saw the bike leaning up against the side of the porch.

"Can I come in?" she asked in a rush.

It might be a trick. I studied her for a few seconds and then glanced at Jesse, who murmured, "She's scared."

"Sure." I unchained the door and stepped back.

It was a testament to her abstraction that she paid almost no attention to the men flanking me—or maybe they were too old to register on her hot scale. She rubbed her hands on her thighs and then shook hands. This time, I watched for the spark, and as when she'd touched me, it came when she greeted Jesse—not Chance.

That confirmed it. Chance wasn't like Jesse, or me, or Shannon. Whatever he was hiding about his paternity, it had left him with a gift that didn't register as human. I wasn't sure how I felt about that, but it didn't matter. It wasn't likely he was ever going to confide his secrets in me, and without that level of trust, I'd never risk being with him again.

"Let's sit down," Chance said. He'd apparently put aside his feelings about my keeping from him what happened in the woods earlier, at least for the time being.

"How'd you find us?" I asked as we arranged ourselves.

I wound up on the love seat next to Shannon, who shrugged. The guys sat down at opposite ends of the sofa.

"Everybody knows everything that happens in town," she said. "I asked around and found out you rented this place."

I didn't know if we should continue with the questions; teenagers tended not to respond well to them. With a glance, I took a survey. Chance didn't even meet my gaze, but Jesse shook his head slightly. Okay, so we'd let her spit it out in time.

"Well, you found us. Want something to drink? I could make some tea."

Nobody looked enthusiastic, so I didn't bother. Thunder rumbled again; the clarity of the music in the background made this seem like a scene from an old movie.

Shannon hunched forward, elbows on her knees. She was so thin and awkward that she resembled a crow hatchling, down to the blue tips of her hair. I hoped I had the patience not to scare her off.

"I heard about you," she finally mumbled. "People still talk, you know. About how weird you were. But you got away." She looked up, china blue eyes matted with old mascara and too-thick kohl. "That's what I want. I know you're not going to stay forever. You came for a reason, and when you're done here, you'll leave." After drawing a deep breath, she finished in a rush: "I want you to take me with you."

Jesse looked worried. "How old are you?"

"Eighteen," she said, defiant. "I just had a birthday."

"You're still in school," Chance pointed out.

She shrugged. "I have to get out of here. I can get a GED anywhere."

That much was true. I'd stayed until I finished high school, thinking that would help me get a job somewhere else, but her body language conveyed genuine urgency.

"Why do you have to leave, Shannon?" I figured she'd tell me her parents didn't understand her and refused to let her get a barbwire tattoo around her right biceps.

Her face paled even further, going almost gray. "Something bad is going to happen," she whispered. "I've been digging around, and something bad always happens on December 21. That's next month. And I won't be able to get away on my own. I don't have a car or money—" Her voice stressed and broke; her hands went white-knuckled in her lap.

Anyone else probably would have dismissed her fear, but I'd lived in this town, and I needed to know what *she* knew. Though I didn't touch people much, I put my hand on her shoulder, expecting a rebuff. She quieted instead, as if I somehow gave her strength.

"It's okay," Jesse said. "We're not going to let anybody hurt you."

Her blue eyes looked big and guileless in her narrow face. She had him now; he was a sucker for a damsel in distress. If she didn't come with us in the Mustang, she'd go with Jesse in his Forester when we left. He wouldn't leave her. I'd never met a guy with a bigger white knight complex.

"Why don't you tell us the whole story, Shannon?" Chance used his warmest expression, and even a bundle of nerves like the girl next to me couldn't resist.

She relaxed enough to settle against the back of the love seat, no longer sitting as if she might need to run at any moment. "Everyone thinks I'm nuts," she began.

Well, that sounded familiar. I didn't interrupt; I already knew she was Gifted. I wanted to know why the town thought she was crazy. We all sat quiet, offering our most attentive expressions.

"I was around thirteen when it started." She refused to look at any of us, staring fiercely at a worn spot on the floor. "I started reading sad poetry. I guess that's pretty common." She shrugged. "Sylvia Plath, Anne Sexton."

"The death girls," I put in with a nod.

She chanced a look at me. "You read them too?"

"Not anymore," I said quietly.

Shannon accepted that without requesting clarification, but my answer prompted the first smile we'd seen from her, a soft little flutter that dissolved almost at once as she resumed her story. "I started thinking about death a lot. I researched the Holocaust. And I got curious about Kilmer." Jesse started to speak, but she anticipated his question. "How people died here. How often. I spent a lot of time in the library archives."

A morbid curiosity, to be sure, but adolescence took some kids like that. I had a feeling I wouldn't like what was coming, but I asked, anyway. "What did you find out?"

"Bad things happen on December 21," she said simply. "People die."

The date chilled me.

"So it's been more than just my family?" I spoke almost to myself. "There must be a pattern to it."

Shannon nodded. "From what me and Mr. McGee could figure out—"

"You knew Mr. McGee?" That captured my attention.

"Kinda." She scowled at me. Some of the edge had come off her fear. Maybe she sensed she sat inside a well-warded house, or maybe Chance and Jesse reassured her. "We got friendly, I guess, while I was poking around. The librarian didn't like me much, but Mr. McGee was nice, and he let me look in the paper files downstairs."

"Us too," I said. *Well, he used to.* "He was about to answer some questions for us when he . . ." *Had a fit and died, frothing at the mouth like a mad badger.* That didn't seem suitable, so I said aloud, "Passed on unexpectedly this afternoon."

Fear clouded her eyes again as she gazed at the three of us. "I heard. And . . . I don't think that was right. I mean," she hastened to add, "I don't believe you had anything to do with it. But somebody did."

Our sound track suddenly switched from "Fools Rush In," which had been looping seamlessly, to "Bye Bye Love." We'd ignored the phenomenon long enough. I got up and went over to my bag, digging for the old radio I'd stolen off John McGee's worktable. By her look, Shannon recognized it, but I couldn't interpret her expression.

I tried to reassure her. "He was telling us about it when he died. He said—"

"Folks could hear ghosts in the snow between channels, if they're close to death themselves." I heard an echo of old McGee in the words she'd obviously heard from the man more than once. "It's true," she added, not meeting my gaze. "*I* can."

"Is that what you were working on with Mr. McGee?" Chance asked.

Shannon nodded. "Yeah, that and our research. He got interested in all the people dying too. It used to only happen on December 21—and not all the time, either. Sometimes years would pass, and nothing went bad. But lately . . . something's different. I can't explain it." She shrugged helplessly. "I can just *feel* it."

I knew exactly what she meant. I'd sensed it in the forest, but tendrils of it wove throughout the town as well, dank and terrible. I didn't want say so, but Shannon's own mother had scared the crap out of me, as had the librarian, Edna.

Jesse smiled at her, pure warmth and reassurance. "Did you try to warn anybody?"

"Sure. Nobody would listen. I'm a weird kid, and McGee was a crazy old coot. It couldn't have been worse for our credibility if we'd planned it."

As if in response to her words, the song changed to "Ain't That a Shame."

Chance cocked a brow. "You get the feeling somebody's trying to tell us something?"

"That's Mr. McGee's kind of music," Shannon told us.

"You said before, you can talk to dead people on the radio," I prompted gently.

She scowled, checking our faces to see if we were messing with her. "Don't be stupid—I have no mic. I can *hear* them, not talk to them. Just have to find their frequency."

I couldn't imagine how that would work, but she'd fallen among the right crowd to display her talent. She wouldn't find skepticism here. We needed to talk to her about being Gifted, but first things first.

"Here." I handed her the radio. "Knock yourself out."

Shannon studied my face with a half frown that melted away when she realized I wasn't joking. "You believe me?"

"Absolutely." I flashed my left palm, the one with the inexplicable brand. "We're all weird here, Shannon. In one way or another. You came to the right place."

"Okay." She bent her spiky blue and black head to the task, fiddling with the knobs. Once she touched the device, the unnatural music ceased, and I heard only snow, full of echoes and ghostly whispers, too many to distinguish. But Shannon had the power to give one voice dominion over the rest. We all froze as the "station" came into focus in her hands.

"They killed me," John McGee said tonelessly. "The rotten sons of bitches killed me." The ancient speakers crackled, tinny and strange. McGee repeated the words again and again, until they reached a thunderous crescendo, and then fell into a whispered moan. With that much rage, he had a fair start toward turning into a poltergeist, I thought. It hurt me just to listen to it.

I wasn't sure what good this would do, however, if we couldn't ask questions. Interesting though it was, a one-way feed provided limited usefulness. If McGee was out in the ether somewhere, broadcasting his pain and anger, then he wouldn't hear our questions. If we could summon him, somehow—

Well, Shannon had known him best. What could it hurt to try? We might learn something about her gift, as I'd certainly never heard of anything like it. Kilmer *did* birth some weird ones, and yes, I meant myself too.

"Try calling him," I suggested. "If we can get him in the room with us—"

"The wards," Jesse cut in. "He can't come in. We blocked anything that means us harm, and confused as he is right now, he might not know friend from foe."

"Ideas?" I glanced at Chance, hoping he wasn't still mad.

He was. I saw it in the set of his jaw and the tilt of his eyes. That didn't stop him from saying, "If you're determined to do this, we could go out on the porch. That way, if things go bad, we can run back inside."

The notion sent a cold chill through me, and I wanted to immediately reject it. It didn't seem wise to step outside our protective walls after dark, but I waited to see what everyone else would say. Saldana considered.

"We'd need to prop the door open with something heavy," Jesse said finally. "If we get locked out, we're sitting ducks out there, and my gun isn't going to help." At Shannon's worried look, he added, "Don't worry. I'm a cop."

Evidently she didn't like the police any better than I did. If Robinson set the standard in Kilmer, I could see why she shared my bias. But Sheriff Pasco, who had the job when I lived here, had been worse.

I raised a brow. "So y'all want to go outside in the dark—in sight of those scary woods—and call up an angry dead man to see what he has to say?"

The looks I received in answer to my question registered as the facial equivalent of a shrug. Shannon seemed least concerned, but she either figured she could run faster than us, or she hadn't seen as much trouble. Either way, I had a bad feeling.

Butch whimpered.

"Yes or no? Show of hands."

I wanted to vote no; I really did. But it was my fault we were here in the first place, and if Mr. McGee could tell us something about what was killing Kilmer, we had to find out what he knew. It would be better if Chuch were here, but we'd do the best we could under the circumstances. With a sigh, I raised my hand. Slowly, Jesse did the same. Shannon's hand went up next—and when she stopped touching the radio, it lapsed into signal snow. Chance's vote didn't matter.

My ex stood and went rummaging in the house. I heard him looking for something heavy enough to function as a doorstop. He returned with a rusty cast-iron skillet.

Chance propped open the door. Night air rushed in, cool, clammy, and somehow ominous. "If we're doing this, we shouldn't let it get any later."

I hoped he wouldn't make stupid jokes about the witching hour. I tended to take them personally.

I blew out a breath. "What the hell, right?"

In the Still of the Night

Thunder boomed a third time, a ghost storm threatening noise and nothing else.

I noticed a prickle as I passed out of the house, beyond the protection of the wards. Out there, I felt defenseless, and not just because I was barefoot. I sensed the thing in the forest watching from the shadow of the trees, darkness beyond mere night, beyond mere absence of light.

It had a particular smell, thick and cloying, like a stagnant pond grown black and green with dying things. With it came that sense of pressure, as if we were miles beneath the ocean. The thing watched us, listened, but it did nothing. I didn't understand its passivity, and that bothered me.

As we arranged ourselves in a circle, keeping on our feet in case we had to move fast, I had the ill-timed thought that between Jesse and Shannon, we now qualified as a Scooby-Doo unit. Butch watched us from the doorway. Whatever foolishness we were about, he wasn't dumb enough to step outside the house for it. That should have sent us all back inside, I guess, but sometimes necessity outweighed wisdom.

"Call him," Chance said to Shannon.

She cast an imploring look at me. "I don't know how."

"There are no real magick words," I said, quoting my

mother. "Any old words will do, if you put your will behind them."

"Okay," she said. "I'll try." She closed her eyes as if she meant to pray. "Mr. McGee, I'm really sorry I didn't get to say good-bye to you. We both knew things were bad here, but I reckon we didn't know *how* bad. If you can hear me, if you'd come and talk with me a minute, I'd sure appreciate it."

For a moment, nothing happened, and then I felt it in the wind rustling the bushes beside the porch. It picked up speed and curled around us like a small, unearthly cold cyclone. I just hoped Mr. McGee didn't blame us for what had happened to him. We had been talking to him when he died, after all.

"Well done," Jesse told her. "He's here."

Shannon gulped a little. I guessed the certainty of the strange was more intimidating than the idea of it. Things usually sounded cooler in theory than they were in practice.

She didn't hesitate, though. I gave her credit for that. Instead, she fiddled with the knobs, trying to find his frequency. It took a little while for her to tune in; she found him on the AM side of the dial this time.

And then McGee's voice crackled from the speakers, tinny and full of impossible distance. "Can you hear me?"

The eeriness of the moment went beyond anything I could articulate. There were no stars; just a brooding wood beyond, and the heavy feel of a storm that wouldn't come. He'd stopped raging, and sounded more or less coherent— for an angry, vengeful spirit.

It seemed right for Shannon to greet him. She'd known him best. We motioned her onward, so she said uncertainly, "Mr. McGee? It's me. What happened to you?"

I thought that was a singularly unhelpful question, but then, we *had* yielded the lead to an eighteen-year-old girl. What did we expect?

McGee answered, "I died, fool girl. They killed me."

"How?" Chance cut in.

Shannon repeated the question because he didn't seem to hear anyone but her.

The radio speakers popped. "How should I know? Something choked me while two fools stood there, worthless as tits on a bull. But I do know damn well that wasn't natural."

It hadn't seemed so to me, either. It stank of summoning. I'd heard of dark stalkers, malicious energy given purpose by a wicked practitioner's will. Maybe we'd hoped for too much in thinking he'd be able to give us information about his death. Dying didn't give you all the answers, apparently.

"You were trying to tell us something," Chance prompted. "Can you remember what it was?"

The girl passed the question along.

"Yes." The radio cut out, and I glanced at Shannon, who was looking pale. Snowy static replaced McGee's voice. The radio cut back in. "—and Augustus England."

I had the feeling we'd missed some important bits, but the girl didn't look good. Her skin had gone from pale to ash gray. Not good—maybe we shouldn't push further. We didn't know anything about her gift or what it took from her

"Are you okay?" I put my hand on her shoulder because she looked like she might collapse.

"My head feels funny," she whispered.

I touched her cheek and found it clammy. Tremors shook her like an apartment above an overpass. Chance plucked the radio from her hands, probably figuring it was draining her somehow, and Jesse swung her up in his arms.

"Let's get her back inside," I said.

The threat from the woods never manifested. I found that strange—and disturbing. Evil rarely practiced anything so subtle as restraint; I didn't want the thing watching us, learning. I didn't *want* a clever, refined enemy. That might prove more than we could handle. I shuddered, remembering how it had said my name. It had called me "precious child," like Mr. McGee. It had claimed to know my mother.

With a final look down the dark gravel drive, I shut the door behind me. Inside, I found Shannon sprawled on the couch. The radio sat beside her on the table, but I wouldn't ask her to do that again until I knew something more about her gift.

"I think she's hypoglycemic," Jesse said. "She has all the preliminary symptoms: nausea, clammy skin, shakes. I'm going to get her some raisins and make a cup of sweet tea for her to drink. If that doesn't help, she might need a hospital."

I nodded as I sat down beside her. "Get the raisins. Quick."

Shannon tried to protest, mumbling she hated raisins, but I ignored the complaint. She ate a handful at my insistence, and then muttered, "If I hurl, you're cleaning it up."

Recognizing her need for bravado and attitude, I gave her that. "Yeah, of course."

By the time Jesse returned with the hot tea, she looked a little better. Her face had some color again, and she was no longer shivering. She took the mug gratefully and cupped her hands around it.

"Well, that was weird," she said at last.

The guys had given up hovering and dialed back to merely looking worried. In retrospect, this wasn't the brightest thing we'd ever done. If any harm had come to this kid with us, I didn't like to consider the consequences, especially not after Mr. McGee died in our presence. I had no doubt Sheriff Robinson could manufacture enough evidence to see us receive life in the state penitentiary if he felt so inclined—or received orders to do so. We needed to keep our noses extra clean from here on out.

"Weird how?" Jesse asked.

"Well, I've done that before," she told him. "That never happened, at least, not that bad. I'd feel a little light-headed, and then I'd have a candy bar and it would be fine."

"Sounds like your gift converts sugars to energy that lets you power the radio like you do," Chance said. "Do you have to be touching it?"

She nodded. "Never thought of it like that, but yeah. Sounds about right."

Interesting. I made a mental note. Kilmer appeared predisposed to breeding girls who had some special gift in their touch. Even if Shannon and I were the only ones, two people in a town this size seemed remarkable.

I followed Chance's idea to its natural conclusion. "If it took tons more energy to hear Mr. McGee than it usually does, that implies resistance."

Jesse took up the thread as I paused. "Which means somebody is trying to keep that from happening."

"Not a warlock," I said. "Not spirit wrack like we saw with Maris. More like a spell that puts barriers in place."

Shannon regarded us, wide-eyed. "Y'all know . . . warlocks? For real? You aren't messing around?"

I smiled at that, though it felt grim and wry. "Not even close. The one we were talking about is dead, but there are others like him out there. I just don't think we're dealing with one here in Kilmer."

"The magick seems clumsy," Chance agreed. "I don't think whoever we're dealing with really knows what they're doing, but I'd give a lot to get a *good* witch out here and see what she thinks."

"Good, like, powerful, or good, like, not evil?" Shannon asked.

Jesse grinned. "Both?"

I was glad to see she was feeling better. "I'm sorry we put you at risk. We won't do that again."

"No, it's okay," she said, ducking her head. "I wanted to. It's nice to feel like people don't think you're nuts, you know?"

I could relate.

"So, I'm going to make something to eat." I stood up. It had been ages since I had the peanut butter sandwich in the SUV, and Chance had to be starving. It had been an unbelievably long day.

Jesse came to his feet, earning a dark look from Chance. "I'll help."

As we went toward the kitchen, I heard Chance ask Shannon, "Do you know anything about powder lining the doorways outside our room at the inn?"

I wanted to hear the end of that conversation, but Jesse clearly had something on his mind. So I figured I'd get the scoop later, if Chance felt inclined to tell me. Given his current mood, he might not.

"What are we going to do about her?" he asked without preamble. "We need to talk to her about being Gifted. According to precedent, since you found her, you should be her mentor, but you hardly know enough to get your feet wet." He raked a hand through his hair. "And I'm not sure I can handle both of you."

My lips curled up into a slightly mocking smile. "Too many women for Jesse Saldana? I never thought I'd see the day."

"Funny." He glared while I made sandwiches.

More peanut butter. They'd go well with the apples I was slicing up.

"It's more that I've never been a mentor before," he went on. "I learned everything I know from my dad."

Now that intrigued me. "You did? What's his gift?"

Saldana mumbled something.

"What? I didn't hear you."

He regarded me in exasperation. "*Growing* things. He focuses on giant squash and pumpkins mainly. He wins the blue ribbon at the county fair every year."

Laughter bubbled out of me, delightful and cleansing. "That doesn't sound too supernatural. Maybe he just has a green thumb."

"He can do it *overnight*," Jesse told me. "He just doesn't, not often, anyway."

"Does your mom know?"

"She knows he has a green thumb. I think he married her

because she makes such good pumpkin pie." Real affection laced his words. "They're a perfect match."

I tried to imagine the Norman Rockwell sort of upbringing he must have had and failed. It sounded sweet, though. "Does she know about *you*?"

"She thinks I'm too sensitive," he answered with a grimace.

"To answer you," I said then, "we don't *do* anything with her. She's eighteen. Shannon can make up her own mind."

Other people might say we couldn't take her with us because she hadn't graduated high school yet, but I had too much sympathy for her plight to leave her stranded here. If she was determined to go, she'd find someone to take her— and that person might be less than interested in her long-term well-being.

"I'll have a talk with her before we leave about the whole Gifted thing," I went on. "And she's mine, not yours. Maybe that violates some protocol I'm not aware of because I'm not 'fully trained,' but I promise I won't let my Padawan go over to the dark side."

He smiled with reluctant appreciation. "Right. She's your worry then, not mine."

"Like that would stop you." I grinned back. "You'll be riding to her rescue before you know it. No wonder your relationships never last. You can't focus the caring."

Genuine pain flickered in his eyes. "I know. No matter how hard I try, the women I love always say they don't come first with me . . . just before they walk out."

"I'm sorry, I didn't mean to—"

"Take the food to the parlor," he said, not looking at me. He busied himself with the kettle. "I'll make tea for everyone and follow in a bit."

I set my palm on his cheek and forced him to meet my gaze. "All cops have relationship problems. A lot of women can't handle knowing their men are in danger, and it makes them shift the blame elsewhere, so they don't have to acknowledge the real reason they can't deal. If anyone says it's wrong of you to care about people, they're full of shit. There's a difference between being compassionate and falling in love with everybody you save." I paused. "You don't, do you? Fall in love with everyone you save?"

He nuzzled his face against my hand. "No. If I'm in a relationship, I assume I'm being overwhelmed by the other person's feelings and that when I walk away, it will pass."

"And you don't act on it?" I watched his face.

"Never, if I'm with someone. If a woman I meet on the job is overcome by grateful desire and it gets me all charged up, I just go home that way."

"Which means you rip your girlfriend's clothes off as soon as you see her."

A long breath escaped him. "Yeah. Sometimes it happens like that."

"Well, you know what they say: It doesn't matter where you prime the pump, as long as you quench your thirst at home."

"So it wouldn't bother you?" He'd lost his haunted air, thank God, and his mouth was doing some interesting things to my palm. Pleasurable chills ran through me.

"Offhand, I'd have to say no." It was a trust issue to be sure, but not the kind that came from secrets, and there was undeniable appeal in knowing your desire would ratchet up your lover's need.

Jesse's other hand lit on my shoulder and pulled me toward him. His bitter chocolate gaze fixed on my mouth, but he wasn't asking permission. He kissed me with the sweetest demand, pinning me up against the counter with his hips. My whole body thrummed in delicious response.

By the time the kettle whistled, I felt flushed. "Um. Give me a minute. *You* take the tea. I'll be there presently."

Jesse grinned at me. "I need a few too, sugar."

"Why . . . oh. Right."

Soon, we had the meal ready. He brought the tray of tea while I carried the sandwiches. "We need to talk to Augustus England," I said as I came into the parlor with my arms full of plates. I'd mastered that trick during a stint as a waitress, but I didn't like being slapped on the ass by strangers, so I never worked in restaurants thereafter. "He seems to have his fingers in a lot of pies, from newspaper to phone book, and his name came from a dead man, to boot. Thoughts?"

I passed out the peanut butter sandwiches with apple slices, feeling like a third grade teacher. Still, Chance and Shannon thanked me, so they must have been hungry. My ex didn't meet my gaze, but for once, I didn't feel guilty.

"We already decided that," Chance said, tilting his head toward Shannon. "She also said it must've been her mom who left us the present outside. Shannon said she's gotten really weird in the last few months, quiet and secretive and more—"

"Plastic," Shannon put in. "There's nothing real about her anymore. Or at least, if there is, I can't see it. She . . . scares me."

That was a hell of a thing to admit about your own mom. I hated to ask, but someone had to, and I doubted the guys would. "Has she ever—"

"No," the girl said quickly. "I mean, other than the usual. She wants me to dress like her and let my hair go back to its natural brown. She wants me in pearls, and she wants me to stop being weird because, get this, it's not safe."

"It's not safe to be different in Kilmer." I repeated that idea, tested it, and decided it was true. Look at what happened to my mother, after all. I ate in thoughtful silence, more to fill my belly than because I wanted the campground food I'd prepared.

Shannon shook her head. "Not at all."

"Jesse . . . what did you get from Sheriff Robinson?"

"He was annoyed but also frightened."

That surprised me. "Of what?"

"Sorry. It's not that specific. I never know why."

We downed our tea in silence and then decided to call it a night. I gave Shannon my bed, such as it was, and the guys would sleep in the other two bedrooms. That left me on the couch. I sighed a little over that, but at least it was soft and sunken, not hard and lumpy. This flophouse-style arrangement better suited college students, I thought, not that I had ever been one.

Thunderclouds in Chance's eyes said he wanted to fight with me, but it would have to keep.

Except it didn't.

The Sweetest Thing

After the other two retired, Chance came back into the parlor. He sat down next to me on the sofa, wearing a determined look. I watched him warily, not sure what to expect. Wordlessly, he unscrewed the cap from the ointment his mother had made for my burns and then took my left hand in his.

I flinched a little as he covered the brand on my palm. It didn't hurt as much as it should have, considering I'd taken the wound earlier today. The area tingled as the medicine started working. It didn't prevent scarring, but it would stop infection and promote faster healing.

When he was done, he put the top back on and sat looking straight ahead. I had the terrible, dizzying feeling I'd hurt him worse than I knew. His features seemed tight, as if he struggled to restrain a plethora of emotions.

"You should have told me," he said without looking at me.

I went on the attack. "Where? In the car? Or before you kissed me senseless? I wanted to get cleaned up before I settled in for a long talk. I was filthy. If you'd been out there in those woods with me, you'd understand."

"Is that what this is about?" He shifted on the sofa to

look at me, haunted. "How I never seem to be around when you need me most?"

"This had nothing to do with you." I really meant it. "Your luck doesn't even work here, Chance. Sometimes bad things happen, and there's nothing you can do about it. I mean, damn. You went to jail so I wouldn't have to. I wasn't going to leave you there—I just needed leverage. Men like Robinson don't respect women, and I didn't know enough about the law to fling it around like Jesse did. And as for why I didn't tell you sooner"—I shrugged—"there's just no good moment for something like that."

"I guess not," he muttered. To my surprise, he didn't take the argument any further. Instead, he pulled me into his arms and buried his face in my hair. "If Saldana hadn't been with you, if he hadn't known CPR . . ." He trailed off, unable to articulate it.

Well, I wouldn't have gone into those woods alone, not even for Butch. But I rather liked his desperation. His hands sifted through my hair, finding the sensitive spots at the base of my skull.

"I found my mother's necklace out there."

He paused in stroking my hair. "So someone took it from the wreckage."

"Someone or some*thing*."

"What do you mean?"

I told him the whole story then from start to finish.

His frown turned into a ferocious scowl. "I really, really don't like this, Corine. That thing recognized you."

"I know." I shuddered, just thinking about it. "But it tried to convince me it knew my mother, and that it meant me no harm. But it was so . . ." I trailed off, unable to find the word I wanted. "Evil" seemed simultaneously too small as well as too melodramatic.

"You must've been terrified."

I acknowledged that by turning my face into his chest. I didn't know what to make of the new Chance; the old one would've never accepted my motivations so readily. It would have been turned into a wedge to drive distance between us, mitigated only by sex—and even then, not real intimacy—just the physical facsimile of it.

"Let's let Butch out and then turn in," I murmured. "We have a lot to do tomorrow."

In answer, he dropped a kiss on my temple, warming me all the way down to my toes. "Out you go, dog. But no funny stuff—and don't even think about running off to the woods again. We will *not* come find you this time."

The Chihuahua gave an indignant little yap, as if to say, *Hey, I'm not an idiot.* He trotted out into the yard, took care of business, and came right back in. A light rain had finally started, pattering on the roof. Butch gave himself a little shake as I closed the door behind him. Then I turned the bolt.

"Tomorrow we go see Augustus England. Then I think we should have dinner with Miss Minnie. Maybe she won't be so reluctant to talk."

I nodded. "Agreed. I'll call her in the morning to confirm. Let's get some sleep. We have a lot to do tomorrow."

I gave a surprised little yelp when he swung me up in his arms. As he carried me, he spoke in a conversational tone. "If you think I'm letting you out of my sight, even to sleep, you're crazy."

"Chance—"

He ignored my halfhearted protest and took me to the guest room where he'd slept the night before. There was a mattress on the floor in here too, but no box springs. He'd found another torn sheet to cover it, and he'd used what looked like an old couch throw as his covers. Altogether, it seemed a remarkably cozy squatter's nest.

His smile flashed bright in the contrasting darkness. "I know what you're thinking. I really know how to wow a woman when I'm trying to win her back."

I gave a soft, reluctant laugh. "Yeah. The five star accommodations will go to my head if you keep this up."

He squeezed me in answer, and then he amazed me with an acrobatic move that ended with him on his back and me sprawled across his chest. I'd left my backpack in the room I gave to Shannon, so I had nothing to sleep in besides my blouse and jeans. Chance seemed to follow my thoughts.

"I'll get you a T-shirt."

I was tired, and I didn't feel like arguing. When he found me an old shirt that didn't look like anything Chance would ever wear, I took a closer look. I recognized it.

It had belonged to my mother; until earlier today, it was all I had left of her. They found it hanging on the clothes-line in the backyard after the fire, and someone gave it to me. I'd taken it with me through so many moves, I'd lost count—but it hadn't come with me through the last one. I'd been in too much of a hurry to check my belongings that night.

"You kept it," I breathed.

"I knew how much it meant to you."

Without regard for modesty, I wiggled out of my clothes and into the worn cotton. It felt like coming home, a hug from my mother. Tears prickled at my eyes. Until that moment, I hadn't realized how much I missed this silly old yellow shirt.

"Why didn't you give it to me sooner?"

"I forgot," he said honestly. "I stuffed it in my bag before I left Tampa to go looking for you. I meant to send it to you after I tracked you down. It was the one thing I felt sure you'd want out of everything you left behind. But then—"

"Min went missing, and you had other things on your mind," I finished.

He'd arranged himself beneath the throw as I got myself situated. His arms came around me, snuggling me into his side with an alacrity that suggested he missed me more than he'd said. I decided I'd let him snuggle me a little before I kicked him out. It had been a long day for both of us.

To my surprise, he didn't push the situation. "You must have been like Shannon once," he said quietly. "I can see you in her. I imagine you were a lot like her when you ran away from Kilmer. Meeting her, talking to her, well . . . I think I understand you better now."

I saw what he was getting at, but I couldn't agree. "No matter what might be wrong with them, she has a family. She's *not* like me."

"Yes, she is. You're both looking for where you belong."

That stymied me because it was so clearly true. And it was more perceptive than I'd come to expect from Chance. He didn't used to deal well in emotional coin; he preferred to show his feelings through material things.

When we'd have a fight back in Tampa, he'd come home with roses, chocolate, and an expensive piece of jewelry. At first, I found that charming, but eventually, I started wanting him to apologize and tell me how he felt; why he did the things he did. And he didn't want to tell me anything at all.

Now he seemed to be genuinely trying to open up. We'd stopped to pick up some more clothing for me on the way to Georgia, but it had been a convenience, not an attempt on his part to impress me with what he could offer financially. He'd finally figured out I wanted more from him than his magical way of turning a hundred bucks into a thousand.

"You can't stay," I said softly. "If you give me your bed, it's the couch for you."

He pushed off the mattress with a faint sigh. "You can't blame a guy for trying."

"Good night, Chance."

"Sweet dreams, love."

I found myself thinking, *Maybe people can change. Maybe—*

Sleep snatched me before I could complete the thought.

When I woke, the slant of the sunlight told me I'd slept half the morning away, so I took a quick, tepid shower and got dressed. I plucked my cell from where it was charging in the hall and called Miss Minnie. "Good morning. It's Corine. How are you?"

"Old and achy," she said with a little laugh. "How about you, dear?"

"Good. I was wondering if you still wanted us to come to supper."

"I surely do. I'll make a nice big pot of soup and some corn bread. You like peach pie, don't you?"

"Cherry is my favorite," I felt compelled to say.

"Cherry it is. It will be so good to catch up and get to know your young man. I don't have guests as often as I'd like these days. Everyone's just so busy. . . ." She rambled on, giving me some idea why people didn't stop by more often, but I needed any information she might possess.

"I'll have two more friends with me, if that's all right?"

"Oh, more young people." She sounded genuinely delighted. "Soup can always stretch, don't you fret about that. I'll see you tonight at six, then?"

"I'm looking forward to it." And I was. Miss Minnie had been the second-best cook of all my foster mothers, surpassed only by Miz Ruth. And actually Miss Minnie's pies were better. I might as well enjoy some aspects of being back in Georgia.

Though the food was delicious in Mexico, it was also different. You just couldn't find decent biscuits and gravy there, or fried chicken, let alone picnic food like potato salad. And the pie was nothing like the same. If I wanted cherry pie, I had to go to the gourmet foods section at Palacio del Hierro—an upscale department store—and search the shelves for the filling. I'd never been able to find ready-made piecrust, either, which meant making it from scratch, and I wasn't nearly skilled enough for that. Plus, my initial attempts at baking had failed due to the high altitude.

Just thinking of all the delicious Southern food made my stomach rumble, and I realized as I rang off that I hadn't eaten breakfast. The others were waiting for me in the kitchen, drinking coffee someone had made with the old-fashioned pot. Jesse offered me a cup when I stumbled in, still braiding my hair.

"Wow," Shannon said. "Your hair is really long. Pretty. Is it real?"

"Depends on what you mean by that. It's real *hair*."

"The color." She rolled her eyes.

I grinned. "As much as yours is."

That surprised a smile out of her. I guessed she wasn't used to grown women who admitted to coloring their hair; I could hear her mother chiding that it wasn't genteel to discuss such artifice. I ate an apple and drank a cup of sweet coffee, liberally mixed with powdered milk. It was better than you'd think. I followed that up with toast and jelly.

Shannon seemed more relaxed than I'd ever seen her. I could understand why. With men like Jesse and Chance telling you they wouldn't let anything happen, it was easy to relax. I'd learned the hard way—sometimes there was nothing anybody could do.

"Are we ready?" I asked.

"Yeah, we already ate," Saldana told me. "We should take my Forester. People already know the Mustang, if someone tried to run Corine over the other day."

I scowled. I would love to have a talk with the guy who owned the Cutlass. In fact . . . we had a native here. Maybe she could tell us who drove it.

"Good point." Chance seemed more cheerful this morning— less inclined to smash Jesse's head in with a claw hammer.

"Shannon, do you know who drives a dark blue Olds Cutlass Supreme?" I asked. "It was an older car, but very well kept."

As we left the kitchen, she thought about that, pale brow furrowed. "Yeah, actually. Sounds like Little Ed Willoughby. His mother owns the hardware store. She's on the school board and the town council—a real meddler, if you ask me."

When we came into the parlor, Butch raised his head from where he'd been napping on the love seat. He leaped up and trotted to the front door, but he wasn't agitated. His calmness reassured me, though; the wards must be solid.

"You think you're going with us?" I asked the dog.

He yapped once.

Despite her own gift, Shannon gazed at him wide-eyed. "Oh my God, that is the coolest thing ever. You have a talking dog!"

"Kind of," I said.

"How? Is he magical?"

I considered as I swept him into my handbag. "I'm not sure. We didn't train him to do it, that's for sure. Maybe one day we'll figure out what makes him tick."

"He's so cute," she said, going for the sweet spot behind his ears, and Butch wore an expression I liked to call "blissful dog."

As I headed down the front steps, the others followed.

Jesse couldn't stop being a cop long enough for us to climb in the Forester. He prompted Shannon for more info as we opened the doors. "Willoughby's dad is Big Ed?"

"His dad's dead," Shannon said flatly. "Or presumed so. He went missing about three months ago."

"Let me guess," Chance put in. "He went out to hunt and never came back."

Like Glen, Miz Ruth's husband.

She looked puzzled. "I don't know if I ever heard that, but it could be. Men around here do love their guns."

"How many people have gone missing in the last year?" Jesse wanted to know.

"We should put Shannon's bike inside," I said.

"Already did." She climbed in front with Jesse, still thinking about his question. "Hard to say, because I don't always know when someone gets scared—or sick of this town and just takes off—and when they just don't come back. But I'd say ten. At least ten."

Ten was a high number in a town as small as Kilmer. Chance and I exchanged a grim look while climbing in back.

Saldana glanced at me over his shoulder. "We need to

find Little Ed Willoughby and ask him why he tried to use his vehicle as a deadly weapon, don't you think?"

"Yeah," Chance muttered. "I'd like a word."

The rest of the drive passed in silence. I wasn't sure we should have brought her with us. It might dump more trouble on our heads to be seen with her, since we weren't ready to leave town just yet. Then again, I didn't know if it was a good idea to leave her alone in the house, even with good wards. On the balance, it was probably better to keep her close. I didn't intend to let Kilmer claim another victim.

"Where to?" Saldana asked her.

"The newspaper office is downtown," she answered, pointing. "I'm not sure if Mr. England will be in. If not, we can talk to the editor, Sam Proust."

"Does the town have any reporters?" Back when I lived here, there had been one who wrote shiny human interest stories about how great Kilmer was.

"Two. Mr. Proust's daughter, Karen, and that old nut job—"

"Dale Graham." The name came to me before she said it.

Saldana parked the Forester, and Chance helped me out, then fed some coins into the meter. I glanced around at the quiet square, wondering if I imagined being the cynosure of malevolent eyes.

"He's gotten weird in his old age," she went on. But when I asked, she wouldn't clarify. Shannon just shivered a little and pulled up the hood on her black sweatshirt. "You'll find out soon enough."

"Will you get in trouble if you're seen with us?" I asked as we walked toward the newspaper office, a nondescript brownstone building a few blocks from the downtown square. The guys trailed us, talking in an undertone that made me nervous.

She shrugged. "Probably. But I'm not going back."

I understood that well, maybe better than she knew. We came through the front door in a group, visibly alarming the thin, overworked-looking woman who greeted the general public. By her expression, people didn't often turn up unannounced.

"We don't give tours," she said in a preemptive strike. "And the printing is done off-site."

That probably deterred anyone else who stopped by, but we had other needs. "We're here to see Mr. England."

Her eyes widened. "Absolutely out of the question."

"I figured it might be," Jesse muttered.

"Maybe we could talk to Sam Proust," Shannon suggested.

The receptionist became positively frosty. "Young lady, you cannot just waltz into a place of business like this."

I didn't know if she meant me or Shannon, but I answered. "Then how about Dale Graham? This is about a story," I added.

We'd just keep name-dropping until we found someone we could see. She didn't like it, but she got on the phone. A few minutes later, a man in late middle age came out in a pair of ragged jeans, a brightly patterned shirt, and a leather vest. He was actually wearing love beads and cowboy boots, an interesting look to be sure.

"I'm Dale," he said. "Clarissa said you wanted to talk to me about a story idea?"

Obviously, we weren't going to get to see the back of the newspaper office today. "Yes, sir. We'll buy you a cup of coffee," Chance said. "Interested?"

Portent of Things to Come

"This town is cursed," the reporter said around a mouthful of peach pie.

We sat wedged into a booth at Ma's Kitchen, a hole-in-the-wall that looked like it had been decorated just after World War II and hadn't been updated since. Good thing Shannon was small, or we'd never have fit. She huddled on the other side of Chance while Jesse sat beside Dale Graham, who carried the scents of patchouli and hemp. He'd listened attentively to everything we had to say, and then made his somber pronouncement with a glee that contrasted sharply with its portent.

"You think it is?" Jesse asked. "Or you know it?"

Dale Graham took a sip of coffee to wash down the pie, his wooden beads rattling with the movement. "Do I have proof, you mean?"

I could see by Jesse's expression that he thought this was a waste of time, but his smooth voice didn't lose an iota of its patience. I grinned when I realized I could destroy his calm better than anyone else. "That's exactly what I mean."

"I'm working on that," Graham said. He scraped his fork back and forth across his plate, making an irritating sound just a half step above nails on the chalkboard.

"So that's a no," Chance put in.

Well, we wouldn't get anywhere if they alienated him, assuming he had anything of value to tell us. I was starting to doubt it. "What *have* you learned?"

He finally put down his fork and took a quick look around the diner as if he suspected someone of eavesdropping. Maybe his paranoia was persuasive, but I found myself doing the same thing. Men in flannel shirts sat at the breakfast counter, pushing their eggs around their plates while they nursed cups of coffee. Near the back, two old women were arguing over whether grits should be considered a starch. Nobody seemed to pay us any particular attention, but I leaned in so he wouldn't need to raise his voice.

"I keep a journal," Graham confided. "Making notes on the strange events around here. It goes back a long way, but things have really started to step up in the last fifteen years, and events seem to be escalating exponentially."

"Missing pets and people," I guessed.

The reporter gave an approving nod. "The freaky thing is, I don't think anybody is looking for them."

That *was* news. "Miz Ruth said her husband went hunting and never came back. The sheriff supposedly mounted a search, but nothing ever came of it."

Graham shook his head. "Not true. I was in his office when she came in, and old Bulldog Robinson didn't mount anything but his feet on his desk."

"What were you doing in the sheriff's office?" Jesse asked with a raised brow.

Looking put upon, Dale mumbled, "I was detained regarding an allegation of possessing controlled substances."

"So you know for a fact, there was no search party," Chance said, thoughtful.

"He didn't even file the form she filled out," the older man answered. "Just pitched it in the trash as soon as she left."

Shannon articulated what everyone was thinking. "Whatever's going on here, Sheriff Robinson's in on it."

I could tell that idea went down smooth as a truck full of cacti, particularly where Jesse Saldana was concerned. He looked like he hated the idea of another dirty cop. After what had happened with his partner, I couldn't blame him, but at the moment we needed to decide how this information best served us.

"There's something in the woods," I said quietly. "And I think they know about it. So if someone disappears out there, they realize there's no point in looking."

"But they don't want to panic the townsfolk." Jesse drummed his fingers against the tabletop. "So they pretend to go about their business while feverishly looking for a solution to a problem they don't acknowledge."

I remembered the grisly pile of mementos and shivered. Chance's arm went around my shoulders in a casual gesture that stole my breath. He'd never been attuned to me like that before; or if he had been, he never showed it. A surge of renegade warmth curled down my spine as he nestled me against his side. He didn't even seem aware of what he was doing, as he listened to the crackpot theory Dale Graham was espousing.

I tried to be gentle when the reporter finally stopped talking. "I don't think this has anything to do with pixies, killer clowns, or lawn gnomes that come to life in the dark of the moon."

No wonder the authorities didn't consider him a threat. Between the drugs and his penchant for tabloid journalism, nobody would ever take this guy seriously. We gave his words credence only because we'd seen things ourselves—and even then, we couldn't believe everything he said.

"They're watching us," he concluded with a flickered look around the diner. "I haven't figured out how yet, but they know where I am *all* the time."

"Maybe we could see your journal," I cut in.

That would likely prove more helpful than listening to him ramble about secret government bases hidden beneath Kilmer, alien breeding programs, and conspiracies that could only be thwarted with the persistent donning of tinfoil hats. The only guy in town willing to talk to us seemed nutty as a Snickers bar.

"I keep it hidden," he said. "I don't want them to realize how much I know."

Well, I hadn't thought he kept it in his pocket. If it represented years of conspiracy research, it was probably a pretty hefty notebook, maybe even more than one. I guessed it would be secreted in his house somewhere.

"Where do you live?" Chance asked, making the decision for me.

Graham glanced between us with narrowed eyes, as if he thought we might be plants from the establishment. His gaze lingered on Shannon, who said, "It's okay. I know how you feel about my mom. I won't come if you don't want me to."

That seemed to reassure him, though I didn't know why. "Out on Rabbit Road," he said. "All the way at the end, just before the road runs out. You can't miss the place."

"I know where it is," Shannon said.

So did I, actually. He was on the other side of the woods from us, but just as close to those watchful trees. I repressed a shudder.

"Be there at nine tonight," Graham said, and crammed the last bite of his pie into his mouth. "I'll need time to retrieve my journal."

So he didn't keep it at home. Interesting. But then, homes had a way of burning down in Kilmer, didn't they? I couldn't imagine where a half-crazed relic from the sixties would hide something.

The reporter excused himself with a jaunty wave out of keeping with the ominous tone of our meeting. After he'd gone, Shannon scooted out and sat down next to Jesse, who made room in the booth for her. She didn't look at us, instead studying the milky reflection of her hands clasped on the white Formica table.

"I didn't tell you everything," she whispered. "Dale knows that. Whatever's going on, my mom is part of it. That's why

I was so desperate to get away. Because I think . . . whoever
is a part of this mess is planning to do something to *me*. I
heard her arguing with my dad about it one night."

That would certainly explain her father's misery, although
I didn't understand why he hadn't just grabbed Shannon
and run. I could certainly comprehend a parent doing all
manner of things to protect his child. I *didn't* understand
inaction.

"When was this?" Jesse asked gently.

I wondered what he felt from her, this thin, big-eyed girl
who was scarcely more than a child. His hand came to light
on the top of her spiky, blue-streaked head, and she turned
her face into his shoulder. I definitely grasped the appeal of
that. Jesse had a way of making a woman feel safe.

"Last week," she muttered, voice muffled by his shirt.
"Just before y'all got here."

"You must have been terrified." Saldana petted her as if
she were a stray puppy he'd found.

She sniffed. "Yeah. But I couldn't let her know how
happy I was to see somebody who might be able to help, so
that's why I acted like such a jerkwad when we first met."
Jesse looked puzzled, as he hadn't been on-site to receive
Shannon's rudeness firsthand.

I waved that away. Her "rebellious teen" act was the least
of our concerns. Before I could comment on what the reporter had said, the waitress swung by to find out if we meant
to order anything besides coffee. She was a stout woman with
big, stiff hair, a pink polyester uniform, and sensible shoes.
When she recognized Shannon, her brows pulled together
like an angry centipede.

"Shouldn't you be in school, Shannon Cheney? Does your
mother know you're gadding about with strangers?" Her disapproving gaze took in the way Jesse was holding the girl,
and her mouth tightened.

I could have assured the waitress he didn't have las-
civious intentions, but I doubted she'd believe me. She

also wouldn't credit that Shannon was scared of Sandra, who looked like the perfect mother. Appearances could be deceiving—could they ever.

"If she didn't before, she'll find out the minute you get a break." Shannon didn't look concerned. I wasn't sure how I felt about her faith in us.

"Let's get out of here." I didn't want to be here when her mother showed up breathing fire and brimstone. She might not be able to physically remove her child, but she could— and would—make our stay in Kilmer unpleasant. I didn't look forward to the inevitable confrontation.

"Check, please." Jesse offered the waitress his best smile, but she glared at him.

We paid the bill, just coffee and Dale Graham's peach pie, then made our way back to the Forester. It was a gray day, heavy and overcast. A cool, damp wind blew over us, carrying the scent of distant fires. I couldn't imagine what anybody would be burning in the middle of the day, but it sent a shiver of foreboding over me nonetheless.

"Something's going to happen soon," Chance predicted.

"I wish that struck me as a good thing," I muttered as I climbed into the SUV. "But it absolutely doesn't."

"Me either." Chance seemed grim as he settled beside me in the backseat. "Dale said events are escalating."

Saldana started the car, made sure Shannon had on her seat belt, and checked our surroundings in the rearview mirror. I felt like people were watching us from behind their blinds and curtains, planning something so bad I couldn't conceive it. Though I wanted to tell myself I was being irrational, I couldn't.

I'd *died* out in those woods. If not for Jesse Saldana, I wouldn't be sitting here. I found it hard to get my breath. Since my mother's death, Kilmer had shaped my bogeymen and my nightmares, filling them with dark beasts that knew my name.

I scowled in reaction. "He also said we could blame everything that's wrong in Kilmer on breeding experiments instituted by J. Edgar Hoover, using genetic material recovered from the Roswell crash."

Jesse laughed as he pulled onto the road. "He'd make a great poster child for antidrug campaigns, wouldn't he? So where to?"

Mentally I tabulated our schedule. We needed to be at Miss Minnie's house for dinner by six, and we should check in with Chuch, Booke, and Chance's mom before the day got too much later. At nine, we would swing by Dale Graham's house on Rabbit Road.

After a moment's thought, I said, "We should check out Little Ed Willoughby, if Shannon knows where he lives."

"They have a place in the old neighborhood, four blocks from the hardware store." Shannon gave Jesse directions.

Since Kilmer was a small town, it took us only five minutes to get there. We pulled up outside a tiny bungalow that seemed hard-pressed to house three people. The place seemed still and quiet, but as we climbed out of the SUV and went up the cracked sidewalk toward the front door, I heard the sound of a TV or radio from inside.

Chance waved us on, circling around back. I didn't know what he was trying to accomplish until he came around the other side. "The car's parked out back," he said grimly. "Looks like we came to the right place."

My heart gave a little skip. Now maybe we'd get some answers. I pounded on the door and then squeezed my hands together so they wouldn't tremble. I'd never come to visit someone who had tried to kill me before.

It took almost five minutes before anyone answered. A muttered curse sounded as something thumped just inside. I braced myself.

Nothing could have prepared me for the sight of a young man hardly older than Shannon, sitting in a wheelchair. Both his legs had casts on them, signed with colorful get-well wishes. Little Ed Willoughby gazed up at us curiously, smiling with a touch of chagrin when he recognized Shannon.

"Hey, girl." I could tell he was trying to look cool for her, actively hampered by several pounds of plaster and a tatty blue bathrobe.

Shannon seemed just as surprised as the rest of us. "What happened to you, Ed?"

"Fell off my uncle's roof," he muttered.

And broke both his legs? That took some doing.

I felt somewhat nonplussed. I could tell the casts hadn't just been applied yesterday, and I didn't think he could drive like that.

"Has anyone borrowed your car lately?" Jesse asked. Trust the cop to get the interrogation back on track.

Little Ed looked mildly alarmed. "No, why?"

"Because someone tried to run Corine over with a vehicle that looks like yours," Chance put in. "Do you mind if we take a look in your backyard?"

"Not at all," the kid said. If he had anything to hide, he was a hell of an actor. He seemed more confused than anything—and a little sweet on Shannon. "I don't know of anybody else who drives an Olds Cutlass like mine. You sure it was blue?"

"Positive," Chance told him.

Ed shrugged. "Well, feel free to have a look around. Come on back if you need anything else."

We took him at his word and headed out back to inspect his car. It took Saldana only a minute and a half to put the pieces together. "This car's been hot-wired. See the loose wires?"

I blinked at that. "So somebody stole Ed's car, tried to run me over, and then brought it back when they failed?"

"What I wouldn't give for a basic forensics kit, so I could take some prints, but then again, there's no computer to run them through." I'd never seen Jesse so frustrated. "This place is like living in the Dark Ages."

Shannon sighed. "Well, that was pointless. It could've been anybody."

"No." I shook my head. "Just someone who wants me dead."

On second thought, that didn't narrow it down much at all.

Homecoming

After a fruitless stop at Little Ed Willoughby's, we had plenty of time to do something that seemed inevitable. I marveled a little that I'd managed to put it off so long. There was one place we might find answers, however, as little as I liked it.

"What's next on our list?" Saldana asked.

"Out of town," I said, swallowing a wave of pain that threatened to drown me. Jesse cut me a sharp look over his shoulder and started to pull over. "Jesus, Corine, are you all right? What—"

"It's okay. Drive."

Shannon craned her neck to stare, as if starting to grasp that there was a silent subtext she couldn't register. She didn't like it, either. A frown etched delicate lines between her inky brows, out of place on a kid her age.

Chance regarded me with his tiger's eyes, amber latticed through with gold and topaz. They were nothing so simple as light brown; in this moment they seemed to glow with lambent light and quiet secrets. "Are you sure about this?"

He knew? I hadn't said anything. My face must have reflected confusion, for his expression softened, and he brushed a kiss against my temple. His look said simply, *I know you. I know how you think.* In a motion that seemed more than natural, he reached for me, offering physical contact easily, as he'd never done when we were together. God, he felt good; so hot and solid beside me. I drew in a deep breath, filling my lungs with Chance.

"About what?" Jesse's tone reflected mild irritation.

"We need to swing by the place I used to live." My certainty came from beyond my own powers and intuitions. Bleak, heavy knowledge pressed on me from somewhere else, but I didn't want to be beholden to the thing in the woods. Loneliness flooded me, utter solitude. Since I wasn't an empath, I knew it was targeting me on purpose. Loathing crawled through me. I didn't want it helping me—I didn't want it sending me hunches on the smoky wind. I didn't want to be able to feel what it felt, and I didn't want to go to the ruin where my mother died, but I *did* want answers.

She deserved justice.

With a sense of foreboding, I gave directions.

Over the years, the elements had reclaimed the wreckage of our former home. Birds nested in the ruin, and creepers had wound their way through the charred timbers, erasing man's passage. Now there was nothing left but a few fallen beams, old ashes, and a sturdy foundation. The walls had long since fallen down, but in my mind's eye, I saw the way the house once looked; I even visualized my mama standing on the porch.

It hurt like nothing I could have imagined—not even dying. I stood beside the SUV with lead in my limbs, feeling like they wouldn't carry me forward. My left hand curled into a fist, and I rubbed my fingers across the brand from my mother's necklace. To my surprise, it didn't hurt but merely tingled a bit. I glanced down and found the mark had healed overnight. It was impossible; something Kel might've done to make me believe in his otherworldly origins. And yet I had an old brand on my palm.

"This is the place." My voice sounded rusty.

I didn't need to turn to know the others stood behind

me, waiting for an explanation as to why we were here. I hadn't done so *before* our arrival because I knew Jesse would object—and he was driving. Shannon didn't know enough about my gift to understand the risk behind what I intended to attempt.

Maybe I was mistaken, but I felt as though my fleeting death had changed something in me. That might come from facing the worst and coming through unscathed. In the queer half-light cast by the surrounding trees, I felt different, shadow touched, and yet as if the reaper had no dominion over me, at least not here and now. Today I would be like water trickling through its bony fingers.

"Not much to see," Jesse said finally.

Shannon agreed. "How long ago did you live here?"

"I was thirteen," I answered. "So it's been fourteen years."

Nobody made a move to approach the house. I suspected they could sense the residual malice of what had transpired lingering in the earth itself. The woods seemed unearthly quiet, no chattering birds, not even the rustle of squirrels or chipmunks in the underbrush. It was as if the world itself held its breath for my return.

Well, I didn't want to disappoint. Squaring my shoulders, I took the first step and then another, climbing carefully through the wreckage until I stood inside the space that had been our living room. Old anguish rocketed through me in a blazing rush. I didn't want to remember how happy I'd been here, or what came after.

"Corine," Jesse said. I knew he had to be suffering too, and I felt awful for putting him through this. "You don't have to do this. We probably can't learn anything here, not after all this time."

"*You* can't." Chance's voice sounded tight and fierce, as if he wanted desperately to protect me from myself. He also knew I wouldn't let him.

Butch popped up from my handbag and yapped twice in agreement. He sank tiny teeth into the fabric of my shirt, as if he'd forcibly prevent me from doing so. I gently disengaged him and handed the dog to Shannon. Much as I wanted to, I couldn't take his advice. I couldn't opt out. We had to know.

Comprehension dawned in Jesse's bitter chocolate eyes. I could see he wanted to argue against the wisdom of it. If a necklace imbued with the pain of my mother's death killed me, what would the house where she died do? Maybe this time there would be no bringing me back.

I'd never attempted anything on this scale before, but it was an inanimate object, right? The principle should remain the same, and I needed its secrets. The tingle in my left palm became a steady pulse of heat, and following some instinct I hadn't known I possessed, I sank down amid old ashes and sealed my hand against the foundation.

Pain scoured my nerves like wildfire consuming a dry forest. For interminable moments, I knew nothing but agony that spread in a black-red wash across my field of vision. I ceased to hear my own breathing, my own heartbeat. I might be dying again, but I couldn't break the connection. The house wanted to own me in a complete and terrible way. I tried to fight—

It took me.

Heavy. Broken. Lost.

Stones crumbled; burnt wood fell to splinters and dust. I registered each tiny, disparate piece that made up the entirety of this ruin to which I'd joined myself. We sat, silent and untended. Nights ran into days; the seasons turned. Rain poured into my broken shell. I shivered at the cold and the solitude. Then the sun baked me until I felt dry and parched, thirsty unto death.

After eons of waiting, suffering, I remembered I wasn't a rock or a roof tile. I was a woman, or I had been, a million years ago. Impressions came then, quick and fleeting. I didn't want years of observations. I only wanted the one night.

The house didn't want to yield to me. It wanted to suborn me and make me part of it for good. I'd never known an object to have a malign will, but this ruin did.

I imprinted myself on it—pure focus from years of training myself not to read objects with a casual touch. *I will know what you know*, I told it. *Show me the night you died.* For it perished, just as my mother did; the burning of the pretty little house where we used to live had given birth to this thing that squatted in its place.

My head rang with the force of its dissent. It didn't want to share; didn't want to help. It wanted to take and devour, as the flames had done.

For an eternity, we struggled—fought.

I didn't know if I could win.

Pain became a constant, and then—

The images I sought came pouring through me. The house gave me back my own uncertainty and terror; it gave me my mother's anger and determination. She hadn't been afraid. The now-broken windows of our house became my eyes. I watched as they came from the woods; twelve, in dark robes, hoods pulled forward to mask their faces.

They mounted the stairs and did not knock. A woman opened the door for them, then slammed it in their faces. They argued on the porch, brands raised. The tallest of them shook his head, and then they took the door down with their shoulders.

My mother was dead when they reached her. But I'd already known that. I'd lived her death, where she gave everything she was to me in a final working. It wasn't her fault that I was broken.

I watched with the house's peculiar detachment as they carried out a ritual around her body, a circle of twelve in dark robes, lighting candles. I could not hear their chants, but I felt the dark energy curling through the walls, twisting what had been good. I tried to moan, but walls had no mouths.

The twelve poured something from a red can—gas perhaps—and then set the place alight, after they completed their night's work. Nobody stayed to watch the fire. They melted into the woods while my body curled and blackened, killing heat exploding my windows outward. *Agony.*

Death. Vengeance. A house could crave such things until it achieved something like sentience. It had me, and it did not mean to let me go. Helpless, I twisted, immolated like one condemned to hell.

I'd assumed too much. This was more than I could manage, and I wasn't coming out. Satisfied with my torment, the house showed me the scene again and again while I burnt. It craved suffering, and I served.

No escape, it told me. *Mine.*

No. Weak defiance. I couldn't feel myself anymore, only what the monster gave. But I could only take so much. Blackness threatened to flood my mind's eye, giving me nothing in place of agony. At this point I welcomed oblivion.

There was something wet on my cheek, sloppy, small, and insistent. Though I wanted desperately to drop down the dark hole, the tiny thing wouldn't let me. It yapped insistently and tugged on my hair. Such devotion touched me and it kept me tethered, despite the pain and nausea.

Then I heard voices from far away. It sounded like a quarrel, but I couldn't make out the words. I sailed down the dark tunnel, expecting to find those I'd lost, and emerged on the other side. The sky was heavy, overcast. Did it rain in hell?

Jesse's taut face flickered into sight. I tried to sit up, and the full anguish of my maimed hand hit me like a fist in the stomach. I vomited into the damp leaves where I lay, retching so hard that I felt as if I were turning inside out. Someone held my head and murmured. Wracked with dry heaves, I moaned. I couldn't keep my eyes open; it was too much. Without lifting a hand to save myself, I sank.

I surfaced to an argument. Someone's arms were around me. I recognized his scent before I opened my eyes.

"We should get her the fuck out of Kilmer," Jesse was saying. "She's been out for three hours, and that burn on her palm needs medical attention."

I was lying on the mattress I'd surrendered to Shannon, and I felt as though I'd been hit by a truck. That was ameliorated slightly by feeling Chance beside me.

"If you touch her, I'll kill you," Chance said conversationally. "The doctors won't know what to do with her. They'll run tests, stick her with needles, pump her full of drugs, and then say she's a medical mystery." He took a breath, as if trying to rein back his protective instincts. "You don't understand how much she hates hospitals. Just give her time, all right? Corine is strong. If I didn't think she could do it, I'd have tried to talk her out of it. Trust her to know her own limits."

Joy came streaming through me like sunlight. *Trust her.* Stupid as it might seem, that elated me. We were making progress. I wanted to hug him, but at first, my eyelids refused to lift. I could feel my body again, but that wasn't a good thing. If I ever considered reading a whole house again, I hoped someone would shoot me.

"I'm okay," I tried to mumble. It came out unintelligible, but the sign of life rendered both men speechless, I assumed with relief.

Eventually I got my eyes open. Everything looked strange and distant, as if I peered through a gauzy veil. My hand throbbed like a son of a bitch.

Chance's arms tightened around me, and I didn't try to get away. "Shannon, get the salve I left in the living room."

Motion flickered at the edges of my vision, but I still couldn't focus right. She must have fetched it, though, because I felt him applying the ointment to my injured palm as he'd done so many times before. His mother's remedy soothed the worst of the pain. More than once, I'd considered the cream magickal. Now I suspected it just might be.

"What happened?" I asked. That time, the words came out more or less as I intended.

"You were . . . inside a long time. And the pain—" Jesse's voice actually broke. "Christ Almighty, Corine."

"So we pulled your hand off the wall," Shannon continued. "But I wasn't sure we did it fast enough, 'cause it didn't seem to do much good. You puked and then passed out."

"It's an evil place," I said, low. "Hungry. But it's different than what lives in the wood."

"The site needs to be cleansed," Jesse agreed. "But that's not our first priority."

I acknowledged that with a tired nod. My stomach still felt queer and queasy. I was in no condition to argue with anybody about anything.

Shannon added, "You should have seen Chance. He was freakin' out."

Chance gave a wry half smile, but he didn't deny it. "So we came back here to wait it out. Butch is relieved to see you awake, let me tell you."

The dog jumped up onto the mattress and licked the back of my uninjured hand. He yapped once as if to corroborate. In response, still too shaky to get up, I stroked his head.

Shannon sat down at the end of the mattress. "Jesse wanted to take you to the hospital. I was starting to think maybe we should. You gonna tell us what happened out there?"

"Water, first, please." My throat ached as if I had really survived a fire.

I drained two full glasses before I felt any better and pulled away from Chance.

Jesse settled near Shannon, ready to listen. I took that as my cue and set the empty glass on the floor beside me.

"Just tell me it was worth it." Saldana stared at his hands. His voice sounded hoarse, raw. "Tell me you learned something. Tell me you didn't go through that for nothing."

What he really meant was, *Tell me you didn't put me through that for nothing.* I had no doubt he'd suffered everything I had. I wished I could apologize, but that would imply regret, and I'd do the same thing again.

I related what I'd seen in bare-bones terms. There was no point in expressing how bad it had been; Jesse knew, and the other two had some idea, based on my reaction after.

"So," I concluded, "they performed a ritual around my mother's body." It hurt so much to speak the truth. "She killed herself before they came in."

No wonder I'd never felt even a whisper of her. According to nearly every religion's lore, suicides went straight to the worst circle in hell—and they didn't get day passes to come whisper reassurances to the living.

"Why would she?" Shannon asked.

I could only shrug. "To prevent them from getting whatever they wanted from her?"

"Power?" Jesse guessed. "If so, it could be a black coven."

I remembered my mother warning me of those who drained magickal gifts and took them as their own. She'd called them ghouls, though they began as human beings. The process awoke an incessant hunger, so once they began to eat the magick of others, they could never be satiated.

The idea didn't wholly explain things. As far as I knew, she had never revealed how much she could do. Between the orchard and the garden, we'd been close to self-sufficient, and she only made charms and potions on request: minor things, low magick. So why would a black coven decide she had enough to risk exposure in taking her? It didn't add up.

"Why?" I asked, frustrated. "What did they hope to gain?"

"I bet it has to do with that monster in the woods," Shannon muttered.

"Have you seen it?" With some effort, I hauled myself into a sitting position.

Shannon hesitated. "Yeah. Well, sort of. I felt it more than saw anything. We cut school and meant to get wasted out there. When it got all dark and still, Robert Walker pissed his pants. He was small and slow, kind of timid. We all ran back to where we'd parked the cars and they wouldn't start."

She shivered, remembering. "I thought we'd never get out. It felt like the thing was playing with us, enjoying it more when we ran."

"Did you all make it out?" Jesse asked.

She shook her head slowly. "Rob never came home."

Poor kid. She's had a hell of a life.

"When was this?" Chance sat forward, carrying me with him.

"Last April." She considered for a moment. "April nineteenth. With all the weirdness and disappearances, it's just not safe here anymore."

As if it ever was.

But Dale Graham was right about one thing. Events were definitely escalating.

"In my experience," Jesse murmured, "you just don't get an evil monster running amok without somebody raising it."

I sensed Chance's agreement even before he spoke. "So the question is, who summoned it, and why?"

I intended to ask Miss Minnie that very question tonight.

Dinner Plans

To my amazement, Shannon brought me a present before I ever stumbled out of bed. The silver chain glimmered in my hand like a sliver of starlight. Somehow, she'd managed to remove all the years of tarnish and filth. My mother's necklace looked like new—even the delicate curves of the flower pentacle.

"Thank you so much. But how did you—"

"Jesse gave it to me while you were out. He thought you might like to wear it."

A sensitive, yet practical gift. Yeah, that was Jesse all the way down to the ground. He'd known I'd love to have the necklace restored, but giving it to Shannon to deal with made her feel useful and distracted her from worrying about me.

"It looks beautiful. I can't believe how good you made it look."

"Basic science," she said with a shrug. "All you need is baking soda, salt, boiling water, and aluminum foil in a pan." I could tell she was pleased with my reaction, though, despite her ostensible indifference.

"Would you mind helping me put it on?"

In answer, she leaned in and deftly fastened it around my neck. A little spark ran through me at her touch, reminding me that I needed to talk to her about her gift. "Did you notice that when we touched?"

"The static?"

I shook my head. "Wrong. That's how Gifted people identify one another. If you touch Jesse, you'd get the same reaction."

She seemed skeptical. "Yeah? It looked like static to me."

Reminding myself to be patient, I explained, "Growing up in Kilmer, you wouldn't know this any more than I did, but there's a subsection of the populace who can do weird and amazing things, just like we can. If you let me, I can put you in touch with them."

"You're for real about this." Despite her amazement, it wasn't a question.

"Absolutely. You saw what I can do. Jesse feels what other people feel."

"Duh. Empathy." She spoke with a scorn that emphasized her youth.

Ah, bravado. I remembered it well. "Right. And there are more folks like us out there. If you accept me, I'll be your mentor, teaching you as Jesse teaches me. We're both fresh out of the woods, so to speak."

"What does that even mean? Mentor?"

Not too long ago, I'd been asking the same thing. "I'll help you when you need it. Answer questions. Basically it means I've got your back."

A rare smile creased her thin cheeks. "I'm down with that."

That taken care of, I hauled myself off the mattress. I shuffled toward the bathroom. I needed a shower to wash away the stench of the ruin that had nearly claimed me. As I came out of the bedroom, I heard the low murmur of voices that told me the guys were in the parlor.

It took every ounce of my strength to step into the tub. For a moment, I clung to the tiled wall, feeling shaky and nauseated. If I had any sense, I wouldn't push myself; I'd been tested as never before. But then, if I had any sense, we probably would've left Kilmer as soon as the mauled dog ran into the road.

I washed up in stages, sometimes pausing to rest in between. Cursing my long hair, I managed to lather and rinse it. Good thing I had some leave-in conditioner with me. I didn't think I was up to rinsing a second time.

My knees nearly buckled as I came out of the shower. Blindly I felt for the towel Chance had brought me a few days before. I'd hung it on a hook to dry, and happily, it was still there. Shivering, I wrapped myself in it. Brushing my teeth helped steady me too. There was nothing like waking up with the taste of revisited breakfast in your mouth. Once I finished in the bathroom, I traveled back down the hall toward my room, holding on to the wall.

The bedroom was empty when I got back. I guessed Shannon had gone to hang with the guys. I layered in getting dressed: panties, black peasant skirt, red camisole with built-in bra, and black sweater. I'd never be a fashion plate, but I liked being able to strip down if I got too warm. Dizzy from the movement, I sat down on the edge of the mattress and touched my mother's necklace.

That reminded me.

"Call your mother," I called to Chance.

"Already did," he answered. "She's fine."

One worry put to bed, at least. I couldn't remember how long it had been since I checked my cell phone. When I unearthed it, I had voice mail waiting. I dialed, input my code, and listened:

Corine, it's Booke. Call me when you get a chance. I have some news.

A computer told me I had another message, and then I heard Chuch's voice:

Wanted to make sure you're okay, prima. That cop called here asking about you. Now he's gone lookin', and I haven't heard from either of you. Call me back, or Eva will have my ass.

Before we went out and lost service again, I needed to

get in touch. I started with Booke. Doing the time conversion, I realized it would be evening there, not that I'd wake him, no matter what time I called. I wasn't sure he ever slept.

He answered on the first ring, a sure sign he'd been waiting for my call. "Corine?"

"Yep," I said. "What's up?"

"I think I've figured out why your cell phone only worked in the library."

Hm. I didn't have the heart to tell him we'd been banned from the library, and events had outpaced his research. I tried to sound encouraging. "Really? Why?"

His rich, educated voice warmed with the interest he felt toward his subject matter. "Protective sigils are etched into the top of the building; very interesting ones too, from a rare Hermetic tradition, harking back to the Emerald Tablet of Hermes, but also incorporating writings from the Rosicrucian—"

"Good work." I felt bad about interrupting, but he would give me onerous detail if I let him. "That's a pretty strange find for a small town in Georgia," I added.

"To say the least," he agreed. "It looks to me like there used to be a steeple in the center as well. Is there any possibility the library once served as a church?"

I considered. "It's down near the old courthouse, so I'm going to say yes. Land records would probably tell us for sure."

If we hadn't been banned from the library.

"At any rate, that building was blessed and protected at some point."

Which didn't save poor old John McGee. We should probably remember that before putting too much faith in our own wards.

"Anything else I should know?"

"I'm still working on discovering what spell would suck a town into a black hole and create an equivalent dark spot in the ether," he told me.

I wished him luck with that, thanked him, and rang off. I

needed to call Chuch and let him know I was still breathing. That didn't take long. He seemed glad to hear from me,
and warned me that things in Texas were still hot as a nest
of scorpions. Montoya had guys looking for me and Chance,
he said, and it would be smart of us to stay out of sight.

That trouble felt distant at the moment, so I told him to
give Eva my love, and then made my last call. Senor Alvarez reported that the store was doing well, he was taking
good care of my plants, and I shouldn't worry about things
at home. I wished that had relieved me, but I wanted to
book a flight right then. I didn't want Alvarez starting to
feel comfortable in my pawnshop or in the life I'd built. I
wanted to get back to it.

But I couldn't until I finished things here.

Before leaving the bedroom, I plaited my long hair into
a single French braid running down my back and secured it
with a nylon band. I found the others waiting for me in the
parlor. To a soul, they bore the same concerned expression.
Even Butch lifted his head from where he was napping and
gave me a worried glance.

"I'm okay," I said. "Just a bit shaky. I'm sure a home-
cooked meal at Miss Minnie's will work wonders."

None of them looked convinced, but they didn't argue.
Instead I packed up Butch's food and water dishes, along
with some kibble. Depending on what Miss Minnie put in the
soup, it might not be good for the dog. Not that he'd mind.
Dogs tended not to care about their health when food was
at stake.

"We're not late?" I asked as we climbed into the SUV.

"Nah." Jesse shook his head. "We have time. We're supposed to be there at six?"

Chance nodded. "It's half past five now."

I was interested in asking her a number of questions, things
only a longtime resident of Kilmer would know. A smart
woman like Miss Minnie would have missed nothing over
the years; I just had to get her to tell me what she knew.

The ride passed mostly in silence. When we got to town,

I gave Jesse directions, and we pulled up outside Miss Minnie's house at ten to six. Her house didn't seem to have changed at all—a snug little bungalow painted white with cheerful red shutters.

Chance took my arm as I slid out of the vehicle, a little overprotective but nice. If I wanted more physical contact from him, I couldn't complain about the way it manifested, could I? Shannon and Jesse followed us up the four stairs to her door, where I knocked.

Miss Minnie answered promptly. As I'd seen outside the library, she was still willow slim, her hair snow-white, and her face wrinkled. She was clad in a button-down dress patterned with a floral print, and her eyes brightened when she saw all of us.

"My goodness," she said. "It's so good to have young people in the house again. I hope y'all like corn bread."

Jesse nodded, Shannon looked ambivalent, and Chance said nothing. *Mmm.* I remembered her corn bread.

"Thanks. It's really good to see you." I gave her a hug because she looked frail and old and she didn't have her own grandchildren to do it. Sadly, I was probably the closest thing she had to family.

"You too, Corine." She stepped back to usher us into the small living room.

"I hope you don't mind. We also brought our dog."

Almost as if in response, Butch bobbed up from the depth of my handbag and gave Miss Minnie a polite kiss on the back of her hand. She responded with a laugh of pure delight. "Why, he's the sweetest critter I've seen in twenty years."

Butch preened beneath her attentions and then yapped at me. I was starting to recognize the tone of his barks. This one meant he wanted to get down and make sure the place was safe. I bent and let him get to work; his little nose angled down.

I made the introductions and left it to Chance and Jesse

to flatter her within an inch of her life. They didn't disappoint. Chance complimented the décor and Jesse applied his down-home drawl to tell her that something in her kitchen smelled better than the supper his mama used to make. She blushed and dithered, so it took her a minute to realize she already knew Shannon.

But she didn't question, just greeted the girl and then invited us all to take a seat in the dining room while she got dinner on the table. I would have offered to help her, but frankly, I was on my last legs. I sank down into the ladder-back chair.

Chance and Jesse followed Miss Minnie into the kitchen. At first she tried to shoo them out, and then she gave in. "I reckon I can get the food on the table, boys." Shannon and I both stifled a snicker at hearing them called "boys." "But it would be a great help if you'd slide the leaf into the dining room table. It's just right back there. . . ."

She had chairs enough already, so I just kept out of the way as the guys pulled off the tablecloth, fitted the extra wood in place, and locked it. The cloth went back on and we were ready to go. Before long, we all sat down with hot bowls of vegetable soup, a platter of piping hot corn bread, and real butter.

I remembered that Miss Minnie would want to say a short blessing first, so I spared myself the awkwardness of beginning before the hostess. I nudged Shannon, who sat beside me, spoon on the way to her mouth. Fortunately, the lady kept it short. She was a considerate hostess, and she put down a dish of cold minced chicken for Butch. He trotted to the dining room as we all dug in.

While we ate, conversation was sparse. We made small talk about where I'd been since I left, and how I'd met Chance. Miss Minnie was quite taken with the romance of my returning his lost keys, as if it meant I held the keys to his heart or something. She made a little joke along those lines, and Chance slid me a weighted look. Everyone laughed politely, but I could tell Jesse wanted me to say that Chance and I weren't together anymore, not like she seemed to think.

For the sake of honesty, I did. "We're just friends now, though."

Miss Minnie raised her brows in surprise. "Does *he* know that?"

Chance frowned at me. "Unfortunately, yes."

After we traded soup bowls for slices of Bundt cake, I felt almost up to bridging the subject we needed to discuss. Even then, I ate a few bites first, not wanting to miss dessert entirely if she took umbrage and chucked us out. Before I could decide what to say, Miss Minnie stood up.

"Go on, now. You can take your plates into the living room. I'll make a pot of coffee and we'll just visit a spell."

"That sounds wonderful," I said. "Thank you so much. It was delicious."

The other three echoed my words with real sincerity. Living like we did, we missed out on home-cooked meals and grandmotherly kindness. At least, that held true for Chance and me; I wasn't sure why Shannon wouldn't have been eating well at home, unless she suspected her mother of tampering with her food. At this point I wouldn't doubt it. But Jesse was the lucky one; he had a mother and a father waiting at home. She made pumpkin pie from vegetables his father grew at home. His family sounded impossibly idyllic, and I couldn't help but wonder what it would be like, sliding into a Fourth of July picnic at his side.

It sounded like everything I'd always wanted.

Five minutes after we sat down in the living room, Miss Minnie brought in a real silver tray, laid with fine eggshell china and old-fashioned cream and sugar bowls. She set the platter on the coffee table, casting us back to older times when it was actually used for that purpose, just like we were doing now. She carefully fixed each cup according to our specifications and then sat back in her rose velvet armchair, looking pleased.

Butch trotted in with nothing to report and fuzz on top

of his head. I dusted him off and pulled him into my lap. Stroking a dog had to be one of the best relaxation techniques in the world. He burrowed into the crook of my arm and went to sleep.

"I don't get visitors like I used to," she remarked again. "I'm just that happy to see you, Corine. I always did wonder what became of you."

I'd never get a better segue. "I'm well . . . but there's a reason I came back." Chance gave an encouraging nod, so I went on. "I need to find out the truth behind my mother's death. I know something's wrong here. I know about the thing in the woods, and that there's evil running free in town. I already know all that, but people aren't talking. I have no reason to think you will, other than your apparent fondness for me, but I'm willing to trade on that. The fact is, you may be our only hope for putting all the pieces together."

Her hands shook as she curled her thin, blue-veined fingers around her cup, and her lined face went pale as milk. "Lord, Lord," she breathed, turning her face upward as if in appeal to a god I no longer believed in. "The end of days has come at last."

Unlucky Break

Things went to hell without a handbasket.

It was as if I'd flipped a switch, and the nice old lady who had served us supper disappeared. In her place sat a dire Cassandra prophesying doom and gloom. As the shadows lengthened, even her face looked different somehow, full of mad premonition.

"I saw them," she said, staring at nothing. "The Four Horsemen of the Apocalypse. They've ridden through town more than once. At first I tried to pretend I didn't see them, but the way they came and went . . . Oh, I knew." She nodded sagely. "I knew."

"Uh-huh," Chance said, seeming worried.

He wasn't the only one.

"But what they don't know is that four angels come to banish them." She blessed us with a beatific smile. "I should have known about you." Miss Minnie nodded at me. "Eyes full of heaven and such an unearthly power in your hands. I should have had faith."

"In what?" Shannon asked.

I guessed she didn't identify herself as a guardian angel.

"In the Lord," Miss Minnie answered. "The time of tribulation is on us."

What do you say to that, really?

To give him credit, Jesse tried to make sense of it. "What have you seen that makes you think—"

"'There was a great earthquake; and the sun became black as sackcloth of hair, and the moon became as blood.'" The old woman closed her eyes, obviously reciting from memory. "'There fell a great star from heaven, burning as it were a lamp, and it fell upon the third part of the rivers, and upon the fountains of waters . . . there followed hail and fire mingled with blood, and they were cast upon the earth: and the third part of trees was burnt up, and all green grass was burnt up. I saw a star fall from heaven unto the earth: and to him was given the key to the bottomless pit.'"

"It's from Revelation," Jesse muttered. "Obviously those verses hold symbolic meaning for her, but I don't know what she's talking about."

With a little shiver, I realized we'd already found one of the places she was referencing. I'd noticed the ground around the hollow tree in the wood looked as though it had been hit by an asteroid, dead earth, almost charred, where the monster stored its trinkets. *To him was given the key to the bottomless pit*—it sure sounded like Miss Minnie thought whatever lived out there came straight from hell.

"You think we can prevent the earthquake, fire, and blood?" I asked, feeling my way through what felt like a mental minefield.

"You will," she said with certainty. "Or nobody. The Lord's will be done."

Try as we might, we couldn't get any more sense out of her. After that pronouncement, she turned her face toward the wall and her eyes went strange and glassy, as if she gazed at some war-blasted inner landscape. Mentioning the wrongness in Kilmer seemed to have triggered an episode.

Butch leaped down from my lap, trotted over to her, and licked her dangling hand. We stayed until she came back to herself; it didn't take long. She fluttered her lashes at us and patted her white hair nervously.

"Did I doze off? I'm sorry."

"If you're tired, I guess we should go." Jesse pushed to his feet.

He hadn't shaved in a couple of days, so his face looked positively bristly, and dark circles shadowed his eyes. Clearly he hadn't been sleeping well, but I'd been too self-absorbed to notice. What would it cost him, being here? Would he miss an important hearing? Was he allowed to cross state lines while on suspension and under investigation for possible misconduct? For the first time I considered that he might have put me ahead of his career. I exhaled shakily and shoved back the question of how important I truly was to him.

Before leaving, I tucked a white crochet afghan around Miss Minnie's knees. She smiled up at me, drowsy from her spell. "I hope you'll come back." As we stood there, her eyes drifted closed again, as if she were too weary to stay awake a second longer.

I scooped the dog into my arms and we headed for the door. We couldn't deadbolt it for her, but it did lock on the way out. Full dark had fallen while we ate, and the shadows seemed ominous. Pausing on the porch, I scanned the empty street. Butch whined, putting me on high alert.

The nearby houses had their curtains and shades drawn tight, and only tiny trickles of light gave a hint there was anybody home at all. The weather wasn't brilliant, true, but you expected more foot traffic in a town this size, and people being neighborly. But we hadn't seen either at all in Kilmer.

I expected an oily spill to break away from the others and try to drain the life out of me. In Laredo, it had happened more times than I could count. But this was a different enemy, less outright power and more guile. In some ways, our enemies in Kilmer might prove more dangerous.

"Well, that was pointless," Shannon muttered.

She started to say more, and then a sharp sound split the night, like a truck backfiring, only—

"Get down," Jesse growled.

I dove off the porch and behind the hedge as the flowerpot on the wrought-iron patio table broke wide-open and showered me in dirt. Two more shots rang out, and Jesse's body thumped beside me. For a brief, terrifying moment, I thought he'd been hit, and then he rolled, peering backward beneath the hedge. He wouldn't be moving so easily with a slug in him.

"Goddammit," he swore. "I wish I had my gun."

"You wouldn't be able to hit him. It's coming from the rooftop of that Victorian over there," Chance whispered.

I heard a curse from the porch. I cast a glance over my shoulder and found Shannon crouched behind one of the columns. In a normal town, we could expect concerned citizens to call the police. I wasn't so sure in Kilmer. If the sheriff chose to show up, he might find some way to blame *us*.

Butch broke free from my arms and ran back toward the door, scratching furiously. His agitated bark rang out. I'd spent enough time with him to know there was something badly wrong inside.

Another shot pinged into Miss Minnie's porch. *Please don't let her step out to see what the fuss is about.* If anything happened to her, I didn't know what I'd do. She was gentle and kind; the only good thing I could remember about my childhood after my mama died. I only wished she hadn't been so scared of my gift—that she'd let me stay with her, baking pies and cleaning cupboards until I was grown. But I suspected I'd be a much different person if that had happened.

"At this distance, it has to be a rifle," Saldana said. "But at least I could lay down suppressive fire, make him dive while we run for it. But don't worry. I'm counting shots. When I give the word, sprint for the Forester and stay low."

Chance objected, "Doesn't it depend on what kind of weapon he has and what kind of ammo he's using?"

"Sounds like a .22, used for varmint hunting," Jesse told him impatiently. "Generally, you're looking at a ten-round mag. Unless he's a great shot, one hit won't kill us outright. Somebody's trying to put the fear of God in us."

Another shot hit the porch steps, too close for comfort.

"I thought I'd be *safer* with you guys," Shannon mumbled.

"That's half a mag, then." Chance must've been counting too.

In the distance I heard sirens. I guess people didn't go up on rooftops and open fire with impunity, even in Kilmer. Butch continued to bark and scratch. He glanced over his shoulder, eyes bulging, as if willing me to take the hint.

"Oh shit."

If I was right, if Butch was hearing an intruder in there, we had to get back inside. It might already be too late. Accepting Jesse's analysis at face value, I pulled myself back on the porch. One hit wouldn't kill me. A bullet slammed into the wood behind me; I felt the splinters against my calf.

"Corine, get down!" Chance shouted.

Ignoring him, I picked up the patio chair and threw it through Miss Minnie's living room window. Shannon cried out, but she didn't budge from the cover of the column. *Good girl.* I dove, arms first, hit the floor, and tried to roll. I'm sure it wasn't graceful, and I felt the sting of broken glass even through my jacket.

"What are you—fuck!" Jesse's voice split on a cry.

That time, I had no doubt he'd been hit, but I couldn't stop. I pushed to my feet and caught the son of a bitch redhanded. A man in black stood over Miss Minnie—and she was so deeply asleep as to be unconscious. He wore a ski mask, the kind criminals used to wear to commit armed robbery, and in his hand gleamed a knife.

I grabbed the first thing that came to hand, a heavy poker from the fireplace. Glass crunched beneath my feet as I braced myself. Good thing he didn't know how truly useless I'd be in a fight, but I could stall him until the cavalry arrived.

"Cover the back," I shouted, hoping someone could get there.

The sirens drew closer. I could see the glimmer of red

and blue in my peripheral vision. Outside, the gunfire had stopped.

We stared at each other. He couldn't decide whether to take out the old lady, go for me, or run for it. That hesitance cost him.

"You're trapped," I told him.

Brakes screeched, car doors slammed, and then I heard a garbled announcement from Sheriff Robinson. I couldn't make out the words, but I suspected it was some variant of "Come out with your hands up." I didn't imagine he would be happy if he had to come in after us.

And then everything happened too fast for me to track. The man in black spun. Too slowly, I swung the poker at him, whiffing air as he sprinted toward the back door. I heard a scuffle and then the heavy thud of a body falling. When I made it to the kitchen, I found Chance kneeling over the corpse, blood on his hands. His face seemed taut with fear. I didn't know if he'd killed anyone before. And what a strange thing to wonder about a man you once slept with.

"Shit," I said.

From behind me, Miss Minnie said, "Oh, how nice to see you again, dear." She came into the kitchen, took one look, and then fainted dead away.

Before we trudged out to be apprehended like dastards, I couldn't resist pulling the mask off; I had to see who Chance had killed. To my astonishment, I recognized the gas station attendant who had pointed me toward Augustus England. That made no sense at all. We'd hardly spoken to the man.

I sighed, collected my heroic dog, and went out with my hands up.

It took hours of separate interviews to convince Robinson of what had happened. The little jail in the courthouse basement wasn't equipped to handle so many suspects, so he unlocked the surveyor's office upstairs and used it as an interrogation room while the rest of us sat in the tiny cell.

Jesse was pale, but he didn't mention the shot he'd taken

to the upper arm. Calling it a flesh wound, Jesse refused to leave Shannon and me. He sat there, pinch faced, between us and tried to look reassuring.

"It's going to all right," he whispered. "If Miss Minnie doesn't press charges, they can't even do anything about that broken window. And I don't think she will. We saved her life."

I nodded as the sheriff came for me a fourth time and left Chance in my place. No matter how many times Robinson came at me or from what angle, I told the same story. We'd been invited to Miss Minnie's house for supper; I had been her foster child once upon a time. And yes, that could be verified.

Local felons must have targeted her for a robbery—an elderly woman living alone, right? When they found us at the house, they panicked, and one of them tried to scare us off while the other attempted to complete the job. As off-the-cuff theories went, I felt rather proud of that one. The truth would make him lock me up quicker than I could spit.

He pursed his mouth and stared at me, hard. "Do you know that for a fact, Ms. Solomon?"

I think he was hoping to make me admit to being an accomplice, but I opened my eyes wide. "No, I don't know that for a fact. I was just guessing. But why else would anybody shoot at innocent tourists? Why else would a masked man be in an old lady's home?"

Sheriff Robinson had no answer for that, so he asked more questions. "Why do you think they didn't just rob Miss Minnie another night?"

I shrugged. "Maybe they aren't very bright. In fact, I'd say they *definitely* aren't if they're robbing old ladies in a town the size of Kilmer."

The portly lawman growled his impatience. "Tell me what happened next, please, Ms. Solomon." He put exaggerated stress on the *please*.

"We had our meal and visited for a while," I answered. "Then she dozed off, so we saw ourselves out." Best to stick close to the truth, whenever possible. "Someone started shooting at us, and I dove into the bushes. But my dog heard something inside that alarmed him, and I didn't think; I just reacted."

"By breaking her window," the sheriff said in a tone of such dry sarcasm that I knew he didn't believe a word I said. "Most people would've been too scared to move. Most people don't listen to their dogs, either."

I peered up at him through my lashes. "So you're chastising me for being too bold, Sheriff?" Lifting Butch, I added, "It's a good thing I do listen to him. And why wouldn't I? He has good ears. We saved Miss Minnie's life tonight."

"Or you want her to think you did," he muttered.

A lance of genuine surprise ran me through. "Are you accusing me of staging the break-in so she'll feel grateful and put me in her will?"

"Right now I'm not accusing you of anything." His jowls quivered. "I'm just fact-finding."

I wanted to challenge him to find proof I'd had anything to do with the aborted "robbery," which I suspected was something else entirely.

"Who was the guy who tried to kill Miss Minnie?" I asked.

The sheriff sighed. "Curtis Farrell. I just can't believe he'd do something like this. He wasn't a bad kid."

Funny. Nobody ever thinks someone is bad until he up and does some terrible thing. I knew from firsthand experience that everyone was capable of that. It only required the right impetus.

"Well, I'm not sorry we were there to help her."

Robinson frowned at me and kept asking the same questions.

In response, I kept giving the same answers until he returned me to the cell, his face reflecting high choler. Butch whined until one of his deputies took him outside. I further annoyed the man by demanding water for my dog.

"You should be giving him a medal," I said as the man brought a plastic bowl. "I can't believe this is how you treat people who help out. What do you do to the criminals? Take them to the woods to die?"

The deputy's hand shook, slopping water on the cement floor. "That's enough out of you, miss." But his voice was none too steady, either, and he didn't meet my eyes as he hurried away.

Butch yapped, and I picked him up. "You got that right, buddy. There's something rotten in the state of Georgia, and it stinks like hell fire."

One by one, Robinson questioned us, and nobody contradicted my version of events. I found it odd that Shannon's parents never showed up to see if she was all right. Maybe her mother had washed her hands of Shannon . . . but that didn't track. Women like Sandra Cheney didn't quietly concede.

The sheriff spent longer interrogating Chance. I was deathly afraid they'd charge him with manslaughter, even though he'd clearly been defending my former foster mother's life and property. In the end, Miss Minnie came down to the station and insisted he let us go.

She chastised Robinson roundly. "I wouldn't be standing here, if not for these children and that sweet little dog. Curtis Farrell must've been on drugs. I know he wouldn't have tried to steal from me if he'd been in his right mind."

The sheriff complied grudgingly, but he let us know as he walked us to the Forester that he'd be watching us. As he put it, "People didn't die nearly so often before you lot came around."

I paused outside the SUV, unable to resist the reply. "That's not true," I said softly. "You just don't go looking for the bodies anymore."

We left Robinson looking sick in the reflected red glow of our taillights.

By the time we got back to the house, it was well after

midnight, and most of us needed medical attention to varying degrees. I set to cleaning wounds, and Shannon saw to mine.

It wasn't until morning we realized we'd missed our appointment with Dale Graham—and by then, it was too late.

Fire and Blood

"Any chance this could be a coincidence?" Shannon wanted to know.

"None," I said flatly.

We'd managed to save one person last night, but we hadn't been there for Dale Graham. If the wicked twelve wanted to make me feel guilty, they'd succeeded. But I knew this wasn't *our* fault. Bad things had been happening in Kilmer since before I was born. I was just determined to get to the bottom of it.

I stood looking at the smoking ruin of his house on Rabbit Road and wanted to throw up. Nobody suggested I try to read it to find out what happened here. Too much heat remained trapped in the burnt timbers to make it feasible, even if I felt like trying that particular trick again so soon. I didn't.

Volunteer firemen poked through the wreckage, looking for human remains. They seemed inappropriately cheerful, as if they did this all the time. Then again, in Kilmer, they probably did.

"Look at the grass and trees around the house," Jesse murmured.

I shifted focus, along with the other two. It hit us all at the same time, but Chance articulated it. "A third of the trees on his property caught fire, and all the green grass burnt up."

"So Miss Minnie was right?" Shannon asked.

I felt a headache coming on. "Sort of. Just not on a global scale."

"That means we need to take her seriously," Jesse said. "However crazy that sounds."

"An earthquake might not be literal." Chance seemed distant but thoughtful.

Most of me felt glad he had eased off—that he was focused more on solving our problems. I wasn't ready for reconciliation, not when his power was on temporary hiatus and our long-term problems hadn't been resolved. When we left Kilmer for good, his luck would return—and I would become a victim of the need for cosmic balance again. I didn't look forward to it.

"But what causes tremors?" Shannon fidgeted, obviously not sure why we were hanging around the fire scene. I guessed she wanted to be away from here before Sheriff Robinson showed up and decided to hold us indefinitely for being troublemaking pains in his sizable ass.

I thought about that, remembering the crappy places I'd lived over the years, and said at the same time as Jesse, "A train."

Chance nodded, excitement sparking like gold flecks in his eyes. "Shannon, are there any houses built close to the train tracks in town? Close enough that they'd shake when the train goes by?"

"Yep," she said. "There used to be a station, a long time ago, but it closed down in—lemme think . . ." She broke off, pondering for a full minute. "In 1911. Now there's just a cargo line that goes by twice a week."

"Do you know the way?" Jesse asked.

She nodded. "I used to hang out with a kid who lived out there, but my mom made me stop because he wasn't a desirable acquaintance." I could tell from her tone that she was quoting her mother verbatim. "It's the worst part of Kilmer."

Saldana tossed her the keys. "Here you go." At her stunned expression, he asked, "You *do* know how to drive?"

She was speechless, staring at him for a long minute before she managed to say, "Well, yeah. My dad taught me. I
have a license too, but I don't have a car, and the last few
months, I've been grounded for one reason or another."

He smiled at her. "Then you need the practice, and it'll
be easier if you just take us there. That okay with you?"

Her smile could've blinded the lot of us. "Sure. Get in."

Jesse Saldana would make a great dad, I decided, as I
headed toward the workers raking the wreckage. He wasn't
quite old enough to be parenting Shannon, but he had the
older-brother role polished to a fine sheen.

"I'll be right back," I said over my shoulder.

I picked my way toward the wreckage of Dale's house.
Ash sifted from the broken beams, and smoke still curled
from the foundation. There were five men raking the place
down; none of them looked pleased at my approach.

"What do you think happened?" I asked the lead volunteer.

Sooty-faced and weary, he shrugged. "My guess? He fell
asleep with a lit cigarette. It would've spread faster if he was
drinking."

*That was the official story they spread about my mama,
too.* Miz Ruth had said as much a few days back. That seemed
an unlikely coincidence.

"Have you recovered his body?" Maybe it was macabre,
but I had to know.

The volunteer shook his head. "Not yet. We'll keep
looking."

First happy news I'd had all day. "Thanks. Good luck."

Maybe Dale Graham hadn't been home when they torched
his house. I could hope, right? And maybe he had his journal with him, wherever he was. Playing dead might be the
smartest thing he could do.

I pulled Butch out of my handbag and put him down.
"Remember the hippie we ate pie with at the diner?"

He yapped once.

"Sniff around and see if you can find him."

It was probably a long shot. The acrid smoke would likely overwhelm any subtler smells, but Butch appeared keen to try. He put his nose to the ground and sniffed all around the wreckage in a large perimeter, and then trotted toward the road. He barked and then lifted a leg on the mailbox.

I didn't know what to make of that. "He got his mail yesterday?"

Butch gave the affirmative yap. I wasn't sure how that helped us, but I bent to scratch behind his ears and told him, "Good dog."

Then I scooped him up, sprinted for the Forester, and climbed in back, where I found Jesse. With his bad arm, he might've wanted help with the driving and was too much of a man to say so. The idea made me smile.

"What?" Jesse asked.

"How's the injury?"

He glanced at the bandage wrapped around his biceps. "I'll be fine; just a graze. It looks worse than it is."

"I was worried about you."

"Yeah? Well, the feeling's mutual." Jesse took my hand, and I took comfort in that tiny spark. He raised it gently to his lips; the heat sent shivers all through me.

Shannon pulled off the gravel drive and onto the county road smoothly. She looked small behind the wheel of the SUV, but she didn't seem nervous. Chance asked her something, and she spared him a glance to answer. I couldn't make out their words for the rush of the road beneath the tires and the soft crackle of blurry music on the radio. I'd never feel the same about AM/FM stations after meeting her. I wondered idly if she could tune in to the dead in a vehicle too.

For a few moments, I let myself enjoy the heat of his hand in mine, and then I pulled back. Touching him was a distraction I didn't need.

"Couple things we need to talk about," Jesse said quietly. "Sheriff Robinson? I got no sense of guilt off him last night. Even when you made your parting shot, all I felt from him was fear . . . bone-deep terror, in fact. Much worse than the night we sprung Chance from jail."

"So he knows something's wrong, but he's not part of it," I surmised. "Why do you think he threw away those missing persons forms?"

Saldana shrugged. "Don't know. Maybe he didn't want proof of his dereliction of duty, but he didn't want to go poking around out in the woods, either. I'm not infallible." By his bleak expression, I could tell he was thinking of his dead partner. "But I don't think I'm wrong this time."

Frankly, if fear of the forest motivated the sheriff, I couldn't blame him. I wouldn't want to lead a search party out there, either. Too bad, because that was exactly what I needed to do. The only way to gather evidence was to go out there ourselves; I didn't expect to like what we found.

"Good to know. If push comes to shove, Robinson might back us if he wants to get some of his spine back."

Jesse nodded. "Possible."

I watched the scenery for a while, green-brown trees passing in a blur. The filtered air felt damp and cool, as if it blew in from the distant sea. Then it occurred to me that I had no idea how the shooter had managed to peg him.

"How'd you get hit, anyway?" I'd thought he had good cover behind the hedge.

For a moment, Jesse studied his hands, seeming unwilling to answer. He said at last, "I stood up to distract the shooter when you went back onto the porch and through the window like a crazy person."

My breath left me. "You got shot for *me*?"

He scowled. "I would've done the same for Chance or Shannon."

"I know," I said, smiling.

That was the kind of man he was. He took his vows to protect and serve very seriously. Living with him might be just as difficult as being with Chance, but for different reasons. When I'd told him that some women had a hard time handling the constant danger their men were exposed to, I hadn't been exaggerating to make him feel better. The divorce statistics spoke for themselves.

Shannon parked the SUV. "We're here."

I clambered out of the Forester and decided she was right. This was the worst part of Kilmer, a section I'd never seen before. It was literally on the other side of the tracks, and the houses built closest must have shaken like blazes when the train came through. *Like, say, in an earthquake?*

Once more, I deposited Butch on the ground. "You were with me when I went into the gas station, right?"

He yapped in confirmation.

"You remember what the guy smelled like?"

The Chihuahua tilted his head in thoughtful consideration, and it was cute as hell. After a moment, he barked once.

"Can I trust you to sniff around for him?"

Butch yapped twice, but I swear it was sarcastic.

I laughed. "Okay, sorry. I shouldn't have even asked. Let me know if you find anything."

He trotted off without deigning to reply.

It would help if we knew what we were looking for. As it was, we strolled through the run-down clapboard houses, admiring the patchy lawns, filthy gutters, and interesting piles of junk. Though I wasn't inclined to agree with Sandra Cheney on principle, I could almost sympathize with her desire to keep Shannon from hanging around here. The whole neighborhood stank of despair and decay.

"So we had the fire," Chance said, thinking aloud. "The burnt trees and grass. We found the 'earthquake' site. What are we missing?"

"Blood," I murmured immediately.

"There was blood when I got shot," Jesse muttered.

Shannon added, "Hail."

Jesse thought for a moment, and we paused to give him a chance. "Miss Minnie said she saw the four horsemen coming and going."

"People don't ride horses through town," Shannon objected. "Even in Kilmer, it can't have been dudes on horseback."

"So what *did* she see?" I asked.

Unfortunately, nobody could come up with an answer. We continued in a meandering path around the two streets that made up this country ghetto. I kicked at a clump of pigweed straggling up at the edge of the road.

"When does the next train come by?" Chance asked Shannon.

"Tuesday and Saturday, just before six a.m."

I suspected she'd know that only if she'd spent the night with her scruffy "friend" at some point, but that wasn't our business. Time had gotten away from me, so I mentally tabulated how long we'd been there.

"It's Thursday?" I asked aloud, none too sure of my calculations.

Jesse agreed with a nod. "So no trains today."

As we completed the loop and wound up back by the Forester, Chance gave us something else to think about. "We should be looking near the tracks. Right here, in fact."

I agreed with that. Unless we were totally off target, one of these ramshackle tract houses held something we needed to know. Talk about an exercise in frustration. Only Miss Minnie's rambling had guided us here, and maybe we were crazy for putting any stock in it at all. It was unlikely that Curtis Farrell had lived anywhere near here.

We paced up and down the street four times before Shannon said, "That one has a red front door. I mean, it's painted—badly, too."

I saw what she meant. It looked as though someone had slung a paint can to cover up some ugly graffiti. From some angles, it also looked like splattered blood.

Chance saw it too. "Red as blood," he noted as we approached the broken cement driveway.

Butch came around the corner of the house, wagging his

tail fiercely. He yapped at me to tell me he'd found the house. I stared in astonishment.

"Here? The gas station guy's been here?"

The dog barked in confirmation, and I gave him a rub. He leaped into my arms, and I stowed him away safely in my bag.

We proceeded with caution. After all, it was early; we were strangers, and most people around here had never heard of gun control. Nothing stirred behind the curtains. While the others made their way toward the house, I paused at the mailbox, hoping to find out who lived here.

Jackpot. I found a couple of utility bills for Curtis Farrell. I hadn't dared hope we would be this lucky. It would have been simpler to locate him in the directory, assuming he was listed, but this confluence of events suggested Miss Minnie knew something, layered beneath bits of old Bible verse. I wished we could talk to her again, but I was afraid of what more questions would do to her. I didn't want to hurt anyone while I was here. Well, nobody who was *innocent*, anyway.

But how brilliant. We needed to search his house, and here we were.

When I caught up to the others, I found them studying the front door. Jesse was asking, "Can you make out what it says underneath the paint?"

Chance leaned in for a better look. "Mar . . . and some numbers. Eight-three-six, I think."

"March?" I offered. "Is it a date, you think? Or a time?"

The others shrugged.

Shannon stepped to the side and peered through the window between the gap in the ragged sheers. "I don't think anyone's here. Are we going in?"

Since the guy was dead, it didn't seem likely anybody was home, unless Curtis had a roommate.

I cleared my throat. "I'm taking Jesse around back. Chance, if the door happens to pop open while we're gone, give us a holler." I thought that was better than making Jesse watch him pick the lock. Even if he was suspended and well outside his jurisdiction, I figured he probably didn't want to see active lawbreaking.

Rummaging in his pockets, Chance didn't acknowledge me as Jesse and I rounded the house. Shannon stayed with him to watch him work.

"So your ex is a house-breaker too," Jesse said, sounding amused. "As I've said before, you have the most interesting friends, Corine."

I thought about Chuch, the ex–arms dealer, married to Eva, the forger, and grinned. "Yeah. They sure come in handy, don't they?"

He smiled back, bitter chocolate eyes roving my face in an appreciative manner. "I don't think I should comment."

"That's probably wise."

We circled the house and found a bunch of disgusting garbage cans that should have been set out weeks ago. If I were truly devoted, I would have suggested going through them for clues, but you couldn't have paid me enough to touch one.

Instead of calling to us, Chance opened the back door and waved us in. "The front was open," he said mildly.

Jesse raised a brow. "Fancy that."

"Small town," I said. "People just don't see the need to lock up."

I climbed two steps and crossed the sagging porch, stepping into Farrell's house. We'd gotten there before the police, assuming the sheriff would even bother. The place looked like a cyclone had hit it, though; clothes everywhere and dirty dishes piled in the sink. Added to the trash in the back, it seemed as if Curtis hadn't been home in a while—at least, I couldn't imagine a human being living like that.

"Have a look around." Jesse took charge as if this were his crime scene. "I'll take the kitchen. Corine, you search the bathroom. Chance, take the bedroom, and Shannon, check out the living room, please. I guarantee we don't have to worry about leaving DNA on the scene, but don't touch any-thing with your bare hands. They probably have a finger-print kit even out here in Hooterville."

Shannon snickered, but she took his advice and pulled the sleeves of her hoodie down past her hands as she headed for the living room. Once in the bathroom, I did the same with my sweater. Ew. I really had to search in there? It smelled like something had died, and green fuzzy stuff grew in the grout between the tiles. Man, I thought Jesse liked me better than that.

From within my handbag, Butch whined. The smell was getting to him too. "There's no help for it," I told the dog. "We have to be brave."

I heard a thunk from the bedroom and peered out. Using a broom handle, Chance poked gingerly at the piles of cloth-ing spread across the floor. He flashed me a wry smile. "I think Shannon got the best deal in this division of labor."

"Well, she's young. He didn't want to traumatize her—oh dear God." I caught my breath at the sight of a dead rat in the cupboard beneath the sink.

It was going to be a long day.

Unearthed Secrets

In the end, Shannon found what we were looking for.

"Mark 8:36," she called, excitement thrumming in her voice. When we gathered in the living room, she read from the book in her hands. " 'For what shall it profit a man, if he shall gain the whole world, and lose his own soul?' This passage is highlighted." She showed us the Bible, where someone, probably Curtis Farrell, had marked the verse scrawled on his door.

"Sounds like a threat," Chance said quietly.

"Somebody knew something," Jesse agreed. "But were they blackmailing Farrell or trying to get him to stop?"

An excellent question. Farrell hadn't displayed the confidence of a career criminal. He'd seemed hesitant, like he didn't know what to do when confronted with resistance. His job had been spelled out for him—and I still wasn't sure what he'd intended to do to Miss Minnie—and once things went wrong, he didn't know how to respond.

"Is this a religious thing?" I asked. "Or someone just using the Bible for a convenient code?"

"Impossible to say." Jesse took the Bible from Shannon and flipped through it. As he gave the book a last shake, a scrap of paper tumbled toward the floor.

With his preternatural reflexes, Chance snatched it before it touched. He scanned it and then looked at me with a half frown. "Robert Frost? It's that 'Two roads diverged in a wood' poem."

"'The Road Not Taken'?" I took the torn yellow sheet from Chance; it looked as if it had been pulled from a legal pad. "Wish we had a sample of Farrell's handwriting. Then we'd know whether he wrote this down himself or someone else gave it to him."

"Can I?" At Shannon's question, I passed it along. Her eyes widened. "This is John McGee's writing. I'd recognize the crabby little letters anywhere."

"So Farrell had been talking to McGee," Jesse mused. "And they both ended up dead."

I wondered aloud, "Could that have been the point? Someone may have sent Farrell to Miss Minnie's house right then, knowing we were there."

A thundercloud frown knit Chance's brow. "Knowing we wouldn't react well to a robber threatening an old lady."

"If that's the case," Shannon said, "then the guy on the roof wasn't working with Farrell. He was there to keep us pinned down until we noticed something was wrong inside."

Jesse gave her an approving nod. "Good thinking, Shannon."

She flushed with pleasure. "Just makes sense, right? He didn't try too hard to hit us. He might've been trying to drive us back inside the house, and then Butch heard the intruder."

It would've taken a dog's hearing to notice someone jimmying the back door with the varmint rifle pinging away. But then, everyone in town knew I took Butch everywhere. As theories went, this one seemed to make sense.

That put a scowl on Saldana's face. "If that's true, it makes it even more embarrassing that he got me."

I didn't look at him. He'd been shot trying to protect me. I couldn't make light of that, even if it hadn't been strictly necessary, but there was no evidence to support any of our hypotheses, anyway.

"We sound like crazed conspiracy theorists," I said in disgust. "It was this; it was that; it was—"

"Bigfoot," Chance said, deadpan.

He startled a laugh out of me. "Definitely."

"Nothing else was underlined," Jesse murmured, getting
us back on track. "I think it's safe to say our guy isn't a
scholar or a church-goer."

Shannon nodded. "No shit. I expect to find a closet weed
farm somewhere in here. But if you want to scope out the
church scene, there's a potluck dinner every Saturday night."

"That's your grandfather's territory," Chance pointed out.
"Is that going to be a problem for you?"

She shrugged. "Up until we leave, everything here is going to cause problems for me. I'm just waiting for it to hit
the fan."

At that point, Butch jumped out of my bag into her arms.
She caught him with a startled laugh. He was simply the best
dog ever; he seemed to sense that she would derive comfort
from snuggling him instead of thinking about her troubles.

I rubbed my hands against my denim-clad thighs, trying
to scrub away the residual filth of poking around that bathroom. To me, Farrell's home hygiene suggested he didn't
believe he had long to live, and thus, saw no point in keeping up the place. But I wasn't sure I could profile someone,
based on slovenly ways.

"Then I'd say a church social is what we need to scope
out the local color."

"This won't end well," Jesse predicted.

We didn't find anything else of interest, not even that
closet weed farm Shannon expected. I was starting to get
frustrated with all the separate pieces not coalescing into a
recognizable shape. There's a reason I hate jigsaw puzzles.
I don't have the patience to find all the border pieces, especially when they're all the same shade of gray.

When we left Farrell's house, we took the Bible. I'd handle it later, but it didn't seem wise to hang around Farrell's place longer than necessary. If Sheriff Robinson found us here, the consequences would be unpleasant.

"Let's take one last look around," Jesse said.

Shannon cocked a brow. "What're we looking for?"

"Anything that offers a hint at who's been hanging around," he answered. "Corine learned a lot from a button, as I recall."

That much was true. Any small object that might've dropped when people were coming and going might tell us something. Right now we had no clue why Curtis Farrell had decided to trade a life of petty drugs and making change for one big felony.

Chance nodded. "Better to be sure we don't miss anything. Somebody will be along to shovel this place out, so we probably won't have another shot at this. Corine, you want to take a look around back?"

I nodded as they divided up the rest of the small yard. Shannon kept Butch, and he showed no signs of minding the attention. I circled the house. Near the back door, I found some weird impressions in the dirt behind Farrell's garage. It would take a tracker to make anything of the morass of churned mud, unless—

I'd never have attempted, or even considered anything like this in the past, but since dying, my gift seemed to have stretched into unknown dimensions. Before, I wouldn't have tried to read a whole house. I knelt, studying the ground: torn earth and grass pulled up by the roots. I wouldn't be able to do anything with the plants, but what about dirt?

The others were searching the front and sides. If Chance or Jesse had been there, they probably would have tried to talk me out of it. I gazed at the new brand on my palm, the smooth, unscarred skin around it, and felt a cold, eerie certainty. I could do this. I didn't know what the mark portended, but it signified change. Though I had no way to prove it, I suspected I'd received more of my mother's power. Instead of passing to me cleanly during her spell, something must have gone wrong and it had wound up in the necklace instead. Now that I'd touched it, I'd absorbed the rest, but there was no way to know how it would affect me down the road.

But it had made me a more powerful handler, no question.

Without hesitation, I sank my fingers into the dirt. It felt like bathing my hand in chemical fire, but I gritted my teeth and held on. Nobody died here; it wasn't that bad, but it was awful enough.

I became two men at once, locked in a life-or-death struggle. That had never happened to me before because objects belonged to one person. Not dirt—it belonged to everyone, no one, or whoever trod upon it.

Their conflicting emotions swamped me: greed, anger, terror, exhilaration, desperation. I seesawed between the apogee and the abyss while they grappled and tore the earth. I'd have given a lot to hear what they were saying, but it never worked like that for me. I imagined the grunts and gasps of breath while pain washed over me in waves of red fire. Though I tried, I couldn't jerk my hand out of the soil until the vision ended. Immersion, immolation; I hovered but a half step away from one or the other.

Finally, the older man shoved the younger to his knees, both hands on his throat. He spoke, saying something I couldn't hear. I strained to read his lips and failed, not for the first time. For a heartbreaking moment, the man on his knees clawed at his captor's hands, desperate. His fear poured through me, sour and rancid. He didn't want to acquiesce, but he'd die if he didn't. He felt it, believed it, and so did I.

When the beaten man turned his face upward, I recognized him. *Farrell.* Whatever the old bastard wanted, Curtis had been forced to it—throttled into submission. He managed a nod, and the other man's hands fell away just before Farrell blacked out. And I went with him.

I came to on my side, gasping for air. My throat burnt

as if someone had been strangling *me*, and my right hand throbbed with an agonizing pulse. *Jesus. Well, that's new.*

Through sparks in my vision that meant I was close to passing out again, I stared at my fingers, focused on wiggling them, and saw they were fire engine red but possessed no new marks. I lay there, breathing and reflecting. It was all I could do right then.

Dirt was less dangerous than metal. But no wonder the tracks didn't look like much of anything. Two men fighting over the same space created the look of a monster rampage.

Jesse came upon me a few minutes later. "What the hell, Corine—did someone attack you? What happened? Can you talk, sugar?" He did a visual inspection of my injuries, lingering at my throat.

Christ, did I wear marks *there* too?

I managed to push to a sitting position, but standing was beyond me. Oxygen deprivation sent tremors through my limbs; I couldn't seem to convince my body I hadn't been choked. He swung me up into his arms before I could tell him not to, and my stomach whirled in response.

"Slowly," I whispered, sounding hoarse to my own ears.

Jesse called to the others and carried me to the Forester, but he modulated his step so as not to jar me. He smelled of plain Ivory soap and a tangy citrus scent. I breathed him in, trying to identify the cologne, and then gave up, closing my eyes.

Jesse slid into the vehicle with me on his lap, and I didn't try to get away. Then again, I wouldn't have tried to escape unless a killer had a hold of me; I was that tapped out. Two doors slammed, and Shannon and Chance got in the front.

"Drive," Jesse told Shannon, who started the engine on command.

She pulled out, gravel spinning beneath the tires. In making our getaway, we didn't encounter any law enforcement types who'd ask awkward questions about why Chance was hanging around the house of the man he'd killed last night.

"What's going on?" Chance asked.

Jesse answered, "At this point? I'm not sure. But take a look at this."

I felt him angle my head, and then I did open my eyes. Chance swore in an entertaining mix of English and Korean. Mildly curious now that my nausea had started to subside, I lifted my left hand and touched my neck. *Ouch.*

I couldn't remember ever taking an injury apart from my hands. *Unless you count dying*, a cynical voice said. My mother's necklace might well have changed everything I thought I knew about my gift, both its boundaries and its dangers.

"Did someone attack you?" Chance demanded.

I shook my head slowly to make sure that much was clear. There would be no point in Shannon stopping the SUV so they could comb the area for someone long gone days before. Concentrating, I mimed writing.

Chance got it right away. He delved into Jesse's glove box and found a pen and scrap of paper for me. I scrawled what I'd done, what I'd seen, and then passed it to my ex. His jaw tightened as he read, and he slanted a look over the seat that could've cut glass. Before he said a word, I could tell what he thought of my pushing my power.

"You're out of your mind," he bit out. "Are you *determined* to die here? Because I see you taking risk after risk and you don't seem to—"

"Stop," Jesse said quietly. "She's been through enough at this point. She doesn't need you yelling at her too."

Chance's eyes glittered like amber with ire frozen in their depths. "*Don't* tell me what to do where Corine's concerned." He looked as if he would break Jesse's fingers and pull them away from me by force.

"Every time I handle, it's a risk." I pushed the words through a raw throat. "I made the choice; I'll live with the consequences."

"Where to?" Shannon cut in, diffident.

I silently thanked her for the change in topic. I struggled

off Jesse's lap and belted myself with some difficulty into my own seat. My fingers stung like hell.

"I need a drink," I told Shannon. "Strong enough to burn off the clouds. Is there a bar anywhere nearby?"

In answer, she cut right on the county road and headed toward town.

After a short drive, she pulled up outside a roadhouse that sat just outside the city limits, a little way past Ma's Kitchen. No signs revealed the name of the establishment, but small orange neon lettering proclaimed CHEAP COLD BEER. That was probably enough for local clientele.

Refusing Jesse's aid, I slid out of the SUV. I brushed myself off as best I could and then gave up, figuring people who hung around in bars this early deserved my dishevelment. My knees felt shaky for the first few steps, but I declined to take anybody's arm. They would just argue I shouldn't be drinking if I couldn't walk straight *before* I started, and they would have a point.

Chance opened the door for me and I stepped in, squinting at the dim interior. There were no lights on at this hour, just the uncertain light filtering through dirty windows. The place was open for business, though, and decorated with liquor store paraphernalia. Beer signs and old advertisements littered the walls.

There was nobody at the bar, nobody in here at all. A guy in a dirty yellow ball cap paused in stocking the bar when we came in. Did they even *have* tequila here? Drowning in a sudden onslaught of homesickness, I wanted some.

This place was nothing like the warm, inviting cantinas at home. It wasn't even as nice as Twilight in San Antonio. Still, my nerves needed steadying, and I could use something to numb the pain.

The proprietor tried on a smile, as if he hoped we were there to spend money and not just use the toilet or telephone. At a glance, the place didn't seem to have one—a public phone, that is. A handwritten sign pointed toward the restrooms.

"What can I get you folks?" His voice boomed out, jocular and forced.

Shannon asked for a Coke. *Smart girl.* I hadn't even thought of her being underage when I suggested this; I wasn't used to hanging around kids. Chance and Jesse both requested beers, but Jesse said the can was fine for him.

"Hell Fire," I said aloud, my voice low and husky as a phone-sex operator.

He blinked at me. "I reckon I have no idea what that is, but if you tell me how, I can mix it for you."

"Equal parts tequila, vodka, Red Aftershock, and a dash of Tabasco. Mix well, pour over ice."

Their drinks came quick. Mine he had to think about. "I got the tequila and vodka," he muttered, more to himself than me. Cheap stuff it was too. He dumped some ice in a glass, anticipating success. I watched, feeling almost cheerful about his uncertainty. He finally glanced over at me. "I don't have no Red Aftershock."

"Cinnamon schnapps will do," I said, easing down at the bar.

Something spicy might clear my head and burn away the confusion. If nothing else, I needed to hold a drink that reminded me of home, one that burned as it went down. I missed Mexico. Georgia had been my home once, but it wasn't anymore.

After I told him what to substitute, it went quickly for him: tequila, vodka, cinnamon schnapps, a dash of hot sauce. With an expression that said *yuck*, he slid it my way. The bartender studied me as I drank the concoction, as if expecting smoke to rise from my mouth. But I was used to stronger stuff.

I was *made* of stronger stuff.

Bar None

"So does this place have a name?" I asked Stu, my new friend.

His name could've been short for Stuart, Studebaker, or Stupid, for all I knew. After two more Hell Fires, I no longer felt the pain in my throat or my fingers. I'm sure it was still there, but I was nicely numb. Not drunk, mind you—I could hold my liquor. After I left Chance, I'd spent a number of nights doing tequila shots and trying not to wonder whether I'd ever see him again.

"Not really," he answered, wiping down the bar. "But *I* call it Bar None . . . 'cause it don't really have a name, and I bar none from entering who got money. Get it? Bar none?" He laughed, slapping his palm on the counter.

I got it, so I smiled politely. Through my alcoholic buffer, I thought Stu had, perhaps, spent too much time in his own company, but then, something else struck me. He didn't seem to suffer from the downtrodden, nervous fear that plagued everyone else in this godforsaken town. I wondered why.

Jesse and Chance were off at a table by the window, arguing. I didn't know what about, and I didn't care. Shannon sat next to me at the bar, nursing her Coke. Stu hadn't asked her for ID and I had an idea he wouldn't, as long as she didn't try to order booze.

"How long have you lived here?" I asked him.

He smiled, pleased by my interest. The man had a seamed face and a couple of missing teeth, but he seemed happy, an emotion I hadn't noticed a lot of in Kilmer. "About eight years, I guess."

My interest perked up. So he'd arrived after I left. It might be helpful to get his perspective. "Have you noticed anything weird about this town?"

Stu snorted. "Better to ask what *ain't* weird about it. People don't drink much, and the ones that come out here do it sneaky, like they're ashamed, even if they don't get shit faced. Sorry, miss," he added in an aside to Shannon. "Now what kind of sense does that make? There's nothing wrong with having a drink now and again, is there?"

I certainly didn't think so. "Not from where I'm sitting."

He continued. "Not a single liquor store in town, either. It's a weird place. I got lost off the highway, stumbled on this little place, and figured it would be a gold mine. No competition! So I scoped it out and bought this parcel of land. Had my brothers come in and help me put up the bar—it was a prefab kit—and once I got opened up, nothing. Crickets. I'm barely making enough to make it worth my while to stay open, but I don't reckon I could even sell the land without taking a loss at this point." He sighed a little.

"Did you have trouble getting permits or permission?" Shannon asked. It wasn't a question you'd expect from an eighteen-year-old, but she wasn't typical. She'd coped with a hell of a lot the last few days, and probably better than someone twice her age too.

"Might have," Stu conceded. "But since I built here, I went through the McIntosh County zoning office instead of the Kilmer town council, and they're easier to deal with. But they're a little strange too. They kept asking how come I wanted to build a bar in the middle of nowhere. I'll allow I could be closer to the square, but this ain't no more than a mile outside town limits."

I remembered Jesse had mentioned not being able to find Kilmer on a map, Booke telling us about the lack of information on the Internet, and the corresponding black smear in the astral. Stu's story drove the point home; people as close as the county seat had forgotten this place existed. A shiver ran through me.

Shannon regarded me, wide-eyed. I thought it certain she'd put the pieces together too. When Stu went to wash the glasses from my first two Hell Fires, she whispered to me, "We're truly forsaken, aren't we?" She imbued the words with Old Testament weight, as if God himself had abandoned the town.

"They are," I told her grimly. "Not us. Whatever happened here, we didn't do it. In fact, we're trying to fix it. So if there's a right side, we're firmly on it."

By the way she smiled, she liked the idea of fighting evil, crusaders for truth and justice. I didn't have the heart to tell her that after the first time it almost killed you, you lost your taste for it. I did, at least; she might be different. Unfortunately, sometimes you just had to keep pushing. I wasn't the type to leave a job half done.

Stu came back to check on us. "Y'all want anything else?"

I shook my head, lofting my third drink. After slamming the first two, I'd nurse this one. "Who comes in here from town, anyway?"

He grinned at me. "Did you want a list? To tell their churchy friends on them?"

Actually, that wasn't a bad idea.

"Sure," I said. "I could have me some fun at the next potluck, couldn't I?"

The owner gave a booming belly laugh. "You're a tonic, you surely are." Then he seemed to realize I meant it. Stu considered for a moment, no doubt debating on the wisdom of it. If they got chided by friends and family, it could hurt his business. With a shrug, he wrote down the names of his regulars on a cocktail napkin. I wasn't a bit surprised to find Curtis Farrell and Dale Graham among them.

I pocketed the info with a smile. We'd use it to cause all manner of awkwardness at the church social on Saturday.

"Do you ever have trouble getting supplies out here?" My voice still sounded throaty.

Stu huffed. "Ever? Huh. I couldn't get on anybody's shipment list, no matter how many times I called. Stupid computers. I drive clear to the warehouse in Savannah to get my stuff. They load the truck for me, but I swear, if I'd known how much trouble this spot would turn out to be, I'd have taken my court settlement and moved to Mexico instead."

"Funny you should say that," I said, smiling.

I might have said more, but across the room, Jesse and Chance stood up and shook hands. I told myself I didn't want to know what dispute they'd settled.

"You ladies ready to go?" Chance asked politely.

"Yep." I left a healthy tip on the bar for Stu.

I was glad we'd come in. I felt a little sturdier. I wouldn't advocate finding strength in a bottle every day, but sometimes there was no substitute for a good jolt. As an added bonus, we had information that might serve as leverage to get people to talk. Walking ahead with Chance, Shannon jangled the keys, cheerful in her role as designated driver.

"Learn anything?" Jesse fell into step with me as we left the bar.

I filled him in as we got into the backseat. In my mind's eye, I saw Jesse's expression as they shook hands, quiet and resigned. What the hell *had* Chance and he been talking about, anyway? If it had to do with me, didn't I get a say? With a sigh, I checked myself. They'd likely just agreed to stop snapping at each other until we were done here.

Setting that aside, I pondered our next move. Little as I liked it, there was only one thing we could do before the potluck on Saturday: Return to the woods. So I offered the idea for consideration. Chance argued against it all the way back to the house. I knew what was bothering him; I had died out there. It seemed like testing fate to go back and give the forest a chance to finish me off.

Ignoring Chance's objections, I took Butch from Shannon and let him out to run a bit. He'd been remarkably good and remarkably helpful the past few days, but he still needed some exercise. I stood on the porch, keeping a sharp eye on him. Jesse and Shannon went inside; she wanted to change his bandages, and since I felt no real affinity for the Florence Nightingale thing, I was happy to let her.

"What do you think you're going to find out there?" Chance asked.

"Bodies."

"How will that help us?" he demanded.

"We should be able to tell if they were killed by a human being. Or . . . not." I didn't elaborate; he'd sense the thing once we stepped into its domain. Frankly, the idea of doing that made me want to leave Kilmer for good, but I wouldn't. We were too close to figuring things out.

"And if we have bodies, the authorities can't ignore the problem any longer, or sweep it beneath the rug."

I agreed with a nod. "A dead dog on the side of the road isn't the same thing as a dead husband, so if we can, I'd like to find Glen, for Miz Ruth's sake. She deserves to know, one way or another."

"And that sheriff isn't going to look for him," Chance said in disgust.

Wonder of all wonders—I'd *managed* him. I didn't even think he'd noticed my doing it. Instead of thinking about how it could hurt me, I'd presented him with alternative trains of thought with branching benefits. Now, to his mind, the pros outweighed the cons. Could I do that again?

Butch ran around the yard, sniffing, prancing, and eventually looking for the perfect place to do his business. Then he ran over to me and put his paw on my foot. I'd figured out that meant he wanted me to pick him up, so I did.

"There are a lot of people in town with missing loved ones. Consider Rob Walker's family." I named the kid from Shannon's class who never made it out of the woods. "Who's going to give them closure, if not us?"

"Okay," he said, slanting his gaze upward. "It's early enough that we can do it before dark, if you think you're up to it."

The liquor had mostly evaporated, and my new injuries were stinging, but I'd certainly suffered worse. It seemed a dubious accomplishment.

"Yeah, I'll be fine."

He paused. "Corine, I need you to believe this—I didn't kiss you in the bathroom because of Saldana. It may have seemed that way because of what I said afterward, but . . . woman, you were *naked*."

At that, I smiled because there was no mistaking his aggrieved tone. I was willing to concede I might have misjudged him. Maybe I'd seized on the first excuse to push him away . . . because I was scared of where we were headed, and this wasn't the time for distractions like that. I needed a clear head to do some thinking, and Chance kissing me silly wasn't going to get that done.

"Don't worry about it."

Unlike other occasions where I'd said it in a way guaranteed to rile him because I refused to talk, I really wanted to forget the misunderstanding. I wouldn't trot it out later. I wouldn't *forget* what came before, though. My toes curled, just thinking about the way he'd taken control, snagged my hair, and pushed me up against the bathroom door.

"You sure?"

I nodded. "And I'm sorry I thought the worst of you. That wasn't fair."

He hunched his shoulders into his well-cut jacket. "I admit, I'm jealous as hell of him because he doesn't seem to rub you wrong like I do. He makes the right moves with you easily, effortlessly, and I'd like to punch him in the face over it." An astonishing confession, coming from Chance— he never admitted to weakness or uncertainty, never admitted to feeling much of anything at all.

Surprise washed over me. "Why are you telling me this? Before, you never told me *anything*."

"I made a lot of mistakes before," he said quietly. "I'm trying not to repeat them."

"Why?" For all I knew, Chance could be under a geas to make amends with me. Min liked me. Based on what I'd seen in Laredo, it wouldn't surprise me if she could do the spell. Before then I'd never have guessed she could summon the Knights of Hell to do her bidding. "It's past."

"You don't want to think about what might have been? In fact, you'd probably prefer to forget we were ever together. God help me, maybe we can even be friends, right? Well, I *refuse*. I refuse to let you write us off."

I started to say that he hadn't answered my question, but he sealed his fingers against my mouth as if he wanted to kiss me quiet, and then went on. "I haven't forgotten anything. I don't want to. I still have all your books at home—did you know that?"

I did now. Sometimes I missed our place on Harbour Island. I missed swinging by his mother's homeopathy shop and going over to her house for dinner on weekends when we weren't traveling for a job. Chance and Min had become the closest thing to family I'd known in years.

A pang hit me as I remembered decorating the loft with him: how we'd discussed the placement of a statue I set on the corner of the counter that opened the kitchen to the living room and how he hadn't wanted to put any pictures on the brick wall that gave the room so much character. We'd agreed on a fluffy white rug in the center of the hardwood floor. I remembered drinking our morning coffee on the balcony, overlooking the ocean.

In Mexico City, I was hours from the sea. I had mountains instead. Though I'd made a life there, I'd probably never stop missing the one I'd left behind.

My expression must have given away my feelings, because he went on, more gently. "I still have the clothes you left behind hanging beside mine in the closet. I went day by day, trying to pretend you were coming back . . . until I couldn't anymore. But know this: Nobody will *ever* love you like I do."

"Chance . . ."

He hesitated. I could see him trembling, and though it might have been the chill, I didn't think so. "I spent three days at your bedside with neither food nor sleep, Corine, and I promised any god or devil that might be listening I'd give anything for you to walk out of there on your own two feet. And when you left me, not only did I think I deserved it—I thought that was the price I had to pay for your survival. But nothing ever showed up to enforce the terms. Turned out there wasn't any otherworld pact—just good medical personnel." His beautiful mouth twisted. "When you live in our world, you tend to look for that, I guess, even when it's not there."

"That much is true." My voice sounded rusty.

These days, I found myself seeking signs and symbols in the strangest places, some clue that I wasn't making disastrous decisions. Sadly, there were no guarantees, and nobody ever gave you a do-over when it mattered. Butch whined, likely sensing my inner turmoil, and burrowed his head against my arm. I took comfort in his warm little body.

"But the fact is, I'm not willing to let you go. I will do my damnedest to be the man you need—I'll even try to find some way to kill this luck—but you have to meet me halfway. Now, you tell me, should I keep trying? Sometimes I feel like I'm beating myself to death against a stone wall, and it's named Corine."

I found myself getting mad, and it helped banish the ache for what we'd lost. "I don't care! I can't predict how I'll feel ten minutes from now, let alone wrap myself up for you with a bow and an instruction manual. You want me back? Earn me! I'm not giving you shortcuts or promises."

He started to smile. "Earn you? Like a pay increase?"

"Not what I meant," I muttered.

"I know what you mean." Chance sounded impossibly tender as he bent his head and brushed his lips along my jaw. "I think I get it. Finally."

A shiver stole through me. "Get what?"

"You."

"No, you don't."

"Show, not tell, right, Corine? Action, not words. You don't want to hear how sorry I am or how things will be different this time. You want to see it with your own eyes. And until I can show you that, you won't tell me what I want to hear."

Huh, he finally *did* get it.

"What's that?"

His answer came low. "That you still love me."

Oh God. I didn't want to. I wanted to start over, and Chance had no place in my new life. I wished I could cut him out of me. But part of me would always look at him and remember he represented the first home I'd known since my mama died.

"You're right on all counts. It broke my heart to leave, Chance. You'll never know how hard it was for me to walk away from you, or how much strength it took. If we ever get back together, it'll be because you convinced me we can make it work long term, *and* because you trust me with everything you are."

He had been nodding, a smile building on his wonderful mouth, until I said the last thing. The breath ran out of him in a sigh. I hated the haunted look in his eyes, but I didn't back down.

"Some of my secrets could hurt you," he said quietly.

"And your luck could kill me." Maybe that wasn't fair. Maybe I shouldn't have mentioned it. That wasn't something he could help, after all.

"I know," he murmured, tawny eyes full of smoke and shadow. "That's why I let you walk away in the first place."

"But you don't love me enough to let me keep walking?"

His voice deepened, gained a raw note. "There aren't words for what I feel for you."

"You'll have to prove that," I said softly.

"Fair enough."

"And you still didn't answer my question."

Chance raised his brows, plainly surprised. I guess he thought he'd succeeded in distracting me. "The why of it?"

"Exactly. Why are you so determined *now* when you could've tried at any point before I left?" *Or come after me* before *you needed me*, I added to myself.

"Because you're back, and that's like a second chance," he said quietly. "I learned from losing you."

"What do you mean?"

"After you left, I only had my pride for company. At first I was furious, and I tried to tell myself, 'Fine, if that's how she wants it.' Unfortunately, I had plenty of time to think about the things we used to fight about and how none of them seemed to matter. I'm not saying I'd cave on every issue now, but I realized it's important to pick your battles.

"There should've been more give-and-take between us, and a lot of that was my fault. Because I didn't want to share, didn't want to give you insights that would make me vulnerable. So this time I told you how I feel about Saldana. You said yourself—I never would've done that before. I've lost too many people. Now that you're back in my life, I've made up my mind you won't be one of them. But I won't push you."

I considered what he'd said, and it all seemed honest enough; certainly more than he would've offered in the past. If Chance really wanted to change, I'd wait and see. He had been right when he said I wanted proof, not promises. It was easier to say, *Baby, come back. Things will be different this time.* But it could be hard to put the words into practice, and sometimes, good intentions resulted in falling back into old habits.

"Is that what you guys talked about at the bar? You agreed to back off?"

"Pretty much."

"Thanks. It was starting to get awkward. And I appreciate your giving me the space I need to figure out what I want."

"Take your time."

"Talking about your feelings is only the tip of the iceberg, though it's a good start. If you really want me back, you have to tell me who you are ... and part with those closely held secrets."

"I know. Give *me* time too. Rome wasn't built in a day." His tone ached with intensity, but he changed the subject, fixing me with a glare. "Dirt, Corine? First houses, now dirt? I'm worried about you, love. I'm afraid you're going to push yourself too far; that you'll go into a handling and you won't come out again. I had no idea you could do this stuff, none at all."

Well, I couldn't, before I'd died. I didn't tell him that.

Chance went on. "What's it going to be next? Highways? Bridges? I thought your power only applied to buttons, shirts, lost jewelry—"

"I don't know what my limits are," I put in quietly. "But if anyone deserves my best, it's my mom."

He bowed his head then, in silent acknowledgment. I'd given his mother my best—and we'd saved her. When he spoke next, it was only to make plans. "We should eat, gear up, and then get out there."

Food sounded like a good idea. As we went inside for more of my famous peanut butter sandwiches, I remembered I hadn't mentioned the most important thing. "The bad guy ... the one who choked Farrell in my vision?"

Butch wiggled, demanding to get down. He trotted into the kitchen, and I heard him munching his kibble—lunchtime for him too.

Chance paused just inside the front door. "Yeah?"

"I'll recognize him. If we spot him anywhere in town, I will know him. And he's key. I can't imagine having a *good* reason to throttle somebody, can you?"

"Not unless you're Kel Ferguson."

Ah, damn. I wished he hadn't said that. I still wasn't over the uneasy truce we'd struck with the holy killer. He scared me more than demons, missing persons, and accursed towns combined.

Before I went into the kitchen, I hid our clues in a safe place—Curtis Farrell's Bible—along with Stu's list and that Robert Frost poem. Together they went up onto the highest shelf I could reach. I found Jesse and Shannon already eating. Jesse looked a little pale, probably from Shannon's poking around in his wound. She'd already made sandwiches for us too, so I thanked her and took my place at the table.

While I ate, Chance told them the bit of happy news about my being able to ID the guy who'd choked Curtis Farrell into submission. Jesse thought about that, munching on his PBJ.

"That's not all," he said. "Our guy will have scabs on his wrists and hands if it wasn't too long ago. And Curtis may have bruises on his neck like yours."

"His hands might match the marks on my neck," I said, much struck. "You think we should file a police report before the bruises fade?"

Jesse frowned at me. "I'm not letting you file a false report, even here."

"Fine. But there's one more thing."

"What?" Chance asked.

"I recognize the guy. I'm sure my mother saw him just before she died."

Both Chance and Jesse put down the remainder of their sandwiches; I could see questions in their eyes. I hadn't told either one of them how viscerally I had experienced her death; it had been like living inside her skin. And my visions from handling charged objects kept ratcheting up in intensity ever since.

"So the guy who choked Farrell is one of the twelve," Chance said.

Shannon ventured, "What did he look like? Maybe I know him. If I do, I could tell you who he's likely to be working with."

It was a long shot, at best. A maladjusted teenager couldn't possibly know everyone in town, not even one the size of Kilmer. But it might be worth trying, so I described him to the best of my ability.

She shrugged, visibly disappointed. "That could be any of thirty men. Saying 'old, tall, and thin' isn't specific enough."

"I wish I could draw."

Jesse waved that away for the moment. "This is big, folks. We're talking about a solid lead. This guy could be the key to unraveling everything else. Assuming you don't plan to execute him when you find him?"

I *really* wished he hadn't asked that.

Search Party

Luckily, I came up with an answer that satisfied Saldana and had the added value of being true. "I won't execute him," I said in neutral tones.

Until he leads me to the other eleven. Until then, I needed him.

Jesse nodded. "Good to know. I didn't think so, but these folks are to blame for your loss. I'm not sure what I'd do in your shoes."

Most likely, he thought me kinder and gentler than I was. I didn't dispel the ideal right then, but I was afraid he might be unpleasantly surprised if he took a good long look. Deep down, I suspected Jesse Saldana might be a much better person than me.

As we finished our lunch, a thought struck me. "How many people are on the town council?"

Shannon shrugged. "No idea."

"Who's the mayor?" I pushed away from the table and went to the fridge for bottled water. If we were doing this, we needed to be prepared.

"Reverend Prentice," she said.

"Your grandfather." It wasn't a question. Chance leaned forward, finally seeming interested in the conversation.

Shannon looked embarrassed, hunching her shoulders.

"Yeah, we're what you call a 'founding family.' We can trace our line on my mother's side all the way back to the people who first settled here."

"That's a long time," Jesse said mildly.

Something about that revelation nagged at me, but we didn't have time to pursue it. We needed to get into the woods before the day got any later. Jesse insisted we take a couple of backpacks stocked with crackers and water, just in case. Chance added a flashlight.

I changed into old jeans and a faded sweatshirt, layered that with a light jacket, and then put on battered sneakers. The others donned similar uniforms, and then we were ready. Butch trotted after us, so I paused.

"You want to come?"

The dog gave an affirmative yap.

"Promise not to run off this time?"

I swore he sighed. Then he barked once to confirm his good intentions. Before adopting this attitudinal Chihuahua with his lion-sized heart and spiked collar, I had no idea dogs could have so much personality. Half smiling, I picked him up and stepped outside to gaze at the nearby tangle of trees.

Though it was daylight, the forest cast long shadows. Spanish moss hung like spiderwebs, making the woods look even more foreboding. Scaly-bark cedar, white hickories, red maple, sycamore, sassafras, and black gum trees grew here. I'd come to know this wood too well the night my mother died. The hickories, maples, and sycamores guarded the perimeter, and as the terrain grew wetter, they gave way to bald cypress and giant tupelo, but if you found yourself that far in, you most likely wouldn't find your way out again.

On most of the trees, the leaves had turned but not fallen. When the wind kicked up, it carried a desiccated rustle like dying things, and it made me think of the ghosts that whispered in Mr. McGee's radio. The air was heavy with brine and a hint of threatening rain, like a fine static shock lifting your hair a whisper off your neck. It had been a wet November compared to what I remembered as typical. September and October were normally dry and sunny, as I recalled, true Indian summer.

That was very different from where I lived now. In Mexico, spring was the hottest time of the year. If you weren't careful, you could run out of water with the city on rationing. I'd once needed to call a private water truck to refill my tank when I hadn't noticed a slow drip from my outdoor tap. Then, when summertime—rainy season—rolled around, you could set your watch by afternoon storms. Sometimes hail pinged down on the passing cars, filling the air with the wet rush of tires and a peppery serenade. Like a listing iron rooster weather vane on top of a farmhouse, my memories of this place carried a tarnished patina of fear and darkness, making me more reluctant to do what I knew needed to be done.

Shit, I hoped I was brave enough for this. I could sense the thing's sharpening prickle of attention, like it had been watching us the whole time, and now it knew something interesting was about to happen. I started to think better of this idea. I mean, the forest was huge, right? How did we think we could find anything at all in there?

Before I could drown in fear and doubt, the other three filed out, and we set off. Since he'd been there with me, Jesse led the way, Shannon and I walked in between, and Chance brought up the rear. I was pretty sure the guys had come up with that to try to protect us. I doubted it would work, but I appreciated the intent.

As we stepped into the trees, the air chilled markedly.

Behind me, Shannon shivered and pressed closer. "I haven't been out here since last year."

When that kid went missing. She didn't need to provide context; I understood her fear.

The trees loomed over us, bleak and skeletal. Like a lattice of graying bones, the limbs twined heavy overhead. Underfoot, fallen branches crackled as we walked. Ordinarily, silence didn't bother me, but here, it did. There were no birds, no small animals nearby. I told myself it was just the season, but I drew the lapels of my jacket together nonetheless.

"Ideas on where to start?" Jesse asked.

I didn't have any. None of our talents offered any help for this situation. Chance's luck wasn't working at all; Jesse might be able to find survivors; Shannon could only talk to the dead, if—

"We need to go back," I said excitedly. "I have an idea."

To my amazement, they didn't ask, but just tromped back the way we came. They waited outside while I ran in. When I returned, I was carrying John McGee's old radio. Shannon recoiled when she saw what I had, but Chance and Jesse looked intrigued.

"What did you have in mind?" Saldana asked as we retraced our steps.

"I was thinking maybe Shannon only had trouble with John McGee because they"—whoever *they* were—"knew we were trying to talk to him before he died. So they did a little afterlife damage control."

Chance nodded to show he was following. "But to forbid her from communicating with all spirits around these parts would take a major working."

"And I don't think we're up against that kind of magickal mojo. If we were, we'd be looking at sendings such as we had in Laredo, and so far, it's been minor stuff. If there *is* a black coven here, I don't think they have much juice."

"That makes sense," Jesse agreed, "and it fits the pattern."

"What do you want me to do?" Shannon gazed at me wide-eyed, as if worried the trouble she'd had before would revisit itself on her.

That wasn't good; she needed to face that fear, or she'd never get past it. Maybe these scary-ass woods weren't the best place for it, but our enemies wouldn't be able to target a spell if we kept moving; hence the big advantage to doing this on the fly.

"You knew Rob," I said carefully. "There's a good chance you can get in touch with him and maybe he can guide us to his body."

Chance nodded. "That's better than roaming around blindly."

"But if you feel anything's wrong, stop before it gets too tough, okay?"

She considered for a moment and then said, "I'll give it a shot." With some reluctance, she took the radio from me, flicked it on, and started messing with the tuning dial. Her eyes closed as she focused.

The antique radio crackled, hissing as she went point by point along spectral frequencies. Around us, the chill increased, eddying around us in currents that I imagined as spirits drawn to the power she exuded. Such unearthly cold could only come from a complete dearth of life. It reminded me of the shades that nearly drained me dry in Texas; I couldn't repress a shiver.

"Cold—," whispered a fuzzy voice through the old speakers. The person sounded young, frightened. "Shannon, I'm cold."

The girl jerked as if she'd been struck. Hearing her name come through like that had to be unnerving. "He's here with us," she whispered. "Should I ask him?"

Christ, how was I supposed to mentor this girl? The dead were *not* my forte. I had to put her in touch with someone via the Area 51 message board as soon as I could. She needed help and training I simply couldn't provide.

"Ask him where he is," Chance said quietly.

There was no response, so I guessed the rest of us didn't exist for him. One answer about how her ability worked, at least. I'd never met anyone who did what she did in exactly this way.

"Are you okay?" I asked, anxious. "No drain like when you called Mr. McGee?"

She shook her head. "It's normal this time. Just weird because"—she shrugged—"I knew him. It's . . . different."

But she braced herself for the next bit, likely knowing it would be difficult, and asked, "Do you know where you are, Rob?"

"I'm in the woods," he answered at once.

Jesse whispered to me, "She's a lodestone for them. It's uncanny, isn't it? I think they tune in to her just as she uses the radio to tune in to them."

I agreed with a silent nod, letting Shannon work.

"You've been out here a long time," she told him gently. "Can you show me exactly where? I'd like to bring you home. Your mom is worried."

There was a long silence, and then: "I'm dead, aren't I?"

How could he not know? I flinched, thinking he might freak out. But the girl merely replied, "Yeah. Sorry."

Even through the old, tinny speakers, his answer sounded wistful. "I'm glad you made it out. I always liked you, Shannon."

Her eyes looked so old in her small face. "I liked you too, Rob. I need you to lead me to where you died. Can you do that?"

"I—yeah. It's a ways from here," he told her.

"Just give me the directions," she assured him. "We'll get you out, I promise."

Thus followed one of the most chilling hours I've ever experienced; two kids, one of them dead, communicating via a decrepit transistor radio, as we trekked through the tangle of trees. Sometimes we hacked away at the undergrowth in order to pass where Rob's spirit said we must. I think Chance shared my latent fear we might be walking into a trap, but we kept pushing forward because I couldn't think what else to do.

I had to trust in Shannon and her gift. It was damn hard, even for a believer like me. Now I knew how other people must feel when I presented them with some inexplicable truth from touching their father's pocket watch.

The unnatural cold sank into my very bones, making my joints ache. Only the fingers of my right hand contained any heat, still burning from their immersion in the soil. Pain accompanied that warmth, of course, but everything had its price.

Gradually, the ground sloped downward, leading toward a deep gully. I knew what we'd find at the bottom, but we climbed down nonetheless. The radio popped and hissed, revealing Rob's agitation as we grew closer.

Overhead, the trees grew tight overhead, giving the gorge a bizarre greenish hue reminiscent of corpse flesh. My companions looked sick and strange in the primeval half-light. I braced myself for the smell I associated with dead bodies, but I detected only the dank vegetation surrounding us.

"Here." The distant voice crackled from the radio, telling us we'd reached our destination.

The rest would be up to us.

At first I didn't find what we were looking for, as dead leaves littered the forest floor. Shannon knelt, then brushed away some of the desiccated kudzu shroud, and I saw the pallid glimmer of bone. The rest of us joined her in uncovering his final resting place.

A hush fell as we worked, different than the eerie stillness signifying the absence of all life. This silence felt reverent. I'd been wrong, though. We couldn't tell how this kid died. Thanks to scavengers and insects, there was nothing left but his skeleton.

We backed off so Jesse could take a look. Among all of us, he had the most expertise. He spent a few moments studying the remains, and then glanced up with a regretful shake of his head.

"Based on his posture, I'd say the kid died from a fall," he said, pointing to damage on the skull. "To me it looks like he dashed his head on the way down, but I'm just guessing. It would take someone more skilled than me to be sure."

I exchanged a wry look with Jesse. The chances of Kilmer possessing a bona fide forensics expert were less than the possibility of my morphing into a six-foot supermodel. I hadn't expected this, but I guess I should have. A year was a long time for a body to lie exposed.

"We could try asking him," Chance offered.

Shannon didn't look eager, but she said, "Rob, do you remember what happened? How you—"

"Died?" the spirit filled in. "I was running. Scared. That's all I know." The radio popped with his frustration.

"What now?" Shannon sounded anxious. "I promised we'd get him out."

Would a blessing and a proper burial be enough to usher his spirit where it needed to go? I wished Chuch were here; he might know. I made a mental note to call him when we got back to the house.

"We will," Chance said, reassuring her. "We just have to decide the best way to go about it."

Saldana rummaged through his backpack, cursing beneath his breath. "I wish I had flags," he muttered. "We need to mark the site somehow."

"Was anyone paying attention to the route we took?" I asked.

"I was," Jesse answered. "I can get us back here again. But maybe . . ." He pulled out his cell phone and tried about six different angles before pocketing it with a huff of disgust. "Nothing," he growled. "What the hell is wrong with this place?"

I really wished I knew. Or rather, I knew *what* was wrong, but I wished I knew *why*.

It went without saying that Shannon couldn't use her radio trick once we'd notified the authorities. The girl didn't want to leave, but we had to get Sheriff Robinson out here somehow. We couldn't scoop up the bones and deliver them to Rob's family. With our reputation, that would be the last straw.

Shadows curled around my peripheral vision. My skin prickled with awareness of the otherness that chased Jesse and me all the way to the forest edge. It was here now.

Eager as I was to get out of these woods, I suspected that if we walked away now, Rob's remains would disappear in a malicious game of hide-and-seek. There'd be nothing to show for the sheriff's trouble, making him unlikely to believe us ever again. We might need his goodwill down the line. Of course, I could only gauge our moves by Jesse's impression that Sheriff Robinson was scared, not a conspirator.

"I'll stay," I said quietly. "It seems quiet enough right here. It won't take you more than three or four hours to get back."

I expected an argument, but instead, Chance said, "Not by yourself. We can break into teams. Jesse knows the way back, and Shannon knows the town, so they should go. I'll stay with you."

He clearly intended to fight whatever might be coming for us, even if he didn't have his luck. I wasn't sure what lived in the woods *could* be combated with fists or feet. No point in saying so, however; Chance hadn't been here with Jesse and me, so he didn't know how it felt.

Jesse hesitated, obviously remembering our previous ordeal. "I don't like it," he finally said. "But it makes sense. We need a cover story."

"We were hiking," I suggested, kicking my backpack. "And we came across the body."

Coincidental, sure, but as concerned citizens, we just wanted to make sure the poor kid got a proper burial. We might even get some good press out of this.

"And I knew he was missing," Shannon put in. "So I figured it must be Rob, and"—she bent down, checking something—"I confirmed it with his class ring."

"Well done." Jesse looked seriously impressed.

"You should go tell Rob's mother first," Chance suggested. "If she goes with you to see the sheriff, he won't be able to say no."

I agreed with that too.

Jesse took me aside, a good thirty yards away and behind some trees. He grasped my forearms in his big hands.

His palms slid up and down as if chafing me to keep warm. "If anything goes wrong, Corine, I'll know. We'll come back. But *damn*, I don't want you doing this."

"I'll be fine," I said. "If it wanted to hurt me, it would have before."

I didn't completely believe it, but he needed to hear it in order to walk away. Jesse kissed my forehead and my cheeks, and then he brushed my lips with his, as if in benediction. His touch sent a sweet little shock through me, and then we rejoined the others. Chance gave me a cool, measuring look.

A whispery echo spilled out of the radio, making me jump. I'd forgotten about Rob's spirit. "Thanks, Shannon. Will you tell my mom I love her and . . . I'm sorry?"

I never knew regret could have a scent until that moment, but it spilled from the ghost like burnt almonds. So many opportunities lost, possibilities denied, and for what? He probably didn't even remember if he'd had fun sneaking off in the woods to drink cheap liquor with his classmates.

"Yeah," she whispered.

But she would couch his words in ways a regular person could comprehend. *I'm sure Rob loves you and he's sorry you were worried, but he's in a better place now. I'm so glad I could give you closure.* Such normal condolences and comforts could hide the reality of who we were and what we could do. I totally understood her bleak look and gave her a brief hug to show I did.

All too soon, Shannon and Jesse took off, leaving Chance and me alone in the woods.

Burning Visions

Chance and I sat at either side of what had been Robert Walker, aged seventeen.

The bones lay between us.

I stared at them, blind and unseeing, until something occurred to me. Though they had once supported life, these were inanimate now. Maybe we *could* find out what had happened to Rob Walker without a forensic team. My sore fingers flexed. If I did this, I'd have to use my left hand.

Did I really want to cripple myself? Well, if we could do some good with the information, then yeah, I'd risk it.

Chance followed my gaze with his, and I saw the exact moment he realized what I meant to do. He reached for my wrist too late. My left hand made contact with the bones.

There was nothing, not even a small shock of pain. I felt only the cool and pitted surface where scavengers had gnawed. Surprise washed over me.

"There was nobody to imprint them," Chance guessed, as I drew my hand away. "The occasional nibble of wild animals wouldn't do it."

I conceded that with a nod. "I should have thought of that."

"Truthfully," Chance said, "I'm glad it didn't work."

"Truthfully?" I repeated. "Me too."

It felt oddly like we were keeping vigil for Rob. There were no candles or holy words, but the intent remained. He'd been out here alone too long. I wondered—could he see us or sense us? I already knew he couldn't hear anyone but Shannon. Was that all that awaited us? A lonely afterlife filled with tormenting glimpses of the living?

A heavy, sorrowful feeling came over me, too much work to move. From that point, I must have daydreamed. I didn't think I had spoken to Chance in a while. He seemed to be feeling that same pressure, as if it would be easier just to topple over.

Lethargy trickled through me, weighting my limbs with lead. *So tired.* I wanted to curl up on my side and go to sleep. Through layers of exhaustion, I knew a spike of alarm. This wasn't like me. I wouldn't doze off in the middle of a scary wood. Nearly too late, I recognized the swirling darkness around us, deeper and darker than any shadow.

It carried with it the faint scent of decay and decomposition, not of meat, but of vegetation. The smell was pungent, but not revolting. I breathed it in, feeling dizzy. I forced my eyes open—or thought I did—but I couldn't seem to move. Fear slalomed through me like an Olympic event. The heaviness all around us increased.

Shit, we hadn't accomplished anything at all by staying. It would devour the bones and this time, us too. The futility enraged me; I couldn't even turn my head to see if Chance was all right. If anything happened to him because he'd wanted to protect me . . . damn. I should have insisted he go with the others. He was helpless without his luck, and I should have thought of that.

"What do you want?" I managed to push the words past numb lips.

Tendrils so cold they burnt brushed my lips and cheeks in an unholy caress. I couldn't sense malice in the touch, but I was damn near freezing to death. It was possible my brain no longer functioned at peak efficiency.

"This is my dominion, darling child."

With an inward shudder, I recognized the voice from the last time. Any last shred of uncertainty dissolved. I imagined a certain cloying fondness in the endearment it spoke, and I remembered the dark thing had claimed to know my mother.

"I was granted this territory in a pact I have honored even when others have not. So what do I want? I want redress."

Pact. The word resonated, lending unmistakable significance. It confirmed what I half suspected when first we discovered Chance's luck didn't work here.

"Who made the pact?" As the dark mist roiled away from me, it grew easier to speak. I even managed to turn my head, but Chance seemed to be asleep. I told myself not to make any sudden moves. This thing might take pleasure in talking to me—and then it might decide it would enjoy rending me limb from limb. *Best not to provoke it.*

"The twelve," it said, "long since gone to dust."

If they'd long since gone to dust, how did they manage to burn down our house? I wouldn't start with that, though. Part of me couldn't believe I was sitting there, talking to the thing, but I didn't have much choice. Though I could speak and turn my head, I still couldn't get up. Certainly I couldn't run, not with Chance comatose.

Since it seemed to be in an expansive mood—and who knew how long that would last—I asked the obvious question. "Why did you have my mother's necklace?"

Icy phantom fingers lingered at my throat. I imagined it tracing the curls and curves of the flower pentacle and tried to suppress a shiver.

"I was fond of her," it answered at length. "I had a forest creature bring it to me. I kept it for you. . . . I *remember* you, darling child. She asked me to keep you safe."

She asked. It could only mean Cherie Solomon, my mother.

Demons lied. It was what they did. So I don't know why the words rocked me so much. I should have been able to shake them off, dismiss them as false. Instead, they ate into my psyche. Perhaps it was because I'd recently seen how little Chance knew his own mother. No matter how much we loved, how could we ever truly know anyone else's heart?

"How . . ." I cleared my throat and started again. "How did you know her?"

"She left gifts sometimes. She knew I was lonely." The earth itself shivered a little with the last word.

Could that be true? Had my mother been kind enough even to take pity on an exiled demon? Well, exiled or bound. It said it was granted these woods as its territory, but in exchange for what? What were the terms of the agreement? If I thought it would answer honestly, I might ask.

Instead, I asked something that had been bugging me. "How come you let us go before?"

"Darling child, I would never harm you."

Huh? "Why not?"

Its amusement rippled all around me. "Have you not guessed? Hadn't you noticed the hell fire that powers your rather unusual gift?"

Oh, Jesus. I had a feeling I wasn't going to like this.

"Corine . . . I am your father."

"Bullshit!" I might not remember much about Albie Solomon, but I was sure he hadn't been a demon. Maybe he couldn't put up with being tied down or my mother's eccentricities, but he hadn't possessed a drop of infernal blood. I'd stake my soul on it.

Well, maybe not literally . . .

"Kidding. I'm *kidding*. I always wanted to say that." To my astonishment, the dark mist coalesced into the shape of a small man, not much taller than me. He hunkered down next to me. I didn't know if that was good or bad. "Between you and me, little one, I get tired of the whole I-will-devour-your-soul routine. Sure, I feed off the visceral terror, but where's the spontaneity, you know?"

"Uh, right," I said. "So what's your name?"

He answered scornfully, "Do you think I was summoned

yesterday? First I give you my name and we're talking and having a good time; then you bind me to something worse than this forest. Forget it. You can call me Maury."

I stifled a laugh. "Okay then, Maury. Did you kill this kid?"

The demon seemed affronted. "Certainly not."

I raised a brow, waiting. Maybe that was true, but it wasn't the whole truth. I knew enough about demons to be sure they told you whatever they thought you wanted to hear.

"He might've been fleeing from me in fear," the demon admitted, after a lengthy pause, "but the *fall* killed him."

Semantics. No wonder attorneys and demons got along so well.

In quasi-human form, the bane of my existence was short and dumpy, a little round about the middle. He had bushy salt-and-pepper hair and robust sideburns. The demon could've easily been someone's uncle. And I realized I wasn't scared anymore, not even a little bit. That could've been a failure of some self-preservation instinct, but I was inclined to believe the thing didn't mean me any harm.

I just didn't know why.

"Seriously, why aren't you terrorizing me?"

He looked at me in disgust. "Because I don't want you to die."

"But *why*?"

"You're my ticket to freedom," he said.

Direct questioning didn't seem to be getting me anywhere, so I tried another tack. "Who were the twelve?"

"The ones who summoned me."

"How long ago was that?"

Maury shrugged. "How would I know? I spend my time in a forest. Do you see a clock out here?"

"Corine!" Booke's voice boomed out of nowhere.

That was my first clue I wasn't awake. "What are you doing here?"

Our contact in the UK came toward me through the woods. "I don't think you should be here with me right now," he told me. I remembered he'd said he could find me anywhere in the world. "And it doesn't feel like real sleep; something's wrong with it."

He touched my cheek gently—

—and I snapped awake.

Chance cradled me close, his face livid with worry. "Are you all right? You've been out for ages."

"Cold," I managed to whisper.

Damn, was I ever. For the second time that day, I found myself lying in the dirt, this time on a bed of decomposing leaves, next to a pile of bones. But at least I had Chance underneath me. I gazed up the heavy lattice of tree limbs overhead and couldn't tell how long I'd been out. Butch whined and licked my cheek.

"All right, I've got you," he murmured. He took my hand between both of his, chafing the skin. I could hardly feel it at all.

"Talked to a demon named Maury." Or had I dreamed that? Had I dreamed about Booke saving me? I licked my lips and my tongue stuck. It took me a couple tries to get out, "It must've been a nightmare for you. I'm sorry."

No working phone. No luck. I couldn't imagine his fear.

"Don't worry about me," he said. "Here, drink a little." Chance held a water bottle to my mouth, and my throat ached as I swallowed. "Stay with me. Don't close your eyes. Tell me about this demon. Did you really say Maury?" From his tone he was humoring me.

I refused on principle to answer questions when I knew he didn't believe me. I tried to struggle upright.

"I'm better; fine, in fact. What time is it?"

Before he could answer, I heard the crunch of footsteps. Thank God—the cavalry had arrived at last.

When Sheriff Robinson, Jesse, Shannon, and three people I didn't know strode down the slope and into the gully, I'd never been so happy to see other human beings in my life. Mrs. Walker had insisted on coming along with Sheriff Robinson and the two men he'd drafted to accompany him.

When the woman recognized his class ring, as Shannon had, she sank down on her knees and wept.

It would likely take them hours longer to deal with the situation, but Chance conferred briefly with Jesse, probably telling him I'd had another one of my "episodes," which made me sound nuttier than a fruitcake. Jesse agreed I needed to get home, get warmed up, and eat something. He slanted a hard look at me, as if he suspected something had happened that we weren't telling, but he had yards of red tape to deal with.

Butch tucked under his arm, Chance set off with me through the woods for home—well, our temporary one, anyway. My real home was warm and sun drenched. I hoped I still had it when all this was over.

I missed the pawnshop. I missed good tacos al pastor. I missed Tia, the local *curandera* who had a stall on market days. I missed the peace.

Nothing bothered us on the way out of the forest. Maybe Maury figured he had tormented me enough.

When we came trudging out of the woods and across the yard, Butch was happy as hell to see the house. He yapped like a wild thing and wagged his tail until Chance put him down and let him run. I gave him a quick pat on my way to take a hot bath. Forget a shower—I intended to soak away the cold that had seeped into my very bones.

By the time I got out of the tub, my skin was pink and wrinkled. I dried off on one of our contraband towels, got dressed, and went to look for Chance.

To my amazement, he'd made soup for me. Just bouillon and rice, but I'd never known him to cook before. I arched a brow, standing in the kitchen doorway.

"Did you think I was dying?" I asked.

Without turning, he answered in neutral tones. "Yes."

"Oh, Chance."

He spun, slamming his hand against the cupboard. "We're done, do you understand me? I can't take this. We don't even know what we're fighting, and I'm sick of seeing you nearly kill yourself when I can't do a goddamn thing to protect you. Are you *trying* to punish me, Corine?"

I found myself smiling. It would only make things worse, but I couldn't stop my lips from curving up. Chance was losing his temper. *Chance.* I didn't dare speak for fear I'd laugh out loud. Instead, I sat down, trying to compose my face.

"Is this funny to you?" he demanded, shoving my bowl of soup across the table.

"A little," I admitted. "Your clothes are dirty and wrinkled. Your hair's a mess. Your luck doesn't work for shit here, and I'm apparently driving you crazy. So why are you sticking around?" I spooned up some broth, waiting for his answer.

The simple soup was good, exactly what I needed. It soothed my sore throat. I picked up the bowl, forsaking the spoon, drained the broth, and then scraped up the rice.

He hesitated, seeming unsure of himself. "Because I promised you I would."

Ah. My smile faltered. I didn't like remembering how I'd bound him, making him promise to come here with me in exchange for my help in finding his mother.

I leveled a look on him. "You can go. I release you of all obligation to me."

Chance shook his head, dropping to his knees beside me. His inky hair was tousled, windblown, and his cheekbones seemed sharper than usual, as if he hadn't been eating. I hadn't paid that much attention before now.

"I won't leave you," he promised. "Not for all the spirits and demons in the world. I will stand with you." His voice softened then. He reached out, stroking the loose, damp mass of my hair. "I don't know what to do here, though. I'm not used to being unable to impact events. I'm not used to being powerless. I *hate* it."

An ache started in my chest. I couldn't imagine the old Chance confessing this to me in a million years. He'd rarely talked about his feelings. He never shared himself. This

Chance knelt on a battered Linoleum floor and gazed up at me as if I were his sun, moon, and stars, wrapped up in one slightly bedraggled package.

Oh God. I didn't know whether I could survive him a second time. I couldn't speak for the pounding of my heart. A multitude of words crowded my throat, and I couldn't decide which ones to use.

He took in my stillness and went on speaking, doggedly, I thought. "It seems everyone in the place is more use to you than I am. I hate that too. But even weak, even useless, I will not leave you."

"You're not useless. You're not weak, either."

Before he could press for more, Jesse and Shannon came in. They made toast and dished up some of Chance's consommé. The girl sat down across from me, thin and pale, but seeming no worse for wear. It occurred to me then that we looked oddly like a family, sitting around the table in this worn, outdated kitchen.

"Did someone check the wards?" Jesse asked.

Chance stood up. "I'll do it. You two eat. Be right back."

While he was gone, I explained what had happened in the woods. Both Jesse and Shannon wore a frown when I finished.

"That's so not cool," she said, "knowing that thing can put a brain freeze on you in the woods anytime it wants."

I considered that. "Have you ever heard of that happening to anyone else?"

She shook her head. "But people don't always live to tell, either."

"Comforting." Jesse eyed me over the rectangle of bread he was munching. "I knew there was something wrong, but it didn't seem like the time to ask."

"I appreciate that. We don't need any more attention from Sheriff Robinson. How's Rob's mom doing?"

Shannon studied her hands. "She was pretty busted up, but I think she was glad too—to finally have an answer."

I could feel good about what we'd accomplished, then. It

was worth spending a little time with a demon to put a mother's uncertainty at rest. Now at least she could start grieving instead of clinging to false hope.

"Wards are solid," Chance reported, coming back into the kitchen.

"Do me a favor?" I asked Shannon.

"Sure, what's up?"

"Bring me the Bible we stashed earlier."

Her expression brightened. "Are you going to handle it?"

I couldn't help smiling back. "Seems like somebody ought to."

Shots in the Dark

The girl crossed the black-and-white linoleum in a shot. Within seconds, she was back, worn leather book in hand. I despised handling two objects in the same day because the next day I wouldn't be able to touch anything without paying the price. But sometimes it was worth it. November was rushing to a close—it would be Thanksgiving soon—and then December would start trickling away. I had a bad feeling we didn't want to be there on the winter solstice. We needed to complete our business and make our getaway before then.

That meant doing my part. With a faint sigh, I put my uninjured hand on the good book and closed my eyes. It took longer than I'd expected to relax my guard; I was even more reluctant than usual to do this—and that was saying something.

To my surprise, there was nothing significant about the book. There were only simple images about where it had been manufactured. Some concerned evangelical type had given it to Farrell—and only that person's profound faith had left much of a charge at all. The item hadn't been special to the gas station attendant after all.

When I opened my eyes, I found Jesse, Chance, and Shannon regarding me expectantly. I shook my head. "Dead end."

"Damn," Jesse muttered.

I sympathized with his frustration, as I would very much like to know why there was a demon in those woods, what pact he was talking about, who made it, why, and what it had to do with my mother's death. It didn't seem likely anyone would volunteer those answers, so we'd have to force the truth out of folks.

"That wasn't as exciting as I'd hoped," Shannon said.

I grinned at her. "Between you and me, your gift is way more impressive. You could make a TV show out of it, if you really wanted to."

"That would be wicked."

Jesse frowned at me. "I wholly advise against that, Shannon. We've stayed healthy by keeping a low profile for the last four hundred years."

"Like anyone would believe it wasn't fake."

The girl had a point. I listened to them bicker for a bit before I remembered the scrap of paper that had been in the Bible, marking the verse numbers Farrell had haphazardly painted over on his front door. So I flipped to that page. Chance was watching me, and I think he knew what I intended, but he seemed resigned to letting me take all manner of risks.

After scanning the poem penned in Mr. McGee's crabbed handwriting, I sealed my hand atop the page. Pain shot through my palm and up to my elbow. I moaned, but the scene tore through my barriers, so I had no time to prepare—I was simply yanked in headfirst, whereupon I once more became Curtis Farrell. His immense shame and anger slammed through me. He and Mr. McGee were arguing about something.

They stood in the basement of the library, though what the gas station clerk would've been doing down there, I had no idea. He slammed something down on the workbench and shook his fist at Mr. McGee. The old man didn't back down; he had the air of a man chastising somebody who deserved it.

I focused on his lips. *Don't be an idiot, boy. You could get out of here.* I wasn't sure about all of that, but I knew I'd gotten the first bit right, because McGee exaggerated his mouth movements as if he was, in fact, talking to an idiot. And that was all.

My palm throbbed, matching the pain in my other hand. *Great. Nothing like a matched set.* I exhaled in a shuddering sigh and opened my eyes. The others were staring at me in alarmed silence. I had no idea why until I glanced down.

The paper had burnt to ash beneath my fingers.

"That's too much power," Jesse said uneasily.

A hard tremor rocked through me, and I thought I might be sick. It took all of my self-control to battle it down. I knew Jesse suffered everything I did when I handled, and I felt bad for inflicting that on him. At the same time, it was also comforting to know I wasn't totally alone with it, even if I didn't choose to talk about it. It almost seemed like he was beside me on the path.

"Did you get anything helpful?" Chance asked quietly.

"I'm not sure. Shannon, did Curtis Farrell have any kind of personal connection to Mr. McGee?"

"I have no idea. I didn't know him that well, really. But I can find out."

I nodded. "If you don't mind, it might be helpful." In a few words, I summed up what I'd gleaned, which wasn't much when you got right down to it.

More than we had before. My fingers stirred in the ashes and gray motes twirled on the kitchen table. *Nothing like this has ever happened before.* Like Chance, I was wondering where it would stop. My gift had taken a decidedly dark turn.

"No problem," she said.

The others let me fill the silence—or not. I did, by telling them all about the girl I'd glimpsed in the attic and how I thought she'd been Gifted too. They all appeared thoughtful when I finished.

"Kilmer has been producing Gifted for a long time," Jesse murmured. "I don't know what to make of that. It usually runs in family lines."

I nodded. "From what you said, it's more genetic, and it

shouldn't just randomly appear in different families who have never known the likes before."

"Maybe it just skipped a generation or two," Shannon offered. "Like a recessive gene or something."

Chance drew a complex pattern on the kitchen table. "Could be. But that's probably not the whole answer."

"I'm sure," I agreed. "But we won't solve it tonight. We should get some rest."

Shannon slipped from her chair and peered at my hands. A little shiver went through her. "No offense, but I'm glad I don't do what you do."

"Me too." I wouldn't wish that on anyone, not even somebody I didn't like.

"G'night."

Her exit sparked the rest of us into motion. The guys cleared the table, and I made my way down the hall to what had been Chance's room. Since he'd offered it to me, I wasn't going to argue. He could sleep on the couch. I'd done it at Chuch's place, after all.

Crap, that reminded me I'd meant to call the mechanic about Shannon's gift and see if he had any advice. It was too late now. *In the morning.*

Jesse caught up with me before I reached my door. "You can take my room. Chance and I are switching off on the couch, and it's my turn."

Such gentlemen. But I just gave a weary nod and turned my steps in that direction. To my surprise, he followed me. When I turned, I saw he had the salve; it was good he remembered, or I would have paid for it in the morning.

Sitting down on the edge of the mattress, I offered my hands palms up, as if he were trying to arrest me. Amusement flickered in his dark eyes, but he merely knelt and started tending my wounds. His ministrations stung like a bitch, but I bore them with stoicism. This wasn't my first time, after all.

"You are *such* a bulldog," he murmured, tawny-streaked head bent.

"Wow, that's uncommonly sweet talk, even for you."

He offered me a wry half smile. "I meant once you lock your jaws into something, you just don't turn loose. I admire it. If you didn't hate cops so much, you'd make a heck of an investigator."

"I don't hate *you*," I said softly. "It means a lot that you came all this way."

"Yeah?" Jesse skated a thumb down the curve of my cheek to my jaw. The touch sparked gently, and I was starting to see that tiny blue flicker as a sign of connection. It meant after so many years of searching, I'd found somebody like me. "I'd love to pull you up against me until we both stop hurting."

"But you won't."

He shook his head. "I promised Chance I'd back off if he did."

"Like I told him . . . thanks."

"God, Corine, you've put me through more in a few days than Heather did in a whole year—and *she* was half crazy."

"I'm sorry."

"Don't be. I'm not."

After Jesse left, sleep didn't come easy, and I dreamed of laughing demons with hands full of fire.

Potluck

I woke up with both hands shiny with salve. The blisters around the brand on my left palm had gone away entirely, leaving the smooth imprint of the flower pentacle. For a while, I lay there savoring the peace and the softness of the mattress beneath me.

Even minor creature comforts impressed me these days. I'd driven myself long and hard, and I desperately needed a break. But I couldn't relax until we'd finished there. Then I'd go home and ease back into my old routine at the pawnshop. I'd take Shannon with me, if she wanted to come. I even had a spare bedroom. Otherwise, I'd help her get wherever she wanted to go.

Butch bounded in, made the short leap to join me, and curled up beside me. "What do you think?" I asked him. "Do we do more legwork today?"

He yapped in the negative. It seemed he'd had enough of crawling around in the woods. Sadly, he was probably smarter than the rest of us put together.

That day we listened to the dog and didn't move much. To my amusement, the other three joined forces to keep me under house arrest. They didn't want me doing anything more strenuous than sitting on the couch.

For the most part, we passed the time talking with Shannon about the Gifted community. She had a number of questions about the kinds of powers other people had. We explained the way Chance's ability usually worked. I was glad of the quiet, for all it reminded me of the calm before the storm.

In the afternoon, I called Booke to thank him for saving me—and to confirm I wasn't losing my mind. He picked up on the second ring.

"I'm so glad you called," he said.

We then spoke at the same time.

"Did I imagine—"

"What happened to you—"

"It was real," I breathed in relief. "I wanted to thank you."

His deep voice revealed his abashment. "It was nothing." Booke hastened to change the subject. "But I did find something out about the spell components you sent me."

My interest sharpened. "Oh?"

"After a number of esoteric tests, I'm relatively certain it was meant to be used in a binding spell."

"Like to bind demons?" *Unexpected.* Had Sandra been trying to sic a monster on me while I was in the bathroom? That didn't seem sporting.

"No," Booke answered. "If it had worked, it would have prevented you from moving until something more . . . permanent could be done to you."

I cast my mind back to that day. Sandra had seemed insistent that we stay to dinner, and her husband had been quietly miserable. *Plan B?*

"So it would've immobilized me," I guessed. "But something went wrong. Do you have any idea what?"

"If I had to speculate," Booke's tone became a touch pedantic, "well, I'd say it could have been any number of things. The person may not have been skilled enough in the dark arts. It is rather a precise business. The spell may also have failed because there were two of you in a small space she'd guessed would contain only one."

"The not-being-skilled part tracks with our observations here," I said.

"Perhaps they are dabblers." His voice reflected his disdain for such dilettantes. "Did you find anything out about the library?"

Crap, I hadn't even asked. I made a note to check with Shannon. After a few more pleasantries, Booke advised me to take care of myself and disconnected. While I was making calls, I checked in with Senor Alvarez, who assured me everything was fine at the pawnshop. Then I went looking for our resident speaker for the dead.

When she heard what I wanted to know, she said, "Yeah, actually. The library used to be a church, a really long time ago. My grandpa had the new one built in . . ." She thought for a moment. "I'm not sure when, actually, but it was before I was born."

"Thanks."

In late morning, Shannon took a trip with Jesse to find out whether Mr. McGee had any connection with Curtis Farrell. She came back aglow with her success.

"They were related," she said with a bright smile. "I had no idea, but apparently Farrell was Mr. McGee's great-nephew on his mother's side."

"So McGee had a stake in anything Farrell might've been doing."

She nodded. "That's the size of it."

Shannon and I talked all afternoon. Chance holed up in his room, trying some experiment related to his luck. I didn't know what Jesse was doing, but from Butch's excited yapping, they must be playing in the yard. All in all, it was an odd, domestic day. We all came together in the kitchen for dinner, a makeshift meal cobbled together from our survivalist-style supplies.

That evening, I called Chuch's place, intending to see if he knew how to send spirits to their final rest. From the looks of things, Kilmer had a number of restless ghosts. But Eva answered, and she wasn't interested in why I'd called. She had her own agenda.

"Oh my God, I can't believe I haven't talked to you in

weeks! How are you? How's Chance? I heard Saldana took off after you like a bat out of hell. So did you make up your mind yet?"

I laughed as I tried to answer her questions in order. "Well enough, fine, yes, he did, and no, I've had other things to think about."

We talked a little more, and then she dropped a serious bomb on me. "Guess what?" Eva didn't wait for me to guess. "We're having a baby!"

The news hit me hard. I imagined a sweet little boy or girl who would round out the normalcy of their lives. They wouldn't want weirdos like me traipsing in and out; they had a real family to think about now. So distance offered the best solution. Considering Montoya's vendetta could endanger them, I couldn't be sanguine about losing the few friends I had.

"Congrats," I managed to say. "That's fantastic, Eva. When are you due?"

"Summer," she answered, chattering on about needing to see a doctor to get an exact date.

I listened quietly, smiling. When I got a chance, I said, "I really need to talk to Chuch. Can you put him on?"

More small talk, but Chuch wasn't a phone guy, so he asked what I wanted pretty fast. I told him. Jesse came along as I was explaining my question about Shannon's gift and restless spirits, and stood behind me, shamelessly eavesdropping.

Unfortunately, Chuch didn't know. "Sorry, *prima*. That's not my thing. You take care of yourself, okay? I want you here after the baby's born. We're naming you and Chance godparents."

"Really?" That surprised me. I'd expected him to make excuses about why we shouldn't come around anymore.

Then I grinned, thinking I'd figured it out. *Lord, save me from Chuch's matchmaking.* I got off the line quickly after that.

As I turned, Jesse looked thoughtful.

"What?" I asked.

"I can post that question to Area 51," he answered, producing his cell phone.

He had Web access, and inside the house, technology worked just fine. It took him a while to get the message typed on his tiny keypad, but he seemed confident we'd have an answer by morning. That was good; I suspected we'd need it.

I borrowed his phone and looked at the post I'd made requesting a witch to do a cleansing. We had one taker, but she couldn't leave Atlanta for two weeks. That might be too late to do any good, but I slowly typed a thank-you on the message board.

I picked Butch up and went to bed shortly thereafter. You'd think the nightmare would have come like it always did when times got tough. But maybe I'd simply reached my tolerance threshold. Thankfully, my mind shut down, and my sleep was dreamless.

In the morning, I felt ready to tackle whatever might come. We had to be getting close to the end of the line. I took a quick shower and ate a PBJ for breakfast.

Jesse spent the day banging around in the kitchen. Chance was still meditating, or whatever he'd been working on the day before. I suspected it had to do with his confession of how much he hated being helpless. If I had to guess, I'd say he was trying to jumpstart his luck. Shannon listened to whispery music on the old transistor radio; if she was bored, she didn't complain, but she did spend a lot of time looking out the window at the woods.

I spent the day doing laundry. Ever since Mexico City, I'd been living out of a backpack, and I hadn't washed my clothes since we left Chuch's house, weeks ago now. Though we'd picked up a few things on the way here, I still didn't have an extensive wardrobe. Then I had to decide what would be suitable attire for a church social.

Shannon wore black leggings, a plaid skirt, combat boots, and a black T-shirt, layered with a black and white flannel.

I'd never gone through a Goth phase like that, but I could see myself in her, especially the attitude she projected. Deep down she was nothing like she looked at all.

As for me, I chose a demure black peasant skirt, a black camisole, and a black lace sweater. My long red hair streamed over my shoulders, contrasting with the sober attire. Studying myself in the mirror that gave a wavering reflection reminiscent of a fun house, I realized I looked like a witch. All I needed was a pointy hat and a broomstick. As Butch trotted in, I realized I even had a familiar.

Had I intended to do that? To drive home the point about the witch's daughter? Well, I didn't plan to change, so this would have to do.

But I'd sure get my share of attention at the church social.

By early evening, we were ready to go. I stood waiting in the living room, tapping a dainty ballet flat against the hardwood floor. Chance came in, wearing charcoal dress slacks paired with a black and silver striped shirt. He flashed me an admiring look.

"We match." He seemed pleased, reaching out a hand to smooth the hair that fell past my shoulder. "You look gorgeous. Witchy hot."

I felt the sheepish curve to my answering smile. "Too obvious?"

Chance shook his head. "No, it's great. Should be funny."

From her place at the corner of the sofa, legs curled under her, Shannon stifled a snicker. "For sure."

"What's wrong with you people?" Jesse asked. "You don't show up empty-handed." With a grin, he flourished a pan.

I stepped forward for a peek beneath the foil and then blinked at him. "You were making a *cobbler* in there?"

Not being overly domestic, I hadn't recognized what he was doing when I'd wandered in and out. Impressive—he'd baked dessert out of the bare staples we had on hand. Jesse Saldana would make a *great* husband, no doubt about it. For a few seconds, I imagined him in nothing but an apron, but

I didn't know where else to go with that mental image, so I shooed it out.

Jesse playfully smacked my hands away, giving me a little grin. "Yeah. My mama taught me. I have two older brothers, and she got tired of waiting for a daughter."

"So Jesse is short for Jessica," Chance said with a smirk.

Was Jesse's family worried about him? Shit. I had nobody, and Chance had only his mom. We weren't exactly poster children for normal relationships. Maybe that was why we'd gravitated together. I tried to see myself assimilating into what I imagined to be the big, boisterous Saldana clan.

Jesse slapped Chance upside the head in answer as he went out to the Forester.

I glanced down at Butch, who was waiting expectantly by the front door. "You want to come?"

He yapped once.

Why did I bother asking? This dog didn't like letting me out of his sight. Given what he'd been through, I couldn't blame him. There was no point in asking him to behave himself, and he seemed to find the request offensive. It wasn't like he'd ever given me any trouble, apart from the time he'd run off into the woods. I wished he could give me some more insight as to why he'd done that, but we were limited to yes and no questions.

As I headed out; I reflected that it was sweet that Officer Saldana had church-going in his past. That certainly dovetailed with his becoming a cop to fight for truth and justice. Climbing into the front, I realized I could easily fall in love with him.

"I got an answer about the restless dead," Jesse told me, sliding in back. "But we need a witch or a medium to lead us in the ritual."

Well, the witch from Atlanta might be able to take care of that, but I hoped we wouldn't be here in two weeks. So it looked like we were on our own. Given the state of the town, it was probably just as well.

Shannon drove because she knew the way. The guys didn't

seem to mind that we were both in the front, and I figured it was my turn. I brooded all the way to the Methodist church, a sprawling white stone building with an ostentatious steeple.

"Someone's compensating," I muttered. I quite forgot I was talking about Shannon's grandpa.

She cut me a disgusted look. "That's . . . so wrong."

Belatedly, I remembered she had said he had the place built before she was born. The lot was lit up like a bingo parlor in marked contrast to the dark all around the place. Cars crowded the parking lot; some had overflowed to the street and the neighboring field. It seemed everyone who was anyone in Kilmer attended the weekly potluck.

"You guys ready for this?" I asked, hopping down from the SUV. The chill in the night air swirled my words around in a white mist.

"Absolutely," said Chance.

With no forethought, we fell into *Reservoir Dogs*–style formation, with Jesse leading the way. I had to admit, it amused the crap out of me to stroll into this holiest of holy buildings behind a blue-haired septuagenarian. If she hadn't been tiny and doddering, I have no doubt she would have favored us with a sniff and a disapproving glare.

My first thought as we stepped into the hall was, *Who the hell knew there were so many flowered dresses in the world?* Older women stuck to gray, black and white, or navy; young ones ran around in pastels. They were unified by the floral prints.

Men, on the other hand, wore button-up shirts and belted slacks in varying hues. Everyone milled around, talking a mile a minute, while a handful of women fussed over a table laden with food. Kids wove in and out, playing tag around the masses. It was at once completely wholesome and achingly foreign.

Despite the darkness plaguing this town, I sensed such genuine warmth. The normal folk here cared about one another. When a stout, middle-aged lady crossed the room and gave a hugely pregnant young woman a hug, she meant it.

I smiled as she rubbed the woman's stomach. "Oh, you're carrying low this time, Millie. Must be a boy."

The younger woman giggled. "I sure hope so. Dan's out of patience with the girls."

Conversation paused as people noticed us. All of us wore black in some form, but Shannon and I stood out more than the guys. In button-up shirts and dress slacks, they both fell within the bounds of normal for this gathering, even if Chance was one hundred percent more urbane than the elder gentleman wearing polyester pants and a plaid shirt.

Before I could think better of this idea, Jesse took my hand in his and led me toward the buffet. I followed since he qualified as our ranking expert on such occasions. He gave the woman in charge his extra-sweet smile and proffered the pan.

"Here you go." At her questioning look, he clarified. "Peach cobbler. Mrs. Walker invited us here tonight."

I didn't know whether that was true, as Chance had spirited me away before they finished in the forest. Even if it wasn't, her suspicion melted into a warm welcome. A round little pigeon of a woman, she came around the table, practically cooing with delight.

"You're the hikers," she exclaimed. "The ones who found Robert Walker. Oh, mercy me, I'm so glad you came. I heard on the prayer chain all about how you waited with the poor boy out in the woods. Not everyone would've done that." I had no idea what a prayer chain was, but she seemed to think our actions stemmed from respect rather than a fear the corpse would vanish. She couldn't know too much about the secret workings of Kilmer, then.

Jesse made small talk, thanking her for making us feel at home, while Chance and Shannon stood mute. The woman introduced herself as Alice Buckner, chair of the social committee. We shook hands, and I must admit, she seemed genuinely pleased to see us. I wasn't used to that.

Alice pointed out various people of interest from the Who's Who of Kilmer. I recognized Phil Regis, the real estate agent, towering over a truly diminutive woman. Why did giants always go for the daintiest flower they could find? He raised his glass in my direction, and I smiled. His wife caught my gaze and gave a sweet little nod. I spotted Ms. Pettigrew watching them from across the room with sadness in her eyes.

"Have you ever been out to the bar outside town?" I asked Alice, somewhat abruptly, if her expression offered any clue as to her feelings.

"Oh my, no," she said. "I think my Harold has a nip out there every now and again, but it's not really a respectable place."

"Because they sell liquor?" Chance asked. "Or because it's a new business?"

Interesting question. Perspicacious too, I thought. I waited for her answer.

Alice thought about that. "A bit of both? We're not a dry county by any means, but too much drinking leads to"—she struggled for the right word—"shenanigans."

Shannon looked like she wanted to laugh. "What exactly is a shenanigan, Mrs. Buckner?" she managed to ask with a straight face.

The older woman leveled an assessing look on Shannon. "You think you're so clever, missy. But here you are in church again, no matter what you told your grandpa."

If I wasn't mistaken, that qualified as a polite, ladylike burn. I smothered a grin as Shannon lapsed into disgruntled silence. Jesse covered the slight awkwardness with more of his honey-sweet Texas charm.

Alice lapped it up, concluding her admiring remarks. "And here you've brought another lost lamb back into the fold." She nodded at Shannon. "After a row in the middle of the parking lot, she swore she'd never set foot in this church again, oh, four months ago or so. Is there any limit to the good you'll do here in Kilmer?"

Could she be flirting, despite the mention of her husband?

"I never get tired of good deeds," Jesse said with a straight face. He'd probably been a Boy Scout too.

Mrs. Buckner took us onward then, introducing us to every last soul in town. They all professed to be pleased to meet us, so tickled we'd set Mrs. Walker's mind to rest at last. Some of them muttered about the worthless nature of local law enforcement.

By the time we'd been there an hour, I'd received hateful looks from Shannon's mother and her grandfather, Reverend Prentice, but they didn't dare make a scene—not here, not now. But it was coming; I could feel it. Shannon's dad was nowhere to be seen. That worried me.

Concern didn't stop me from enjoying the homemade food: fried chicken, green beans with bacon, sweet potato casserole, ambrosia salad. I slipped bits of chicken to Butch in my handbag. Every now and then he'd growl low in his throat and I'd make a mental note of the person he didn't like. His instincts were excellent.

In this setting, it'd be impossible to poison us, as much as Sandra Cheney would like to. If she didn't want to kill us when we first arrived, she did now. As she saw it, we'd stolen her daughter, but I didn't trust her intentions toward Shannon. Studying Sandra, I suspected the girl had been right to fear. The woman's expression didn't contain maternal concern; instead, it was all thwarted rage. By helping Shannon, we'd interfered with something she planned. Sandra's icy gaze followed me as I wove through the room, tugged by Alice Buckner as if I were a barge.

Single church-going females snagged Chance and Jesse early on; every now and then, they shot me a desperate look, but they needed to man up and pump for information. If I could handle charged objects when my gift had clearly gone haywire, then they could take a few hours with marriage-minded Southern belles.

Shannon stayed close to me. I didn't blame her.

I was about to call the whole endeavor a bust, when I saw a tall, thin figure across the room. The church hall spun, then seemed to recede. *Well, holy shit.* Maybe I went pale, because Shannon clutched my arm.

"What's wrong?" she whispered.

I waved the question away. "Who is that?"

I pointed at the gray-haired man who stood a head above everyone else. It wasn't the real estate agent; Phil was much beefier. This man looked like he lived on pickled beets and malice. And he wore a horseshoe tie tack. Remembering what Miss Minnie had said about the Four Horsemen of the Apocalypse, I knew that couldn't be a coincidence.

Now we had to find the rest. We were looking for twelve total, but I had an idea the others followed the lead of the top four.

Shannon searched the crowd, trying to follow the trajectory of my gaze. In a crush like this, it was impossible, so I described him, leaning toward her so nobody could overhear.

She stared at me, wide-eyed, before answering. "Augustus England. He practically owns the whole town. Why?"

"Of course he does," I muttered. "He's *also* the man who choked Curtis Farrell behind his garage until Farrell promised to do his bidding."

My mother had glimpsed this man pushing back his cowl as she died. She hadn't seen the others—and so neither had I—but I'd never forget. *Oh, blessed day. At long last, our enemy has a face.*

White King

Shannon stilled beside me. Obviously she registered the significance, but she said only, "We need to find Jesse and Chance."

I agreed wholeheartedly; it was time to rescue them from the clutches of a few hopeful Southern belles. We needed to keep an eye on England because I had a feeling he was the key to the whole mess. After thanking Mrs. Buckner for her time in introducing us around, I wove my way through the crowd.

Before we found the guys, I spotted another horseshoe tie tack. I didn't recognize the man who wore it, but I knew his type. He stood just under six feet, but broad and solid, shoulders straining his navy blue suit jacket. His hair had been shorn close to his skull, leaving a salt-and-pepper buzz. I put his age around forty-five, but he had the fit, powerful body of someone who took physical fitness seriously.

When his gaze met mine, I felt a sudden shock of cold. He had a predator's eyes, cool and watchful. I *absolutely* didn't like the way he smiled at me and took a sip of his coffee, as if he knew something I didn't.

I turned to Shannon. "Do you know who that is?"

She followed the cant of my head and made a face. "Mr. Cooper. He's the high school principal, a real tight-ass. I don't know how many times I was in his office last year, just for violations of the dress code. They were always looking in my locker too, as if I'd be dumb enough to take anything to school with me." Then she noticed why I was looking at him. "Shit. He's wearing a horseshoe, just like England."

"So Phipps retired. Where did this guy come from?"

"I dunno." She shrugged. "I never had a reason to give a shit about the high school principal before. Lemme ask around."

I followed her while she made some quiet inquiries, and I noticed that Cooper never stopped watching us. His interest registered like that of a hunter, checking out his prey's behavior patterns, scanning for weaknesses. A shiver ran through me.

Folks were able to tell us the following: Harlan Cooper had grown up here, but unlike most, he'd gotten out of Kilmer for a little while. Again, unlike most who escaped, Cooper returned. He'd apparently spent some time in the military, though nobody knew which branch. When Phipps was near retirement, England had applied pressure to get Cooper hired as school principal, and Cooper had been his man ever since.

"Oh, and he likes to hunt," one matron added. "My husband is always turning down his invitations to go prowling around. Harlan just loves those woods."

Oh, really? Now we had something truly interesting to tell the guys. Chance seemed improbably happy to see us.

He removed a girl's hand from his arm with a polite smile and turned to me. "Are we leaving?"

"We might be," I answered.

As we went to get Jesse, I whispered to him what we'd learned. Chance tilted to get a look at the tall, angular man filling his plate at the buffet table. Augustus England had a subtle air of superiority about him; I noticed as he moved away that he made sure not to brush up against other people.

I also noticed the way Cooper watched England from a distance. To the best of my recollection, I'd seen such vigilance only in those paid for protection. Chance took a look at him too, and then scowled.

"He's a bad one," he muttered. "And he won't go down easy."

Frankly, I was surprised to find the town moneyman at such a function, but when he made for Sandra Cheney, I understood the draw. Her manicured fingers lit briefly on his sleeve, an intimacy he welcomed with a quick, cool pat of his long fingers. *Aha.* I wondered if Shannon's dad knew; his overall misery seemed to indicate he did.

We found Saldana standing in a ring of females, none of whom could've been more than twenty-five years old. They all looked as if they'd like to hit him on the head and take him home to a shotgun wedding. Jesse excused himself as we walked up, but he managed to look reluctant when he did so. His good manners went all the way down to the bone.

Shannon relayed our news, and then he too looked for England. "We're tailing him from here?" he guessed.

I hesitated. I wanted to, but I wasn't sure it was a good idea. Kilmer wasn't a big city, and he'd notice a vehicle departing directly after his and making all the same turns.

"Options?" Chance asked.

"Any possibility you know where he lives?" I asked Shannon.

"Sorry," she said with a touch of bitterness. "My mom never took me along to her monthly meetings at his place."

Jesse asked, "What meetings?"

We all favored him with a "Come on, really?" look.

Shannon said, "The Rotary club."

I saw where she was going with that. "Yeah, her rotating her heels behind his head."

She smirked a little. "Again, I'd rather not imagine that. I've known for a while now. My dad's really bummed about it."

Saldana nudged me. "They're on the move."

I turned to see England heading for the door. Cooper immediately put down his paper cup and headed for the exit; he took his bodyguarding seriously. Sandra must have intended to count to a hundred before following or whatever chicanery they practiced to fool the good church-going souls in Kilmer. Instead, she gave him a full five-minute head start before she began making her excuses. When she pulled her keys out of her handbag, another piece fell into place; she had a horseshoe on her keychain.

"I don't know what we should do," I muttered. "But we can't go home, and—"

"We can't stay here," Chance finished with a half smile.

"Maybe we can tail them to the turnoff," Jesse offered, "but keep going straight and then double back."

"We'll get lost," Shannon predicted. "It's fuckin' dark out there." She looked at us as if she expected us to chide her for her language, but that wasn't a priority for me. Besides, with all the ambient conversation, nobody seemed to have noticed.

That did it. "Let's go, then."

A few people stopped us on the way out, wanting to shake our hands and thank us for finding Rob Walker. I wasn't used to townsfolk reacting to me that way. They weren't even giving the witchy outfit a second glance anymore. I felt oddly out of sorts; I had hated this whole town for so many years, and now I was finding that some of them were genuinely nice people, just making the best of their crappy lives in a terrible town. I didn't like realizing I'd been just as judgmental and intolerant as folks had been to me so often.

As soon as we could, we hurried out to the Forester. While Jesse unlocked the doors, I bounced with impatience. Each second that passed increased our chances of losing Sandra Cheney, who was our only hope of finding England's estate.

My heart nearly stopped when somebody stepped out of the shadows near me. I stumbled back a few steps. Chance slid in front of me in a smooth motion, ready to fight. But then, he'd been looking for a fight ever since we hadn't had sex up against the bathroom door.

"Easy, easy." Dale Graham, still wearing the clothes he'd had on when we bought him coffee, came out into the overhead light, his palms spread. "I don't want anybody else to know I survived the fire, so why don't we get in the car and drive?"

With a quick, furtive look around the parking lot, we did. Jesse got in front with Dale; Chance, Shannon, and I crammed in back. But Jesus, Dale smelled evil. Whatever he'd been doing to lie low hadn't involved personal hygiene. Eyes watering, I cracked the back window and wished I could crawl all the way back to the cargo area.

"You've fingered Sandra and August, am I right?" He rubbed his hands together like a gleeful child. "I have *proof*. And I have the book with me, thank God."

"More important, do you know the way to his place?" Jesse asked.

He'd taken the wheel because Shannon wasn't trained in tailing, but it looked like we'd missed Sandra Cheney. I hadn't seen her leave the parking lot. Dammit. We'd spent too long saying our good-byes to friendly parishioners. At Dale's gesture, Saldana pulled out from the parking lot and onto the road.

"Absolutely," Graham assured us. "I've been following them for weeks, and it's even worse than I thought. In fact, they haven't been conspiring with an alien race to subjugate all humankind."

I blinked and slid a look at Chance, who asked, "What could be worse than that?"

The reporter shifted on the seat, peering at us over his shoulder. "Demons," he whispered. "I think they're summoning demons."

"At least one," I agreed. "And I don't know what we're going to do about it."

"Do you think they're going to summon more? When?" Shannon asked.

Dale sighed. "I wish I knew."

He turned back around then and focused on giving directions to Saldana. The night was black as ink, starless, cloudless. The farther we got from Kilmer, the more my flesh crawled. Shouldn't there be a moon somewhere up there? I thought about what Booke had said concerning the stain upon the astral. Could it be spreading? I wondered if there would come a time when there was no longer any blue in the sky at all; if the town was being slowly sucked elsewhere, so when the odd stranger came by here, there would one day be nothing but a stretch of weirdly empty road.

I shivered, and Chance wound an arm around my shoulders. "Do we trust this guy?" he whispered.

"They burnt down his house," I answered quietly. "They must think he knows *something* incriminating."

"Or they're just crazy," Shannon put in. "I know my mom is."

I couldn't argue that, and there was no point in speculating. We'd be there soon enough—and I'd rather not breathe any more than I absolutely had to.

"We'll have to park here," Dale said abruptly. "We're going in the back. I know a way around the fences."

"Are they electric?" Jesse asked.

The reporter shook his head. "No, but he has dogs."

"Of course he does," Chance muttered.

I glanced down at my skirt. Well, at least I was wearing black, but if I'd known ahead of time, I probably would have dressed down a little. We pulled off the road just inside a stand of trees. It offered basic cover for the SUV, but it wouldn't stand up to prolonged scrutiny. The good news was, most of Kilmer was at the Methodist church.

We hiked a short way past the road and into the field. To get through Dale's gap in the fence, we had to crawl. My sweater caught, but Jesse unhooked me before it could tear. I flashed him a smile as the others came past.

"Which way to the house?" Jesse whispered.

At first I wasn't sure why the hushed voices, and then I realized our words would carry twice as far in the still night air. It was so dark I had a hard time seeing anything, let alone minute gradations on the ground. Dale led the way with surety, which I hoped came from frequent reconnaissance, not from being England's secret minion. Burning down his house seemed extreme for a cover story, though.

As we crossed the hilly field, we didn't talk. A somber mood had fallen upon us, driving home the idea that we were trespassing. Anything could happen to us out there. Death didn't have to come from some exotic source. A knife or stray bullet would do the job more permanently than any of us liked. Butch whined a little in my bag, and I gave him a reassuring stroke.

As we crested what Dale said was the final hill, a mansion worthy of a Gothic novel sprawled before us. I took in the mullioned windows, graven arches, and the crumbling, ornate stonework. We stood closest to the back door, or the servants' entrance.

Maybe that would be our ticket in; I just didn't know how yet. Not for the first time, I wished I had my mother's affinity for real magick, not just a touch that crippled me whenever I used it. Wouldn't it be awesome if I had a bag of tricks full of prepared spells? Chance could pick the lock, but what would we say to the cook? A concealment or disguising charm would have come in handy right about now.

Too bad I wasn't a witch.

"We can't just stand here. Anybody looking out those windows"—Jesse gestured at the upper stories—"could see us. Let's take cover." He led the way toward the hedges.

Because I couldn't think of a better plan, I followed.

Once we were hidden, I noticed Chance craning his neck to get a better look at the symbols etched into each stone that composed the arches. I looked too, figuring it might be important. And then it clicked.

"They match the ones on the library," I whispered.

Shannon added, "Which used to be a church."

"They're Rosicrucian," Dale put in.

Hey, I could show off my Booke learning. "But they also draw from the Emerald Tablet of Hermes."

The conspiracy theorist looked suitably impressed. "Oh, excellent." He took a notebook out of his man purse and scrawled something.

Saldana's leashed aggravation added a lovely edge to his Texas drawl. "I don't mean to interrupt the ramblin' about architecture, but unless you have a point to make, I think we need to focus elsewhere. Otherwise, the butler's gonna come out this back door and find us squattin' in the bushes."

"I do have a point to make," Chance said, unexpectedly, and with a hint of steel in his tone. "Our technology worked at the library. My *luck* worked at the library—"

"Which means it might work here," I breathed. "We're right under the sigils."

Chance favored me with a smile. "Exactly. So how about I concentrate on finding us a way in there?"

Sounded good to me.

Shannon didn't really know what we were talking about. Chance had been mundane for all the time she'd known him, and Dale squinted at us like he thought we were crazier than him. That took some doing.

As Chance focused, the air seemed to thicken around us, as if charged with electricity. I could feel the hairs on my arms prickling. Yep, his gift was definitely working here, and it seemed stronger than ever. Could it have built up power from not being used? An interesting question, but I needed to take a few steps away from him. I didn't want to see what would happen if the bad-luck polarity had ramped up too.

It occurred to me I ought to put Butch down and see if he could find anything useful as we walked. I slipped him out of my purse, set him on the ground, and said, "Sniff the place out, but don't rush off."

He gazed up at me with big bulging eyes. Though he didn't bark, he gave the impression of understanding me. How had the not-so-bright security guard wound up with a genius dog anyhow? The Chihuahua trotted along beside me, snuffling in the flowerbeds.

"This way." Chance followed his luck as if it were a lodestone.

We circled the house, staying low and close to the walls. I didn't want to risk getting too far from the protective runes and having his talent kick off like cheap cable TV. Midway around, Butch stopped, sneezed, and pawed at the ground.

I knelt to see what he had. Jesse dropped to his knees beside me. Dale shone a key chain penlight over the area, and with sure hands, Jesse raked the topsoil, examining the herbs. "Looks like the remnants of ward preparations, but not the general kind, like we learned from Chuch."

My brows went up. "Maris?" That was his now-deceased ex-girlfriend, who had been a talented and powerful witch before a warlock murdered her to prevent her from telling us what she knew. "So, what's this used for?"

He nodded. "To prevent demons from crossing your threshold."

That served as confirmation that England was in this mess up to his neck, not that I'd needed it. I trusted my mother's memories, but others probably appreciated concrete evidence since we were going after the most powerful man in town.

I gave the dog a pat. "Good work."

We moved on then. With deliberate malice, Shannon scuffed her feet all the way around the house, tearing up the protective measures at every possible opportunity. Eventually Chance stopped outside a darkened window.

"This is it?" Dale asked. Without waiting for an answer, he pushed on the window and it slid up.

"Incredible," Jesse muttered. "A place like this, and he leaves a ground-floor window unlocked."

It might be the only one too. Jesse made quick work of the screen; given his profession, he showed an unexpected talent for B&E. Then we climbed inside, trying to be quiet. As my eyes adjusted to the darkness, I saw we'd come into a formal study. The hulking desk by the window hunched before us like a monster, and two wing chairs sat nearby as its minions. For a moment, I heard nothing but our rustling movements, and then our breathing. Then I picked out the distant murmur of voices. We'd found them.

"We need to find out what they're up to," Shannon whispered.

But it didn't make sense for all five of us to go banging around in the dark. In the end, it came down to Jesse and Chance. The cop had the skill set for sneaking, but Chance's luck might guarantee he wouldn't get caught. They eyed each other for a few seconds before agreeing to a coin toss.

"Not you," Saldana muttered. "I get heads."

Chance just grinned and put away the silver coin he liked to roll along his knuckles. He kept it in his pocket for when he needed to think. Back when we were together, he'd often spin it on his hands while working out the solution to a knotty problem. I'd always liked watching him.

Our girl dug out a quarter and flipped it. The coin gleamed in the dark and she caught it cleanly, then peered at it. "Tails," she said unnecessarily.

Luck always favored Chance. With a quick smile, he set off to spy on the twelve.

The Devoted Dead

Fifteen minutes passed.

Dale slipped back outside and sat, just beneath the window, drinking from a flask. In a way, I envied his alcoholic purple haze. The rest of us might as well see what we could learn in here.

Time to loot the desk. Quietly, I rummaged through the drawers, looking for anything of interest. In the bottom-right one, I found an interesting manila dossier full of pictures, old-fashioned black and whites that would've required a dark room. Among them, I found shots of us. So I hadn't imagined that "being watched" sensation.

More telling, I found shots of Curtis Farrell half naked with a girl who probably wasn't even eighteen. That would've been why England fingered him for a dirty job, but when blackmail didn't work, he moved to brute force. What the hell had England wanted him to do to Miss Minnie?

Rob her? Frighten her into a heart attack? *Silence* her?

Or maybe I'd been right the first time. If England had been monitoring our movements and he'd known we would be there that night, maybe Farrell wasn't supposed to do anything but die. Did Farrell know something about England, then?

Shannon came over, peering across my shoulder. "Holy crap," she whispered. "I didn't know Missy was sleeping with Curtis Farrell."

Aha. "That would be—"

"England's daughter," she finished.

So England used his leverage with Farrell to get him where he wanted him. What then? Well, let's see. If you had all the money and power in town and you caught a dirty, weed-smoking gas station clerk messing around with your daughter, what would you do? Find some schmucks to kill him for you, of course. *The perfect crime.*

Mr. McGee must've found out that Farrell was running around with Melissa England; hence the argument. He'd wanted Farrell to stay away from the girl, hoping he could get out of Kilmer. Neither one of them would be going anywhere now.

We can ask the sheriff to look at the scratches on England's hands before they heal and at the bruises on Farrell's neck. If only they had DNA testing there . . . but I might as well have been wishing for the moon. I thought about that for a moment; I could accuse him falsely and blame England for the bruises on my neck too, if I believed the end justified the means. Of course, we couldn't be caught poking around his property for that to hold. He could say he'd acted in self-defense since we'd broken into his home.

Dammit. Where the hell was Chance?

As if in answer, he slipped silently around the corner and back into the study. Relief surged through me. He held his finger to his lips and motioned that we should go. I didn't need a second invitation.

I slipped over the windowsill, and the others followed me. Jesse went last and secured the screen behind him and then slid the window back down soundlessly. It took a kick in the side to rouse Dale. He'd been drinking steadily since we arrived, but somehow he managed to stagger back to the SUV along with the rest of us.

My heart didn't stop its wild hammering until we were well away from there. Chance kept looking over his shoulder like he couldn't believe we'd gotten away clean, but his luck held until we were a good distance along the highway. I sensed it cutting out that time, similar to leaving the range of a radio station. I wondered if anyone else had heard it.

"Details," I demanded.

Chance sat between Shannon and me in the back. We hadn't been willing to share the seat with Dale, so he rode up front with Jesse. Even with the windows cracked, my eyes watered. We needed to hose him down and dose him with hot coffee in order to get any sense out of him.

"So here's the deal," Chance said. The vehicle's interior fell silent, everyone ready to listen. "There was a lot of bitching about us and how we're messing everything up. I'm paraphrasing, of course."

"Were there any complaints about us meddling kids?" I asked.

Chance flashed me a grin. "Not exactly, but close. Keep a tight hold on your sense of humor, Corine. You're going to need it." He paused and took my hand. Oh, that couldn't be good. "They didn't mention the particulars, but apparently your surviving that house fire put a huge crimp in their plans. They seem to think killing you will resolve all the trouble that's been plaguing the town in the last year or so."

Holy shit. I tried to wrap my mind around that.

"You mean . . . like a human sacrifice?" Shannon asked.

Jess agreed. "That's what it sounds like."

So the townsfolk wanted me dead—and the demon didn't. The bizarre juxtaposition seemed almost funny. "I wonder why they didn't try to kill me when I was a kid, if that's the case."

"At that point . . . I'm sure they didn't know what the recup . . . repercussions would be," Dale slurred. "'Sall in the book."

Jesse tapped his fingers on the steering wheel as he drove,

thoughtful. "And people might talk if a little girl who'd lost her mama suddenly turned up dead. People were watching, after that."

It was as good a theory as any. I turned to Chance. "What else?"

"They plan to mount a 'search,'" he told me quietly. "Tomorrow they're going to invite you to lead the party, looking for more missing persons. They think you'll feel flattered and obligated to assist."

I blew out a breath. "All twelve of them will be out there 'helping' me?"

"Yeah." His unease communicated itself to me in the way he gripped my hand.

"Perfect," I said at once. "I'll never get a better crack at them." Then I sighed. "You don't think I should do it."

Chance parried that. "It's not my decision to make."

Well, I'll be damned. He'd learned.

"There will be a hunting accident," Jesse predicted as he turned down the long road toward the house. "People running around the woods? *These things happen*, they'll say. *Such a shame when she was just trying to help.*"

Shannon took my other hand. "Then they'll have a big potluck and talk about how nice you were. Corine, I don't think you should do it, either. It's a trap."

"Duh," I mumbled. "But forewarned, we can turn things to our advantage."

Beside me, I could feel Chance squirming with the need to tell me how dumb this idea was. But I trusted in my team. We'd be on guard and could make them rue the day they decided to mess with us. Face it; they had to be desperate to consider venturing to a demon's home ground.

Some might argue that loosing a demon on the world would be worse than letting a few people in a small town get away with murder. I didn't agree; they were responsible for my mother's death. Besides, maybe out there in the woods, we could accomplish both—see justice done *and* deal with the demon.

I wouldn't hold my breath, but if I had to pick? The twelve were going down. I didn't know how, but we had twenty-four hours to work it out. We pulled up at the house and found everything quiet, thank goodness. Tomorrow they'd come with their request for our help. We had plans to lay.

The guys dragged a protesting Dale Graham off to the bathroom and tossed him in the tub. He sat under tepid water, cussing his head off for a good ten minutes before he sobered up enough to strip and actually shower. Shannon and I avoided that duty by virtue of being female.

She'd come up with an idea. "So you guys were talking about the sigils, right? The ones built into the library and England's house."

I nodded. "Right, what about them?"

"If we painted the symbols onto a clay token and Chance kept it in his pocket, wouldn't that protect him? He'd have a little traveling luck shield wherever he went."

I stared at her, impressed. The girl was brilliant. "That's one of the best ideas I've ever heard."

She flushed with pleasure, ducking her head as if she couldn't believe my response came without being laced with criticism. Damn, her mother had a lot to answer for.

"I've been thinking of something else too," she went on.

If this idea was any indication, this would be genius too. "Shoot."

"You know the mix of herbs we used for the wards?"

"Yep," I said. "We still have plenty."

"I was wondering . . . if wards work on a building, would they work on a *person*? I mean, if we mixed up a little sachet bag full of them and kept it in a purse or pocket?"

I thought about that. "Well, vodoun practitioners do mix up gris-gris bags for people, and witches make charms. . . ."

She shook her head. "No, that takes special training and/or power, but anybody can lay wards, as long as they use the right ingredients. So why couldn't anybody make personal protection packs if they used the same stuff?"

Wow. I couldn't believe I'd never thought of this. Compared to this kid, I felt dumb as a stump, but I was very proud of her.

"It should work," I said. "Let's find some old linens and my sewing kit, and we'll make up some Tri-Ps."

Her smile became radiant. "Tri-P. Did I just *invent* something?"

"You most certainly did."

"I can't sew," she told me. "But I know how to make homemade clay. Flour, salt, water, et cetera. Bake it for an hour and you have a permanent object. So I can make a little tablet for Chance."

"Girl Scouts?" I asked.

She grinned. "Yep. I dropped out in sixth grade. I thought my mom would kill me." Those words fell heavily into the room, and her smile faltered.

"I'll get you out of Kilmer," I told her fiercely. "Don't worry about that."

Shannon nodded and went on into the kitchen while I sliced a worn pillowcase into fourths. The nice part was that the sides of the bag would be consistent, just from that one cut. As I worked, I remembered making doll clothes with my mama. This seemed bittersweet, yet oddly fitting. Here I was outfitting us for the final showdown, using a skill my mother taught me. She'd like that, I thought.

With her, I'd spent long hours learning those woods. She had taught me about medicinal plants and the names of the trees. Because of her, I could identify the calls of the mockingbird and the whip-poor-will. Before her death, the woods had been like a second home to me, not the nightmare I remembered now.

After I finished stitching the four little bags, I measured out herbs in their proper ratio to fill them. The guys came in after dealing with Dale, who'd passed out in Jesse's room. We still hadn't gotten a look at his mystical book. By this point, Shannon and I had stuffed a couple while her clay cooked. I had to admit, our Tri-Ps didn't look special, crafted out of a worn daisy-print pillowcase and tied off with yellow string.

"What the hell are you two doing?" Chance wanted to know.

Since it was her idea, I let Shannon explain. She did so quietly, seeming abashed until she saw how impressed the guys were. Then her face lit up like a sunrise.

"It'll work," Jesse said. "And it really is brilliant."

It was frosting on the cake when she told them about the luck bubble. To my surprise, Chance grabbed her up in a huge hug and whirled her off the ground. Shannon squealed, her face bright with pleasure. I guessed being luckless had been harder on him than I knew.

Earlier, when he said nobody would ever love me like he did, he'd proposed finding some way of getting rid of his luck for good in order to be with me. Watching the exuberance in his face now, I realized that loss would be like severing a limb for him. Being with me, he'd sacrifice part of himself.

How could I permit it?

I *couldn't*. I wanted him to be better because of me, not less. I didn't want him to kill his luck, but I didn't want to die, either.

Over Chance's shoulder, Shannon cut me an odd look. "You okay?"

Yeah, I was fine. I'd just realized I didn't want him to change enough to make me both happy and safe, but I didn't know if I could live with the risk. I waved them both away with a smile as fake as a three-dollar bill.

"Get your Smartphone," I suggested to Chance. "You took pics of the library for Booke, right? You should help Shannon figure out the sigils so she'll be ready to draw them when the clay cools."

"That'd be great," she answered. "I have a notebook in my backpack. I'll get it."

They went into the kitchen together, but not before Chance

gave me a last penetrating look. I hadn't fooled him, but he wouldn't push. He'd finally learned to read my cues for when I wanted to be chased and when I wanted space. With a faint sigh, I finished stuffing the last two Tri-Ps. We needed any edge we could muster.

Ignoring the way Jesse tracked me with his eyes, I went outside—yes, beyond the protection of the wards. My enemies here were human, and none too skilled in the dark arts. I didn't fear the woods any longer. For whatever reason, the demon was the least of my problems—and wasn't that simply too weird?

I sat down on the top step of the front porch and dropped my head into my hands. I didn't know how to reconcile my surety that Chance wouldn't be happy if he changed as much as I needed him to. I couldn't be with him, not when I knew how happy it made him to get his luck back; not when I knew how much he hated being powerless. This wasn't a relationship issue anymore. Those things could've been fixed, and he'd been working so hard to show me he could change.

Just not in ways I could allow.

I remembered how I'd felt when I dropped through that burning floor and during those long hours in the hospital with him at my bedside. His eyes burnt with guilt, and I'd found it hard to look at him. That was when I started thinking about leaving him. Though I might always want him, I couldn't get past the idea that he was bad for me, dangerous—and not only in a sexy, irresistible way.

I wasn't surprised when Jesse slid out the door and sat down beside me. My feelings would register on his white knight radar and render me irresistible to him. *Here's a woman who needs your TLC, Saldana. Go get her!*

"Go away," I muttered.

"You just realized it's not going to work," he said quietly. "Been there."

I didn't look at him. "It's worse for you, though. You can feel what they feel, even when you're ending it."

He shrugged. "I feel what everybody feels. Never learned to shut it off."

I'd rather talk about his gift than my feelings. "What about proximity? I mean, you're not being bombarded by the whole world?" That would drive anyone nuts, surely.

"Generally, we have to be in the same building," he agreed. "When I feel strongly about someone, the range amplifies."

He'd felt me all the way in Texas. Did that mean what I thought it did? Then I glanced over and found him sitting in a similar posture, elbows on knees. He wasn't looking at me, either.

"Are you distracting me with this on purpose?"

"Maybe I just want you to know you have options," he said quietly.

I let that be for a minute. "Tell me about her."

"Heather," he answered without even thinking about it.

"The pyro girl." I remembered his talking about her back in Laredo.

"Yeah."

"What happened to her, anyway?" I knew they weren't together anymore, but that was *all* I knew.

Jesse stiffened. If I were an empath, I'd be feeling waves of pain washing over me right now. I could see it in his body language. In fact, I was surprised he answered.

When he did, his voice was raw. "Two years back she went to prison for arson, and she died in a fire inside."

"I'm sorry." I took his hand.

Our fingers tangled and clung. We sat beneath the heavy dark of a moonless night and reflected on the weight of those we had not been able to save.

Butterfly Girl

Dawn came slowly.

Jesse had bunked down on the floor in Chance's room, unwilling to share with Dale. Shannon still had the mattress where I'd been sleeping before she arrived. Unable to doze off, I lay on the soft, sunken sofa, staring up at the dusty ceiling. The guys had been taking turns, and since I was feeling better, I figured I could do my part.

Around three a.m., someone tiptoed along the hall toward me. I shifted and saw it was Shannon. She wore a T-shirt that came nearly down to her knees, and I was struck by how young she was, no matter how readily she'd adapted.

"Can't sleep?" I whispered.

She shook her head. "I keep thinking about that girl you saw locked in the attic."

Though it hadn't been my primary concern, I wondered what happened to her. The idea of being confined in that attic for being different made me shake all the way down to my bones. If my mama and I had lived a hundred years earlier, our lot might've been even worse. Judging by the way she'd been dressed, the poor kid was probably long dead.

"Maybe you can ask her," I offered, lifting my legs so she could sit down.

"I've never contacted a spirit I didn't know in some way."
Shannon sounded doubtful, but interested.

"I don't see what it would hurt to try. Doesn't look like
we'll be sleeping much until we resolve this, one way or
another."

"Agreed."

We crept through the house. I climbed onto a chair to let
down the ladder by increments, so softly it made no noise
at all. Getting upstairs took some doing, and I was a little
concerned that we'd wake the guys with our clambering
overhead, but it seemed as if the night itself wanted us to do
this.

Sounds seemed muffled, cloaking our movements. Not
entirely understanding the impulse, I tugged the ladder back
up after us. I felt like this was a private ceremony between
females, and the guys shouldn't be a part of it.

In a low whisper, I explained how to traverse the boards
without bouncing them. We inched toward the windowsill,
but I didn't touch it. This was Shannon's show.

As if in concert, we sank down opposite each other. The
girl turned her radio on low, and the static hiss filled the
dark space. Maybe I was just tired and suggestible, but I
sensed something. The hair on my forearms stirred; my skin
prickled.

Shannon whispered to the girl's spirit as she fiddled with
the knobs. I couldn't make out what she was saying, but it
sounded imploring. I sat quietly, trying not to distract her.

I don't know how long we sat in the dark, but as she spun
the dial farther along the bar, a tinny voice finally crackled
into focus. "Hello. I'm here."

A hard shudder wracked me. This was a child no older
than the one I'd seen by the window. Whatever happened to
her, it hadn't been long afterward. She hadn't escaped or
lived to a ripe old age. She wasn't an angry ghost, or she
would have tried to take her wrath out on us, but she didn't
rest in peace, either.

"Who are you?" Shannon asked softly.

"Martha," came the slow, crackling reply. Her words carried impossible distance, echoes of the grave. "Martha Vernon. It's dark in here. Have you come to let me out?"

Oh God. Sucking in a sharp breath, I wrapped my arms around my knees. She thought she was still trapped in here. And, well . . . she was.

Shannon looked very pale, arms wrapped around the radio. I could tell she was as chilled as I was, but her answer sounded composed. "We're going to try. What happened to you, Martha?"

"Same thing that happens to everyone who's different around here."

In the stillness, I heard the soft shuffle of someone who wasn't there. The boards creaked lightly beneath Martha's invisible weight. As she'd done for countless years, she paced her prison. I thought my heart would explode when the footsteps, accompanied by terrible cold, stopped beside us.

Shannon managed to ask, "What's that?"

The non sequitur came, low and almost toneless, full of hissing, static snakes. "They found I can call things to me, things that fly, things that crawl. I can fill a tree with butterflies, spell your name in lightning bugs, or send a plague of locusts to their houses, but I cannot get out of here. Won't you let me out?"

I ached for her. Kilmer wasn't a good place to be different. That had still been true in my time. I couldn't imagine what it would have been like in hers.

"I'll try," Shannon assured the child's ghost. "But I need to know what happened to you first."

"Same thing that happened to Holly Jarrett, Timothy Sparks, David Prentice," Martha sang out. An eerie, tuneless humming poured out of the radio, and it made my head feel strange, almost disconnected from the rest of me. Eventually, the sound evolved back into words again, leaving me numb and frightened. "And more, and more."

"Tell me what that was," Shannon begged.

"They fed us to the thing in the woods. 'Two roads di-

verged in a wood, and I—'" the ghost in the machine whispered, "'I took the one' . . . 'I took the one' . . ." Her tinny
little voice repeated, a scratched phonograph phantom.

Mr. McGee must've been researching the dead children
and he'd located Martha Vernon on his radio—not because
he was Gifted, but because he was old and near death. He'd
said I could understand the whispers, whereas Chance could
not because I was soon to die myself . . . and I did.

He'd scrawled down the poem at some point, and Curtis
Farrell took it with him. Maybe I didn't know all the reasons why yet, but I was starting to find connections. Once I
had all the pieces, the big picture would take shape.

"That's the link," I said aloud. "Remember how you and
Mr. McGee found a pattern for the 'bad things' that happen
every so often on December 21? They targeted families who
were different and sacrificed them to the demon. I saw them
performing the ritual when I read the wreckage."

My mother and I had certainly qualified. If anyone knew
about Shannon's gift, it would have qualified her for the
purge. I could imagine Sandra Cheney's chagrin when she
realized her family wasn't perfect enough for her perfect
town. Maybe she thought sleeping with August England would
change his mind. If she'd only taken a good look in his
eyes, she would have seen he had no heart, and hence, no
reason to change his mind.

"But *why*?" Shannon's question came out anguished.

I shrugged. "That's the million-dollar question, isn't it?
Why did they hang so many witches in Salem?"

"'I took the road less traveled by,'" Martha announced
at length.

The radio crackled and spat. I could sense its vibrations
against Shannon's chest. A cold breeze poured over us, stirring the dust in the attic until it became hard to see.

"She's getting agitated," the girl said in a rush. "What
should we do?"

Right, *I* was the mentor here. I didn't have time to think
or ask for a second opinion; Martha was working her way

up to a poltergeist tempest. Like most children, she wasn't
long on patience, and the years alone in the attic hadn't helped.

I decided swiftly. "I'll pry open the window."

A child's strength wouldn't have been sufficient, not when
the nails were new and the boards were at their best. Years
of dry rot and rust had weakened the slats over the window,
though, so I pulled them off, one by one, not trying to be
quiet any longer. I yanked them away, tearing my fingers on
the splintering wood, and still didn't pause until I had the
whole thing cleared. Fresh air poured into the attic for the
first time in I don't know how many years, mingling with
the spirit storm.

I nodded at Shannon. "Tell her the way is clear."

Who knew if removing the symbol of her imprisonment
would be enough? The girl relayed the message, standing
up to thrust an arm through the triangular window. A queer
pop emerged from the radio as if something had passed
through its ancient speakers, and then wind gusted outward.

Surely we'd set her free. In another moment, we had our
answer. Though it was too late in the year for fireflies, they
twinkled outside the house, glimmering in sequence to spell
out the words, "Thank you."

Shannon whispered, "Good-bye, butterfly girl."

The radio went dead silent. In response, Shannon clicked
it off. I stretched, arms over my head, just as we started to
hear commotion downstairs.

"Where the hell are they?" Jesse asked.

"Hell if I know." Chance wasn't a morning person, let
alone a middle-of-the-night person. "Did you hear a car
pull up?"

"Didn't hear anything," he answered. "The Forester and
the Mustang are still here. You think someone took them?"

Chance's voice became panicked. "They wouldn't have
gone out to the woods without us?"

That tore it. If we let them, they'd go running around looking for us, trying to play heroes, and wind up lost. Then we'd
have to go save them before the demon scared the piss out

of them and they broke their necks falling in the gully like Rob Walker.

"We should nip this in the bud," I said.

Shannon grinned. "Yeah, they're about to have twin aneurysms."

In response, I unhooked the catch and gave the ladder a good kick. It dropped with a thunk; then I waited. Both guys came running, armed with makeshift weapons. Their fear turned in unison to absolute exasperation.

"What are you two doing up there in the middle of the night?" Chance demanded.

Shannon told him pertly, "Exorcising a ghost."

Excellent. I couldn't have done better myself.

Jesse thought better of whatever he'd meant to say. "Did it work?"

"Yep." I knew I sounded smug. "Didn't you feel all that wind blow through here?"

"Well," Chance muttered. "Yeah. It woke me up, in fact."

"But I thought something was wrong and that the windows were open when they shouldn't be," Saldana added.

"That'd be a reasonable assumption under any other circumstances . . . ," I began.

"And with any other combination of people," Shannon finished.

Lord, I loved this girl. I gave her a quick hug around the shoulders, surprising both of us. Sheepish, I grinned and indicated with a gesture that she should precede me down the stairs. We went into the kitchen and fixed pancakes, even though it was a few hours before dawn. It didn't look like any of us would get back to sleep anyway.

The guys bitched us out soundly for not waking them, but neither of them had much to say when I asked, "Just what would you two have contributed to the occasion?"

Frankly, Shannon hadn't even needed me. Unless she wouldn't have thought to open the window. In that case, I'd been mildly useful.

After conceding the point, Chance made a pot of his deluxe coffee, and I didn't try to talk Shannon out of having some, well doctored with sugar and powdered milk. I figured we both needed the warmth and the kick, after the serious eeriness of the last hour.

An hour later, Dale staggered in and put away two mugs of java and two plates of pancakes. He didn't seem to suffer from hangovers in the usual sense, but he did ask for some aspirin. None of us had any, and we were apologizing for that when a knock sounded at the front door.

I think our collective response to that was . . .

Oh shit.

At this hour, it couldn't be the twelve, coming to invite us to partake of our civic duty. Somehow I wasn't a bit surprised to open the door and find Sandra Cheney standing there, perfectly groomed even at six in the morning. Not a single blond hair stirred from her attractive bob. Her fingernails shone pearly in the half-light.

She fixed a smile on her face as I might hammer a nail into a wall: doggedly and with force. "I've heard Shannon is staying with you. I've come to take her home."

Behind me, the girl made an awful little sound. I made a show of looking at her. "Do you want to go?"

"Fuck no," she answered deliberately.

"I'm pretty sure you can't remove her against her wishes," I said with saccharine sweetness. "Is that right, Jesse? How does the law stack up on that?"

"Once kids turn eighteen, they can't be forced to return to a home they've left," he agreed. "And I think her wishes are clear at this point."

I smiled. "It was kind of you to come out and check on her, though."

"Well then." Sandra fidgeted with her pocketbook. In her icy eyes, I saw livid anger. She wanted to rant and say we'd all rue the day, but that wouldn't be polite. Plus, you shouldn't threaten people you actually meant to harm. Sandra might be evil, but she wasn't stupid.

"I'm so distressed to hear that, Shannon. I know we've

had our share of troubles, and you think I don't understand you, but the truth is, your father and I love you very much. He's going to be so sad to hear this."

"He's been sad a long time," Shannon muttered pointedly. "And it wasn't because of me. I'll write to him when I get settled."

Sandra ignored most of that. "No idea when you're leaving, then?"

"Probably soon," Chance said,. "I believe we've just about tapped the tourist attractions around here."

To say the least.

"Then take care. I love you, sugar bean." To my surprise, Sandra said that with evident sincerity. Her two-inch ladylike heels clacked as she hurried across the porch and down the stairs toward her shiny, understated luxury automobile.

When she drove away, I honestly didn't know what to make of the visit. "Could you be wrong about her?" I asked Shannon, shutting the door. "Could she have started sleeping with England when she realized you had a gift, trying to *save* you?"

That didn't clear her of the charge of trying to kill us and deliver us up as alternate sacrifices, but it might mean she wasn't as bad as we thought. It was a rare she-viper who could slay her own young without batting an eye.

Shannon thought about it for a moment and then shrugged. "Don't know. Possible, I guess, but I wouldn't stake my life on it."

Well, neither would I.

"Come on," Dale roared from the kitchen. "Time's a-wasting! Will you ungrateful devil-seekers come look at the book or not?"

As it happened, we would.

"Waiting for Godot"

The book was a gold mine.

Crazy Dale Graham had all kinds of news clippings coinciding with the December 21 disasters. He also had a mess of pictures documenting the secret meetings, and everything he'd compiled corroborated our theories. Mainly, it was good to see pictures of our enemies; we'd be out in the woods with a bunch of different people today, and I didn't want collateral damage if we could help it, so I memorized names and faces.

This would be a different sort of final showdown, not of weapons, but of wits; not of action, but attrition. I didn't intend to fight fair.

After the sun came up fully, I took the list of casualties to Shannon. "Can you call them to you?" I asked. "I know it'll take a lot out of you, but I think it'll be worth it. We've got a stash of chocolate you can have if you need it."

"Everyone but Mr. McGee," she said. *Right, the block-age.* "Why?"

I told her.

"Oh, that's fiendish," she breathed. "I'm on it. What're you going to be doing?"

"Waiting for Godot."

At nine a.m. sharp, he arrived in the form of Sheriff

Robinson. When I opened the door, he doffed his hat and twisted it in his hands. His brown uniform pulled across his gut as he fidgeted. I didn't make things easier on him, but just stood there studying him.

"Morning," he said.

I nodded. "What brings you out this morning? Not bad news, I hope?"

His answer came in a rush. "The good people of Kilmer have taken heart from your bravery. They'd like y'all to lead a search party for the other missing folks."

I couldn't seem to acquiesce too easily. Robinson might not be in on this, but England would doubtless ask for a recap of the conversation. So I furrowed up my brow, feigning puzzlement. "How come? We're not professional search and rescue."

"Well, I reckon they're hoping your good luck will rub off," Robinson offered.

I barely stifled a snort. *If only he knew.*

"To tell the truth," he went on, "those woods spook a lot of folks around these parts, but y'all have shown us there's nothing to be scared of out there."

I wouldn't go that far.

He peered at me a little closer. "What happened to your neck anyhow?"

Oh, here was my chance. I could level charges now, and England *might* pay for what he'd done to Curtis Farrell. But if I blamed August England at this point, it would queer the whole deal, and they'd doubtless wonder why I hadn't come forward before. In a town like Kilmer, you could accuse England of anything and he'd likely walk away clean.

No, this was the better opportunity. How else would I get all twelve of them in one place outside of their secret meetings?

"Got it stuck in the can ring of a six-pack of cherry cola. People should really take more care not to litter." He responded to that with a puzzled blink, but before he could say that didn't make a lick of sense, I added, "I'll ask the others if they're game for another hike, then." I called out, and the guys appeared within a few seconds.

"What's up?" Chance asked.

I filled them both in.

Civic-minded soul that he was, Jesse nodded first. "Sounds like a good idea. What time should we meet you?"

"And where?" Chance added.

"Three . . . the access road at mile marker forty-seven," Robinson suggested.

I thought it might seem suspicious if I agreed too readily. They knew I wasn't stupid, so I pretended to haggle. "Now that's not going to give us enough daylight, is it? Make it two."

"Done." The sheriff squeezed my fingers, then briskly clasped hands with Jesse and Chance.

I gave a sweet smile in parting. "Looking forward to it. Let's bring some of those poor souls home."

Chance grinned as I shut the door. "Your accent becomes pronounced when you talk to the locals, you know that? I keep expecting you to fling your hand to your forehead and say, 'Tomorrow is another day.'"

I smiled back, but my heart tugged because I knew that when this was all over—and it would be soon, one way or another—we were going to talk, and he probably wouldn't like the outcome. After calling to Shannon and Dale, I led the way into the front parlor. With the couch and the chairs, we had just enough seating for everybody.

Settling with Dale's book of secrets in my lap, I rubbed my hands together. "We have a little less than five hours 'til showtime. Let's get to work."

At one forty-five p.m., we sat waiting near mile marker forty-seven. We'd left Dale at home keeping an eye on Butch. The little dog hadn't been happy, but I knew damn well this would be dangerous. I only wished we could have left Shannon there too, but she wouldn't have stayed put. I'd seen the movies where you forbade the teenage girl to do something, and then she would run off to do it all by herself. We weren't going to let that happen.

Thanks to Dale's good records, I'd recognize the twelve when they arrived. I just hoped a lot of innocent townsfolk wouldn't volunteer for the search party, as it would shortly turn into a wicked game of cat and mouse. In that case, things could get . . . complicated.

Well, we'd cross that bridge when we came to it.

To my delight, they arrived in just two vehicles, which meant they hadn't brought any bodies along for the ride. I signaled, and Jesse pulled in behind them. We'd agreed it wouldn't be smart to let them block us in.

I hopped out of the SUV, settling into my role as cheerful, helpful former resident. It probably wouldn't fool anyone, but it might annoy them. As I'd already known, mostly men climbed out of their vehicles. Only Sandra Cheney and Regis's receptionist added estrogen to the mix.

Agnes Pettigrew? Really?

That revelation startled me. I hadn't sensed any killing animosity from her—just the typical bureaucrat's annoyance at having her system circumvented. Even now, she didn't look frightening—just a plump, middle-aged woman geared up for a ramble in the woods—but I did notice she wore a horseshoe pin on the lapel of her jacket. She must have been in the top tier, part of the council leadership.

August England, Harlan Cooper. I located them with a casual glance and covertly watched them as they discussed their options in a low voice. I wished I could read lips. They had no visible weapons, but I would have been surprised if they didn't have guns beneath their jackets. They even wore orange vests so they wouldn't be mistaken for game if someone happened to be hunting. I glanced down at my black hoodie. So that was how they meant to play things. It was strange how they saw me only as an old mistake to be erased.

The rest of the men looked like they must have been retired; I recognized none of them from prior encounters in town, but they matched the dossiers Dale had compiled. I twitched, knowing I was standing before the men and women who had casually decided to feed my family to the demon. I wanted to scream, to spit at them, but that would have tipped our hand. They thought they'd been so clever, running me around town looking for answers.

By the goddess, I had them now.

I pinned a smile on my face. "Are y'all ready to take a look around out there? There's a lot of ground to cover."

Sandra Cheney looked as if she'd had a bad face-lift. "That's why we're wearing our walking boots."

We set off in two groups: us and them. I think they expected me to lead the way, but they were crazy if they thought I intended to let them get behind me. Once we stepped into the woods, all bets were off.

The path narrowed as we stepped into the trees. A chill wafted all around us, telling me we weren't alone. I recognized the heavy, watchful feeling from the other times I'd ventured in here. By the way the twelve reacted, they hadn't expected the demon to find us so quickly. A few of them shifted, looking restive.

Don't run, I told them silently. *Yet.*

I patted my pocket where I'd stashed my Tri-P. The others caught my movement and did the same. We were protected from bad magick, but not from bullets, stab wounds, or being rent limb from limb. I wouldn't think about any of those possibilities. Sometimes you just had to gamble.

"Remember the plan," Jesse breathed. "Chance, you stay with Corine. She'll need the most protection because they're gunning for her, and I have a bad arm."

I acknowledged him with a nod. Chance stepped closer to me, tugging lightly on one of my braids. Smiling at him hurt because I knew what was going to happen after we left the forest.

"Who brought the maps?" I asked brightly. "We'll divide the territory and split up into teams of two so we can cover more ground."

After some mumbling, the Kilmer crew worked that out

among themselves. Taking care not to touch him, I discussed the division of forest with England. "We'll take this section over here." I pointed to his map. "Jesse, Shannon? Would you take this part?"

Yeah, I wanted them close by, preferably within screaming range. But I wasn't prey like they thought. No, indeed. Instead, I was bait.

"Sounds good," Saldana said.

"We'll meet back at the vehicles in three hours," England said. "If you find something, mark it with one of these stakes." He handed two DayGlo orange wooden markers to each of us. "Then make sure you map a route to the body, so we can locate it and give that person a proper burial."

Oh, well played, sir. Makes it seem like you mean business. Makes it seem not your fault.

I tucked them into my backpack. "You ready, Chance?"

"Absolutely."

We set off, ostensibly to search our quadrant of woods for missing persons. In fact, I wanted to get some distance between us and everyone else. Instead of searching, they'd be stalking us. There was no telling what would happen now.

The wind kicked up, whistling through the skeletal branches. I recognized the feeling from the attic; it meant Shannon had done her part. The restless dead had arrived, searching for those responsible for their wretchedness. She'd called them to her and whispered how they could confront their tormentors at last. I didn't know if they could inflict physical harm, but mental damage and hallucinations might be enough.

A shiver rolled through me. In the distance, I heard the staccato report of gunfire; then screaming. Yeah, it had begun.

It seemed much later than midafternoon. Within the shadow of the trees, the wan sunlight struggled to penetrate the tangle of wintry limbs. As we walked, I lost all sense of direction. I couldn't tell how far away the noises were.

And then I heard the unmistakable sound of a weapon

being cocked. I froze, surprised I didn't feel a bullet tearing into me right away. Beside me, Chance spun in a slow circle, looking frantic.

Of all the hunters in the woods, I felt mildly astonished to see Agnes Pettigrew step from the trees. Her hands trembled visibly on the grip. Unsteady as she was, she had as good a chance of hitting the man beside me or a squirrel in a distant tree. Her moon face was tinged green, pallor so profound I thought she might be in shock.

Chance measured the distance between us with his gaze. I could see him weighing the risk she might get a shot off before he took her down. Then I saw him decide not to risk it. He couldn't be sure how effective Shannon's charm was; if it was even slightly off-kilter, in this scenario, if anyone got shot, it would be me. He knew that—his luck would see to it. So he stood still and quiet. I sensed how difficult that was for him and spared him a smile. I knew he hated being powerless.

Would it do any good to bluff?

"What's wrong, Ms. Pettigrew?" I ventured. "Is everything all right?"

When she spoke, her voice sounded shrill. "Nothing will ever be all right. Not until you're dead."

"Do you really think that will fix it?" I asked, trying to keep my tone steady and gentle. "You've always known there was something wrong here. You couldn't have approved of going to people's houses in the middle of the night, doing what you did there."

Pure anguish flashed in her wild, glittering eyes. "It doesn't matter what I think. I'm a legacy."

"What does that mean?" Chance asked softly.

"My father participated in the initial summoning. Our family has been part of this since the beginning—and I don't have a choice." Agnes shook even as she raised the gun. "Once I . . . take care of you, things will return to normal. We'll have our sweet, quiet little town back again."

"You'll have to live with killing me," I whispered, watching her finger tighten on the trigger. "Not just standing by while someone else does the dirty work."

The wind whipped up, cold as ice as it wailed in the trees. To me, it sounded like a storm was coming, but by the way Ms. Pettigrew's eyes widened, she'd heard something else entirely. She stared past me. I didn't dare turn, but from Chance's puzzlement, he didn't see anything else.

"No!" she screamed. "You're dead. We killed you!"

As she raised her hands to cover her ears, her gun dropped to the forest floor and she turned to flee. I still didn't see anything, but I thought she might do something stupid, and to my surprise, I no longer wanted anything awful to happen to her. She seemed to have suffered enough. I snagged her weapon as I went by, thinking I might need it.

Chance and I gave chase, following her through the underbrush. Ms. Pettigrew fled in a blind panic, disregarding the branches that tore at her clothes and slashed at her face. I called out to her, breathless, as we ran, but she ignored us. Maybe she thought we were part of her horrific hallucination; maybe our pursuit was only frightening her further.

I heard her sobbing as she ran, but she never called out to God, never asked for aid or deliverance. I heard a crack and a thump, as if she were rolling. And then all sound cut off. We burst from the trees to a small clearing and teetered on the edge of the gully. Chance grabbed my arm and pulled me back. My heart pounded in my ears.

Halfway down the steep incline, I spotted Ms. Pettigrew's body. She'd fallen at an odd angle, twisted so it was obvious she'd broken her neck.

And she wore a positively beatific smile.

No Fear

My teeth chattered. Chance wrapped his arms around me and rubbed his hands across my back, murmuring comforting words. I clung to him, hating myself for the weakness that would make him believe in possibilities between us.

"I don't want this anymore," I muttered into his shirt.

"I don't think there's any stopping it," he said gently. "There are forces unleashed here that we don't control."

Yeah, it came back to being careful what you wished for because you might get it. Somehow this revenge didn't taste as sweet as I'd expected. And I didn't entirely understand. Agnes Pettigrew had been a middle-aged spinster with lovely penmanship; she had suffered from unrequited love for her boss and wore her skirts a little too tight. She hadn't been vicious or evil that I could tell, so it made no sense that she'd been part of the group that showed up the night my mother died.

I didn't understand any of this.

"You're right." At this point, we could only ride it out and try not to get caught in the cross fire.

That cold wind rolled over us again, carrying with it an actual physical darkness. The small clearing grew smoky, a tiny pocket hell, where I'd led twelve souls to be tormented. A man burst past us, screaming with raw horror. Before I could move or speak, he too plummeted over the edge, crashing down the slope to find his eternal rest just a few feet from Agnes Pettigrew.

"We shouldn't stay here," Chance said then. "You don't really want to see . . . ?"

No, I didn't. Nausea and horror warred within me. I'd wanted justice, but I'd never foreseen the horror-laced madness that led them along the same path like lemmings. Demon darkness and the wailing of the wretched dead drove them along, scared almost to death even before they fell.

With some effort, I asked, "You have your little tablet?"

In answer, Chance pulled it from his jacket pocket. "Yeah. Shannon's sharp as a tack, isn't she?"

"You feel like testing her invention?"

He arched a brow. "What'd you have in mind?"

"I thought maybe we could really find some lost souls."

Maybe if we did some good out here, it would outweigh the rest. I didn't put too much faith in that, of course, but I wanted to feel like more than an agent for destruction. In this way, I could give comfort and closure.

Thanks to his luck, we found two bodies in the first hour. They both lay in varying positions along the bottom of that gully. They'd run from the demon, fleeing it in terror, and plunged to their deaths.

I tried to ignore the screaming as others broke down, forgetting everything but the need to flee that devouring darkness, further agitated by angry spirits whipping through the trees. It couldn't be easy, knowing they were the reason such evil surrounded the town. But they hadn't realized when they set out to hunt me here that the demon wanted their deaths more than anything else. I hadn't been sure of that, but I did know monsters didn't like being bound, cheated, and forgotten. And I'd been willing to bet it wouldn't hurt me.

I knelt to mark the second corpse, which had rolled beneath a scrubby little bush, and said, "I think this is Glen Farley."

Chance didn't answer. I stilled, scenting danger like a living thing all around us. Scarcely moving a muscle, I glanced up to find Sandra Cheney, filthy and bloody faced on the rise above. The wind whipped at her clothing and lifted her platinum hair in a way that made her look utterly mad—and terrifying. She held no weapon, but she didn't look as though she had mind enough left to remember why she'd come out here in the first place.

Her hands curled into claws as she screamed for her daughter. "Shannon! Shannon!" She threw back her head, wailing in wordless grief.

I heard the crunch of approaching footsteps, and then I saw Jesse and Shannon approaching from the southwest. Sandra hadn't noticed them yet, keening like a bereaved woman from ancient times. The gale amplified her pain, and all around her, the shadows gathered. From my angle, they looked hungry, swollen with sharp anticipation.

I didn't know if the deaths of those responsible would be enough to give the phantoms rest or if they'd passed beyond the human afterlife—and were now feeding on pain, terror, and grief. They had been paler wisps, facsimiles of those they'd known in life, but we'd turned them into something else, and I didn't know what exactly they could do.

Shannon had called them. Perhaps she could send them away too.

"I'm here, Mother." The girl stepped forward, but not close enough for Sandra to sweep her over the edge, and Jesse stood within a safe distance.

"I did it for you," Sandra moaned above the rising wind. "I didn't want them to know you were Gifted. If only you'd listened to me—"

"So this is *my* fault? You could have warned me. Instead, you plotted and schemed, fucked that filthy old freak, and made Dad miserable. He loves you, though God only knows why."

"It was for you," Sandra said again. But she didn't sound as sure as she had. "I didn't want to let them take you."

Shannon snapped. "Right. And when exactly were you going to get me out of here, Mommie Dearest? When did you plan to save me, if you couldn't convince England with your bodily charms?"

"So you will not forgive me?" It was such a melancholy question, but I knew the answer before Shannon spoke.

"Never." The girl's tone echoed with ice.

To my absolute horror, Sandra did a swan dive then, landing in a broken heap near where we stood. I shuddered . . . because I was pretty sure she'd died in midair. That image would haunt me—the shadows closing in on her, swallowing her as her flesh fell and then passed into an inert state, before she touched the ground.

"Are you guys okay?" I managed to call out.

"A little beat-up from playing *Survivor*," Jesse answered, "but nothing serious."

"There're only two left," Shannon said.

Harlan Cooper and Augustus England.

"Should we go hunting?" Chance asked as he helped me climb out of the gully. I think he knew I'd go nuts if we stayed down here a minute longer.

Jesse nodded, offering me a hand to tug me the last few feet. "It's about time."

As much as I wanted to run, I couldn't bring myself to leave the job unfinished, not after all we'd been through. If I didn't put an end to things, once and for all, I'd likely never forgive myself. Especially not when we were so close.

I raised a brow. "Any idea where we should start?"

Shannon raised her antique radio, looking cool and remote. "They'll find the last two for me, if you want me to ask."

Something about her expression made me shiver a little. I glanced at the guys to get an idea what they thought. Chance was nodding; Jesse looked unsure. Would it warp her gift, asking spirits to do her bidding instead of merely communicating with them and offering information? She'd asked Rob Walker to find his own body, but that had the whisper of altruism attached. This, most assuredly, didn't.

Since the alternative was knocking around the woods all night—and it was already starting to get dark—I gave a curt nod. "Let's finish this."

The girl powered the radio on and fiddled with the dial until the hissing static coalesced into a comprehensible, in-human whisper. "Thank you," it said. "Thank you, Shannon. They're almost all gone. We made them pay. And . . . I'm not so cold anymore." It gave an awful little giggle.

Shit. That couldn't be good.

"Tell me where England's hiding," she bade it.

The rest of us stood stock-still, distrusting the give-and-take between Shannon and the thing on the radio. I was afraid to move. I sensed the shadows pooling all around us, drawn to her like a lodestone. She almost seemed to glow with a dark, unholy light, feeding them even as she conversed.

I exchanged a look with Jesse. We really had to get a handle on her gift before something terrible happened. Shit, it might have already.

The whisper lapsed into a soft sibilance that the rest of us couldn't understand, but Shannon nodded and responded as if the thing made perfect sense. It was eerie as she led us along the gully to the south, skirting the slippery edge. A soft rain began to fall, making progress more difficult.

We came upon England from behind. He was crouched in a blind, trying to be patient, but I could sense his fear like a living thing. He just had more control than the rest of his people. And he held a hunting rifle with the surety of someone who knew what to do with it. If he hadn't been so distracted by the swooping shadows and the icy wind, he would have heard us approach.

Shit. Shit, shit, shit. I was supposed to end this. If I were really the instrument of vengeance I'd tried to become, I wouldn't hesitate to end him. In the distance, thunder rumbled, but no lightning accompanied it.

How fitting, I thought, disgusted with myself. *All sound and fury.*

Chance broke the stillness, going after England with such

speed I could have blinked and missed it. My heart clenched until I remembered he had his luck back. He wrapped an arm around his neck and knocked the rifle out of England's hands. To his credit, England didn't even struggle.

He stilled, eyeing me with pure hatred. "Shoot me," he spat. "You've won—and destroyed Kilmer in the process. Now it will fill up with franchise stores, fast food, Internet cafés, and pornographic bookshops."

I'd tucked Ms. Pettigrew's pistol into my bag, and now I drew it out slowly, as if it were a snake about to bite me. Could I really do this? Execute a man in cold blood? I knew he was responsible for my mother's death, but I'd never felt any closer to her here, never felt she was watching with approval. Now he was beaten, broken at my feet, and I cringed to think of putting a bullet in him.

Darkness flooded the woods, carrying that particular scent of dying vegetation. The wind kicked up, full of echoing whispers of murdered souls. Though I knew I had nothing to fear from either the cold or the dark, I couldn't help but shudder. The demon had come to witness this moment.

England set his jaw, straining against Chance's hold. "We should've killed you when you were a kid," he told me. "I wish to hell we had. But mark me, only one of us will walk out of here, Corine Solomon. I don't make the same mistakes twice." He slammed his head into Chance's chin, loosening his hold, and then kicked backward.

Chance went sprawling, and his luck tablet bounced out of his pocket when he hit the ground. It tumbled into the underbrush, shrouded in darkness. We couldn't take our eyes off England long enough to go searching for it, and I couldn't live with myself if anything happened to Chance.

"Stay back," I begged him.

For an old man, England had some vicious moves, but he was unarmed and I had a gun. I knew how to shoot, if not well, and at this distance, even *I* couldn't miss. My blood cooled as I leveled my weapon on him.

"Get out of here," I told the others. "This is between him

and me." When they hesitated, I added, "You'll just distract me and give him an opening. Let me end this."

I must have sounded cold—and sure—because I heard them moving off. England's pale eyes held a mad, fervid light, as if he debated coming at me with his bare hands. "You murdered my mother," I said quietly.

As good as, anyway. She wouldn't have taken her own life or tried to pass me her power in a failed ritual if there hadn't been a hooded mob outside her door.

He didn't deny it. "She didn't belong. Neither do you. I've dedicated my life to keeping Kilmer a quiet, clean, peaceful place where people can be proud of living. I've kept the filth of the modern world at bay, just like my father before me. And now"—he dove for his boot—"it's time for you to go."

When I saw him come up with a holdout pistol, I fired. The pistol report rang like an explosion in my ears, and the kickback hurt more than I'd expected. He got a shot off as he fell, but it went wide, up in the air as he toppled back. I'd hit him in the gut, maybe not a fatal shot if he got medical attention right away. He wouldn't.

The rain beat down in a savage fury. Then the lightning came, flashing above the trees as if in fierce celebration. Blood spread across his abdomen, trickling down his sides and into the damp forest floor. The earth itself rumbled as if with pleasure. I should've walked away, not watched whatever would happen next.

But England raised a hand, as if beckoning me closer. I knew he didn't want forgiveness. He'd probably try to stab me if I crept up to him, and I didn't think I had the strength to shoot him again. I backed away, knowing I had to find the others.

The ground shuddered again, like the earthquake Miss Minnie had predicted. As I scrambled backward, the forest floor gave way, and England went sliding down in a mad muddy rush. I tried not to imagine him suffocating as he bled out, buried with those he'd led to their deaths.

A landslide like that would hide a lot of bodies.

I lost my breath, running blind. I didn't care where I was going, as long as it was away. The rain lashed at my face, stinging along with wild branches. Darkness writhed all around me with tormenting shapes. I tore my hands when I fell.

Someone jerked me to my feet. *Chance.*

His hands framed my face, his gaze anxious as he searched my face. "Did you really think I'd leave you? You did good, Corine. It's almost over."

I tried to wipe the mud and water out of my eyes, but only succeeded in smearing it further. "We have to find Cooper," I agreed. "Where are the others?"

"Right here," Jesse said.

Shannon smiled at me; at least I thought she did. Between the wild wind, the driving rain, and the swirl of shadows, I couldn't be sure.

Destination Darkness

The radio stopped working.

Shannon fiddled with it, but try as she might, she couldn't get a response. Finally, she glanced at me, brow furrowed. "I don't know what's wrong."

I shrugged. "It could be that killing England gave the spirits closure and now they're gone. But we still have Cooper to deal with."

"And that's not going to be easy," Saldana predicted.

Chance stared beyond us into the dark tangle of trees. The wind wailed through their skeletal limbs, giving no hint of human movement. "What do you know about him?"

"He's a hunter," Shannon answered.

That meant he wouldn't have panicked, wouldn't have broken beneath the mental strain. He'd probably hunkered down somewhere until the smoke settled. Now he'd be clearheaded and rested, ready to stalk his prey. A shiver ran through me.

My voice sounded thin. "So what do we do?"

"Get off the path," Saldana said at once.

Chance led the way into the undergrowth. I couldn't help the prickling sensation that we were being watched, but that might be the demon, though I couldn't smell the dank, decaying vegetation that marked his presence. Shannon stuck close to my side, and I ached for her. Though she might seem cool, soon it would hit her that her mom was dead—and how Sandra died couldn't help but scar her. I could still see the shadows swarming as she fell, as if feeding on her despair.

"Here are the problems as I see them," Chance said quietly. "One, this is Cooper's home ground, and he's had ample time to lay in snares for us. Two, he's an expert tracker and hunter. Three, we're tired and shaken, not at the top of our game anymore. Four, I lost my luck tablet back there, so we can't expect things to swing our way in this fight."

Summed up that way, it sounded worse than I'd realized. Stillness and silence seemed to offer some protection, so we didn't move as we tried to hammer out a plan in nearly inaudible whispers. As if to exacerbate our situation, the rain shifted from drizzle to downpour, inhibiting visibility further. Between the dark, the trees, and the weather, we'd be lucky to make it out of these woods.

"We could make for the SUV," I murmured. "Try to avoid Cooper. And then get the hell out of town."

At my suggestion, the earth trembled with outrage. The wind whipped up, tearing at our clothing. Two tree limbs cracked and fell, crashing to earth nearby. I, for one, took that as a threat.

Shannon leaped backward. "I don't think that's an option, Corine. If we leave, Cooper will just recruit eleven more. Missy England will take her dad's place. I have cousins. This will *never* end, and Kilmer will never be free, unless we finish it here, now."

"She's right," Chance said softly.

"I wish Butch were here," I muttered. "He might be able to track him."

Everyone regarded me dubiously. Who ever heard of a Chihuahua being used as a bloodhound? But Butch wasn't your average purse dog.

Jesse stilled. "I might be able to too."

Shannon and Chance looked puzzled. After a moment, I remembered how he'd sensed Butch, homing in on his location. Tapping into the emotions of someone like Cooper might drive Jesse crazy. It was his call, though.

"How?" the girl asked.

"I'm an empath," he explained. "I can scan, pick up all emotional states within a certain radius. Takes a lot out of me, hurts like hell, but I can do it."

Based on what I'd seen previously, that was an understatement.

"Go for it," I said, before I could change my mind.

Jesse closed his eyes. I studied him in the half-light, watching his face go vacant. We stood motionless for a good two minutes before he jerked and staggered. He would have fallen if I hadn't caught him around the waist. Jesse twitched and Shannon came to his other side, her big eyes round with worry.

"West," he rasped out. "Lying in wait. He's the only thing left alive out here besides us. But Jesus. Jesus . . ." Jesse fought free of me and bent at the waist, wracked with endless waves of dry heaves. "I've never felt anything like him."

"Inhuman?" Chance asked.

"I . . . don't know," Saldana answered at length.

After a couple of minutes, he managed to straighten up and put on his game face. His skull probably felt like it was splitting in two, but I didn't step close as I'd done before and let him put his head in my hands. I didn't want to hurt Chance, nor was I ready to declare myself open to a relationship with Jesse. It didn't seem like the time. I needed to get back to the pawnshop; needed some time to mourn and move on.

"Can you walk?" I asked.

Jesse gave a curt nod, but he let Chance take the lead. Shannon kept a hand on Saldana's arm, as if she thought she could steady him. Even if I thought it was fruitless, it was still sweet. And maybe she was stronger than she looked.

There was no path. We pushed west, forcing our way through underbrush and dead wood, avoiding sinkholes and tangled vines. I could sense the demon lingering nearby, but it didn't interfere with us, nor did it try to communicate. The rain spilled down my hoodie, soaking me to the skin. I doubted the others fared any better, but nobody complained.

"The ground's softer up ahead," Jesse said. "Watch your—"

Chance dove wide as a bed of leaves gave way. I skidded downward, grasping in vain at slick roots that gave no purchase. Someone snagged the back of my sweatshirt, and I tried to scramble backward, heels digging into the slick soil.

Stomach churning, I shuddered as my gaze dropped and I saw that I was hanging above a pit trap full of spikes. *Jesus.* I whimpered as my shirt began to slip upward. I tried to raise my arms, but the movement made Chance swear.

"Be still," he begged. "If we're not careful, we'll both end up down there." I couldn't see what was going on behind him, but he added to the others, "No, don't come up here. The extra weight might crumble the edge. I've got her—you hold my feet."

I don't know how long I hung there, feeling my shirt slip, and then tear. A sob shook me. I found myself dependent on Chance's strength. He cursed low and virulent in Korean as he worked me upward. His arms had to be burning, but he never faltered until he had his arms all the way around me.

Then we wriggled backward inch by inch until I felt the solid ground beneath my back. It seemed safe, so I began to use my heels to push upward until we fell back onto Jesse and Shannon. She looked pale as milk, rain slipping down her cheeks like tears.

"Everyone okay?" the girl asked shakily.

"More or less. Did you tear your wound?" Chance checked Saldana's shoulder and found blood trickling down his biceps.

Jesse waved a hand. "It's nothing. Let's move before he has time to leave us any more surprises."

Chance took the lead again, but this time he tested the path with dead limbs and heavy bark. He chucked them as we walked, triggering the traps Cooper had left for us. We found two snares and a trip wire that way as we pushed west. I stood watching the blades dance on the line, silvered with rain. Though that trap might not have killed us, it would have sliced us up, weakened us for the final confrontation.

"This is one sick son of a bitch," Chance said softly.

A cold chill ran through me. I'd nearly been impaled. I'd have nightmares about falling now, but at least it would be a change from the fire. In my mind's eye, I could see the spike piercing my guts, and I imagined the way blood would burst from my mouth as I died.

"Stop," Jesse whispered. "We need you here with us. He didn't get you, and he's not going to. I promise."

As if in answer, a shot rang out. If not for the darkness, wind, and rain, it would have drilled through my skull instead of into the tree beside me. Splinters and bits of bark sprayed my face, and I hit the ground.

Shannon crouched next to me, hand on my back. "Did he get you?"

"No." My voice sounded thick.

But damn near, closer than I wanted to think about. I wasn't bulletproof.

"Where the hell is he?" Chance demanded.

"It came from over there," Jesse said. "Not sure how far. Visibility's not good."

And the night got darker. The demon might not be able to attack Cooper as part of the terms of its binding, but it could shroud him in darkness.

But the hunter didn't panic. Besides weather and forest noises, I heard only silence. If he sat still and quiet, we'd have to come looking for him, and the odds were good he'd get one or two of us at close range. *Shit.*

I pushed into a kneeling position and met Shannon's gaze. "I don't want you going any farther," I told her quietly. "Jesse, would you stay with her? I don't want to give this guy a body count."

Though I didn't say so, he shouldn't wade into a fight wounded. If I could, I'd make Chance stay behind too, but I knew he wouldn't do it. Plus, I couldn't kill Cooper. I knew that. I needed Chance. At this point, he was the strongest and fastest. He'd have to finish it for me. And then I'd call us even for everything I went through in Laredo.

"I think it sucks," Jesse bit out, "but I see your point. We'll wait here. If he tries to circle around behind you, we'll take him out."

I knew he wouldn't have conceded except for Shannon. Jesse Saldana could always be counted on to safeguard the innocent. The girl glared at me, but she didn't argue.

"Meet us back at the Forester in an hour. If we don't show . . ." I trailed off. "Well, give us fifteen minutes leeway and then get the hell out of here."

Nobody said it out loud, but they knew. If we weren't out in seventy minutes, we weren't coming back. Shannon hugged me fiercely around the neck. I patted her back, feeling the rain ease up, no longer stinging the skin as it came through the bare trees.

Stepping back, I pulled my hood up, and the black cloth helped camouflage me. My face was already liberally smeared with mud, so I went with it, covering every inch of pale skin. Chance did the same, and then we slid away into the dark.

He went first, slow and quiet as he listened. Maybe he imagined he could hear the other man's breathing. In this demon-dark soup, our one advantage was that Cooper couldn't see us any more than we could see him. It would come down to reflexes, and Chance had those in spades.

I don't know what warned me—it wasn't quite a sound, but as we went past a tangle of bushes—I spun. Instead of catching me to the left of the spine for a clean kill, the knife went into my side. The pain was agonizing. I fell back as Chance lashed out, snagging Cooper's wrist and hauling him forward.

My knees crumpled as they fought. I felt my hands wrap around the hilt of the blade still lodged in me, but I retained enough presence of mind not to yank it out. I might bleed out before we could find help.

Chance was fast, so fast. I could see his training in the way he lashed out again and again. Cooper blocked, then kicked. He connected with a brutality and strength that sent Chance reeling back. They didn't speak. With the strange distance in my head, it was almost like watching a movie.

But I didn't see the big finish. The rain blinded me. Pain broke me. I fell forward into the mud and woke up somewhere else.

Before my eyes focused, I recognized the rank smell of dying vegetation. Maury. Shit, I didn't have any reserves left to fight a demon. I didn't have any tools with which to banish him. If he meant to kill me now, I was utterly defenseless.

"Did we win?" I asked.

Maybe I'd died. Maybe this was hell.

"It's not hell," he told me. "And yes, you did. Well, *Chance* did. After you passed out, he broke Cooper's neck."

"I thought I dreamed you." Well, part of me had. "Am I dreaming now?"

He didn't reply directly. But when did demons ever give a straight answer?

"You're used to this face," he said. "What are dreams but a way for your brain to say, 'Hi, here's something you need to know'?"

"So you need to tell me something?" I shook all over, both from cold and nerves, and I was covered in mud. I could feel the stab wound like a phantom pain, but when I looked down at my midriff, I saw nothing. This wasn't the real world, then.

"You set me free, so you get to ask a boon before I go."

For obvious reasons, I didn't trust demon favors. I had to think quickly, something that wouldn't backfire. There was a lesson to be learned from that whole monkey paw deal. Then it occurred to me: I could ask it to shield me from the ill effects of Chance's luck.

I couldn't breathe for wanting it.

"Will there be side effects? Catches? Hidden faults that the human brain can't conceive until it's far too late?"

Maury grinned. "What do you think?"

I exhaled slowly. "Then I guess I'd better go with a selfless wish. I'd like you to mark all the bodies of the innocent people who died out here, and then provide me with a map. I want to give their loved ones closure."

His eyes opened wide, brows shooting up into his busy hair. "Seriously? Nothing for you? Not fame, fortune?"

"Trying to cut down on the infamy. And I have enough money to get by. At this point, I just want to go home. Now, you heard my wish. Make it so."

"Are you sure?" he asked. "You won't live to see it done."

That hit me hard. "I won't?"

"Cooper caught you in an artery." The demon sounded genuinely regretful. "The minute anyone pulls out the knife, you'll start hemorrhaging. Sure you don't want to change your favor? You could wish for eternal life."

Ah, Jesus. I recognized the certainty of its words. Sometimes demons needed only to tell the truth to torment you best. Well, the people of Kilmer—those who were innocent of this madness—would still appreciate finding their loved ones. I squared my shoulders.

"Yeah, I'm sure."

He closed his eyes for a few seconds and then handed me a folded sheaf of paper. "Done. There's your map."

"Thanks," I said. "Before you go, before you send me back . . . could you . . . *would* you tell me what happened here? What was this all about?"

"In a nutshell? Well, the original twelve wanted to keep Kilmer safe and clean, uncontaminated from the outside world. They wanted to pick and choose what technologies were acceptable. They wanted to shield their kids from unwholesome influences."

I blinked at that. "So they summoned a demon?"

"Yours truly. What better way to safeguard the town than to put a demon of entropy and decay on the job?"

"And they paid you in sacrifices." I got it now. The pain from my body came in a raw, red wave. I wouldn't remain here in this half dreamworld much longer.

He agreed with a nod. "I prefer the Gifted ones. Tastes great, more filling. Ironically, I think my presence here made Kilmer something of a hot spot. Once they summoned me, you Gifted started being born like there was something in the water supply."

"Martha Vernon, Holly Jarrett, Timothy Sparks, David Prentice—"

"And their families. It was a package deal, remember. When you ran to me and hid during the fire, you broke the terms of the pact. Since you didn't die, I didn't get my sacrifice that year, and that was a deal breaker. Every year thereafter my bonds weakened a bit more, and I could roam a bit farther and cause a little more trouble closer to town. When you came back, I guess they thought they could fix things by killing you now, but it wouldn't have helped. And with the twelve dead, I'm free now."

Ah, damn. I could have lived without knowing that.

"Uh, you're welcome. I guess."

His expression became grave. "I never wanted your mother, Corine. She was one of the truly good souls. They started using my price to purge the town of those they considered undesirable. But I didn't take her, even when they performed the ritual around her body. Her death was clean. I don't know where she is now."

"I guess it's time for me to go," I said.

"I won't see you again," Maury answered with finality. "Unless . . ." His expression became crafty. "Oh yeah, I like that idea. I like it a lot."

Before I could ask, I spun outward, hurtling back toward my injured body at breakneck speed. With a strangled cry, I struggled upright to find myself in Chance's arms. He ran full out, carrying me. I felt every jolt, every rough patch. I moaned, both hands going to the knife in my side. I'd gotten what I wanted; they were all gone.

Why didn't I feel better about it? I should have felt vindicated. The twelve had to be stopped; their ancestors had done a terrible thing to this town, and their descendants had been carrying on their work.

Instead I only felt sick. We'd loosed a demon on the world, even if we hadn't conjured the thing in the first place. Then it got worse.

Last Call

The knife . . . melted into my skin, and I felt a searing heat against my wound. I screamed, startling Chance so that he nearly dropped me. I rubbed my fingers downward, back and forth across my side. My fingers came back slippery with blood, but they found no wound.

How was that possible?

His voice sounded raw. "I've got you, love. You're going to be fine, I promise. We'll get you out, and—"

"Put me down," I demanded.

Chance stopped running. I guess he noticed that my voice sounded stronger, because he complied, keeping a hand on my shoulder. "We need to get you to the doctor, Corine. We're done here."

I raised my shirt, twisted, and peered down at my bloody torso. Healed. But I hadn't imagined the pain that felt like the hole had been cauterized and plugged with metal. I pressed harder. Had the weapon actually become part of me? I knew I hadn't removed it.

"Did you pull the knife out?"

Chance, now studying me with equal parts fear and confusion, shook his head. "No, that's too dangerous if you don't have a med kit at hand."

I exhaled slowly and then spun in a circle. It wasn't gone.

I could feel it watching; sense its amusement. "What did you do?" I shouted.

The earth rumbled, and its voice boomed like thunder, sending an awful chill down my spine. "Why, I healed you, darling child. It seemed a fitting tribute to your mother. But now you owe *me* a boon. I'll see you soon, Corine. . . . You know my people never forget a debt. So long, and thanks for all the fear."

Darkness split in a white beam that made it seem as though lightning had hit nearby. Once my eyes adjusted, I could tell we were alone. We stood in a dark forest now, where fell a soft and natural rain.

I owed my life to a demon? Owing Maury a favor would obligate me to any number of horrible things, and it didn't matter that I hadn't agreed to the terms. Unless I killed myself *right now*, I'd have to pay up because I was enjoying the extension of life it had provided. My mother had explained this kind of thing; it was called tacit acceptance. I sank to my knees, shaking.

Chance pulled me upright, not understanding what had happened, but his determination to get us out of the woods hadn't waned. I ran with him, feet sliding in the mud. His hand felt warm and firm on mine. He hadn't left me; hadn't given up, not even when I fell over with a knife in me.

We ran until we broke from the trees to the quiet of the access road. When we reached the SUV, Jesse and Shannon were waiting.

"Done?" Jesse asked. "Are you guys okay?"

My instant recovery would cost a pretty penny down the road, but yes, I was. I didn't want to talk about it. "I'm fine."

Chance donned a pair of driving gloves. "I'll move their SUVs so it looks like they didn't go missing right here. Maybe park them off road somewhere."

Jesse nodded. "Good idea. I'll follow you, but not into the fields. We don't want two sets of tire tracks."

I thought that plan might be overly cautious, but I didn't

want anyone asking questions later. As far as I was concerned, the sooner we left Kilmer now, the better. I kept seeing the shredded meat of England's stomach. Jesus, I'd put a bullet in another human being. I suspected I might also set off metal detectors at the airport.

The whole endeavor took half an hour, and then Chance wiped down the trucks quickly. I could tell by Saldana's expression that he thought Chance was a former criminal, based on his ability to dispose of a vehicle like this, not to mention the smooth way he managed the hot-wire.

Saldana drove us to the house, glancing at me every now and then in the rearview mirror. I knew I looked pale and shocky. After so much death, after a demonic intervention, I couldn't appear otherwise.

I'd done this. I'd wanted this. I hadn't stopped until I accomplished it. And I'd set a demon loose in the world. My insides felt tied in knots.

"The trucks were still there when we left," Jesse told us. "That's the official story."

"Got it," Shannon said with a nod. "In one sense, it's even true."

When we got back, we found that Dale had made soup. It gave the place a ridiculously homey smell. The crazy reporter seemed to like the farmhouse, where he wandered around describing every little thing as "cool" and "groovy."

I had a feeling he'd stay on after we left. It wasn't like he had anywhere else to go, and he had a hell of a story to write, assuming they'd let him. The body count astounded me. Could I honestly say it had been worth it?

Then I looked at Shannon, who might've been sacrificed in my stead. Yeah. On the whole, I'd do it again. She smiled at me, bare faced from the shower, full of trust and sweetness. Before we left town, we'd go looking for her dad. He deserved a good-bye.

Butch ran up to me, yapping his discontent about being left behind. I ran my hand over his head and said shakily,

"You wouldn't have liked it, boy. You'd be as dirty as me if we'd taken you out there."

He yapped his agreement and followed me to the bathroom, where I tried to clean up without him. But the dog whined until I let him in. He hopped up on the lid of the toilet seat and stood guard while I bathed.

I huddled in the shower until the water ran clear, washing away the traces of blood and mud. The *ground* had swallowed up the dead. I kept replaying the way it buckled under my feet. I wondered if the others had felt the tremor.

The next few days we devoted to playing with Butch, letting Jesse recover, and tying up loose ends. Honest to God, the sheriff thanked me for finding the bodies. He didn't say a word about new missing persons. Maybe their families hadn't filed reports yet.

Kilmer held a party in our honor. We ate lemon cake at the church and drank sweet tea. People seemed livelier, their spirits almost joyous. I think they knew they'd turned a corner. Now this was just a normal little dying town in the middle of nowhere—nothing spooky, nothing unholy.

More people should start arriving. Tourists might even find the place charming now, a well-preserved slice of Americana. Missy England would take over when she realized her dad wasn't coming home, and she'd probably do a better job. She seemed a smart young woman, even if she had slept with Curtis Farrell. Her brown eyes were sad and grave as she thanked us for our efforts. Maybe she already knew, deep down.

On our last day there, we found Shannon's father. Sandra had locked him in the cellar so that he wouldn't interfere with her plans. She'd left him food and water, and the time to go quietly mad with grief and fear. Mr. Cheney hugged Shannon so tight, I thought he'd break her bones.

"I'm sorry," he wept. "I'm sorry. Months ago, when I first suspected what was going on, I should have—"

"Don't worry." Shannon managed a smile through her tears.

"It's okay. But you understand why I have to get away from here, right? I'll write."

"I understand," he said gravely, but his misery never lifted. I suspected he would always feel he'd failed her. "I'm leaving too. I can't stay here. I'm sure I'll be able to get work somewhere as a handyman."

That left them standing there, awkward, trying to figure out how they'd stay in touch when neither of them had cell phones—and they didn't know where they'd end up—so I gave him my address in Mexico. "You can write to Shannon there. I'll know where she is, if she doesn't come to stay with me."

Mr. Cheney thanked me with an overbright smile. "I will never forget you for this. If you hadn't come . . ."

They'd have sacrificed her—and probably Sandra and Jim as well—on December 21. They would have tried to make good with the demon, even though they'd been failing each year I remained alive and well. I just nodded a "You're welcome" as we headed out.

We went back to the house to get our stuff. Before we left town, I called Chuch and Eva to let them know the job was done and everyone was more or less in one piece. To my amusement, Eva stole the phone from her husband and regaled me with anecdotes about her pregnancy. I marveled at the normalcy of it all and promised I'd come to her baby shower in a few months.

"Yes, I'll stop by on my way home," I agreed.

Then I rang Booke, who confirmed the black stain was gone from the astral. He could explore the place at his leisure now, but there didn't appear to be anything unusual to see. I fancied I could almost feel him next to me, watching me, but that was ridiculous. He couldn't go out of body and talk on the phone at the same time.

"I'm so glad you're safe," he said quietly. "I just wish I could've done more."

"You did plenty. I'll call you soon—and *not* just to ask for help."

I hung up and collected my things. Knapsack in hand, I took one last look at the farmhouse. We'd done good work here, almost like the old days. Except you can never go back. Thomas Wolfe was right when he said *you can't go home again*. Nothing ever looked or felt the same. It was an appointment with disappointment.

But now that we'd sorted things in Kilmer, there would be no putting Chance off any longer. His truce with Jesse was over, and I knew he was eager to hear how I felt.

Well, here I stood, cursed and demon touched, and I didn't want to see him broken over me. I didn't want him to bear the weight of my death any more than I wanted to die.

The cost was just too high.

"You all set?" Chance had his duffel in hand, ready to load the trunk.

He expected to take me home with him. My things were still there, just as I'd left them. To his mind, we could simply make the decision and start over. I could stroll back into the life I'd left behind.

Just before she died, Mama had started telling me the rules of riding in cars with boys, as she understood them. I was twelve, and she thought I should learn about that kind of thing. *Always leave with the boy you came with*, she'd told me. *It's not polite otherwise.*

I knew that. Oh, I knew.

But I couldn't abide by the rules this time.

"No," I told Chance. "I'm going with Jesse and Shannon as far as Texas."

Eva had a passport waiting for me there. After visiting with them for a while, I'd take the bus to Monterrey. From there, I'd hop a flight to Mexico City. But he didn't need to know my plans.

"I don't understand." His face was stark and pale.

"It just doesn't make sense for you to drive me all the way back home when you're so close to Florida now. That's where you live, Chance. And it's not where I live anymore. We're going two separate ways now. It's not fair of you to expect me to give up everything for you. I have a new life. I love my pawnshop. It's not just what I do to pay the bills. I've finally found a place where I can use my gift quietly, turn a profit, and not suffer for it. You really want me to give that up for you? Would you give up your life in Tampa for me and move to Mexico City? Do you want this thing bad enough?"

Maybe it wasn't fair to ask him that, but it wasn't only a matter of our conflicting geographic locations. There would always, always be the insurmountable matter of his gift. I didn't want to be another victim to his luck, like the lover he refused to tell me much about. And I would never again sacrifice so much of what made me happy for a man. I'd found a core of steel inside myself, and it wouldn't let me make so many compromises. Maybe it wasn't fair, but he had to show me he'd follow me to the ends of the earth—or at least to Mexico City.

"I can't do that at the drop of a hat," he protested. "There's too much I need to be on hand to manage there."

"And yet you expect me to sell my shop for you," I said.

His hands clenched into fists, a muscle ticking beside his mouth. "Are you saying what I think you are?"

Oh God, I didn't want to be.

I was.

"Yeah," I said softly. "I'm saying that. Tampa is where Min is, where the store is. Your mom's waiting. She needs you. Keep the Mustang—you earned it. It's a cherry car and Chuch would kill you if you sold it."

"He would." His voice sounded odd and hollow. "That's it, then. I . . . I'll send your stuff. I know you'll want your Travis McGee books for sure."

A knife twisted in my heart. *Twist*. I swore I could feel the blade lodged just so. That meant he'd accepted I wasn't coming back; hence time for him to move on. I didn't want to hear about him with someone else. Part of me would always love him, but I wasn't going to let that part's play-in-traffic attitude get me killed. Maybe one day he'd love me enough to change all the way, put his promises into actions, but that wasn't now, and I wanted to go home.

"You don't have to."

"It's no trouble."

I leaned in to hug him, but Chance stepped back. He didn't want anything of me in parting, heartbreak burning in his eyes. When he climbed into the Mustang, I didn't watch him drive away. Instead, I slithered into the backseat of Jesse's SUV and drew my knees up to my chest. Butch popped out of my handbag and hopped onto the seat beside me, snuggling as if he knew I needed comfort.

"You gonna live, sugar?" I heard warmth and concern in Jesse's voice.

Shannon didn't know what had passed between Chance and me, but she took one look at my face and said, "Drive."

Clever girl. Couldn't have said it better myself.

I closed my eyes. I had a long way to go and miles of hard road before I got there.

Read on for an exciting excerpt from
Ann Aguirre's new Sirantha Jax novel,

KILLBOX

Sirantha Jax is a "jumper," a woman who possesses
the unique genetic makeup needed to navigate faster-
than-light ships through grimspace. With no tolerance
for political diplomacy, she quits her ambassador post
so she can get back to saving the universe the way she
does best—by mouthing off and kicking butt.

And her tactics are needed more than ever. Flesh-
eating aliens are attacking stations on the outskirts of
space, and for many people, the Conglomerate's forces
are arriving too late to serve and protect them.

Now Jax must take matters into her own hands by re-
cruiting a militia to defend the frontiers—out of the worst
criminals, mercenaries, and raiders that ever traveled
through grimspace. . . .

Coming in September 2010 from Ace Books

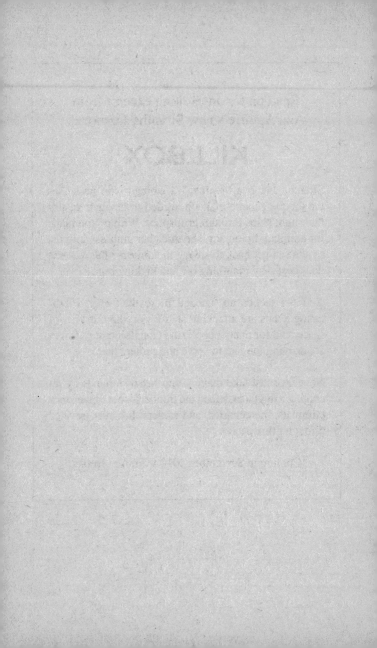

Grimspace blazes through me like a star gone nova.

I'm the happiest junkie who ever burned chem, because this is where I belong. Kaleidoscopic fire burns against the hull, seeming as though it should consume us, but we are the only solid things in this realm of ghosts and echoes. Sometimes I think this place holds all the potential for everything that ever was, everything that ever shall be. It's a possibility vortex, and thus lacks any shape of its own.

I glory in the endorphins pounding through me. Cations sparkle in my blood, marking me as unique even among thrill seekers. You see, my life started here.

Unfortunately the rush is fleeting, and I need to carry us safely through. I focus on the beacons; they pulse as if in answer to my command. Here, I feel powerful, damn near invincible, however much a lie that proves to be. Jumpers almost never die old and gray.

March—my pilot and lover—swells inside me, filling my head with warmth. He feels natural there. Anybody else would wonder at that, but if you're a jumper, you get used to sharing mind space. In fact, I'm lonely without him there.

He manipulates the ship so we can jump. The phase drum hums, all juiced up, and we swing out of grimspace. Homesickness floods me at once, but I battle it back. No point in dwelling in what can never be—staying in grimspace would kill me. At least I'm jumping again. Not too long ago, I thought I'd have to choose between my addiction and my life. The decision isn't as obvious as you might think.

I unplug, still savoring the boost, and check the star charts. *Oh, nice, a clean jump.*

"Good work." March grins at me and steals a kiss.

I'm so happy that he wants to.

He's not as pretty as the men I've been with before. I used to have an eye for the lovely androgynous ones, but I guess deep down, I don't mind a bit of the brute. March has strong, angular features and a nose that's obviously been broken. But his eyes . . . his eyes shine like sun through amber. I could spend hours looking at him.

But business before pleasure—I have an important message to send. With a jaunty wave, I leave the cockpit and head for my quarters. I share the space with March. Despite that, it's an austere environment: plain berth, terminal, lighting fortified by solar simulators to compensate for lack of nutrient D_3, in case you spend too much time on board.

Constance greets me, flickering into a 3-D image projected from my terminal. She's everywhere and nowhere, blazing her way through the ship from terminal to terminal. I don't know whether we'll ever convince her to come back to a physical shell now that she's tasted the power and freedom a starship can offer. She's either fused with the vessel's limited AI or overridden it. Regardless, I suspect there's something illegal in what we've done, and I couldn't care less.

"All systems indicate a smooth arrival, Sirantha Jax."

I smile. "You got that right."

Since we jumped from Ithiss-Tor to the beacon closest to New Terra, the crew could be forgiven for thinking we intend to land there. That's what our orders demand. Instead we're heading away from the planet. We're not operating on the Conglomerate's credits, and this is a vessel out of La-chion, so I can do something I've been longing for since the minute I acceded to that rock-and-a-hard-place decision. Jael was right about one thing: People seem to think it's all right to force me into choices that range from bad to worse.

No longer.

I add, "Activate comm. I need to bounce a message to Chancellor Tarn."

"Acknowledged."

The system glimmers to life before me, and I sit down to record. This won't take long. Constance zips through the protocols, leaving the proper software in place. In the shadowy light, I can see myself in the terminal, and it's an eerie feeling—alone but not.

I could make this a lot more detailed. Instead I go with blunt, which is my favorite style of communication. If I never have to dissemble again, that will be wonderful. My time on Ithiss-Tor damn near killed me, figuratively and literally.

I imagine Tarn playing this message and smile. Then I deliver two words: "I quit." Satisfied, I stop the program and tell Constance, "Send it right away, please."

"My pleasure, Sirantha Jax. Do you require anything else?"

"Not at the moment. Feel free to go back to exploring the ship."

Standing, I consider the consequences of what I just did.

Tarn may reply with bluster and words of obligation; he might say I have a duty during mankind's darkest hour. Maybe he'll even accuse me of turning tail when the chips are down. Once, those accusations might have even been true.

Now my skin is too thick with scars for such barbs to draw blood. I know my own mettle. I've glimpsed my breaking point. And Tarn will never, ever have my measure.

I choose not to serve the Conglomerate as an ambassador, but that doesn't mean I've given up on humanity. Surrender isn't a word in my personal lexicon; there are other ways and means. If nothing else, Ithiss-Tor taught me there's always a choice.

Now we're heading for the last place anyone would ever look for us: Emry Station. It will be a long haul in straight space, but this isn't a frequently traveled trade route, and there's nothing here to attract pirates and raiders. We should pass unnoticed.

We've been cruising for about four days, heading away from New Terra, when disaster strikes.

I awaken to the sound of sirens. Next to me, March bounds to his feet and starts scrambling into his clothes. His face seems all hard planes in the half-light, softened by the shock of dark hair and his hawk's eyes. Though this is new to me, I recognize the warning even without Constance on the comm.

"This is not a drill or a technical malfunction. Your vessel is under attack." She sounds so polite and unruffled that I cannot help but smile.

My hands feel clumsy as I tug up my black jumpsuit. Mary, it feels good to be back in familiar gear. "What do you want me to do? We can't jump from here."

"Check in with Dina at weapons," March says over his shoulder, already on his way out.

No time for other niceties.

The ship rocks. In a vessel this size, that can't be good. Even without seeing it, I know we're taking heavy damage. It doesn't make sense, though. We're not a merchantman or a freighter. We're not hauling contraband and we're well off the beaten path.

I take off at a dead run for the gunnery bay. Dina's already there when I burst in. She's got lasers, but she can't work those as well as the particle cannons. We also have old-fashioned projectiles from an ancient rail gun, but those are best directed at personnel attempting to board, not ships.

"I'll take cannons," she snaps. "Get your ass in the chair. Besides March and me, you're the only one with any interstellar combat experience."

High praise, indeed.

"Is that why you're not trying to keep this thing in one piece up in engineering?"

"The only reason," she mutters. "I hope those clansmen know what they're doing."

"How're we holding up?"

"Better than expected. Our hull's been reinforced."

I bring the sighting apparatus down over my head, and suddenly I'm out in space, part of the fight in a way that scares the shit out of me. I tap the panel and the system whines, telling me it needs time to power up. This is a hell of a cutter we're fighting, slim but fast, and outfitted with enough ordnance to destroy a small planet. Whoever these assholes are, they're serious. To my eyes it looks like a Silverfish adapted for space flight, but I don't know if that's possible.

Their shots nearly blind me, but they soar wide, striking the Gunnar-Dahlgren vessel far starboard. I don't know what they were aiming at, but they missed weapons. Maybe our engines?

I can see but not hear Dina's first volley; she hits the other vessel in a clean blow that takes out the aft shields. This is more advanced than the technology on the *Folly*. For a second I can't breathe because of all the black space around me. There's no air here.

With sheer will, I choke it back and tell myself this is only a sim. *Focus on the other ship.* The system cycles and then shows readiness. I just have to point and shoot.

"Do we want to disable or disintegrate them?"

Before her next shot, Dina taps the comm. "Use deadly force?"

March's voice fills the room, giving me courage as if he's beside me. "Confirmed. We are at war."

That's all I need to know. I spin the sight and target the panel where they're trying to restore shields. A tap magnifies my target; then I fire until the lasers whine, telling me they're out of juice for the time being.

It's oddly pretty.

And there's no boom.

But a panel flies wide. They have a hull breach. We probably do too, but we've given them something to think about.

Muffled through my headgear, I hear Constance on the comm. "I have identified the vessel. According to the registration on the hull, this is the *Blue Danube* out of Gehenna. Data on the ship is scarce, but I found reference to an unpaid tariff on trade goods."

"Speak plainly," I mutter.

"In its hold, the crew had concealed four human females, two Rodeisians, and three male humanoids of unknown origin, possibly from some class-P world."

Slavers. Well, shit.

It makes sense they'd be getting bolder along with everyone else, and Gehenna does a brisk business in the flesh trade. I just didn't realize they do it literally. I thought it was more of a rental than a purchase.

"Did they have slaves on Tarnus?" I ask.

"Yes." Dina is too distracted to care I'm prying. "Aren't those lasers ready to go yet?" She lets fly another burst from the particle cannon, focusing on the weak spot. More bits of metal break off in slow, graceful chunks.

Our ship spins. How much damage have we taken? I can tell it's March or Hit in the pilot seat because we're taking evasive action that has us rolling and twirling. If nothing else, our fliers outclass theirs.

"Almost. Is there anything critical where we're aiming?"

I can hear the evil grin in her voice. "Only little things like power and life support."

"No wonder we're shooting that way."

Slavers. Random evil. They're not part of any grand conspiracy. They just want to buy and sell us like livestock.

Like hell.

I'm ready for round two. Red beams burst forth, slicing the dark between the pearly gleam of our hulls. Luck or Dina's calculations—either way, I hit a stress point and the back half of the ship cracks wide, the stern going dark, adrift in space. At that point, the *Blue Danube* starts trying to pull away from the fight. Their engines are crippled, which is a good thing; otherwise, they'd leave us sniffing their trail.

There could be slaves on that ship.

I wonder whether March has thought of that. It reminds

me unpleasantly of Hon's Station, where he tried to save people who were beyond hope of rescue. In doing so, he proved himself a hero, but he also endangered all of us. It never would've even occurred to me to look. But now here I sit, worried that we might be blowing innocent people to cosmic dust.

My breath skitters. I shouldn't say anything. I absolutely should not.

Even as I think it, there's a warm tingle at the back of my neck. He's there. The gun bay must be just below the cockpit or he wouldn't be able to do this. His gift has limits.

What's wrong, Jax? You're scaring me.

No turning back now. *There could be innocents aboard.*

His surprise crackles through me like footsteps on fresh snow. I know what I've done. Seconds later, I hear his voice on the comm. "Dina, belay the order for deadly force. We have to board."

"Are you out of your mind?" she snarls.

"No," he answers. "Take out engines and weapons array if you can. I'll get the tow cables on them to hold 'em still."

"You heard the man," she says, yanking the headgear off me. "He wants precision, and for that I need lasers. I guess you're done here."

"I'll go prepare the boarding party."

"You'll need me," Dina calls. "Don't leave without me."

I'm already thinking about who else we should take. Hit, March, and Vel for their hand-to-hand skill, Doc in case anyone is wounded. Dina and I round out the group. Of them all, I'm the most expendable. That's an interesting sensation.

Once I'd have protested at the stupidity of this. We should've just blown them to atoms and went on to Emry Station. For good or ill, I don't think that way anymore.

It doesn't take me long to assemble my gear: shockstick, torch-tube, a few packets of paste. You never know when that will come in handy. If we manage to save anyone over there, they might be starving. Slavers aren't known for their kindness.

Once prepared, I head over to the hatch to wait. With the tow cables in place, we'll launch the boarding apparatus and connect to their hatch doors. Vel has the expertise to get us in, even from the outside. I pull on the full compression suit, but leave the helmet off. It gets sweaty in there fast, and I don't want to wear it longer than I have to.

I'm slightly queasy over the idea of entering the boarding array. It's no more than a few thin centimeters of an alloy allegedly perfected for use in space. Seeing how Farwan "perfected" other technology, it leaves some room for concern.

One by one, I notify everybody who'll be going with us. I don't need to check with March on that. I know he'll agree with my call. Too many, and we'll hinder one another in the close confines of the smaller ship. Too few, and we won't have the skills we need to make this work. It's a delicate balance.

Maybe that's the mistake we made on Hon's Kingdom. We tried to do it on our own. I just hope history's not repeating itself, because it was *my* idea this time.

ABOUT THE AUTHOR

Ann Aguirre is a national bestselling author. She has a degree in English literature and a spotty résumé. Before she began writing full-time, she was a clown, a clerk, a voice actress, and a savior of stray kittens, not necessarily in that order. She grew up in a yellow house across from a cornfield, but now she lives in sunny Mexico with her husband, two children, two cats, and one very lazy dog. She likes books, emo music, action movies, and *Dr. Who*. You can visit her on the Web at www.annaguirre.com.

Also Available from

ANN AGUIRRE

Blue Diablo
A Corine Solomon Novel

Eighteen months ago, Corine Solomon crossed the
border and wound up in Mexico City, fleeing her past,
her lover, and her "gift." Corine, a handler, can touch
something and know its history—and sometimes, its
future. Using her ability, she can find the missing—and
that's why people never stop trying to find her. People
like her ex, Chance...

Chance, whose uncanny luck has led him to her
doorstep, needs her help. Someone dear to them both
has gone missing in Laredo, Texas, and the only hope of
finding her is through Corine's gift. But their search may
prove dangerous as the trail leads them into a strange
dark world of demons and sorcerers, ghosts and
witchcraft, zombies—and black magic.

**"Gritty, steamy and altogether
wonderful urban fantasy."**
—#1 *New York Times* bestselling author
Patricia Briggs

Available wherever books are sold or at
penguin.com